CRITICA[illegible]DSEY

'No one writes with more wit, warmth and insight about the law and its practitioners than Peter Murphy. He has no equal since the great John [illegible]rtimer' – **David Ambrose**

'Though his exasperation is sometimes palpable, what triumphs over everything is his sense of humour. And it is the humour that makes *Walden of Bermondsey* such a delightful read. Think of him as what Rumpole would be like if he ever became a judge, and you get some idea of his self-deprecating wit and indomitable stoicism. Add a dash of Henry Cecil for his situation and AP Herbert for the fun he has with the law, and you get a sense of his literary precedents' – **Paul Magrath**

Also by Peter Murphy

Removal (2012)
Test of Resolve (2014)

The Ben Schroeder series
A Higher Duty (2013)
A Matter for the Jury (2014)
And Is There Still Honey for Tea? (2015)
The Heirs of Owain Glyndwr (2016)
Calling Down the Storm (2017)

Walden of Bermondsey (2017)

First published in 2018
by No Exit Press,
an imprint of Oldcastle Books Ltd,
PO Box 394,
Harpenden, Herts,
AL5 1XJ
noexit.co.uk

A CIP catalogue record for this book is available from the British Library.

ISBN

978-0-85730-203-8 (print)
978-0-85730-204-5 (epub)
978-085730-205-2 (kindle)
978-0-85730-206-9 (pdf)

Typeset in 11.5pt Minion Pro
by Avocet Typeset, Somerton, Somerset, TA11 6RT
Printed in Denmark by Nørhaven, Viborg

Judge Walden
Back in Session

PETER MURPHY

CONTENTS

FOREWORD

By Lord Judge, former Lord Chief Justice
of England and Wales

Charles Walden, the Resident Judge of Bermondsey Crown Court, is amply qualified for inclusion in any list of fictional National Treasures.

With the support of his delightful wife, the Reverend Mrs Walden, he is able to fulfil his judicial, pastoral and administrative responsibilities at a small Crown Court. He has the advantage that his cases are always interesting. In this second collection of his experiences, for example, he describes how the defendant in one case was mortified at the deliberate insult paid to him and his family when the police sought to treat him as a minor criminal; in another, the defendant is a vicar seeking mortification of the flesh for penitential relief. Beyond the ongoing trials themselves there is always a simultaneous compelling outside distraction impacting on the work of the Court, not least the discovery of an ancient artefact, now, after a struggle with bureaucracy, forever to be identified as the Bermondsey Cannon.

Judge Walden is a wise, patient and thoughtful judge, cocooned by his self-deprecating humour against that dreadful disease, 'judgitis'. He is not anxious to emerge from the 'jurisprudential shadows' into the 'predatory' sights of the Court of Appeal. He is acutely aware of the foibles, and prejudices of his colleagues, but recognises that together they form a sound judicial team. He notices the qualities of the advocates who appear in front of him, describing one advocate who prefers to muddy the waters rather than pour oil on them, and another who is excellent, short and to the point. The forensic process is examined in a light touch, good-humoured style, which will evoke a constant stream of smiles, and chuckles from nonlawyers and lawyers alike.

At times there is a sharper tone to the humour, never departing from the humorous but occasionally touching the satirical. At these times, the defendants, the witnesses, and indeed all those directly participating in the judicial processes form the backdrop, while the main focus shifts to others. Sometimes this focus falls on the senior judiciary. But Judge Walden's particular anxiety is the way in which the 'Grey Smoothies', as they call them at Bermondsey, do not always appreciate the true nature of judicial responsibility. When they are being obtuse, he is nevertheless extremely skilful at finding or waiting for a satisfactory solution to emerge. Within this sharper tone you can discern some of the frustrations and anxieties of the judiciary in the Crown and County Courts. This collection is much more than a series of funny legal stories.

I like Judge Charles Walden, the human being as well as the judge, and I have come to relish and respect his subtle, thoughtful insights into and observations arising from all the processes by which justice is administered in his Crown Court.

Igor Judge

WHO STEALS MY PURSE

WHO STEALS MY PURSE

Monday morning

Few words uttered by a member of staff at any Crown Court are more calculated to strike fear into the heart of a judge than those our list officer, Stella, spoke this morning when she came into my chambers to go over the week's schedule. Stella is given to sounding rather like the voice of impending doom, but I don't blame her for that at all. There's a lot that can go wrong in Stella's job. She has the unenviable task of making the work of four judges and four courtrooms run smoothly, in the face of the constant efforts of defendants, solicitors, barrister's clerks, the Crown Prosecution Service, and not infrequently the judges themselves, to throw spanners into the works. Stella has learned to see catastrophe lurking just around every corner, and as a result, often sounds rather fraught. So I make every allowance. But her tone has conditioned me to expect the worst whenever she comes into chambers, and this morning my expectations have been fully realised.

Such a shame. I'd passed a very agreeable weekend with my good lady, the Reverend Mrs Walden, priest in charge of the church of St Aethelburgh and All Angels in the Diocese of Southwark. On Saturday, the parish held its annual spring fete – insofar as any parish in Inner London can credibly hold an event with such a bucolic ring to it as a spring fete. It was all very Jam and Jerusalem: the choir belting out a selection of thoroughly modern hymns no one else seemed to know, accompanied by the church's resident guitar and vocal duo, Ian and Shelley; a bouncy castle for the children; stalls selling candyfloss and ice cream and doubtful-looking hot dogs; others inviting you to throw a ball and knock various items off a shelf, or score a double twenty at darts, to win a stuffed animal or a box of chocolates: and of course, the inevitable tombola and raffles to raise money for various parish projects.

It was the kind of thing that would have seemed more natural in a churchyard in rural Lincolnshire, surrounded by open fields and ancient trees, than one in Bermondsey, surrounded by your stereotypical inner city decay. But due in part perhaps to the beautiful weather, it was surprisingly well attended, and the Reverend Mrs Walden pronounced it a great success, which it therefore was. This led to a very pleasant evening for the two of us at La Bella Napoli, where we partook of sea bass baked in salt, roast potatoes, spinach with garlic, and a bottle of the house's special reserve Chianti to wash it down. And on the following morning, the sermon had positive, cheerful themes – not always the case with the Reverend Mrs Walden, who can sometimes give way to a certain judgmental tendency when it comes to the perceived shortcomings of her congregation.

In addition, this morning I have a very pleasant stroll in to work. As always, I call into my favourite coffee and sandwich bar, which is run by two ladies called Elsie and Jeanie in a small archway under the railway bridge, not far from London Bridge station. It gets crowded if they have more than two customers at a time, but they do a wonderful latte. The only slight downside is that often, while it's being prepared, I have to listen to a litany of complaints. Jeanie has a husband who likes a flutter on the horses or the football; Elsie has grandchildren I'm probably going to see in court one of these days when they've graduated from the Youth Court. But not this morning. This morning,

Jeanie prepares my latte with unusual enthusiasm, the result, she confides in me, of her husband's success in his betting activities over the weekend. Jeanie's report of this is highly technical, and features such terms as accumulators and cashing out early, which rather elude me; but the net result is that he has done very well for himself, and she is understandably pleased that the rent money is safe for the month – which isn't always the case. Elsie tells me proudly that her grandchildren have managed to stay out of trouble for the second consecutive weekend – which also isn't always the case. Next door to Elsie and Jeanie is my newsagent, George, who is in just as good a mood, handing me my copy of the *Times* with a cheerful, 'Good morning, guv', and not a bad word about the Labour Party. So I arrive in chambers in an excellent frame of mind. But a matter of seconds after I take my seat behind my desk and start to savour my latte, Stella enters in full Angel of Doom mode, and announces –

'You've got Lester Fogle, Judge, and he's representing himself.'

A defendant acting in person is the prelude to a nightmare of a trial. American lawyers are so traumatised by it that they try to cover up the horror by putting it in Latin – they refer to it as the defendant acting '*pro se*'. I don't see how that improves the situation; I suspect that trials with a defendant acting '*pro se*' are just as bad as those with the defendant acting in person. Mercifully, despite the ravages wrought by the government on the legal aid system, we have not yet reached the situation in the Crown Court in which defendants have to represent themselves because they can't afford a lawyer and the state won't provide one. So defendants representing themselves are still something of a rarity, and when you encounter one, it's almost always because the defendant thinks he can do a better job than a barrister or solicitor of convincing a jury that there may be some reasonable doubt about his guilt. The statistics don't support this brand of optimism; in fact, the reverse is true. But the kind of defendant who prefers to act in person is not the kind of person who sets great store by statistics, and even when they are brought to his attention by the judge, he remains convinced that he is the exception that proves the rule. When convicted, he will complain that the judge or jury, or both, were biased against him, or that the police engaged in some skulduggery to take him down; but never that he was just another statistic.

During the trial itself, he can be his own worst enemy. The judge is legally obliged to bend over backwards to help a defendant acting in person, and we do make a sincere effort. Every stage of the trial is explained to the defendant, he is told what options he has, and the judge will always give assistance if he can't think of the right question to ask a witness. Defendants often don't have the first idea of how to examine a witness; or of the difference between asking questions and hurling abuse; or between asking questions and making a speech to the jury. But however helpful the judge tries to be, the defendant often interprets it as an effort to prejudice him in the eyes of the jury. So towards the end of the trial, it's usual for a certain tension, if not outright animosity, to have developed between judge and defendant, and it can occasionally get out of hand. Trials with a defendant in person take longer, and involve many more headaches than trials in which the defendant is represented, even by a lawyer who's not one of the stars of the Bermondsey Bar.

In addition to that, the defendant is Lester Fogle. I don't know Lester personally, but I know *of* him, and I am well acquainted with his family. I had a considerable number of professional dealings with them in the old days, when I was in practice as a barrister. The Fogles are one of a group of local families known affectionately to the Bar as the 'Disorganised Crime Families', or to the more cosmopolitan as '*Le Cinque Famiglie di Bermondsey'*. There's no reason for the Gambino or Genovese families to lose any sleep over *Le Cinque Famiglie di Bermondsey.* The Fogles in particular have a delusional view of themselves as Bermondsey's undisputed crime lords, but their main claim to fame within the criminal justice community is their propensity to get nicked and sent down on a regular basis. Indeed, they are notorious for having perpetrated some of the most spectacular cock-ups in the annals of London crime. But their attrition rate has never seemed to discourage them from leaping headlong into the world of serious crime on a generational basis, and apparently Lester is one of the current cadre of Bermondsey 'made guys' who thinks he's terrorising South London.

Sitting in chambers waiting for the day's proceedings in court to begin, I scan the file and go through Lester's antecedents. His record follows a familiar pattern. It begins with the exploratory minor offences typical of young offenders starting out – shoplifting, criminal damage and the like – and gradually escalates to handling stolen goods, and finally to robbery, the family's main business. When Lester's father Bill and his uncle Tony – my main client in the family – were active, the fashion was for hijacking lorries. Today it seems to have moved on to knocking over jeweller's shops and the occasional building society. It's all rather depressing. Lester is thirty-five now, and hasn't learned at all from the experience of his father and uncle, both of whom spent long periods of their lives inside, leaving their world-weary wives to carry on as best they could. This time, I glean from the indictment, it's a bit less serious. He's charged with stealing a car. Not just any car, admittedly: a classic 1965 Volkswagen Beetle lovingly preserved in pristine condition by its owner, one Raymond Hunter Lewis, which was found by police parked in the driveway of Lester's house, standing there for all to see, two days after Mr Lewis had reported the theft. Lester was duly nicked.

I'm not going to get to him immediately, needless to say. It's Monday morning, and I have a courtroom full of advocates waiting to make and oppose bail applications, and to conduct plea and case management hearings in cases to come to trial in the future. The first three of these involve defendants in custody appearing by way of live link from the prison. The live link system was introduced several years ago by the Grey Smoothies – the name we use at Bermondsey to refer to the civil servants responsible for the running of the courts – as a measure designed to save time and expense, specifically the time and expense of the prison authorities in bringing defendants to court in time for their hearings. Saving money for the taxpayer is the Grey Smoothies' consuming passion; which would be all well and good but for the magical thinking that goes with it, according to which the courts will continue to function just as efficiently, regardless of how much of our resources they take away by means of cuts, and regardless of how much they dismantle our proven methods of working.

The live link is a prime example. You have to book appointments for each live link individually, at intervals of fifteen minutes. If a hearing runs longer than expected; or if the defendant hasn't had the chance to confer with his counsel or solicitor beforehand; or if the prison has overlooked a defendant and left him in his cell; or if the link goes down because of one of any number of technical problems, any subsequent hearings may have to be abandoned and the defendants brought to court later in the week for a personal appearance. If the defendants made a personal appearance in the first place there wouldn't be any technical problems, and I could juggle the list to take whichever case was ready at any given moment and give the others time to get ready. With live link that's impossible, and with all of this going on, it's not unusual for it to be eleven o'clock or later before I get to whatever trial I may have in progress or about to start. Meanwhile I have a jury of taxpayers cooling their heels upstairs, doing nothing and wondering why everything in court takes so long. Today, I lose two plea and case management hearings until Thursday because we are late for our appointments.

Lester has dressed up nicely for court, in a smart light blue suit and tie, his shoes nicely shined. I'm not surprised. That would be the influence of his uncle Tony, who always looked the very image of the innocent businessman whenever I represented him – which was a fair bit over the years. He's been on bail, and my court clerk, Carol, tells me that he arrived at court at nine o'clock sharp. I'm not surprised by that either – Tony was always scrupulous about arriving at court in good time for every hearing.

I notice, too, that he's brought *Archbold* with him. That's something else I remember from the old days. Some families have family bibles. The Fogles have *Archbold*, and in my day never came to court without it. I remember fondly sitting in a conference room at the Inner London Sessions, listening to Tony explain to me, referring me to the text, why his appropriation of a huge quantity of railway signalling wire from the side of the tracks couldn't amount to theft because it appeared to have been abandoned. 'I mean, it says it right here, it's "*res derelicta*", innit, guv?' But the volume Lester has brought with him looks as though it may be seriously out of date. Tony and Bill wouldn't have been seen dead with anything other than the current edition, but with the younger generation it seems standards have slipped. I ask our usher, Dawn, to borrow a copy of the current edition from the library and loan it to Lester for the duration. There are few things more dangerous than an out-of-date edition of *Archbold*; indeed, with the possible exception of the *Physician's Home Companion*, the 1924 edition of which I remember as the medical bible in my grandparents' home, none springs immediately to mind.

Carol identifies Lester formally, and we are ready to go. Lester is fairly soft-spoken, I notice immediately – another family trait; I was forever telling Tony to keep his voice up when he gave evidence. But Tony was always legally represented, so apart from his time in the witness box, it didn't matter. Now it does. I can't have the jury struggling to hear Lester in the dock throughout the trial. Having consulted Susan Worthington, who's prosecuting, I release Lester from the dock and ask him to sit in the same row as Susan, nearer to the jury. He wishes Susan a polite good morning as he takes his seat, calling her 'madam'; she gives me a quick grin.

'Mr Fogle, stand up, please,' I begin. 'I can't help noticing that you're not legally represented today.'

'No, sir.'

'Would you mind telling me why? Were you refused legal aid for some reason?'

'No, sir. I just prefer to represent myself.'

'Mr Fogle, a barrister or solicitor with experience of these courts is likely to be more effective in presenting your case than you would be yourself. If you want to represent yourself, of course, you're free to do so, and if you do, I will give you any help I can. But I have a duty to tell you that you would be well advised to have someone to act for you, and I will adjourn the case for a short time if you would like to make arrangements.'

Lester nods. 'Thank you, sir. I do know how helpful barristers can be. My uncle Tony has told me how much you helped him when you represented him.'

Susan starts to giggle, and has to hold a hand in front of her face.

'Yes, well, it's very kind of your uncle Tony to say so, I'm sure –'

'He remembers the birdcage case with great fondness, sir. He asked me to remind you of it.'

I need no reminding. The birdcage case was a classic Fogle

family disaster. Tony 'masterminded' the hijacking of a lorry without much prior intelligence of what it might contain, the assumption being that any given lorry must contain something worth nicking. The job followed the Fogle family's trademark routine. The lorry was diverted into a side street using fake road works signs. When it stopped, Tony and his crew hauled the driver out and slapped him around a couple of times. I should point out that the slaps were strictly token, and the driver was always offered a good drink for his trouble; to their credit, the Fogles had no truck with violence. Tony then commandeered the lorry and drove it to a warehouse where the goods would be unloaded. Unfortunately, on this occasion, due to an administrative oversight, the warehouse was still full of gear from one of Bill's capers and wasn't available, and so Tony had to unload the swag into his own garage at home. Even worse, the lorry proved to contain nothing except three hundred odd wicker birdcages.

Tony struggled valiantly for some weeks with the problem of how to fence three hundred wicker birdcages. It wasn't the kind of gear he could sell to his usual customers or offload at the pub. In the end, he resorted to advertising in a number of bird-fanciers' magazines, which had some limited success in terms of sales, but was ultimately to prove his downfall when the owners of the consignment, noticing the close resemblance between the advertised goods and their hijacked load, put two and two together and made four. When the police came, Tony, weeping with relief, led them straight to the garage and told them he was having a nervous breakdown trying to work out what to do with so many cages. He pleaded guilty, and, I suspect largely because the judge found it all rather amusing, was given a charitable twelve months, a good result for a man with his record, for which I took some largely undeserved credit. The birdcage caper represented the high-water mark of

Fogle family disasters for some three years until Bill hijacked a lorry containing a contingent of shoes – all of which turned out to be for the right foot, a simple but effective security device.

'I should have thought, Mr Fogle,' I say, 'that with your family's experience, you would know by now that having a barrister to represent you is the wise thing to do. But it's up to you. I can't keep the jury panel waiting indefinitely, but if you would like to change your mind…'

'No. Thank you, sir.'

'Very well. Are we ready to go, Miss Worthington?'

'We are, your Honour. It should be a fairly short trial. As Mr Fogle is unrepresented, I will call the owner of the car, Mr Lewis; we also have the officer in the case, DC Hemmings; and the investigating officers, PC Jenkins and PC Hartley. In addition, Mr Fogle has asked me to make one other police officer available, a DI Venables. The prosecution is not aware of any connection DI Venables may have with this case, but since Mr Fogle wants him, we have no objection to making him available.'

Having read the file, I can't see any connection either, but the name of DI Venables rings a bell immediately. I'm slightly surprised he hasn't retired by now. My curiosity is aroused.

'Would you like to tell me in outline what kind of defence you will be offering to this charge, Mr Fogle?' I inquire.

'No, thank you, sir. I'd prefer to keep it to myself for now, so that I don't lose the element of surprise, if you take my meaning.'

With or without schooling from Tony, Lester has just homed in on one huge advantage of being unrepresented. Any defence lawyer knows that the courts no longer allow trial by ambush. These days, under the Criminal Procedure Rules, the defence is obliged to serve a defence statement on the court and the prosecution, outlining the nature of the defence, and giving details of any witnesses to be called. This means that the court and the prosecution have some idea of what the case is about, and can prepare accordingly. It appears that Lester has overlooked this procedural step. In theory, the rules apply equally to defendants acting in person, but as a matter of practical reality, it's a waste of time trying to make a defendant acting in person comply. We shall just have to wait and see what the defence is.

Unfortunately, by the time we've had this conversation, my colleague Judge Rory Dunblane – 'Legless' as he is known to all, as a consequence of a now obscure incident after a chambers dinner while he was at the Bar – has grabbed a jury panel for his trial, and the jury bailiff won't be able to sort out another panel until two o'clock. I extend Lester's bail for the duration of the trial, send everyone away until after lunch, and retire to chambers to reflect further on how to deal with Lester Fogle representing himself. No great ideas come to me, and eventually it's time to join my colleagues in the judicial mess for lunch. But just as I'm about to leave chambers, Carol puts her head around the door.

'Sorry, Judge, but I've got a bit of an unusual situation. Counsel in the trial in Judge Drake's court have asked to see you.'

'Counsel in Judge Drake's court?'

'Yes, Judge.'

'If they're in Judge Drake's court, why aren't they seeing Judge Drake?'

Carol nods. 'I did ask. They say something has come up that they haven't been able to resolve with Judge Drake; it's delaying the start of the trial; and they need to see you as resident judge to see if you can sort it. Will you see them?'

I think for a moment or two.

'I don't think I should do that without speaking to Judge Drake first and finding out what's going on, do you?'

'I suppose not, Judge, no.'

'He is here, is he? He hasn't pushed off to the Garrick Club or anything?'

'No, Judge, he's here.'

'All right. I'll see him at lunch. Tell counsel to report back at two o'clock – but no promises.'

'Right you are, Judge.'

And so to lunch, an oasis of calm in a desert of chaos.

I'm the last to arrive. Judge Drake, Hubert, is tucking into the kitchen's dish of the day, billed as home-made lasagne with garlic bread. Hubert's courage in tackling the kitchen's dish of the day on a regular basis is something the rest of us all admire. Legless and my remaining colleague, Judge Marjorie Jenkins, have gone with variants of the baked potato, tuna for Marjorie, baked beans for Legless, and I've selected the cheese omelette – all of these being regarded as safer bets by connoisseurs of the court cuisine. There are many days when I pick up a ham and cheese bap from Elsie and Jeanie, just in case there's nothing reasonably safe on the menu. But Hubert grapples with the dish of the day every day of the week, and today he is attacking his lasagne with a vengeance. He says nothing to explain why counsel in his trial might want to see me. I decide to approach with caution.

'How are everyone's trials going? Have you all got started?'

'Mine's fine,' Legless replies. 'I'm sorry I tied the jury panel up just before lunch, Charlie. I gather you needed a jury too. But I had a couple of long sentences this morning, and I couldn't get to it any earlier.'

'Not a problem. Marjorie?'

'Yes, all set. Conspiracy to supply class A drugs, probably take until towards the end of the week, but no problems.'

'Good. Hubert?'

'Yes, Charlie?'

'How's your trial going? It's a GBH, isn't it? Have you got it started?'

Hubert looks a bit shifty, and keeps his eyes down on his plate.

'No... not as such... not just yet, Charlie. We've had a... a legal question come up, that's all. I've sent counsel away to think about it over lunch. I'm sure we'll get underway this afternoon.'

'Difficult one, is it, the legal question?'

'Difficult? No. As far as I'm concerned it's perfectly simple. Why do you ask?'

I put my knife and fork down.

'I ask because, just as I was leaving my chambers to come to lunch, I received a message from counsel in your case, saying they want to see me. They say there's some kind of difficulty they haven't been able to sort out with you. It seemed a bit odd, and I was wondering whether you'd care to enlighten me before I decide what to do?'

Marjorie and Legless both raise their eyebrows in my direction.

Hubert finally looks up from his lasagne.

'It's nothing I can't deal with, Charlie.'

'So I would have assumed. But apparently, counsel don't agree.'

Hubert takes a deep breath and lets it out in one heavy, frustrated, exhalation.

'Very well, if you insist. I had to tell the advocate for the defendant that I couldn't hear her.'

We all consider this for a moment or two, and I note the coded language. When Hubert uses the term 'advocate' he means that she is a solicitor advocate rather than a barrister. If she were a barrister, Hubert would have referred to her as 'counsel'. We've had solicitor advocates in the Crown Court for many years now, but Hubert has never reconciled himself to them. He still believes that solicitors should know their place – namely, sitting behind counsel – and that barristers should have a monopoly of advocacy in the Crown Court.

'I take it, Hubert,' I comment eventually, 'that you were using the phrase "couldn't hear her" in the legal sense, not in the sense that she wasn't speaking loudly enough.'

'Obviously,' Hubert replies. 'I'm not a complete fool, Charlie. If she wasn't loud enough I'd tell her to bloody well turn up the volume, wouldn't I? I can't hear her because she's improperly dressed.'

'In what way, improperly dressed?' Marjorie asks. 'Do you mean she forgot to bring her robes to court, or left them somewhere else? I get that sometimes; I'm sure we all do. It shouldn't happen, but it does, and in the end I let them get on with it rather than waste the court's time.'

'No, I don't mean that, Marjorie,' Hubert replies. 'I'm not always as charitable as you are. If the robes are anywhere within striking distance I send counsel off to fetch them. I agree – there are times when you just have to overlook it and move on. But not in these circumstances.'

'What circumstances?' Legless asks.

'The circumstance that Miss Gloria Farthing has bright pink hair under her wig.'

Marjorie giggles momentarily, but quickly recovers by putting her napkin over her mouth. Legless and I exchange glances and have much the same reaction, but it's pretty obvious that Hubert doesn't see a funny side to it, so we, too, compose ourselves as best we can.

'Pink hair?' I ask.

'*Bright* pink hair, and it's protruding from under her wig on both sides of her head, and at the front.'

'Gloria Farthing?' I muse. 'I'm not sure I know her.'

'She's one of those *solicitor* advocates,' Hubert replies with distaste. 'I have counsel prosecuting – Piers Drayford, who's all right, of course. But it's always the same with these bloody solicitors.'

'Oh, come on, Hubert,' Marjorie intervenes. 'Some of them are just as good as counsel, and let's be honest, we all know barristers who are not exactly ornaments of the profession.'

'I agree, Marjorie,' Hubert replies. 'But these solicitors don't get enough training in advocacy; they don't have to study the rules of evidence; and they don't have the Bar's ethical standards. It shouldn't be allowed.'

I know from previous experience that it's pointless to argue with Hubert about this.

'What exactly happened, Hubert?' I ask. 'What did you say?'

'Miss Farthing had some submissions to make to me about the evidence before we swore in a jury,' Hubert replies. 'And that's when I noticed the hair. Obviously, I couldn't let her get away with pink hair, so I did the only thing I could do. I told her I couldn't hear her.'

Legless laughs. 'I didn't know anyone still said that,' he says. 'I thought that was a thing of the past.'

'Certainly not,' Hubert replies indignantly. 'It happened to Sammy Mountford when I was at the Bar. We were down at Surbiton or somewhere, at the Sessions. Sammy's train was delayed and he was late getting to court. And you remember Frank Godwin, the Chairman of Sessions down there, I'm sure. Dreadful man, terrible temper. We were all terrified of him. If you were a minute late for court he'd come down on you like a ton of bricks. So anyway, on this particular day I was prosecuting Sammy, and I was already in court. So was Godwin. We were all waiting for Sammy, and suddenly I saw him rush into court and begin to apologise and explain about the train and so forth. And I'm waiting for Godwin to land on Sammy, but instead he starts laughing and can't stop, and he keeps saying "I can't hear you, Mr Mountford." Sammy has no idea what's going on. He raises his voice as much as he can until he's virtually shouting at the bench, but Godwin is still saying "I can't hear you" over and over again. Sammy looks at me as if to ask what on earth is happening, and it's only then that I notice the same thing as Godwin, and I start laughing too, so much so that I can't get a word out to tell him.'

'To tell him what…?' Legless asks. Hubert had stopped and seemed poised to turn his attention back to his lasagne.

'What? Oh, yes. Sammy had been in such a rush that he'd forgotten to put his wig on. He was wearing his wing collar, bands and gown, but instead of his wig he was still wearing his bowler hat. So, you see, that's one example. Judges still say they can't hear counsel if they're not properly dressed.'

'It's been a few years since you were at the Bar, Hubert,' I point out.

'What's that got to do with it?' he asks. 'We still wear robes. What's the point of wearing robes if advocates are going to turn up improperly dressed?'

'But you could argue that Miss Farthing *was* properly dressed,' Marjorie suggests. 'She wasn't wearing a bowler hat. She was wearing her robes. All that's happened is that you don't like her choice of hair colour.'

'I'm not sure about that, Marjorie,' Legless says. 'Hubert has a point, doesn't he? You can't claim to be properly dressed if you're making your robes look ridiculous.'

'What's ridiculous about it?'

'With pink hair? Come on, Marjorie.'

'No really. I'm serious. I –'

'Look,' I interject. 'I understand what Hubert's saying. In our day, if you'd appeared in court with pink hair you would never have heard the end of it. You'd probably have been drummed out of chambers.'

'There weren't any women at the Bar in your day, Charlie,' Marjorie replies.

'Of course there were –'

'A few, a very few. It was a man's world, and they had to dress and behave themselves in ways men approved of, and in those days men didn't approve of hair if it was pink, red, blue, or anything other than one of the natural colours. Times have changed.'

'That doesn't mean that advocates can appear in court dressed as if they were on their way to a party,' Legless insists.

'I'm not saying it does,' Marjorie protests. 'All I'm saying is that most people today feel that women are allowed to make choices about how to colour their hair, and that men shouldn't be telling them that some colours are out of bounds.'

'I have no problem with women with pink hair in a social context,' Legless insists, 'if they're going to a party or a rock concert or whatever. God only knows why any woman would want pink hair, but if she does, good luck to her. But if she's appearing professionally in court she must respect the dignity of the court, and I don't see how she can respect the court with pink hair under her wig. It undermines the whole system.'

'Oh, come on, Legless. That's a bit anachronistic, isn't it?'

Before Legless can respond, I decide it's time to jump in. My RJ's instincts are beginning to whisper to me that an academic discussion about changes in societal attitudes to hair colour isn't going to produce an end to this matter.

'Look, fascinating as this all is,' I say, 'it seems we have something of a situation on our hands. Hubert has refused to hear Gloria Farthing, a solicitor advocate, because she has pink hair. Now she wants to see me about it, as RJ, at two o'clock. Meanwhile, she's representing a defendant charged with GBH who's expecting a trial in Hubert's court, and what I need to know is what, if anything, I can do to get the case back on track?'

No one responds immediately.

'I'm not sure you can do anything today,' Legless offers after some time. 'Even if Miss Farthing has seen the error of her ways – which I doubt, given that she apparently wants you to intervene – she can't change the colour of her hair while she's at court, can she? So unless Hubert changes his mind, he'll have to adjourn until tomorrow in any case.'

'I'm not going to change my mind,' Hubert insists. 'Someone has to keep standards up in this place, and I don't hear anyone else volunteering to do it.'

'How long is her hair?' Marjorie asks him.

'How long is it? I don't know. Long enough to be seen. What's that got to do with it?'

'Well, I was wondering whether she could put her hair up and stuff it all under her wig so that it can't be seen,' she suggests.

'That's not a bad idea, Hubert,' I agree. 'An advocate's hair is supposed to be covered by the wig, isn't it, if she's properly dressed? So if you can't see it, there's no problem, and honour's satisfied on both sides.'

'But her hair would still be pink, wouldn't it?'

'So what?' Marjorie demands. 'If you can't see it, why should you care? For that matter, why is it any of your business? Are you going to ask her what colour knickers she's wearing?'

'Because she would be in my court, and I would still know that her hair was pink, wouldn't I? She would be mocking the court under her wig.'

'Oh, for God's sake,' Marjorie says.

'All right, look,' I intervene, seeing that things are getting a bit out of hand, 'we need to find a solution of some kind.'

'The solution is perfectly obvious, Charlie,' Hubert says. 'She can get rid of the pink hair, or she can get someone else to take the case over. Perhaps she'll instruct counsel. That would be better all round, anyway.'

Marjorie snorts.

'Do you want to deal with it?' Hubert asks me.

'No. You're the trial judge. You're the judge who's refused to hear her, so it's up to you to say what solution is acceptable.'

'Fair enough,' Hubert says, standing. He seems to have lost interest in the lasagne, and is ready to return to chambers.

'I'm not sure about this, Charlie,' Marjorie says after Hubert has gone. 'I think perhaps you should deal with it. You know what Hubert's like, and it occurs to me that he may not be on solid legal ground.'

'Oh, come on, Marjorie,' Legless protests.

'No, I'm serious. Hubert's saying that Miss Farthing can't exercise her profession with her hair a certain colour. What gives him the right to do that? What colours are acceptable and what aren't? How is she supposed to know? Are there any rules about it? Because if so, I've missed them.'

'You don't need rules to tell you that pink hair is unacceptable,' Legless insists sullenly.

'That might have been true in the 1960s or whenever it was that Frank Godwin and dinosaurs like him roamed the earth,' Marjorie replies, 'but it's not true today. I wouldn't want to be defending that proposition in the High Court if Miss Farthing were to challenge it. I think we ought to move carefully, Charlie, and I think it would be better for you to handle it.'

I shrug. 'I don't see how I can, Marjorie. Hubert is the trial judge. It's his court. It's up to him. Perhaps he'll come round to the idea of her putting her hair up. Let's just hope that Miss Farthing's hair isn't too long.'

'Or too short,' Marjorie points out. 'That would be just as bad. It won't fit under the wig properly unless the length is just right.'

'What would you have done, Marjorie?' Legless asks. 'Nothing, I suppose. You would have just let her carry on.'

'I'm not sure,' Marjorie replies. 'But I would have seen her in chambers on her own before the trial started, rather than raise the subject in open court.'

'That would have been better,' I agree, 'but it would be easier for you, as a woman, wouldn't it? If I had to do it, I'd ask you to see her with me, or at least have Carol or Stella sit in with me. I wouldn't fancy talking to a woman about the colour of her hair on my own.'

'But if she insisted that her hair colour was her choice,' Marjorie adds, 'I think I would have to let it go at that.'

* * *

Monday afternoon

'We're now going to start the trial, Mr Fogle,' I begin once court has been assembled. 'The first thing we have to do is select a jury. The jury bailiff will bring a jury panel into court; the clerk will pick twelve names at random from the cards she has in front of her, and these twelve will take their seats in the jury box. You're only allowed to object to a juror for cause – in other words, you can't ask me to excuse a juror just because you don't like the look of them. Do you understand?'

'You didn't need cause or nothing in my uncle Tony's day,' Lester complains. 'You could just object to up to seven of them for any reason you wanted, and the judge had to sling them off the jury. He told me all about it.'

'Well, you can't do that now. You can only object if there's a real problem, for example if the juror is someone you know, or someone who's had some involvement in the case, or has some knowledge of it.'

'That's not fair,' Lester protests.

'That's the law,' I reply.

Are you beginning to see now why trials with defendants acting in person take so long?

This afternoon my panel consists of fourteen good citizens of Bermondsey, thirteen of them wearing what I call Bermondsey smart casual – an open-necked shirt with jeans or tracksuit bottoms for the men, a brightly coloured blouse and tight black slacks for the women – plus one woman who is quite differently dressed. I confess that my first reaction on seeing her is to ask, 'Why me?' and then, 'Why today, when I'm dealing with a defendant representing himself, and why today when that defendant is Lester Fogle?' There's no answer to that, of course, except the obvious one: it's Sod's Law. Obviously, it has to be today, and no other day, that the jury bailiff sends me a female juror wearing the hijab, including the black burqa and niqab, which conceals her entire body apart from the eyes. Glancing at Lester Fogle, I see the spectre of cause arising in his mind.

It's not the first time we've had a woman wearing the hijab at court, of course. These days, it's not uncommon at Bermondsey or at any urban court centre. They may come as jurors, or as witnesses, or occasionally as defendants, and whenever they come, they pose one or two practical problems. The first is identification. How does the court know that she is who she claims to be? The second is a certain feeling of discomfort at not being able to gauge someone's reaction to what's going on in court, which, without a view of the face, you can't. Then there's the case where she's the defendant and wants to give evidence without letting the jury see her face, which is another matter entirely.

We've asked the Senior Judiciary – their Lordships of the High Court and above – for guidance on how to deal with these issues a number of times, but our pleas have fallen on deaf ears. Guidance isn't usually hard to come by from the Senior Judiciary; often you don't even have to ask for it. In general, they take great pleasure in trying to micromanage the work of the Crown Court, and explaining to us how much better they would run things, if only they had the time. But faced with a sensitive question such as the hijab, which has the potential to propel their images on to the front page of the *Daily Mail*, they tend to fall prey to a sudden attack of the vapours. They tell us it's nothing to do with them: we're the judges of the Crown Court; we should stop bothering them, get on with it, and use our common sense. So we do, and for the most part, with the assistance of the Bar, it seems to work out well enough. Today, however, I don't have the assistance of the Bar on the defence side, and I'm not sure how happy Lester's going to be with my application of judicial common sense.

Of course, there's always the chance that fate might let me off the hook, that she won't be one of the first twelve jurors selected from the panel at random; but when Sod's Law is the governing principle, you just know you're not going to get off that easily. Sure enough, at Carol's bidding, she takes her seat in the jury box as Juror Number Six. Once all twelve are in the box, Carol formally advises Lester that if he wishes to object to the jurors or any of them, he must do so 'as they come to the book to be sworn and before they are sworn'. Lester knows all about that already, of course, courtesy of his uncle Tony, and when Juror Number Six stands and takes the Holy Qur'an, carefully wrapped in its green cloth, from Dawn's outstretched hand, he duly objects.

'What's your objection to this juror, Mr Fogle?' I ask innocently.

'I can't see her face, can I? How do I know what she's thinking?'

'I'm not sure we ever know what jurors are thinking, do we?' I reply. 'At least until they return a verdict.'

'No, but if I give evidence or speak to the jury, I at least want to see who I'm talking to.'

'I understand that, Mr Fogle, but I'm afraid that's not enough to object for cause.'

'And in addition to that, how do we know who she is? What if she can't be bothered to turn up tomorrow and asks one of her mates to cover for her? We'd never know, would we?'

'I'm sure that the jury bailiff will check her identity, as she does with all jurors,' I try to reassure him.

'And the other day – it was in the *Sun*, wasn't it? – there was a lady on a jury wearing this get-up who was listening to music all day during the trial using her headphones, and nobody knew because she was hiding it under the... whatever you call it, the veil.'

'I'm aware of that incident, Mr Fogle, and I seem to recall that the juror in question was fined for contempt of court when it came to light.'

'And in addition to everything else, your Honour, her culture is different to ours, innit? I mean, she comes over here from Saudi Arabia, where they cut your hand off just for stealing a loaf of bread, and here I am charged with nicking a motor. What chance do I have with her on the jury?'

This, of course, is Lester's real point. I'm about to address it, when to my considerable surprise Juror Number Six decides to do it for me. She's a tall, imposing figure of a woman, and when she draws herself up to her full height, shrouded in black, it's actually a quite intimidating sight.

'What did you say?' she demands loudly of Lester.

Lester falls silent. I don't suppose Tony has prepared him for the experience of being interrogated by a juror, and he's not sure whether or how to respond – which is fine because I don't want him responding in this situation. It could get out of hand pretty quickly. For the second time I'm on the verge of intervening, but once again Juror Number Six beats me to it.

'Now look here, my good man,' she continues. 'I'm sure you

have all the usual depressing prejudices against people who look different from you. But I will have you know that I did *not* come over here from Saudi Arabia – or anywhere else, for that matter. If you must know, I'm from Chippenham. My name is Mary Elizabeth Green. My maiden name was Winslow. I read law at Cambridge. I'm a solicitor, and I'm on the selection committee of my local branch of the Conservative Party. And yes, I happen to be a Muslim. Is there anything else you'd like to know about me?'

She subsides a little and turns towards me.

'I'm sorry, your Honour. I do apologise. I didn't mean to get carried away, but when people start to talk about cultural differences…'

'That's quite all right, Mrs Green,' I reply, 'quite understandable. Let me just ask you one question. If you are sworn as a member of the jury, you will have to promise the court to try the case fairly, based on the evidence. Is there anything that would prevent you from doing that in Mr Fogle's case?'

'Nothing whatsoever, your Honour.'

I turn back to Lester.

'Do you still want to object, Mr Fogle?'

'No, sir, not in that case. And I would like to point out to Mrs Green that I'm not prejudiced against anyone. In fact, I'm proud to be part of a multi-faith, multi-cultural Britain.'

'Mr Lewis, what is your full name?' Susan Worthington asks.

She has opened the case to the jury with admirable brevity, less than ten minutes. In the course of her opening, Susan has explained to the jury that if they are not sure that the defendant intended to deprive Mr Lewis of the car permanently, and is therefore not guilty of theft, they can still convict him of taking the car without Mr Lewis's consent. It's sensible for Susan to hedge her bets. If Lester had intended to keep the car and sell it on, he probably wouldn't have left it sitting there in his front drive for all the world to see. So she offers the jury an alternative narrative. Perhaps this was more a borrowing than a theft, a way of ensuring that Lester had a ride home, the culmination of a night's drinking. For some reason, Lester, who has listened to the rest of the opening impassively, seems to be quite disturbed by this part of it. Shaking his head furiously he consults the index of the current *Archbold* we've loaned him, and scribbles some notes in a loose-leaf notebook.

'Raymond Hunter Lewis.'

'And do you live at an address in Canonbury, Islington?'

'That's correct.'

'Are you the owner of a 1965 silver Volkswagen Beetle, registration number EDB 726E?'

'Yes, I am.'

'And a beautiful car it is, too, to judge by the photographs.'

Lewis smiles fondly. 'It's my pride and joy. I take very good care of it.'

'That's obvious, Mr Lewis. On the evening of the twenty-fifth of February of this year, did you go out in your car?'

'I did. I drove from my home to the Lamb public house in Bloomsbury, Lamb's Conduit Street. I was with a friend, and we were going out for a couple of pints.'

'Where did you park?'

'Nearby, in Great Ormond Street. You can't park on Lamb's Conduit Street at that point; it's too crowded. But where I parked was just a minute's walk from the Lamb.'

'Yes. Mr Lewis, do you now realise that you made something of a mistake while you were parking?'

'Yes. It was stupid, really. I must have left the keys in the ignition and forgotten to lock the car. My friend and I were talking about Arsenal's chances for the rest of the season and getting a bit carried away, and I didn't think about it.'

'At what time did you arrive at the Lamb?'

'Eight thirty, eight forty-five.'

'And at what time did you leave?'

'Just after eleven.'

'What did you do on leaving the pub?'

'We walked to the spot where I'd left the car in Great Ormond Street. But the car wasn't there. That was when I also realised that I no longer had my keys.'

'Did you report your loss to the police?'

'Yes. Holborn Police Station is close by, at the top of Lamb's Conduit Street, so we walked there and reported it.'

'Two days later, on the twenty-seventh of February, did you see your car again?'

'Yes. I got a call from PC Jenkins, the investigating officer. They had recovered my car in South London and they had it at the police station in Bermondsey. They wanted me to come and identify it.'

'Did you do that?'

'Yes, I did. They had my keys, too.'

'Did you notice any damage to the car?'

'No, thank God, there didn't appear to be any damage.'

'Mr Lewis, did you give anyone permission to take or to drive your car on the evening of the twenty-fifth of February?'

'No, I did not.'

'Thank you, Mr Lewis. Wait there, please; there may be some further questions for you.'

Lester consults his notes before rising to his feet. He knows the drill. But, as I'm obliged to, I explain to him that this is his chance to cross-examine.

'So, Mr Lewis, you left your motor unlocked, did you?'

'Yes.'

'Careless.'

'Yes.'

'And you left the keys in the ignition?'

'Yes.'

'Even though you tell the jury it's your pride and joy? Plus, it's a bit of an antique now, innit? Worth a few bob, I daresay?'

'Yes. I'm embarrassed. But it happened.'

'So literally anyone could have nicked it, couldn't they?'

'I suppose so, yes.'

'It didn't call for your master car thief, did it?'

'No.'

'No need to finesse the lock or hot-wire it, was there? All they had to do was jump in and start the engine?'

'Perfectly true.'

Lester looks up to me with a smile.

'That's all, your Honour.'

'Your Honour, I'll call PC Jenkins,' Susan says.

PC Jenkins is a young, energetic officer, who almost bounds into the witness box. He's wearing a suit and tie for the occasion.

'PC 1521 Avory Jenkins, attached to Holborn Police Station, your Honour.'

'Officer, were you on duty at Holborn Police Station on the evening of the twenty-fifth of February this year?'

'Yes, Miss.'

'At about eleven twenty-five, did you have occasion to speak to someone?'

'May I refer to my notebook?'

After a few necessary questions to establish the circumstances in which he made his notes, I agree that he may; another process we could have short-circuited if Lester had been represented.

'Yes,' the officer replies after consulting his notes. 'At about that time, a Mr Raymond Hunter Lewis came into the police station with another gentleman, to report the theft of his car which he had left parked in Great Ormond Street earlier in the evening. My desk sergeant assigned me to talk to Mr Lewis and investigate the matter.'

'What did you do?'

'I took statements from both gentlemen, and gave Mr Lewis some paperwork to prove to his insurance company that the theft had been reported. I advised him that we would let him know as soon as we had any news, and I circulated the vehicle as missing, so that it would be on the radar of officers on patrol generally.'

'And in due course did you receive some information about Mr Lewis's car?'

'I did, Miss. This was two days later, on the twenty-seventh of February. In the afternoon, I was contacted by an officer based at Bermondsey police station, who informed me that Mr Lewis's car had been seen in their bailiwick, and was being kept under observation. He invited me to meet him at his station, which I did.'

'Who was that officer?'

'PC Robin Hartley.'

'Yes. After arriving at Bermondsey police station, did you go somewhere in company with PC Hartley?'

'Yes, Miss. At about seven fifteen that evening, PC Hartley and I visited an address at 161 Lynette Avenue, SW4, in Clapham. We parked a few yards down the street and walked to the property.'

'What kind of property is that?'

'It's a detached house with a garden and a driveway in front.'

'How were you and PC Hartley dressed?'

'We were both in uniform, Miss, and we were in PC Hartley's marked police car.'

'And what did you observe at 161 Lynette Avenue?'

'Parked in the front drive of the address, we observed a silver Volkswagen Beetle, registration number EDB 726E.'

'Was that the vehicle that Mr Lewis had reported to you as having been stolen?'

'Yes, that's correct.'

'What did you do?'

'I made a note of what we'd found, and took several pictures of the car and the scene using my phone. We then knocked on the front door of the address.'

'Did anyone answer?'

'Yes. The door was answered by a white male who appeared to be late thirties, early forties, wearing a floral open-necked shirt and khaki trousers. I asked the male if he was the owner of the property, to which he replied that he was. I asked his name, and he gave me the name of Lester Fogle.'

'Pausing there, Officer, do you see that man in court today?'

'Yes, Miss, he's the man seated to your left, Lester Fogle.'

'Thank you. Did you ask him any questions?'

'Yes, Miss. I said, "This vehicle parked in your drive was reported stolen two days ago in Bloomsbury. It belongs to a Mr Lewis. Can you explain why it's parked on your front drive?" I then cautioned Mr Fogle.'

'Yes. Tell the jury the words of the caution, Officer, please.'

'You do not have to say anything, but it may harm your defence if you do not mention when questioned something which you later rely on in court. Anything you do say may be given in evidence.'

'Did Mr Fogle say anything in response to the caution?'

'Yes, Miss. He said, "I've never seen that before." I said, "What? This car's been nicked two days ago and we find it in your drive, and you've never seen it before?" Mr Fogle then said, "That's it. I'm not saying nothing else. I want to see my brief".'

'What did you do then?'

'At seven thirty, I told Mr Fogle that I was arresting him on suspicion of theft, and again cautioned him. He made no reply to the caution. PC Hartley and I then conveyed Mr Fogle to Bermondsey police station.'

'Later that evening, with the assistance of the officer in the case, DC Hemmings, did you interview Mr Fogle in the presence of his solicitor?'

'Yes, I did.'

'And did he reply "no comment" to all the questions you asked him?'

'Yes, he did.'

'Officer, when you found Mr Lewis's car in the defendant's front drive, were any keys found?'

'Yes, Miss. The doors were unlocked and we found the keys in the ignition.'

'Was the car later tested for fingerprints?'

'Yes, Miss.'

'We have the report in case Mr Fogle wishes to refer to it, but please tell the jury whether any significant fingerprints were found.'

'Yes. Mr Fogle was fingerprinted on arrival at the police station, and we established that his prints were on the steering wheel and the driver's side door.'

'Thank you, Officer, wait there please.'

Lester gets to his feet again.

'Constable Jenkins, do you know me?'

'Do I know you, sir?'

'Yes. Do you know me?'

The officer gives me a quick glance to indicate that he's not quite following the question. Neither am I, yet.

'Well, I know you from having arrested you in this case, sir, yes.'

'Do you know me apart from this case?'

'Apart from this case, sir, no, I don't believe so.'

'But you know *of* me, don't you?'

'Know of you? I'm sorry, sir, I don't understand the question.'

I do. I'm beginning to see where Lester's going, but the problem is, I have no idea why. He's about to perform the sensitive operation lawyers call 'putting his character in'. He wants the jury to know about his criminal record. This is a classic example of the horrors of dealing with a defendant in person. In most cases, the defendant's previous bad character plays no part in the case; the prosecution can't use it against him except in particular circumstances, which aren't present in this case. Defence counsel will sometimes tell the jury all about it for tactical reasons, and I can generally trust counsel's judgment and not worry about it. But the effect of this kind of revelation on a jury can be considerable, and with Lester apparently steering the Titanic in the direction of the iceberg in person, I have some responsibility to suggest that he change course before he's holed below the waterline.

'I'm a villain, aren't I, Officer?' he asks.

'Are you, sir?'

PC Jenkins has been properly brought up – a rarity in this day and age. Many officers today would be only too glad to agree with Lester and jump headlong into the details. But Jenkins knows better, and very fairly gives Lester a chance to retreat. Before the exchange can go any further I send the jury and PC Jenkins out for a coffee break. It's the only way to try to regain some control over the ship, even though the jury have already heard a bit too much, and I've noticed that Juror Number Six is paying close attention and taking copious notes.

'Mr Fogle,' I begin once the jury are safely out of earshot, 'I've sent the jury out because I must explain to you that you don't have to tell the jury about your previous record. The prosecution can't ask you about it, and it doesn't need to play any part in the case.'

'No, obviously,' he replies, picking up *Archbold*. 'I know that. But I want them to hear all about it.'

'Are you sure?' I ask. 'You should understand that it may do some harm to your case to tell the jury about your previous convictions. Would you like to tell me why you want them to hear about your past record? Perhaps I can give you some guidance?'

'No, thank you. As I said before, I'd prefer to keep my defence to myself for the moment. All will become clear before long.'

'By then the damage may have been done,' I point out.

'Yes, sir, I realise that, but I don't think I have any choice, and I have consulted *Archy-bald* about it.'

'You understand that if you put your character in, Miss Worthington will also be entitled to go into it?'

'I do understand that, yes.'

He's up to something. I'm not sure whether this is his idea, or whether the Fogle family brains trust has come up with it while poring over their collection of old *Archbold*s during the long winter evenings, but there's nothing I can do. If he wants to go down this road, all I can do is warn him. He's free to disregard my advice. I see Susan licking her lips in anticipation.

'Very well, Mr Fogle,' I say. 'Let's have the jury back.'

'I'm a villain, Officer, aren't I?'

PC Jenkins is a bit out of his depth now. His professional instincts are to keep well away from this subject, but he's beginning to realise that he's getting dragged into it.

'If you say so, sir.'

'If I say so? Officer, you've got my previous convictions, haven't you?'

He looks to me for guidance.

'You can answer, Officer,' I say. 'I'll stop you if there's a question you shouldn't answer.'

He nods. 'Yes, sir. I have a copy of your antecedents.'

'Well, in that case, you know I'm a villain, don't you? Why did you say, "If you say so"?'

'Because he's trying his best to be fair to you, Mr Fogle,' I intervene.

Lester nods. 'All right. But I'm asking him.'

Whereupon Lester takes PC Jenkins line by line, with painstaking thoroughness, through his own antecedents. I still can't see where he's going, though the jury are all ears, and Juror Number Six is scribbling furiously.

'I'm a robber, PC Jenkins, a big-time robber,' he concludes after a dramatic pause. 'Wouldn't you agree?'

'You have been convicted of robbery, sir,' Jenkins agrees. 'It's not for me to say whether you're a big-time robber or not. I should think that's a matter of opinion.'

'Did I or did I not, on two occasions, rob commercial premises in company with others with the aid of an imitation firearm?'

'You did, sir.'

'Thank you, Officer. Oh, yes, one more thing. When DC Hemmings was briefing you before you interviewed me at the police station, did he describe me as a "big-time local villain"?'

Jenkins thinks for a moment.

'I can't remember him using those words, sir. But he did indicate to me that you were known to the police in Bermondsey.'

'You were a visitor to the Bermondsey police station, weren't you? You're based at Holborn?'

'That's correct, sir.'

'But, by any chance, did PC Hartley direct your attention to a list of names posted on a notice board in the canteen at Bermondsey police station?'

'I believe he did, sir.'

'Was my name on that list?'

'Yes, sir.'

'And what was the title of the list?'

'It was entitled, "Local Villains", sir.'

Lester turns triumphantly to the jury, arms in the air, like a Premier League footballer who's just scored the winning goal. If there had been grass on the floor in court, I think he would have fallen to his knees and slid all the way to the jury box. The jury are chuckling. Actually, I can't tell whether Juror Number Six is chuckling or not, which causes me a momentary feeling of guilt. If I can't tell what she's thinking, neither can Lester.

'That will do, Mr Fogle,' I say. 'Do you have any further questions?'

'No, thank you.'

I'm intrigued by the fact that Lester knew about the 'Local Villains' list. Initially, I can't work out how that could have happened, but then I remember that we are going to be hearing from DI Venables, and a glimmer of light enters my mind.

'I have PC Hartley, your Honour,' Susan says. 'The prosecution doesn't really need him, but if Mr Fogle wishes me to call him and tender him for cross-examination, I'm happy to do so.'

'I do have a few questions, as it happens,' Lester replies.

PC Hartley, in uniform, is called into court, enters the witness box and takes the oath in a brisk monotone. Susan asks him to answer any questions Lester may have.

'PC Hartley,' Lester begins, 'do you know me?'

'Yes, sir. From this case.'

'From this case? Not otherwise?'

'No, sir.'

'But you know *of* me, apart from this case, don't you?'

'Do I sir?'

He's looking at me, and I don't want to go through the charade again.

'It's all right, Officer. The jury have already heard Mr Fogle's record.'

He nods. 'Thank you, your Honour. In that case, sir, yes, I was aware of you before this case.'

'And that's because I'm a local villain, Officer, isn't it?'

'If you wish to put it that way, sir, yes.'

'I'm simply quoting from the list of names displayed on the notice board in your canteen, Officer.'

'Sir?'

Lester does a fine job of affecting surprise and indignation.

'You're not saying you haven't seen the "Local Villains" list, are you, Officer?'

'I can't immediately recall –'

'Can't you, Officer? I find that rather strange because PC Jenkins told us that you showed it to him.'

There is an awkward silence while PC Hartley appears to search his memory banks.

'Oh, *that* list…' he manages after some time.

Lester sits down without comment. It's all I can do not to applaud. It was very nicely done – almost as well as I would have done it, I reflected, and almost as well as Tony probably saw me do it at some time or other. Susan looks distinctly put out, and she still doesn't know how any of this relates to whatever defence Lester thinks he may have. Neither do I, but I'm enjoying the show.

'If there's nothing else,' Susan says, 'may we adjourn until tomorrow? DC Hemmings is giving evidence at the Old Bailey this afternoon, but he will be with us first thing in the morning.'

I agree readily, and release Lester and the jury until the next day.

I've been focusing on Lester Fogle so much during the afternoon that the matter of Gloria Farthing's pink hair, on which her client's chance of having his day in court seems to depend, has receded in my mind; but passing Hubert's chambers on my way to mine, it returns. I knock and go in; no sign of Hubert. I stroll down the judicial corridor to Hubert's courtroom; empty, no sign of activity of any kind. Finally, I make my way down to the list office, where Stella is busy charting our work for the next week or two.

'Did Judge Drake get his trial started?' I ask as casually as I can.

Stella shakes her head. 'No, Judge. He only sat for a few minutes and then adjourned for the day. He's ordered everyone to be back at ten o'clock tomorrow.'

I feel frustrated. 'Tomorrow? For God's sake, what was the problem? Was her hair the wrong length?'

Stella stares at me blankly. 'I'm sorry, Judge: what?'

'It doesn't matter,' I reply. 'I'm sure he'll sort it tomorrow.'

I'm not sure of that at all, but I've had enough for one day. Home beckons.

* * *

Tuesday morning

On the way to work this morning, thinking about Hubert, an association of ideas occurs and I suddenly have a vision of yesterday's dish of the day, the lasagne. The memory disturbs me, and as the prospect of the court salad or baked potato doesn't appeal either, I am prompted to take the safe route of a ham and cheese bap from Elsie and Jeanie. I pick up my latte as well, of course; no better way to get my morning started. George is the next stop, and as usual he has my copy of the *Times* ready, but this morning he's proposing some additional reading.

'You might want a copy of this too, guv,' he says with a disconcerting grin on his face, pressing a copy of the *Daily Mail* into my hand together with the *Times*. George knows better than to offer me the *Mail* – or indeed anything other than the *Times* – under any normal circumstances, but once in a while he has a good reason to suggest an alternative source of news. I've always been able to rely on George to sniff out any news items affecting the court or myself from the vast assortment of newspapers and magazines he has on any given day. I assume it's a service he performs for any of his customers who may attract the attention of the press. I'm not quite sure how he does it, but he always alerts me when one of my cases is getting some publicity, or when the court is mentioned because of a high-profile case or some unusual event.

The most spectacular example was when Legless tackled a defendant who was trying to escape from his court, and detained him at the cost of some, fortunately minor, injury to himself. That was easy to spot. Legless was the front page headline, his fifteen minutes of fame garnering him national attention. But George can flush a news item out even when it's buried on page forty-eight of the *Economist*. As he hands me the newspaper, he's grinning from ear to ear, which strikes me as ominous.

Seated at my desk with my latte, it doesn't take me long to find the reason for George's grin. On pages four and five of the *Mail*, under the byline of someone rejoicing in the name of Michaela Fabricante, there appears an article entitled, 'Keep your Hair on, your Honour! Judge sees Pink over Gloria's Glamour look.' It doesn't take me long to get the gist of it.

If you were an elderly gentleman who regularly appears in public in a wig and a purple dressing gown, you might think twice before telling women what colour their hair should be. But Judge

Hubert Drake apparently thinks there's nothing wrong with laying down the law to women if they are sporting a colour he doesn't approve of. When glamorous solicitor Gloria Farthing arrived in Judge Drake's courtroom at Bermondsey Crown Court yesterday to represent a client charged with a serious assault, the judge refused to allow her to do her job. Why? Because he didn't like the colour of her hair.

The judge, 66, who wears a purple dressing-gown-like robe and a white wig when in court, refused to hear Gloria because she had her hair coloured pink. 'I was properly dressed for court,' Gloria told the Mail. *'I was wearing my wig and gown, but the judge objected to the colour of my hair and wouldn't even discuss it with me. As a result, my client's trial has had to be delayed, and I don't know where I stand.'*

That was yesterday morning. After lunch the judge renewed his attack, telling Gloria that if she wanted to appear as an advocate in his court, she must change her hair colour to one 'normal women would have'. Gloria declined to comply. 'It's become a matter of principle now,' she said. 'It's incredible in this day and age that any man should try to dictate to a woman what colour her hair should be. If Judge Drake had approached me privately I might have tried to come to some understanding with him. But when he gave me a public dressing down in court, I decided to stand my ground. The prosecuting barrister agrees with me. The judge has ordered us back to court tomorrow, and I have no idea what will happen then.'

One experienced female barrister, who prefers to remain anonymous, told the Mail *that there is no list of approved colours for women's hair in court. 'This judge obviously thinks Queen Victoria is still on the throne,' she said. 'Perhaps in her day male judges could tell women how to dress, but I don't think that's the case today. I'm not even sure it's legal.' The barrister added, 'I wouldn't dye my hair a bright colour like that myself, but that's just me, and if Gloria wants her hair pink, I think the judge has to respect that.'*

This newspaper has often pointed out that most judges are still white males, and most of those white males were educated at private schools and graduated from Oxford or Cambridge University. Their privileged backgrounds make them out of touch with the public, and they seem to relish clinging to the traditions of a bygone age. Judge Drake is also a long-time member of the Garrick Club, which has always refused to admit women as members. Perhaps he would prefer to have only men in his courtroom as well as his club.

Gloria tried to have Judge Drake's decision reviewed by the court's resident judge, Judge Charles Walden. As resident judge, Judge Walden has overall responsibility for the judicial work of the court. But Judge Walden refused to see her. He was too busy dealing with women's headwear in his own court. When Lester Fogle, 35, appeared in front of Judge Walden on a charge of stealing a car, the judge permitted a woman wearing the full veil to serve as a juror, despite Mr Fogle's protests that he could see nothing of her except her eyes. The Mail *is not prejudiced. But when people are allowed to dress in this way regardless of the effect it has on the working of our cherished national institutions, something is going wrong. The* Mail *has consistently urged the people of Britain to take back their country, but as long as out-of-touch, unelected judges stand in the way…*

And so it goes on. I'm just finishing my reading, and realising that my latte is getting cold, when Stella walks in and immediately notices the *Mail* open on my desk.

'I wondered if you'd seen it,' she says.

'The question is whether Judge Drake has seen it,' I reply.

'Not as far as I know, Judge. I'm sure we'd have heard about it if he had. We're screening his phone calls, and being Judge

Drake, fortunately there's no chance of him finding out via the internet, but even so…'

'Even so, he's going to have to know.'

'Yes.'

'I'll talk to him myself. What have you done about the press?'

'I've notified the Judicial Press Office. They said we should refer all phone calls to them, and they're going to put out a press release during the morning.'

'Good.'

'But we've got reporters arriving at court, Judge. I think both you and Judge Drake will have something of an audience this morning. And the Grey Smoothies are sending someone to talk to you at lunchtime.'

'The Grey Smoothies? What have the Grey Smoothies got to do with it?'

'I don't know, Judge. But you know how funny they get whenever a court's mentioned in the news.'

I nod. 'Yes. Well, we'll worry about that at lunchtime, shall we? I'd better go and show this to Judge Drake. And you'd better have Miss Farthing and Mr Drayford available. I may have to talk to them myself.'

'Right you are, Judge.'

By the time I've calmed Hubert down, it's almost ten o'clock and I have to send a message to everyone in the Fogle case that there's going to be some delay and they have time for coffee. It's required all my powers of persuasion to talk him down from issuing warrants for the arrest of the editor of the *Daily Mail* and Michaela Fabricante, and a further warrant for the search of the *Mail*'s offices and the seizure of any further subversive material found there. And that was after I'd talked him down from dragging Gloria Farthing into court there and then and banging her up for contempt until she apologised and returned her hair to whatever colour it is naturally.

Odd as it may seem, I don't think it was the suggestion of his being out of touch that upset Hubert. That's an image he enjoys and cultivates. He's a natural and enthusiastic reactionary, and I'm quite sure that he has never for one moment doubted that he has power to dictate to female advocates what colour their hair should be in court. The image of the ancient judge wedded to an anachronistic tradition is one he relishes, not to mention that it should be worth a congratulatory drink or two from his friends at the Garrick Club. I think what upset him was the reference to his age. He's sensitive about his age because many of us suspect he's older than he lets on. I don't buy sixty-six, and one day not too far off there's going to be an almighty row about the date of his retirement; so age is a subject he prefers to avoid, especially when the Grey Smoothies may be paying attention.

Eventually, Hubert agrees that diplomatic relations between Gloria Farthing and himself have broken down beyond recall, and we are past the point where he can deal with this as the trial judge. We further agree that I should have a word with her and see if I can get the trial back on track before it becomes too much of a *cause célèbre*. I return to chambers and ask Carol to find Miss Farthing and Piers Drayford and bring them in. I'm sure the press are wondering why nothing is going on either in my courtroom or Hubert's, but they will just have to be patient. I have a crisis to manage. I ask Carol to stay. I don't want Michaela Fabricante demanding to know, in the columns of tomorrow's *Mail*, why Gloria Farthing was the only female in the room when she was grilled by the resident judge.

Having nothing to go on except Hubert's account of events and the report in the *Mail*, I must admit that I'd formed a mental image of Gloria Farthing as a kind of legal Boadicea, ready to die in the cause of pink hair, rushing into my chambers with bloodcurdling screams and brandishing a battle axe, her face smeared with woad – or at least threatening me with dreadful reprisals at the hands of the Supreme Court if I don't immediately declare pink hair to be an acceptable fashion statement in Bermondsey Crown Court. I couldn't have been more wrong. In fact, I find a visibly distressed young woman, who is obviously mortified by the predicament she's got herself in. Even now, she looks teary. I ask Carol to bring us all some coffee, and we sit around my table – Gloria, Piers Drayford, Carol and myself.

'You asked to see me yesterday, Miss Farthing,' I begin. 'But I thought I should speak to Judge Drake first. After all, it's his case and his courtroom. So I've heard his side of it. Why don't you tell me yours?'

'I never dreamed my hair would be a problem,' she replies. 'I was totally shocked when Judge Drake refused to hear me. Piers suggested coming to see you. He's been very kind, very supportive. I've only been qualified as an advocate for a few months, less than a year, and I've only done a couple of trials. The judges in those trials didn't comment on my hair, and you can't see much of it anyway under the wig.'

Well,' I reflect aloud, 'it's a new experience for all of us. I must admit that when I spoke to Judge Drake yesterday, I had some sympathy with him. In his days at the Bar, and mine too, I suppose, no one would have thought of coming to court with brightly coloured hair, and if they had, they'd have got short shrift from the judges.'

She nods. 'I understand, Judge. My grandmother gives me a hard time about my hair, even when I'm not going to court. But you see coloured hair everywhere now, and to be honest, I never thought about it. I didn't intend to offend Judge Drake. It's just that this is how I do my hair.'

'Are you with a firm of solicitors?'

'Yes, Judge.'

'Well, when you did your advocacy training, didn't anybody talk to you about how to dress for court? Didn't the partners give you any tips?'

'About dress, Judge, yes. We were told to wear a dark suit and black shoes, but they never said anything about hair.'

I shake my head. I suppose it's a generational thing. No woman lawyer in my day would have had to be told not to come to court with pink hair. They wouldn't have dreamt of it. But now, apparently, there are more things in heaven and earth than are dreamt of in our philosophy, and no woman lawyer today would dream that she isn't allowed to. Perhaps my day has passed, I reflect, but in any case, whether it has or not, there's no point in brooding over it. I need to work out what to do.

'Well, I'd like you to find a solution to the problem if you can,' I say, 'if only because your client is charged with a serious offence, and the court has a busy schedule, and we need to get on with his trial. So I'd like you to reach some accommodation with Judge Drake, if possible. I'm not sure how easy it will be, and frankly, having his name plastered all over the *Daily Mail* hasn't exactly improved his mood.'

'Or yours, I'm sure,' she smiles. 'Michaela shouldn't have mentioned the juror in your court. It had nothing to do with the story.'

'I'm not concerned about that,' I reply, only half truthfully. 'But I am concerned about Judge Drake. When I saw him this morning, he was contemplating having you arrested and taken down to the cells, and dealing with you for contempt of court. I managed to talk him down for now, until I'd had the chance to speak to you, but I'm not sure I can hold him off indefinitely. It would be in your best interests to find a way to resolve this quickly.'

She bites her lip and nods. 'I understand, Judge. But he humiliated me in open court, and I don't see how I can back down now.'

'You said you didn't intend to offend him,' I point out, 'and you didn't think your hair would be a problem. I accept that, and I think we can get Judge Drake to accept it. But I don't see any way out except to put your hair up under your wig, or ask for an adjournment until tomorrow and wash the dye out of your hair overnight.'

'I can't do that,' she replies quietly. 'I know I've only been doing this job for five minutes, but I think I've got to stand up for myself. It's not about pink hair now; it's about the way I'm being treated, that I can't be an advocate unless the judge approves of the way I look, unless the judge signs off on my hair. That's not acceptable. We're not in the Dark Ages any more, Judge. It's become a matter of principle.'

'Really? We're going to the Supreme Court over this, are we, or perhaps even to Strasbourg?'

'Perhaps so, Judge.'

'Judge Drake was pretty rough with her, Judge,' Piers adds. 'I understand his not hearing her, but some of the things he said after lunch, about the kind of hair colour "normal women" would have, were very harsh. I hope you don't mind my jumping in…'

'Not at all, Piers,' I reply. 'Most helpful.' I think for some time. 'Look, let me make one suggestion, and I make it because this situation could have serious repercussions for your career. Do you understand that?'

'Yes, Judge. I've been thinking about that this morning, and getting quite depressed about it.'

'Well, this suggestion might help. Get some advice from someone more senior in the profession. Ask your senior partner. Tell him it's urgent, that you need an answer by tomorrow morning at the latest. I can hold Judge Drake off until then. But your trial has to get underway tomorrow, one way or another. If it doesn't, I won't be able to protect you from the list officer, never mind Judge Drake.'

'That's a good idea, Judge. I do feel rather alone and vulnerable. I would feel more confident if I could get some advice.'

'Good. Then let's not waste any more time. I'll speak to Judge Drake and tell him what you're doing. Keep me up to date on progress.'

'I will, Judge. Thank you.'

As she is leaving, I call her back.

'Miss Farthing, how did this Michaela Fabricante get hold of the story so quickly?'

She smiles. 'I didn't leak it, Judge, if that's what you're asking. Michaela and I are best friends. We were at university together. She had asked some time ago whether she could come to court with me one day. It just so happened she came yesterday, and she saw the whole thing.'

Sod's Law again. I might have known.

Before I can do anything else, I have to see Hubert again and tell him to await events, just to make sure he doesn't have a rush of blood to the head and try to have Gloria Farthing committed to the Tower. I add that he can make himself useful by talking to Stella and offering to take any applications or sentences that may be keeping Marjorie or Legless from their trials. By the time Carol has assembled the court for Fogle and DC Hemmings makes his way to the witness box, it's already almost eleven-thirty. There are a number of reporters present. Most would have drifted over from Hubert's court, once they realised that nothing was going to happen there. If Juror Number Six is concerned about them, she doesn't show it, and if the reporters think there's going to be a big story about her today, they're sadly mistaken. They're welcome to report the landmark case of Lester Fogle if they're so minded.

'Leslie Hemmings, detective constable, attached to Bermondsey Police Station, your Honour.' He returns the book to Dawn and folds his hands behind his back.

'Officer,' Susan begins, 'are you what's known as the officer in the case?'

'Yes, Miss.'

'Would you explain to the jury, please, the role of the officer in the case?'

'Yes. The officer in the case is in overall charge of the investigation, and so is responsible for collecting and preserving the evidence, making sure that witnesses are interviewed and make statements, working with the Crown Prosecution Service to make sure the charges are correct and the case is ready for trial; and generally doing whatever needs to be done.'

'And when did you take over as officer in the case?'

'Soon after Mr Fogle had been arrested, Miss. I spoke to PC Jenkins, who was the investigating officer from Holborn, and PC Hartley from my police station. I made sure that the latent prints from the vehicle were sent for analysis. That was about it, really. It wasn't a complicated case.'

Not until now, I sense Susan thinking.

'As officer in the case, you've been in court during the trial so far, haven't you, except for yesterday afternoon, when you were giving evidence at the Old Bailey?'

'Yes, Miss.'

'So you know that the jury has been made aware of Mr Fogle's previous convictions, and I assume you are familiar with his antecedents?'

'Yes, Miss.'

'You also know that the jury has also been told about a list, entitled "Local Villains", pinned to a notice board in the canteen at Bermondsey Police Station. Yes?'

'Yes, Miss.'

Excellent. Ten out of ten to Susan for bringing this up before Lester has the chance to make yet another officer look dodgy just for exercising his professional discretion. She's going to take the wind out of his sails if she can.

'Were you aware of the list?'

'Oh, yes, Miss. All of us were.'

'What can you tell us about it?'

'It started out as a bit of a laugh. Some of us in CID made a list of well-known names we came across all the time when we were investigating local crime, and then someone had the idea of a wall of fame, where we could list them in order of how much of a nuisance they were. So we put it up in the canteen. But the Detective Chief Super thought it was actually a useful thing, especially for the younger officers coming in who didn't have the experience of the area yet and didn't know who was who; so he asked us to keep it up there, and bring it up to date from time to time. Everybody knew about it.'

'Is the name of Lester Fogle on the list?'

'Yes, Miss, it is.'

'And in terms of how much of a nuisance he is to the police, how high up the wall of fame is Lester Fogle?'

'Oh, not very high; somewhere around the middle of the table, I would say.'

Lester looks outraged.

'That's not a fair assessment,' he complains. 'That's outrageous. You've got some total wankers on that list. I should be at the top.'

'That will do, Mr Fogle,' I reply firmly. 'You'll get your chance to question the officer in a few minutes.'

'Well, it's not fair.'

'That will do,' I repeat.

Gradually, Lester subsides. The jury are chuckling again, but again, whether Juror Number Six is chuckling is unclear;

though I do catch a glimpse of her eyes, and I suspect she is. So is Susan.

'Mr Fogle may question the officer now if he wishes,' she says. 'I have nothing further.'

Lester stands and stares at DC Hemmings for some moments before beginning. Was that something Tony saw me do at some point? I realise I'm in danger of getting a bit paranoid on the subject of Tony, and try to put it out of my mind. But then things take an unexpected and rather dramatic turn. He shifts his gaze to me.

'Your Honour,' he announces in a formal tone, 'I am now about to reveal the nature of my defence in my cross-examination of this witness.'

It takes me a moment to react.

'I'm delighted to hear it, Mr Fogle,' I reply. 'The jury and I have been waiting with bated breath.'

'Right. Well, here we go, then. Officer, you told the jury that, as the officer in the case, it's your job to make sure all the evidence is available for the trial. Yes?'

'Yes, it is, sir.'

'If there was any CCTV footage of the theft of Mr Lewis's car, that would be useful evidence, wouldn't it?'

'I would agree, sir.'

'Was there any CCTV footage?'

'Not to my knowledge.'

'Not to your knowledge? As the officer in the case, did you make any inquiries to find out whether there was or wasn't?'

'I asked PC Jenkins to look into it, but he never got back to me.'

Susan closes her eyes briefly.

'Well, PC Jenkins isn't the officer in the case, is he? You are.'

'Yes, sir.'

'Where Mr Lewis parked, in Great Ormond Street, can't be very far from the children's hospital, can it?'

'I assume not, sir.'

'You assume not? Didn't you go to the scene yourself to have a look around?'

'No, sir, I didn't think it was necessary.'

'You'd expect to find some CCTV close to a hospital, wouldn't you?'

'Again, I assume so, sir.'

'But you can't confirm it because you never went there and PC Jenkins didn't get back to you?'

'Correct.'

'So the jury will never know whether there was CCTV footage that might have shown the theft in progress, will they, Officer?'

'We had the fingerprint evidence, sir. I thought that ought to be enough.'

'What? The fact that my fingerprints were on the steering wheel?'

'And the driver's door, sir.'

'Right. My prints were found on a car that someone left in my driveway, and it didn't occur to you that I might have been curious about finding a strange car in my driveway? I mean these days, with car bombs and what-have-you everywhere…'

Lester turns to me before Hemmings can reply.

'I'm sorry if I appear to be giving evidence, Judge, but I want to make my point. I will say all this on oath when I give evidence.'

I shake my head. Now I am truly amazed. I've already deduced that Tony has been doing some coaching behind the scenes, but now I see that 'coaching' doesn't do him justice; he's been giving Lester a master-class. All those hours poring over *Archbold* have had their reward.

'Your question was perfectly proper, Mr Fogle,' I say. 'Answer, please, Officer.'

'That did not occur to me, sir; no.'

'Right, well let's turn to something else, shall we? I put it to you, Officer, that my ranking on the "Local Villains" list should have been well above middle of the table. I should have been right at the top. I'm a big-time robber, aren't I?'

'I wouldn't agree with that.'

'I'm from a family of big-time robbers, aren't I? I mean, let's be honest, everyone in Bermondsey knows the Fogles, don't they? '

DC Hemmings looks at me anxiously, but I do nothing to suggest he shouldn't answer the question.

'Yes, sir. Your family is very well known in the area.'

'My dad and my uncle Tony used to hijack lorries.'

'So I understand, sir. A bit before my time, I'm afraid.'

'And I've done my best to continue in the family tradition.'

'Let's not get carried away, Mr Fogle,' I intervene. 'What's the point of these questions?'

Lester nods. 'My point, Officer, is: you took the chance to fit me up for an offence I didn't commit and would never have committed.'

'Fit you up, sir?'

'Do you understand that expression, Officer?'

'Yes, sir, I do, and I'm highly offended by it. I don't fit people up, and in any case, why would I fit you up with stealing a car?'

'To destroy my credibility as a member of the Fogle family,' Lester proclaims triumphantly. He turns to me. 'That's my defence, your Honour.'

DC Hemmings is obviously anxious to respond, but I hold up a hand.

'Let me see if I understand this,' I say. 'You're suggesting that it harms what you call your credibility to be falsely accused of stealing a car?'

'Of course it does. I'm a big-time robber. Have you got any idea what it does to my reputation if people around Bermondsey think I've been reduced to nicking motors? And not only that – no disrespect to Mr Lewis – but if I was going to nick a motor, it wouldn't be a Volkswagen Beetle would it? I mean, Gordon Bennett, give me *some* credit. If I was going to have a car away, it would be a Mercedes or a BMW, wouldn't it? But now, I'm a laughing stock in Bermondsey. I can't go down the pub without all my mates laughing at me. It's right out of order.'

'I see. And your suggestion is that this officer falsely accused you of this offence to make you look ridiculous in the eyes of your peers? Is that what you're saying?'

'That's exactly what I'm saying.'

I nod. 'Well, that makes it clear. What do you say about that, Officer?'

'That is completely untrue, your Honour.'

'Anything further, Mr Fogle?' I ask.

'Yes. Officer, is the name of Jimmy McGuigan on the "Local Villains" list?'

Susan springs to her feet. 'Your Honour, I must object to that. Whoever Jimmy McGuigan may be, he's not here to defend himself, and it's quite wrong for the defendant to attack his character in this way.'

'With all due respect,' Lester replies at once. 'According to *Archy-bald*, I'm entitled to attack Mr McGuigan's character if it's relevant. Miss Worthington is entitled to attack my character in turn if she wishes.'

Susan is beginning to seethe now, but as she couldn't really attack Lester's character any more than he's already attacked it himself, there's nothing much she can do. She sits down again with clenched teeth. I signal to DC Hemmings that he may answer.

'Yes, sir. Jimmy McGuigan's name is on the list.'

'He's generally known as Jimmy "Wheels" McGuigan, isn't he?'

'Yes, sir.'

'Where does that nickname come from, I wonder?'

'It comes from Mr McGuigan's propensity to steal and fence cars, sir, for which he has a number of previous convictions.'

'Does he specialise in exotic and unusual vehicles?'

'Yes, sir, that would be a fair statement.'

'Such as a classic Volkswagen Beetle?'

'I couldn't say, sir. It doesn't strike me as all that exotic.'

'Isn't it true, Officer, that you had evidence that Jimmy McGuigan was the person who stole Mr Lewis's Beetle?'

'No, sir, certainly not.'

'And didn't you and other officers recover the motor from Jimmy McGuigan, and tell him that it was his lucky day because you needed to fit someone else up for it, namely myself?'

'Absolutely not.'

'And didn't you leave the motor in my front drive in the early hours of the morning, to make it look like I'd nicked it?'

'Absolutely not.'

'I bet you didn't check for CCTV in the area near my house either, did you, Officer?'

'No sir, I did not.'

'Thank you, Officer, nothing further.'

Next, Susan formally produces written evidence proving that Lester Fogle's fingerprints were indeed found on the car, though somehow this evidence now comes across as rather less compelling than it did in her opening speech. She then calls DI Venables. It's been a few years since I saw Freddy Venables. He was a DC and then a DS when I dealt with him in several Fogle family cases. I've always liked Venables. He is a fair officer, and he always gave me the impression that he had something of a professional affection for the family based on long association. He is also the officer who once confided in me that the Fogles were opposed to violence, particularly against police officers, and sometimes quietly grassed up members of other families who committed such offences. He smiles and nods to me as he enters the witness box and takes the oath.

'DI Venables,' Susan says after he has introduced himself, 'I have no idea why I've been asked to produce you. I have no questions for you, but I believe Mr Fogle may. Please answer them.'

'Yes, Miss.'

Lester stands.

'Mr Venables, you've never dealt with me personally, have you?'

'No, sir.'

'And you've never been involved with this case?'

'That's correct.'

'But I believe you have had extensive dealings with my family, the Fogle family of Bermondsey, over the years?'

'I have, sir.'

'Could you please tell the jury what these dealings involved?'

'Well, in short, sir, I've had occasion to arrest various members of your family over the years for various offences of dishonesty.'

'Including my dad, Bill, and my uncle Tony.'

'Especially Bill and your uncle Tony, sir.'

'And at that time, would it be fair to say that the Fogle family ranked as one of the leading local crime families, if not *the* leading local crime family?'

'Yes, I would agree with that.'

'And Mr Venables, would it also be fair to say that on one

occasion – and I want to make it clear that I'm not saying you fitted him up, I want to make that clear –'

'Thank you, sir.'

'Because I know you didn't. Tony and my dad always said you were very fair to them.'

'Thank you, sir.'

'But would it be fair to say that on one occasion, you caused a rumour to circulate in Bermondsey about my uncle Tony?'

'That's quite correct, sir, yes.'

'What was the rumour?'

'I put the word out on the street that Tony was planning to target small shops in the area, sweet shops, newsagents, tobacconists, that kind of thing.'

'Which he never did?'

'Which he never did.'

'Mr Venables, please tell the jury why you did that.'

Venables smiles and shakes his head, looking up at me.

'It was a stupid idea, really. I can't remember who came up with it, me or DS Johnson. But Tony was so into himself, the big-time lorry hijacker. We'd nicked him for it more than once, and there were some other jobs that we knew were down to him, but we couldn't prove it. So we thought if we could make it look like he was reduced to knocking over sweet shops, we might put a dent in his reputation and discourage people from working with him on the big-time stuff.'

'Did it work?'

Venables laughs. 'No, sir. No one believed a word of it. I mean, with some others I could mention it might have worked a treat, but not Tony Fogle. He had too much of a reputation. But to give Tony his due, he didn't hold it against me. In fact, years later, we saw each other down the pub and had a good laugh about it.'

'But did this episode become well known to officers at Bermondsey Police Station?'

Venables laughs again. 'It became part of the folklore, as you might say. They still tease me about it today. But I've only got another month to go before I retire, so I'm not too bothered.'

'Thank you,' Lester says, sitting down.

'It's nice to see you again, Mr Walden,' Venables says, as he turns to leave the witness box. 'I never got the chance to say congratulations on becoming a judge. Well deserved. I'm very pleased for you.'

I smile. 'Thank you, Mr Venables,' I reply. 'My best wishes for your retirement.'

Susan closes her case, and it's time for lunch. Not an oasis of calm in a desert of chaos today, sad to relate. The Grey Smoothies want to talk over a sandwich; never a good omen.

It's a high-level delegation today, led by none other than Sir Jeremy Bagnall, the former Mr Jeremy Bagnall CBE, of the Grey Smoothie High Command, who is reputed to have the ear of the highest in the land. Sir Jeremy was knighted in the New Year's Honours list, for services to the court system: a citation which defies satire. He is accompanied by Meredith, our cluster manager, who is wearing her customary two-piece suit, flamboyant scarf and high heels. Her title indicates that she has responsibility for more than one Crown Court, the term 'cluster', in Grey Smoothie-speak, being used to denote any quantity greater than one. Meredith has brought her flunky, Jack, a graceless young man who looks as though he can't be older than fourteen, and wears an ill-fitting grey suit and a pink tie, horribly mangled with a miniscule knot scrunched under his collar. We are in my chambers, eating some dreadful canteen sandwiches with cheese and onion crisps and drinking cans of Coke Light.

'Something has to be done, Charles,' Sir Jeremy is saying. 'Judge Drake is giving the impression of being some kind of antediluvian nitwit who thinks he can dictate to women how they should appear in public. Can't you have a word with him?'

I notice that Meredith is sporting a few green streaks in her otherwise brown hair, so it's probably not the day for any show of frivolity on my part.

'I've had several words with him,' I reply.

'Well, they don't seem to be doing any good, do they?'

'It's not a matter for me, Jeremy. I can't tell another judge how to run his courtroom just because I'm RJ.'

'Well, if you can't control him,' Jeremy retorts, 'it may be that the ministry will have to intervene.'

'It's a judicial question, Jeremy,' I reply as mildly as I can. 'It's not something the ministry has jurisdiction over.'

'But the minister is concerned about it. The *Daily Mail* is pursuing him and he's worried that questions may be asked in the House. How is he to respond?'

Ah, yes, of course. The perennial ministerial nightmare: the question in the House.

'He should respond by pointing out that he has no legal power to intervene,' I insist. 'It's a judicial matter on which Hubert made a ruling during judicial proceedings. If he's got it wrong, a higher court will put him right further down the road. It's not a matter the minister has any power to intervene in.'

'*If* he's got it wrong?' Meredith interjects incredulously. 'The man is refusing to let a woman do her job because he doesn't like the colour of her hair.'

'Judge Drake made a judgment that Miss Farthing was not properly dressed to appear in his court,' I reply, doing my best to keep my frustration in check. 'That's something judges still have power to control. Judge Drake is within his rights. It may not be what I or the other judges here would have done, but that's not the point. Judge Drake is entitled to control proceedings in his courtroom until a higher court rules that he's doing so improperly.'

'It's a political issue,' Meredith fumes. 'Not to mention that he's violating her rights under the European Convention on Human Rights.'

'That would only be true,' I reply, 'if the right to appear in public with pink hair is a fundamental Convention right. I'm open to correction, but I don't think that's the case.'

'It's still a political issue,' she insists.

'I think pink hair looks cool,' Jack interjects as his contribution to the discussion. 'My sister has hers silver and light blue, but I don't think it's half as cool as pink.'

We all stare at him for some moments.

'Look, Jeremy,' I say, 'I know you have the ear of the Lord Chief Justice, as well as the minister. Why don't you ask the Lord Chief to have a word? I'm sure he will agree with me, and it may put the minister's mind at rest if he hears it from the Lord Chief rather than me.'

Jeremy doesn't reply this time, and contents himself with an unenthusiastic effort to take another bite of his mackerel sandwich. I decide to press my initiative.

'If the minister really wants to do something helpful,' I continue, 'he might have a word with the Lord Chief and ask him to issue a practice direction, so that trial judges know what to do with women who come to court wearing the hijab.'

'Yes, I was reading about that juror in your court,' Jeremy replies. 'Isn't there any rule about it?'

'No, there's no legal rule. We've been asking for guidance for ever, and, unlike pink hair, this really *is* a political issue. We want the Lord Chief to issue a practice direction. The trouble is that the Senior Judiciary run for cover as soon as we raise the matter. If the minister would tell the Lord Chief that he would provide cover – perhaps make a request for a practice direction himself – it might make a difference.'

'I'm surprised you allowed her to serve on the jury,' Meredith says sullenly, 'when you can't see her face.'

'I'm sorry you disapprove, Meredith,' I reply, 'but I thought I'd heard you say that judges shouldn't be telling women how to look when they come to court. Did I misunderstand you?'

She glowers at me, and I seem to see the green streaks getting progressively more luminous, as though they were radioactive.

'I very much hope,' Jeremy says as a final salvo, 'that you can sort this out by tomorrow, Charles. Any later than that and the minister's going to come under pressure.'

'I'm sure it will be sorted out one way or another,' I reply, 'for the very good reason that we need to get on with the trial of Miss Farthing's client. She knows that, as does Judge Drake. I will monitor the situation and help to the extent I can, but I'm afraid that's all I can promise.'

'What's a hijab when it's at home?' Jack asks Meredith.

* * *

Tuesday afternoon

As I'm bound to, I go through the motions of explaining to Lester that he isn't obliged to give evidence; that the jury are not allowed to convict him just because he doesn't give evidence; but obviously, in that case, the only evidence they have will have come from the prosecution; and that, if he does give evidence, Susan will be entitled to cross-examine him. Lester knows all this from *Archy-bald*, of course, but I have to do it. He listens politely, then strides boldly into the witness box and takes the oath. There's no one to ask him questions, of course, so he has to offer the jury his own narrative. I've assured him that I won't interrupt as long as he doesn't stray into areas he shouldn't.

'Right. For starters,' he tells the jury, 'I didn't nick Mr Lewis's motor, did I? I wasn't in Lamb's Conduit Street that night. I was at home, watching TV. Alone, for once; the missus was with her people in Wales, so I don't have any witnesses. But that's where I was. I don't go north of the River, do I? South London's my patch. If I go out drinking, or what have you, for the night, I go out locally. I don't know my way around up there, and I don't know anyone there.

'Look, I don't nick motors. I'm offended by the suggestion. I'm a big-time robber. I come from a family of robbers, and I'm very proud of my heritage. We don't nick cars in our family. It's the way I was brought up; it's just not something I would do.

'Anyway, on the night in question, in the early hours of the morning, this was – I couldn't tell you what time exactly – I was in bed asleep, but I was woken up because I thought I heard a car pulling up in my front drive. You know, it was quiet at that hour, and I heard the tyres on the gravel. I thought, "Oh, here we go", because I wasn't expecting anyone at that time of night and there was obviously something out of order going on.

'I went downstairs as quietly as I could. I didn't put the lights on. I kept waiting for whoever it was to knock on the door, but no one did. I waited for a long time, and eventually I drew the curtain back a bit and looked out of my window. I saw the motor there on the drive, but I couldn't see anyone around, so eventually, I went out to have a shufti at what was going on.

'I don't know anyone who has a Volkswagen Beetle. That's not my scene, if you get my meaning. But there it was, and it did occur to me that perhaps one of my mates might have had it away, and might have left it because he didn't want to be found with it. So I tried the driver's door handle. It wasn't locked. I climbed in and had a good poke around, but I couldn't find anything to say whose it was. I noticed that the keys were still in the ignition, and I left them there. I thought, perhaps whoever it was would come back for it. So I decided to go back to bed and if it was still there in the morning, I would deal with it then. Nobody came the next morning, and I sort of forgot about it.

'But the following evening the Old Bill came round and told me it was stolen, and accused me of stealing it. I could see straightaway how it was going. I was nicked, but I didn't answer any of their questions. But now, I'm a laughing stock in Bermondsey. Like I said, I can't even go down the pub without all my mates laughing at me. "Here he comes", they say, "Mr Grand Theft Auto. Fancy one of the old Minis, Lester? I know just where you can find one." It never stops, and no one's thinking about me as a serious robber any more. And that's about it, really.'

'So this is all a wicked plot by the Old Bill, is it, Mr Fogle?' Susan asks. 'A wicked plot to destroy your reputation, just as they tried to bring down your uncle Tony in the old days?'

'That's right.'

'Except, of course, they didn't fit your uncle Tony up with anything did they? DI Venables told us that. All they did was plant a rumour?'

'Yes, but it didn't work, did it? This time, they had to go a bit further, innit?'

'And they had to destroy your reputation because you're such a big-time robber? They had to go further to get you than they did to get your uncle Tony. Is that right?'

'That's right.'

'Well, let's look at that for a moment, shall we? How many convictions for robbery do you have, Mr Fogle?'

'Two, but I'm just getting started. And they don't know what else I might have done.'

'Really?' Susan asks. 'Are there any others you'd like to confess to now, while DC Hemmings is here taking notes? Anything you'd like to add to your CV?'

No reply.

'Well, let's stick with what we know, then, shall we? One conviction for robbery of a betting shop on London Bridge Road, in which the swag amounted to three hundred pounds and some change – to be split between three of you?'

'With a weapon, a firearm.'

'An *imitation* firearm. One conviction for robbery of a post office near Waterloo Station, resulting in a gain this time of two hundred and forty pounds and change, again to be split three ways. And that's it, isn't it, Mr Fogle, as far as your career as a robber is concerned?'

'As I say, that's as far as they know. But, see, they know I'm a member of the Fogle family. They know I have the gene. I'm on my way up.'

Susan is nodding. 'By the time he was your age, your uncle Tony was hijacking lorries and fencing thousands of pounds worth of merchandise on a regular basis, wasn't he?'

'It was easier to get started in his day.'

'All you've got apart from the two robberies is a few convictions for shoplifting and criminal damage and such like.'

'Everybody has to start somewhere. I'm a member of the family. My day would have come.'

'Come off it, Mr Fogle. You're not in your uncle Tony's league, are you? And you never will be. DC Hemmings's got you pegged, hasn't he, Mr Fogle? Middle of the table. That's where you are on the list, and that's where you are in reality.'

'That's not true. You're just as bad as them, the Old Bill. You're trying to make me look bad.'

'The truth is: you were up in Bloomsbury for the night; you needed a ride home; and you took Mr Lewis's car because it was easy – it had been left unlocked with the keys in the ignition. You took a car without consent, didn't you, Mr Fogle? That's how close to the big-time you've come.'

'That's not true.'

'And but for the vigilance of the police, you would have sold it on. But you couldn't even get that right, could you? You left it in plain view on your front drive for the police to find.'

'That is a wicked lie.'

'Admit it, Mr Fogle, you're a car thief.'

'No. That's not who I am. It's not what I do.'

Susan sits down with a knowing smile in the direction of the jury. She obviously thinks she's nailed it, and perhaps she has. But what Juror Number Six makes of it all, we don't know. That's the end of the evidence. Lester has no witnesses to call. As he's unrepresented, Susan honours the tradition of foregoing her closing speech, so all that remains is for Lester to make his. I give him overnight to think about it.

* * *

Tuesday evening

'So I'm caught between a rock and a hard place,' I complain to the Reverend Mrs Walden over dinner. We are enjoying her fettuccine primavera with slices of garlic bread, accompanied by a bottle of Lidl's Founder's Reserve Valpolicella, a welcome repast after the trials and tribulations of lunchtime.

'I can't interfere with Hubert's running of his courtroom without getting myself in trouble with the Lord Chief. But on the other hand, I can't let him continue as he is without having the Grey Smoothies on my case. And whatever I do, the *Daily Mail* is going to complain about it.'

'Yes, I see your dilemma, Charlie,' she agrees. 'What on earth has got into Hubert? I mean, he's always been a bit eccentric, but

I never thought he would be so mean to this young woman in his court. What's the problem?'

'I don't know. He's getting more and more eccentric – if that's the right word – as he gets older. But the trouble is: he's right in a way – Miss Farthing should know better than to come to court with pink hair.'

'Are you saying you would have done the same as Hubert?'

'No. I would have said something to her quietly in chambers. I tried to do that this morning, but it's all escalated to the point where nobody's listening.'

We are silent for a few moments, savouring the aroma of the Lidl's Founder's Reserve with its reassuring reminiscences of Italian summer evenings.

'Well, it seems to me,' she says eventually, 'that both Hubert and Miss Farthing should be paying more attention to her client, who's been waiting for his trial. What's he charged with? Is it serious? Is he in custody?'

'Yes. It's a very nasty GBH, a glassing during a pub brawl, causing permanent scarring.'

'Well, there you are, then.'

'Clara, I've made it clear that they need to get on with it, but no one's listening to me.'

'Then you're not using the right weapon,' she suggests. 'Borrow one from my armoury.'

'Really? And what might that be?'

'Guilt,' she replies.

I make a face.

'You've heard enough of my sermons, Charlie. Try a big helping of good old-fashioned guilt. Works every time.'

* * *

Wednesday morning
I'm in early today. I have Jeanie's latte but I have foregone the pleasure of the ham and cheese bap in the interests of time. To my relief, Hubert is also in early. When I present myself in his chambers, he's trying to convey an impression of relaxed indifference, apparently engrossed in the *Times* crossword. It's not convincing.

'We've got a man in custody awaiting trial for a serious offence, Hubert,' I begin. 'It's not your fault, but I need this trial to get underway. It's not fair to the defendant otherwise, to say nothing of the fact that it's playing havoc with the list. Stella's having kittens.'

The Reverend is right. To inculcate a feeling of guilt about inçonvenience to the court, and to Stella, is the way to go with Hubert, I'm sure. The one subject I'm not about to bring up is the Grey Smoothies. If Hubert suspected that the Grey Smoothies had anything to do with it, he would hold out until next Christmas as a matter of principle.

'It's nothing to do with me, Charlie,' he insists. 'I'm not standing in the way of the trial. I'm perfectly prepared to start the trial as soon as I have a properly dressed advocate representing him. If Miss Farthing doesn't want to do it, she should instruct counsel.'

'I understand, Hubert. I'm not suggesting you've done anything wrong. But I need you to help Stella out. We've got a nightmare of a week coming up as it is. If your trial runs over, it's going to cause all kinds of problems for all of us.'

He thinks for some time.

'Have you spoken to the pink-haired one this morning?'

'Not yet. I wanted to make sure I saw you first. Stella and I really need your help, Hubert.'

Finally, he puts the *Times* down on his desk.

'What do you want me to do, Charlie?'

'I want you to promise me that if you can't see any pink hair this morning, you will hear Miss Farthing and start the trial.'

'If her hair isn't pink, I have no reason not to hear her.'

'Well, actually, Hubert, my point is: not whether her hair is pink, but whether you can *see* her hair. If you can't, you would have no reason to inquire whether it is still pink or not.'

'Even if I suspected that it was?'

'Even then.'

'She would still be playing games with the court.'

'Perhaps she would. But I'm asking you to rise above it and maintain a dignified silence on the subject: just long enough to allow the trial to take place. If you want to take some action after the trial ends, of course, you're perfectly free to do so.'

I try to put on my sternest stare.

'But please, Hubert, for the sake of the court, let this trial go ahead if there's no obvious contempt of court going on.'

He says nothing for some time, but then gives me a perfunctory nod.

'Thank you,' I say, 'on Stella's behalf, as well as my own.'

I've arranged for Carol to bring Gloria Farthing into chambers on her own this morning. I'm sure Piers will understand. I don't want her to be worrying about opening up to me with her opponent present. But Carol is going to remain, to see fair play – for both of us. The hair, I note with some feeling of discouragement, is still the same bright pink.

'Did you think any more overnight about what we discussed yesterday?' I ask.

She nods. 'I did speak to my senior partner, Mr Daniels. He reminded me that we have a duty to represent our client, and he suggested that I shouldn't be doing anything to stand in the way of that.'

I've never met Mr Daniels, but I like him already.

'He's quite right, Miss Farthing. You don't want to cause any injustice to the defendant, do you?'

'No, of course not, Judge. But after the way I've been treated...'

'May I make a further suggestion?' I ask.

She nods.

'What if you could go into Judge Drake's court with your pink hair, but in such a way that Judge Drake couldn't see what colour it is?'

'So that he couldn't see it?'

'Yes. Technically, to be properly dressed, your hair should be concealed by your wig in any case, whatever colour it is. So why not put your hair up under the wig?'

She thinks about this for some time.

'But then he would have won, wouldn't he? What message does that send to other women advocates?'

'Your job at the moment is not to send messages to anyone,' I point out. 'As Mr Daniels said, your job is to represent your client. Don't let your client suffer over this.'

I attempt my most entreating look.

'I suppose what I'm asking you to do is to rise above it and maintain a dignified silence on the subject: just long enough to allow the trial to take place. If you want to take some action to send a message after the trial ends, of course, you're perfectly free to do so.'

She considers for some time.

'I'm not sure it will work,' she replies at length. 'My hair's a bit too long to go under the wig, but not long enough to put it all up at the back.'

I look at Carol. She and I have already had that discussion.

'No problem, Miss Farthing,' Carol says. 'I trained as a hairdresser before I came to work for the court service. I'll fix you up in no time. Grab your wig and come with me. We have a nice quiet staff bathroom. We won't be disturbed, and you'll be ready to go by ten o'clock.'

Lester, resplendent in his suit, a clean white shirt and an immaculately knotted tie, is ready to make his closing speech. I tell him that the floor is his and ask if he has any questions.

'There was one thing. Is it all right if I quote some Shakespeare to the jury? My uncle Tony said he remembered you quoting some once when you represented him, but he couldn't remember which bit it was.'

Neither can I. Susan is holding a handkerchief over her mouth.

'It was probably Portia's speech from *The Merchant of Venice*,' I suggest.

No one reacts to this except Susan – and Juror Number Six, who laughs out loud and seems momentarily tempted to applaud.

'You're quite free to quote Shakespeare if you wish,' I reassure Lester.

'Members of the jury,' Lester begins, 'I don't suppose you like me very much. I understand that. I'm not asking you to like me. I'm a villain. I'm a robber. I come from a family of robbers. But in a way, that's the point I've been trying to make. I was brought up in a criminal family, a very famous family in Bermondsey, the Fogle family. For years, my family was responsible for more thefts in South London than any other family. By the time I was ten, I was helping to unload the lorries my dad or my uncle Tony had hijacked, and by the time I was fifteen I was helping to fence stuff down the pub. That's how I grew up.

'I'm not making any apologies for myself. But the point is, I was also brought up with certain principles. One is that you don't use violence. I know that may seem a strange thing for a robber to say, but that's what I was taught. You might threaten violence, but you don't use violence. Another thing they drummed into me is that you don't do petty crime. You don't want to get the reputation of being a petty criminal. Once you get that reputation, people aren't going to work with you on the serious stuff. They feel they can't rely on you any more.

'Like I said in evidence, I didn't nick Mr Lewis's motor. I wasn't north of the River that night. The first I knew about it was when the car appeared in my driveway. I didn't know how it got there, and all right, I should have done something about it straightaway. I should have called round to my mates to see if anyone knew anything, or perhaps I should have called the Old Bill. But I didn't, and that's my fault. So I got nicked.

'But it's my belief that the Old Bill have fitted me up with this. How do I know? Because a little bird told me that it was Jimmy "Wheels" McGuigan that nicked this particular motor, and that's all I'm going to say about that. Whatever happened, it's been a disaster. Like I said, I can't even go down the pub any more. If I was in America, it would be one thing, because I would have been charged with Grand Theft Auto. That wouldn't be so bad, would it? Nothing petty about that, is there? I mean, if you can say you've got form for Grand Theft Auto, that's got a bit of a ring to it, innit? But here it's just theft. In fact, it's even worse than that. The prosecuting barrister said I might not even be a thief. I could just be a twocker. A twocker is someone who takes cars without consent: taking without consent, twocking. That doesn't have much of a ring to it, does it? I mean, which would you rather have: Grand Theft Auto or Twocking? And that's all I am now in the Bermondsey community, a twocker.

'They could have given you evidence about who stole Mr Lewis's motor, couldn't they? It was parked close to Great Ormond Street Children's Hospital. They have to have CCTV there, don't they? But DC Hemmings, the officer in the case, whose job it is to get the evidence, didn't bother with it, did he?

He didn't even go there himself to see if there was any. He didn't look to see if there might have been some in my street. There isn't, by the way. It's something you notice in my line of work. So you will never know if there was CCTV footage that could have shown who stole that motor.

'The prosecution barrister laughs at me for suggesting that I've been fitted up. But DI Venables told you that something similar happened with my uncle Tony years before. All right, he wasn't fitted up, it was just a rumour they spread, but the principle's the same, innit? They were trying to do him in by attacking his reputation. And that became part of the folklore at the Bermondsey nick. Is that where they got the idea?'

Lester picks up his notebook.

'And lastly, members of the jury, I want to leave you with these words written by the Bard of Avon that I think describe my situation very well. This is spoken by Iago in *Othello*, act three, scene three.'

He holds the notebook up and reads.

Good name in man and woman, dear my lord,
Is the immediate jewel of their souls,
Who steals my purse steals trash; 'tis something; nothing;
'Twas mine, 'tis his, and has been slave to thousands;
But he that filches from me my good name
Robs me of that which not enriches him,
And makes me poor indeed.

After which, Lester sits down without another word. I see Juror Number Six nodding.

It doesn't take me long to sum up. I outline the facts and I explain the jury's choice between labelling Lester a thief or a twocker, adding a witticism to the effect that they have no power to convict him of Grand Theft Auto. I point to the prosecution's failure to search out evidence in the form of CCTV footage. In conclusion I remind them of Lester's defence, and warn them that regardless of their personal feelings, they must give that defence a fair hearing. They may only convict Lester if they are sure of his guilt. If the evidence, including the allegations of a fit-up designed to make Lester look like a loser and a disgrace to his family, leaves them feeling unsure for any reason, they must find him not guilty. I have them out deliberating on their verdict before noon.

And so to lunch, an oasis of calm in a desert of chaos.

Having finished my summing-up relatively early, I'm the first to arrive today. I've ordered the baked potato with baked beans, usually a safe enough option. Legless and Marjorie arrive together just before one. Both confirm that their trials are going well. I regale them with the tale of Lester's literary prowess, by which we are all suitably impressed. Hubert is last. It's almost one-fifteen before he makes his entrance, which is unusual for him; he is rarely even a minute late for lunch, and his dish of the day, a chicken jalfrezi with basmati rice, is waiting for him threateningly. I allow him time to make a start on it.

'How are things going, Hubert?' I ask tentatively once he is tucking in.

'Very well,' he replies brusquely. 'We've started the trial. It will finish this week, so no need for Stella to worry.'

He's not going to add anything to that. I see both Legless and Marjorie poised to ask questions, but I hold up a hand and shake my head. I don't want anything jinxing it now. I know he's had a sprinkling of reporters in his court all morning, as have I, and I don't want to stray into contentious areas.

'You'll never guess what happened in my trial this morning, Hubert,' I say.

* * *

Wednesday afternoon

Carol comes into chambers at three thirty to announce that the jury in the case of Lester Fogle are ready to return a verdict.

When court has been assembled we bring the jury in, and I am intrigued, not to mention slightly anxious, to see that the former Juror Number Six has been elected foreman of the jury, and is sitting in her proper place in the front row closest to the bench. Lester looks at me like a man bereft of hope, and I turn away to avoid his gaze. Out of the corner of my eye I see him rubbing his right hand, almost as though he is imagining himself in the public square in Jeddah, awaiting his sentence for stealing a loaf of bread. The reporters are poised, pencils in hand.

'Would the foreman please stand; would the defendant please stand?' Carol says briskly. Both comply.

'Madam foreman, please answer my first question either yes or no. Has the jury reached a verdict on which they are all agreed?'

'We have,' the former Juror Number Six replies, quite clearly, through her veil.

'On the sole count of the indictment charging Lester Fogle with theft, do you find the defendant guilty or not guilty?'

She turns with obvious deliberation to face Lester.

'We find the defendant not guilty,' she replies firmly.

'You find the defendant not guilty, and is that the verdict of you all?'

'It is,' she replies, equally firmly.

I tell Lester he is free to go, and thank the jury for their service. I think of making a short speech for the benefit of the press to the effect that, in this country, jurors from any background and of any faith can be relied on to play their part in the proper working of the criminal justice system; but reflecting on how that would be likely to be translated in the pages of tomorrow's *Daily Mail*, I think better of it, and make my way back to chambers.

Five minutes later, Stella arrives to update me on our work for tomorrow.

'I don't suppose,' I ask tentatively, 'you've heard anything from Judge Drake's court?'

'Oh yes,' she replies at once. 'Didn't you hear?'

My heart sinks and I close my eyes. Cynic that I am, the only question in my mind is, not whether there has been a catastrophe, but the scale of the catastrophe.

'Judge Drake stopped the case,' she continues.

I look up. 'What?'

'Judge Drake stopped the case about half an hour ago. The case depended on identification evidence. Judge Drake didn't think the evidence was reliable enough to leave to the jury, so he directed a verdict of not guilty. I've got a new trial for him to start tomorrow.'

I shake my head. Before I can say anything else, there is a knock on the door. Carol enters.

'Judge, sorry to disturb you, but Miss Farthing asks if she can see you for a moment?'

'Yes, of course.'

She enters, still fully robed, including the wig, and there is not a pink hair in sight anywhere. I smile appreciatively at Carol. She smiles back proudly.

'I'm sorry to barge in, Judge,' she announces, 'but I'm sure you've heard what happened.'

'I've only just heard about it,' I reply. 'My own trial only finished a short time ago.'

'Well, I just wanted to let you know that, after he dismissed the jury, Judge Drake asked me to come into chambers – on my own.'

I feel my body tensing up again, and the thoughts of catastrophe return. What has Hubert done now? But to my amazement…

'He asked me to have a cup of tea with him,' Miss Farthing continues, 'and he told me what a good job I'd done showing up how weak the evidence was; and he thanked me for putting my hair up; and he said that he admired me for standing up to him over the hair; and that if I showed the same courage during the rest of my career I would do very well; and that he would be very pleased to see me in his court again.'

There are very few times when I am literally speechless, but I confess this is one of them. I must have muttered something in the minute or two before Miss Farthing left, I suppose, but I have no earthly idea what it was or whether it made any sense.

'Oh, Judge,' Carol says on her way out, 'you know that *Archbold* from the library we lent to Mr Fogle? I can't seem to find it anywhere. You don't happen to know what became of it, do you? Did someone retrieve it?'

'I have no idea,' I reply. 'But I'm sure it will turn up.'

Actually, at the time, I felt pretty sure it wouldn't. In fact, if I'd had to put money on it, I would have guessed that it had found its way into another Bermondsey library where it would probably be used far more often than if it had been left to languish in ours. But as it turned out, my words proved to be prophetic. Early in the following week I came into chambers to find the missing volume lying on my desk in a large brown envelope. The envelope also contained a letter from Tony Fogle. In it he thanked me for making sure that Lester had a fair trial; apologised for the 'lad's' lack of judgement in having the court's *Archbold* away after we'd been nice enough to lend it to him; and hoped I would understand that such a thing would never have happened in his day, adding that Lester was a grave disappointment to the Fogle family. He also wished me well, and said that I knew where to find him if I ever fancied a pint with him and DI Venables to reminisce about old times.

On my way out of court, I call into Hubert's chambers. He's about to leave for the day to take his accustomed place in the bar at the Garrick Club.

'I'm proud of you, Hubert,' I say.

'What?... Oh, you mean Miss Farthing... yes, well... I'd rather you didn't spread that around too much, Charlie. I don't want people thinking I'm going soft in my old age.'

'I don't think there's any danger of that,' I reply.

'And it doesn't mean that I approve of pink hair.'

'Of course not, Hubert. But well done, anyway.'

Hubert sniffs dismissively.

I wish him a good evening, and make a quiet exit, leaving him to his thoughts.

* * *

Wednesday evening

'So,' the Reverend Mrs Walden says, starting work on her second Cobra, 'Hubert's reputation has emerged intact after all?'

We are dining at the Delights of the Raj, which tonight has a particularly delicious lamb dupiaza on offer. All in all, it's been a highly satisfactory day, and although the *Daily Mail* will no doubt put its own characteristic spin on it tomorrow, the tradition of being properly dressed in court has been preserved, as has the right to be seen in public with pink hair in all appropriate circumstances. Neither Hubert nor Gloria Farthing will be taking further action. There is nothing left for the Grey Smoothies to get excited about; there is little risk that anyone is going to disturb the minister's repose by asking him a question in the House. And a jury led by a woman wearing the hijab has returned a verdict in favour of the scion of one of *Le Cinque Famiglie di Bermondsey.* There is as little hope as ever that we will get a practice direction from the Senior Judiciary on the subject of women wearing the hijab in court. But all in all, it's been a very good day for Bermondsey Crown Court.

'Yes,' I agree. 'It would have been a shame for it to get out of hand. Hubert may be eccentric, but he's a kind man at heart. If he'd banged Miss Farthing up, the press would have had a field day.'

'He wasn't going to let that happen,' she smiles. 'Hubert knew what it would mean for him and he knew he wasn't going to come out of it well. He was protecting himself.'

'Yes. I'm sure that's what it was.'

'Well, of course it was. He's just as concerned for his reputation as anyone else. And we know what Shakespeare had to say about that, don't we?'

I smile back. 'We do indeed. "Who steals my purse steals trash; 'tis something, nothing; 'twas mine, 'tis his, and has been slave to thousands."'

'"But he that filches from me my good name,"' she adds, '"robs me of that which not enriches him, and makes me poor indeed."'

We touch bottles and drink a silent toast to the Bard.

ARTHUR SWIVELL SINGS COLE PORTER

ARTHUR SWIVELL SINGS COLE PORTER

Monday morning

Sitting as I do most Sundays in my pew at the church of St Aethelburgh and All Angels in the Diocese of Southwark, I'm often tempted to compare what the Reverend Mrs Walden does when she delivers her sermons with what I do when I sum a case up to a jury. You might not think there's much of a connection between the two, but in my experience there's a remarkable degree of similarity. We both get dressed up in our robes of office; we both have an essentially captive audience; and we both spend a lot of time talking about law and the consequences of breaking it. True, she has a significant advantage when it comes to influencing our audience; I'm confined to the uncertain remedy of contempt of court, whereas she can summon up far greater powers. But all in all, the two processes have a lot in common, not the least of which is that we both repeat ourselves endlessly using time-honoured language: much of hers from the Bible, and much of mine from *Archbold*, which in the Crown Court is more or less the same thing.

There are substantial parts of any summing-up that hardly change from case to case. It's one of the comforting aspects of summing-up, that there is always quite a bit I could do in my sleep and that I can trot out without really having to think about it. This is a great boon if I have to start late in the afternoon;

I can get half an hour's worth in by rote, after which I can respectably leave the parts that require some thought until I'm fresh in the morning. For example, the burden and standard of proof: the jury can't convict unless the prosecution prove the defendant's guilt so that they are sure; anything short of that and the defendant must be acquitted. Once you've got a form of words that works to convey that idea, you can use it in every case. It seems to be much the same with the Reverend's sermons. There are certain constants, such as sin, repentance, and forgiveness, which always seem to attract the same familiar words and phrases.

The detailed content of a sermon or summing-up, on the other hand, varies considerably from case to case, and that's where the work comes in. In my case, the work consists of going over the law and my note of the evidence, and trying to summarise it so that it makes sense to twelve people with no legal training. For the Reverend Mrs Walden it involves summarising theological propositions so that they make sense to a church full – well, half full, anyway – of people with no theological training. One advantage the Reverend Mrs Walden has is that she's free to seek inspiration outside her study. I can't visit the crime scene, however much it might inspire me; I'm not allowed to, unless we have a formal view and I'm accompanied by counsel and the jury and the whole panoply of the court – a potential forensic disaster, and a mercifully rare occurrence. But the Reverend is free to seek inspiration in places which in her mind have some connection with the theme of the sermon. She often takes me with her on such quests. One of the staple themes of her sermons each year is the old chestnut of trying to serve God and Mammon at the same time, and whenever it comes time to retrieve those sermons from the archives, we seem to find ourselves prowling around Bermondsey market.

Bermondsey market is one of the great institutions of South

London. It's a vast sprawling street market, not too far from Elsie and Jeanie's archway coffee and sandwich bar, with canvas-covered stalls selling anything you could ever want to buy. We're all hooked on internet shopping these days, but I reckon Bermondsey market could give Amazon a run for their money when it comes to being able to find almost anything you want. Some of the stalls are small, basic affairs, and some are huge, almost like permanent shops, that make you wonder how on earth they ever get them assembled and disassembled in a single day, trading profitably in between. I'm always fascinated by the fruit and veg vendors with their exotic wares from foreign climes. I can browse around for an hour and not find more than one or two kinds of fruit and veg I can actually identify. Then you have your bakers and butchers and candlestick makers – literally – not to mention your fishmongers and your clothing retailers, offering complete wardrobes for the price of a decent lunch. And, speaking of lunch, there are several stalls providing refreshments, everything from burgers and fish and chips to kebabs, from curries to paella. There are stalls selling ordinary household items like sets of kitchen scales, tea and dinner services, coffee pots, mugs and plates featuring happy events in the life of the Royal Family down the ages, and things your parents and grandparents gave away because surely no one would ever want them. There's even a chap – he's not there every day, but often enough – with a selection of antiquarian books for sale.

And then, there are the vendors of electrical goods, tapes, DVDs and the like, which is usually where the courts and the church can get involved. In this area of the market, you have a fair chance of running into items that have fallen off the back of a lorry – or, in this day and age, more likely through the bottom of an ocean-going container. If you have the right contacts, the market is a perfect place to fence stolen goods of this kind; and so in addition to the traditional fencing of everyday commodities, which has been with us since the dawn of time, you now have the more sophisticated trade in counterfeit goods, everything from electrical devices to tapes, CDs and DVDs. All of this interests both the Reverend Mrs Walden and myself; in her case as an example of a blatant preference for Mammon over God, and in my case as a blatant example of the commission of criminal offences. One of those who's flirted with danger, both legal and theological, from time to time is Bert Coggins, an old market hand who, over the years, has sailed close to the wind in terms of suspect goods with some success. But one Saturday morning, his ship was finally blown on to the rocks. Bert's stall was visited by the local council's Weights and Measures Inspectors, and now he's in trouble on both fronts. The Reverend gave a God vs Mammon sermon yesterday; today, I'm dealing with his case.

To my frustration, I can't get to it until almost eleven-thirty. Today I had all the preliminary hearings listed in my court instead of spreading them among all four judges as I normally would. I'll explain why later. It took some time to get through them all, and meanwhile I had a jury panel cooling their heels upstairs, wondering whether we'd forgotten about them. But as I will explain, I had my reasons, and eventually, I'm ready to start Bert Coggins.

I'm amused, and pleased, to see that he's represented by Julian Blanquette. Julian has a reputation in the field of cases involving artistic themes, as he demonstrated some time ago when successfully defending the court's portrait artist, Jan van Planck, on a charge of fraud over a doubtful Dutch master. He's elegant, witty, and acerbic, and has an infectious energy about him. Prosecuting is Julian's antithesis, Piers Drayford. Piers is dry and methodical and rather lacking in style, but he is dependable and thorough, which more than makes up for any defects he may have. It should be an interesting case.

We swear in the jury, having interrogated each juror to ensure that none of them has more than a passing familiarity with Bermondsey market and, specifically, has never bought so much as a pair of bootlaces from Bert Coggins. And then it's time for Piers to take us all for a trip on his forensic magic carpet to the mystical land of bootlegged musical albums.

'Members of the jury, my name is Piers Drayford. I appear to prosecute in this case. My learned friend Mr Julian Blanquette represents the defendant Bert Coggins. Members of the jury, this case is about fraudulent trading and bootlegged CD Roms – albums of music offered for sale as being something they are not. This may all seem rather strange to you now, but I promise you, by the end of the trial you are going to need to know all you need to know about this dishonest trade.

'Members of the jury, the defendant Bert Coggins has a stall in Bermondsey market. He's been selling his wares in the market for more than thirty years; he's well known to the other merchants and to the public, and he's noted for that witty market trader banter immortalised by Del Boy in the classic TV show *Only Fools and Horses*.'

I see Julian think about rising to his feet to object to the comparison between Bert Coggins and Del Boy, but he rightly calculates that it's not going to score Piers any real points; and in the end he takes the far better approach of turning to the jury and sharing a smile with them, which scores one or two for him. Del Boy has many admirers in Bermondsey and I won't be a bit surprised if he comes back to bite the prosecution later in the trial.

'You've all seen stalls like Mr Coggins's at some time or other. He deals mainly in electrical goods, everything from televisions to CD and DVD players, smart phones and tablets, adapters and transformers; and I make clear at once that most of the merchandise Bert Coggins sells, though mostly second-hand, is genuine and above board. But when Weights and Measures Inspectors visited his stall one Saturday morning about six months ago, they found some merchandise that was neither genuine nor above board. This merchandise consisted of a consignment of one hundred bootlegged CD Roms, a musical album to which someone had given the title of *Arthur Swivell Sings Cole Porter.* Members of the jury, you will hear that Arthur Swivell was for many years a popular entertainer in South London, and that he performed with his jazz sextet in and around Bermondsey. Whether Arthur Swivell ever made a recording during his career the prosecution simply don't know, but if he did, members of the jury, the CD Rom offered for sale on the defendant's stand was not it.'

Piers turns to DC Watson, the officer in the case who is seated behind him, and is handed a number of copies of the offending album. 'Your Honour, there are copies for your Honour and the jury, one between two. With the usher's assistance...' Dawn, today resplendent in a violent bright red dress under her usher's black robe, does her usual brisk job of distributing them. 'Your Honour, I don't think there's any objection. May this be Exhibit one?'

I glance briefly at Julian who shakes his head. 'Exhibit one,' I confirm.

'Members of the jury, when I say that the album had been "given the title" of *Arthur Swivell Sings Cole Porter*, I mean that it was given a false title; because in fact, the album Mr Coggins had for sale is a recording entitled *Cole Porter, the Golden Years*, and it is a recording made as long ago as 1962 by a band called the Joe Kingsley Sextet. The Joe Kingsley Sextet was a jazz band based in Los Angeles, California, in the United States. Sadly, with the exception of Joe Kingsley himself, who is in a nursing home in Beverly Hills and is suffering from an advanced case of dementia, all its members are now deceased. So the prosecution is unable to call any of them to give evidence about their work on this album. But the prosecution is in a position to identify it, and you will hear from a Mr Chivers, who works for the company, that the album *Cole Porter, the Golden Years* was issued by the HMV recording company – His Master's Voice, I'm sure you remember, with the image of the dog staring into the big horn of that marvellous old gramophone, as they were called in those days.'

If any of the jury – whose average age looks to be late twenties to thirty – has any such recollection, their blank stares aren't giving it away. Mischievously, Julian grabs his pen and draws a quick picture on a page of his notebook – not at all bad for a few seconds work, especially the dog – and with a feeble effort to seem surreptitious, holds it up to the jury, while making sure that both Piers and I get a good look. The jury nod and have a giggle about it. It is a bit naughty, but if I try to tell Julian off he will give me one of his *faux* grovelling apologies, and it will only make things worse. And it is rather funny, so I join in the smile. Alone among those in court, Piers is not amused.

'Yes, I'm much obliged to my learned friend for his admirable artistic abilities,' he says icily, 'but if he had waited another minute, he could have seen the real thing.' He turns to DC Watson again, and carefully takes possession of what in my heyday as a teenager we called a 'record', a good old-fashioned piece of vinyl to be played on a turntable at 33 rpm.

'I'm trying to be as careful with this as I can,' Piers says. 'It's rather delicate. Members of the jury, this is an example of the original Joe Kingsley Sextet recording from 1962. Of course, in those days, it came out in the form of vinyl and only in the form of vinyl. You will hear this album played to you a little later, and you will be able to compare it with the bootlegged version offered for sale by Mr Coggins.' He turns to me. 'Again, I don't think there's any objection, your Honour. May this be Exhibit two?'

I nod. Piers holds the album on high.

'I'm obliged, your Honour. As I've said, members of the jury, we will prove that the album Mr Coggins had for sale is a bootlegged version of the recording issued by the Joe Kingsley Sextet in 1962, and that it was certainly not issued or released by HMV. Where it was produced, and by whom, the prosecution cannot say with any certainty. According to the cover, it is the work of a company called Young Earth Recordings, and there is what appears to be a website address. But you will hear, members of the jury, that the police investigation suggests that no such company exists, and that the website address leads nowhere. You will hear that it may well have been produced in Hong Kong, which is the origin of many bootlegged albums; but when and by whom it was produced, and how it made its way to Bermondsey market, will probably remain a mystery.

'What is not a mystery is that when local Weights and Measures Inspectors inspected his stall on that Saturday morning, Bert Coggins had one hundred of these bootlegged albums in his possession, and he was offering them for sale to the public at the price of nine pounds ninety-nine. Members of the jury, Weights and Measures Inspectors are officers employed by our local council to investigate all measure of dishonest trading practices, including fraudulent trading. They have powers to search for bootlegged products and on this occasion, they did indeed seize the albums. Having done so they asked PC Franklin, who accompanied them for the purpose, to arrest Mr Coggins, which he duly did. You will hear all about that from Inspector Thwaites in a few minutes time.

'You will see from the indictment, which I will now hand out to you, that Mr Coggins is charged with a single count of fraudulent trading. His Honour will explain the law to you later in the trial, and I won't take up your time with it now, except perhaps to say that as the name suggests, this offence consists of offering products for sale to the public in a deceptive way, using false pretences, pretending that the product offered for sale is something other than it is.

'When interviewed under caution in the presence of his solicitor, Mr Coggins answered most, though not all, of the questions put to him. He wasn't obliged to answer any questions, members of the jury. He was perfectly entitled to say "no comment" throughout if he wished. He did answer some questions, but made no comment with respect to others, including questions about how and from whom he acquired the albums, and again, he was perfectly entitled to take that course. I think it's a fair assessment of his interview to say that he denied all knowledge that the album *Arthur Swivell Sings Cole Porter* was anything other than what it seemed to be. He told the officers that he remembered Arthur Swivell performing in Bermondsey with his sextet years ago at the old Bermondsey Palais de Danse, and he had no reason to believe that the album was anything other than genuine. And it's right to say, members of the jury, that if you're not sure that he was knowingly engaged in fraudulent trading, he is entitled to an acquittal. But I submit to you that when you have heard the evidence, you will reject that explanation, and you will conclude that Bert Coggins knew perfectly well that he was offering to sell bootlegged albums to members of the public.'

He turns to me.

'With your Honour's leave, I will call Inspector Thwaites.'

Inspector Thwaites is a tall, erect man with a military bearing, dressed in an immaculate black suit, white shirt and red tie. He takes the oath in the purposeful tone of voice of a man who doesn't take fraudulent trading lightly.

'Inspector,' Piers begins, 'you are a Weights and Measures Inspector employed by the London Borough of Southwark, is that correct?'

'I am a *Senior* Inspector, sir.'

'A *Senior* Inspector. I do apologise. And for how long have you been a Weights and Measures Inspector?'

'For nearly twenty years now, sir.'

'Would you explain to the jury, please, what it is a Weights and Measures Inspector does?'

'As the name implies, we are responsible for seeing to it that the local traders give members of the public what they expect when they make a purchase from a trader. In other words, that you get full measure when you order a pint in the pub, that you get a pound of meat when you ask for a pound of meat from your butcher, and so on. We investigate and prosecute any cases of dishonest and misleading trading.'

'Yes, I see,' Piers says. 'And today, of course, it goes a bit further than the publican and the butcher, doesn't it? Do you also investigate more sophisticated cases, such as counterfeit or bootleg entertainment products?'

'Yes, as far as we can. We try to keep up with the technology, although it sometimes seems like a losing battle, what with all the resources the criminals have today. You see, our budget just doesn't allow –'

'No, I'm sure,' Piers interrupts wisely. These days, professional witnesses of all kinds love to bemoan their lack of resources while giving evidence, because they think of the court as a captive audience, and because they are deluded enough to think that the court actually has some influence over it all. It's not that we don't sympathise. Over the years, the cuts have undoubtedly made their job much more difficult than it used to be, as they have ours, and no doubt in some instances, have made it impossible. But there's nothing the court can do about it, and it's not the right forum in which to complain. We need their evidence, and in any case we can't let them use us to plead their own cause. With all the depredations visited on us by the Grey Smoothies, we have enough problems of our own.

'Turning now to the case of Mr Coggins,' Piers continues, 'did there come a time, on a Saturday morning, the eighth of September, when you visited his stall in Bermondsey market in company with other officers?'

'I did, sir. This was at about ten thirty on that morning and I was in company with Inspectors Farmer and Winstone, and we had with us a police officer, PC Franklin.'

'Inspector, do you see Mr Coggins in court today, and can you identify him to the court, please?'

'Yes, sir. He's the gentleman in the dock seated next to the officer.'

'What was the purpose of your visit to Mr Coggins's stall on that day?'

'We had received information that he was offering contraband musical albums for sale to the public. The information came from an anonymous call to the office,' he adds in a more confidential tone, looking up to me as if sharing a mystery with a fellow-professional who would understand. I nod briefly.

'What did you find when you observed Mr Coggins's stall?'

'As we had been advised, we found a number of albums entitled *Arthur Swivell Sings Cole Porter.* I made a test purchase of one of these albums from Mr Coggins for the price of nine pounds ninety-nine, which I paid in cash using funds previously authorised for that purpose by my superior officer, Chief Inspector Garwood.'

'Did you identify yourself to Mr Coggins as a Weights and Measures Inspector at that time?'

'No, sir, when making a test purchase I am authorised to represent myself as being a member of the public. I'm technically working undercover,' he adds with another knowing look up to the bench.

'Did Mr Coggins have anyone else working with him?'

'Not as far as I could see, no.'

'So, did Mr Coggins sell the album to you personally?'

'He did, sir.'

'At that time, did the name Arthur Swivell ring a bell with you at all?'

Senior Inspector Thwaites actually smiles.

'It did, as a matter of fact, sir. I used to hear about Arthur Swivell from my parents. Apparently he used to perform at the old Bermondsey Palais de Danse. My parents had met at the Palais, so they were very fond of the place, and they remembered Arthur Swivell from those days. They've knocked it down since, of course,' he adds with some feeling, 'like they do with everything, to build those new flats.'

'Yes,' Piers continues. 'Now, jumping ahead a little, have you since been told that the recording was in fact made in 1962 by a band called the Joe Kingsley Sextet, and that it was released by the HMV label?'

'Yes, sir.'

'That, of course, is the famous label involving the dog?' Piers asks, rather unwisely. The dog theme went wrong for him the first time, and experience surely teaches that it's not likely to get any better the second time. Sure enough…

'If my learned friend would like to borrow my admirable sketch, he's very welcome to do so,' Julian offers, brandishing his notebook. The jury start to giggle, but it's a bit too naughty for me this time.

'That will do, Mr Blanquette,' I say as sternly as I can manage.

'Yes, your Honour,' he replies, with a totally false tone of contrition.

'Please look at Exhibit one, Inspector,' Pier continues, making a commendable effort to ignore both Julian and the jury. Dawn conveys Exhibit one to the witness box. 'Is that the album you purchased?'

'Yes, sir.'

'Is there any sign of the dog or the gramophone horn on it?'

'None whatsoever, sir.'

'Any mention of HMV at all?'

'No, sir.'

'Any mention of the Joe Kingsley Sextet?'

'No, sir.'

'There is a reference to a company calling itself the Young Earth Recording company. Did your investigation produce any information about that company?'

'Both DC Watson and I inquired about that, sir, and we were unable to trace any company of that name in the recording business. Their so-called website stated that the site was in the process of development, and that was all. So we didn't get anywhere with that line of inquiry.'

'How many of these albums did you observe being offered for sale at that time?'

'There were nine in plain view on the stall, including the one I purchased.'

'What did you do then?'

'I identified myself and those who accompanied me to Mr Coggins and asked him how many of these albums he had. He went to the back of the stall and produced a single brown cardboard box, containing a further quantity of albums, which we counted and found to number forty-six in addition to those in plain view. I then asked Mr Coggins if that was all, and pointed out that we had powers of search, and at that point he produced to us a second brown cardboard box which contained a further forty-five. So in total, with those in plain view and the one I had purchased, there were exactly one hundred.'

'What did you do then?'

'I asked Mr Coggins –'

Julian rises to his feet. This time it's not about the sketch, and any pretence at humour has vanished.

'Your Honour, if my learned friend intends to go into his questioning of Mr Coggins, I must object. The Inspector clearly had enough evidence to suspect that an offence had been committed. Once that was the case, he could only question Mr Coggins further in a formal recorded interview at the police station. The police did interview Mr Coggins at the police station later, and of course, my learned friend is entitled to adduce evidence of that interview, but any mention of what was said at the scene is inadmissible. If my learned friend wishes to argue that point, may the jury please retire?'

Julian is absolutely right. Once you are a suspect you are entitled to the protection of being interviewed on tape at the police station. To circumvent that right by asking questions about the offence at the scene is a clear violation of police Code of Practice C. Police officers, as one would expect, have this drummed into them on the first day of training, and perhaps PC Franklin should have stepped in and stopped it. But you can't blame a young officer for not wanting to take on a senior Inspector like Thwaites who did his training long before we were saddled with liberal nonsense like codes of conduct – nonsense obviously designed for the sole purpose of frustrating investigators such as himself. Piers concedes without a fight. I have a shrewd idea that he wouldn't even have tried it on if Julian hadn't messed him around with the sketch of the dog. Fair enough, I think.

'I'll move on, your Honour. What did you do next?'

'Having made further inquiries,' Inspector Thwaites replies with a disapproving glance in my direction and with all the disdain he can muster for Code of Practice C, 'I conducted a thorough search of the stall, and I then asked PC Franklin to arrest Mr Coggins on suspicion of fraudulent trading, which he did. The officer cautioned Mr Coggins in my presence and hearing at about eleven fifteen, to which Mr Coggins replied, "No, these are the real thing, guv. They have to be, don't they? Anything on my stall has the Bert Coggins seal of approval".'

'Thank you, Inspector,' Piers replies. 'Wait there, please.'

'Inspector,' Julian begins, 'after Mr Coggins was arrested, did you make further inquiries about the *Arthur Swivell Sings Cole Porter* album?'

'Inquiries?'

'Yes, inquiries: to see if you could find out who had produced the album; where it had come from, and so on?'

'I did make some inquires about the origin, sir, as I said before, together with DC Watson. There were some details of the wrapping and presentation that suggested an origin of Hong Kong, but that's commonplace in this kind of case, and it didn't take us very much further.'

'I take it from what you say that it's not terribly difficult to manufacture a bootleg recording?'

'It's not hard at all. All you need is a decent copy of the original and the right equipment. Of course, how much equipment you have determines the quality of the product, but it's not hard to churn them out.'

'Well, what about inquiries a bit closer to home?'

'Closer to home?'

'Yes. You told the jury in answer to my learned friend that you were familiar with the name of Arthur Swivell, yes?'

'Yes, that's correct.'

'Did you interview Mr Swivell?'

'No, sir.'

'Really? Because his name was on the album, wasn't it?'

'It was, sir.'

'And for all you knew, Mr Swivell might even have been a potential victim of any fraud?'

'A victim, sir?'

'If Mr Swivell's name was being abused in connection with a fraud, wouldn't it be fair to describe him as a victim?'

'I suppose so, in a sense,' the Inspector concedes after some consideration.

'And, of course, if it happened that Mr Swivell and his sextet were actually the artists on the recording, he would certainly be a victim then, wouldn't he?'

'Mr Swivell wasn't the artist on the recording.'

Julian smiles. 'Well, we'll come to that in due course, Inspector. But leaving that aside, Arthur Swivell was something of a legend in your family, wasn't he, what with your parents' happy memories of the old Bermondsey Palais de Danse?'

'I wouldn't go that far. I never saw Mr Swivell perform myself.'

'No, but how could you resist the chance to speak to him? After all, then you could have told your parents all about it, couldn't you? "You'll never guess who I met today – none other than Arthur Swivell." It would have brought back all those happy memories of the good old days at the Palais de Danse for them, wouldn't it?'

'My parents are both deceased,' the witness replies stiffly.

I see Piers turn his head away and stuff the handkerchief from his top pocket into his mouth in a desperate effort not to smirk, if not to snigger. Fortunately, he's successful. I have to admire Julian. Whom the gods would destroy they first make to look like a total prat. The gods of advocacy deal you a blow like that in the courtroom sometimes, and for most of us there's no quick or easy way to recover. It takes Julian about three seconds.

'I'm very sorry to hear that, Inspector,' he replies with an astonishing show of sincerity.

'Thank you, sir.'

Julian looks up to the ceiling, allowing us all a respectful pause, as if seeing in his mind's eye the old Palais de Danse before they knocked it down to build the flats, taking with it so many memories. The jury follow his gaze.

'So, leaving aside any sentimental aspects of the inquiry,' he continues without undue haste, 'it didn't occur to you that Arthur Swivell might have some light to shed on the matter?'

'No, sir. I can't honestly say that it did.'

'I see. Thank you. Just one more thing: when you visited Mr Coggins's stall, the albums were being offered for sale in plain view, weren't they? There was nothing surreptitious about it, was there? They were there out in the open for anyone to see?'

'They were, sir.'

'So if Arthur Swivell had happened to pass by at that time, he could have seen them, couldn't he?'

'They were there for the whole world to see, sir.'

'Thank you, Inspector. That's all I have, your Honour,' Julian says.

His timing is good. It's almost one o'clock.

And so to lunch, an oasis of calm in a desert of chaos.

I said I would explain my decision to take all the preliminary hearings myself this morning, instead of spreading them around as I ordinarily would; and now I will. I have no real choice in the matter anyway; my colleagues will have noticed that they were able to start their trials on time this morning, and they're bound to be curious about such an unexpected bonus. In fact, Marjorie starts interrogating me before I can even take the wrapper off Elsie and Jeanie's ham and cheese bap.

'I thought I saw La Meredith prowling around the halls this

morning, Charlie. Are the Grey Smoothies making a nuisance of themselves again?'

'The Grey Smoothies want to know why we don't have enough defendants pleading guilty at preliminary hearings,' I confirm. 'Meredith has come to observe for the week and interrogate me about it.'

'Oh, not that old chestnut again,' Marjorie protests.

'How many are we *supposed* to have pleading guilty at preliminary hearings?' Legless inquires.

'How should I know?'

'Well, you *are* the resident judge,' Legless points out tentatively.

'I don't see what that has to do with it,' I protest, rather irritably.

'Well, we're supposed to keep statistics about that kind of thing, aren't we?' Legless asks. Seeing my frustration starting to build, he adds. 'By "we" I mean the staff, Charlie, obviously, not you.'

'Legless, you know we don't have any truck with that kind of nonsense at Bermondsey. We're a small court centre, and if we had to keep up with all the statistics the Grey Smoothies are always demanding, we'd never get any bloody work done and there wouldn't be any statistics.'

'But we must be giving them *something*.'

I nod. 'When they pester us, I sit down with Stella and we put some numbers together for them. Stella knows how many defendants plead guilty, of course. Some of them plead guilty at the preliminary hearing, others at the plea and case management hearing, and some of them leave it till the first day of trial. That's up to them. There's nothing we can do about it. I don't see what good it does to keep statistics about things we can't change.'

I think I can actually feel my blood pressure rising when I have to waste time on this nonsense.

'I've told Meredith that I won't see her until after court ends for the day,' I add. 'She's welcome to sit in court and take notes, but I'm not holding my trial up any more to discuss statistics with her.'

'Quite right, Charlie,' Hubert says, looking up from his sweet and sour pork with rice, the dish of the day. 'These civil servants have too much power as it is. If you play their game, it only encourages them, and there's no point in that. They should stay out of our way and let us do our job, as they always used to.'

'I couldn't agree more, Hubert,' I reply. 'But times have changed, I'm afraid.'

'That's the problem with everything now,' Hubert nods into a mouthful of rice.

'But are they saying we don't have enough early guilty pleas, Charlie?' Marjorie asks. 'And if so, what do they expect us to do about it?'

'We have as many early pleas as there are defendants who decide to plead guilty at an early stage,' I reply. I feel a bit silly about the obvious tautology, but in my mind it's self-evident. 'We give them the officially sanctioned encouragement with the offer of a third off prison time for an early plea, don't we? What more can they ask of us?'

'It's a waste of bloody time anyway in most cases,' Legless adds. 'In most cases Chummy isn't in danger of a prison sentence, and even if he is it will probably be a suspended. So what's the big deal about a third off? We have no real leverage; we can't work miracles.'

'And in any case,' Hubert insists, 'why should we? What's the court for if it's not going to let people take their chance at trial? That's the way we've done it for centuries. Why change now?'

'Well said, Hubert,' Legless comments.

'Because the Grey Smoothies think it would save time, and therefore money, if we put more pressure on defendants to plead without going to trial,' I reply. 'And you know what they're like. They have to make sure the taxpayer is getting value for money. Trials are not good value for money; early guilty pleas are.'

'Well, I still can't see what we can do about it,' Legless says. 'I'm sure it's much the same all over the country – isn't it?'

I nod. Sadly, he's hit the nail right on the head.

'The Grey Smoothies are comparing us with the West Country,' I reply. 'Apparently they've got the early guilty plea rate up above eighty per cent.'

There are audible gasps around the table.

'Eighty per cent?' Legless asks, aghast. 'What in God's name are they doing to defendants down in the West Country, waterboarding them?'

'They're either promising them something over the odds,' Marjorie replies, 'or more likely, they're making the lives of their solicitors a misery to get them to lean on their clients. They must know they're running the risk of pressurising defendants into pleading even if they may have a defence. I'm sorry, but in my book that's not on.'

'Absolutely right,' Hubert agrees.

'It's not fair to compare us with the West Country, anyway,' Marjorie adds. 'What sort of crime are they dealing with down there? Poaching? Supplying unpasteurised cheese? They should come and sit with us for a week or two in London and deal with some real crime. Let's see how close they get to eighty per cent then.'

'Just as a matter of interest,' Legless asks. 'What are our figures?'

'How on earth should I know?' I reply. 'It all depends what Stella and I decide on when the Grey Smoothies insist on having some figures.'

'Well, it rather seems that we may have reached that point,' Legless observes.

He's right, of course. It's bound to happen from time to time, and with Meredith vowing to camp out at the court all week to see for herself how we deal with preliminary hearings in comparison with the West Country, it may be a bit more tricky than usual to come up with some acceptable, albeit random numbers. But what choice do I have? I'm not about to authorise waterboarding at Bermondsey just to keep the Grey Smoothies happy.

'I will do what I can,' I reply without conviction, 'as I always do.'

There is a silence for some time, and I'm watching Marjorie playing around with her fork among the remains of her salad. I could swear that there's something she wants to tell me.

'Actually, Charlie,' she says enigmatically, 'speaking of Meredith, I may just have come across something of interest.'

'All help gratefully received,' I reply.

'There's no real secret about it, surely?' she asks, almost to herself, as if she is talking herself into leaking some terrible official secret. 'After all, it's just a case; it's a matter of public record, isn't it?'

'What is?' I ask.

She hesitates. 'Well, Stella has given me a case she wants me to manage. It's a fraud, looks as though it might be quite complicated. I haven't read the whole file yet, something to do with selling timeshares on the Costa del Sol which might or might not exist, or might or might not be available when you want them – you know the kind of thing. Anyway, I'm fairly sure that one of the defendants, a fellow called Stanley Everett, is the brother of our esteemed cluster manager. Her surname is Everett, isn't it?'

Time for more audible gasps around the table.

'You're *fairly* sure?' Legless asks once it has subsided.

'I made a couple of internet searches. It could be someone else of the same name, but it would be quite a coincidence.'

'Does Stella know Chummy might be Meredith's brother?' I ask.

'I assume not. If she did, I imagine she would have already asked you to transfer the case off circuit, to avoid any conflict of interest.'

Legless sniggers. 'Let's transfer him down to the West Country and have him waterboarded into pleading guilty,' he suggests. 'Let's see how she likes her brother being reduced to a cipher in the great eighty per cent statistic.'

'If Marjorie's right,' I point out, 'we'll have to transfer it somewhere.'

'Agreed,' Marjorie says with a definite suggestion of mischief in her tone. 'But my question is: do we have to do it immediately?'

She smiles at Legless.

'Marjorie makes a good point, Charlie,' he says.

The smile turns in my direction, and I suddenly see where Marjorie is going.

'Well, yes. You may be right, Marjorie. I'm not sure we could transfer it immediately, in any case. After all, we're not absolutely sure that this Stanley Everett is her brother at this stage, are we? But that would be a proper matter to raise at the preliminary hearing. In fact, one would have to go into it then. When is it listed?'

'Wednesday,' Marjorie replies. 'If Meredith is going to be with us, it occurred to me that you might want to take it.'

'Perhaps I should,' I reply, and actually catch myself smiling. 'Actually, I think I may have a duty to take it, as RJ. It's all very unfortunate, but I don't think I have any choice.'

'I'll send the file over to you,' Marjorie says. 'I know you'll make sure that Mr Everett isn't pressured into an early plea.'

I exercise my right to make no comment.

* * *

Monday afternoon

'My name is Henry Chivers,' the witness replies to Piers's first question after taking the oath. He's a short man with a soft American accent, wearing a blue three-piece suit and a violent purple tie, which, someone has obviously convinced him, is normal court dress for someone in a creative calling such as the music industry.

'Mr Chivers, what is your job?'

'I'm an archivist employed by HMV. I'm based in Los Angeles, but I travel abroad all the time to countries where we have a presence.'

'What exactly do you do as an archivist?'

'It's my job, in a sense, to be the company's institutional memory. I make sure we have systems in place to preserve all our original work under suitable conditions, and to be in a position to make examples of our work available whenever required.'

'I take it you don't do all that on your own?'

He smiles. 'No. I have a staff of about twenty working under me in LA.'

'And I take it that the work you do is not just for the sake of maintaining the legacy?'

'Oh, no. It's partly legacy, of course – that's important to us – but there's an obvious commercial side to it also. We have to be able to account to our artists and their agents, and of course, to our own management, at any time.'

'Mr Chivers, in this case, were you contacted by the Crown Prosecution Service and provided with a copy of what we're calling Exhibit one, an album entitled *Arthur Swivell Sings Cole Porter*, and did the CPS ask for your help in analysing that album?'

'Yes, they did.'

At a sign from Piers, Dawn carries a copy to the witness box.

'Is that the album you were provided with?'

'Yes, it is.'

'Had you ever seen it before?'

'No, I had not.'

'Mr Chivers, was that album produced or released by HMV?'

'Absolutely not.'

'And you know that because…?'

'Well, first off, it's not mentioned in our archives. Added to that, it's an obvious bootleg.'

'Why do you say that?'

'There's no trademark, no date, none of the stuff any reputable company would have on the cover when it releases an album. Once you know that the company named doesn't exist, there's no way to identify it. You can see all that just by looking, but in addition, when you listen to it, the quality is inferior. It doesn't come close to the quality we or any reputable company would insist on. In fact, it's obviously been done in a barely professional studio. I can almost tell you what equipment they would have had.' He takes one further look at Exhibit one. 'Plus, the wrapping and printing is vintage backstreet Hong Kong.'

'Mr Chivers, had you ever heard of Arthur Swivell before you came into this case?'

'No, I had not.'

'Having checked your archive, can you say whether HMV has ever recorded or released any work by Arthur Swivell or his sextet?'

'No, we have not.'

'Having listened to this album, are you now in a position to identify it?'

'Yes.'

'Tell the jury, please, how you were able to do that.'

'It took time, I'll tell you. It was obviously an old recording.

I had a pretty shrewd idea that we were talking the early 1960s, if not very late 1950s – it was difficult to tell because of the poor quality of the recording – but you can get in the ballpark just from the style of the music, the arrangements and so on. So I ploughed through our jazz collections from that period, but I still wasn't coming up with it. In the end, I approached one or two of our retired staff who go back to that time, and one of them recognised it as the Joe Kingsley band. This guy had actually worked on some of their stuff – not this one, but it turns out we'd recorded several albums by the Kingsley band. So eventually I ran it to earth. I can now identify this as an inferior quality bootleg of an album by the Joe Kingsley Sextet released by HMV in 1962 under the title, *Cole Porter, the Golden Years*.'

'Thank you, Mr Chivers. And have you also produced an example of the original vinyl recording released by HMV, which we are calling Exhibit two?'

'Yes, that's correct.'

I've been noticing some movement going on behind Piers in the last few minutes. One or two members of the CPS staff have been quietly carrying in items of equipment, one of which looks very much like a turntable similar to the one I had when I was about seventeen. It seems that the afternoon is about to get rather more entertaining. Piers invites me to rise for a few minutes so that the equipment can be set up and tested, which obviously, can never be done before court sits – that would be far too easy. But I'm not complaining today. In a short while the jury and I are going to have to concentrate hard on a long succession of sounds, and a break won't go amiss.

It also gives me the opportunity to alert the Reverend Mrs Walden to the afternoon's proceedings. Not many of her parishioners know this, but the Reverend is something of an authority on jazz, and has a very impressive collection of albums in various formats from vinyl onwards – a relic of her student days. Her main interest is female vocalists; and her collection is rich in Billie Holiday, Lena Horne, Cleo Laine, Ella Fitzgerald and others. But she is very musically aware more generally in the jazz field – and she is aware of Bert Coggins from her own research expeditions into Bermondsey market. I know she's going to be interested in this case, and I've promised to tip her off once the action gets underway.

When I and the jury return to court, the Reverend is just taking her seat at the back of the court. Mr Chivers is standing in front of the bench alongside what is now an impressive array of recording devices and loudspeakers. Piers tells me that we are ready to sample Bert Coggins's wares and compare them with what Mr Chivers believes to be the original source.

'So that your Honour and the jury know what to expect, I propose to play four tracks from Exhibit two, the original vinyl, and after each one, the corresponding track from Exhibit one, the CD offered for sale by the defendant.' He holds up the offending item. 'Your Honour and the jury may already have noticed this, but if not, the prosecution point out that both albums have exactly the same sixteen tracks, all songs by Cole Porter, and both albums have them in exactly the same order. We say that is a compelling piece of circumstantial evidence in this case.'

I don't know about the jury, but I hadn't noticed. Now that he's pointed it out, I'm inclined to agree with him. That is going to take some explaining.

'Your Honour, the four tracks we have selected are: "Anything Goes"; "Just One of Those Things"; "You do Something to Me"; and "Night and Day". We've chosen them as songs most people will be at least somewhat familiar with.'

I glance towards the back of the court, and see the Reverend smiling, as if to confirm Piers's good judgement in the matter. For a few seconds I have an image of Piers as a disc jockey in a leather jacket and jeans, plying his trade in some upscale jazz club, a thought I suppress as quickly as I can.

'Your Honour, it would assist greatly if Mr Chivers could remain by the equipment rather than returning to the witness box.'

'Certainly,' I agree.

'I'm much obliged. Mr Chivers, may we begin with "Anything Goes", please?'

'Yes.'

Chivers presses a button; the turntable begins to rotate at 33 rpm; he lifts the arm from its cradle and expertly places it on "Anything Goes", which, as it happens, is the first track on the album. Instantly, the court is treated to a sound which evokes memories of a vanished era – the gritty crackle of needle on vinyl, anticipating the release of the first notes of music into the air. It is a nostalgic moment for the more elderly among us in court, and I share a smile with the Reverend Mrs Walden; it brings back moments from our courtship. As it ends, Piers, who is far too young for this particular kind of nostalgia, is kind enough to allow us older folk a brief moment of respectful silence.

'Now, that was from the original recording on the HMV label by the Joe Kingsley Sextet: is that right, Mr Chivers?'

'Yes, it was.'

'Thank you. Would you please now play for the jury the corresponding track on Exhibit one, the CD offered for sale by the defendant?'

'Yes.'

This involves somewhat more modern technology, but despite that, the superior quality of the vinyl track is obvious to everyone in court. In fact, to my untutored ear, apart from the fact that both are undoubtedly recordings of 'Anything Goes', I have some difficulty in making any real comparison between them, and I suspect that at least some members of the jury are having the same difficulty. Piers and Chivers, of course, have anticipated that, and are ready to point out the salient features to the untutored ears among us.

'Mr Chivers, the track on Exhibit one is not of a very high quality, would you agree?'

'Yes, indeed; but that's often the case with bootlegged recordings. It all depends on the quality of the original the bootleggers have to work with and the equipment they have available.'

'Yes. With that in mind, what can you tell us about any points of similarity between the two recordings?'

'The first and most obvious thing is that the same instruments are involved: we have piano, guitar, clarinet, bass, and drums, and of course, the vocal. The second thing, which is less obvious unless you listen to music quite a bit, is that the arrangements of the song on the two tracks appear to be identical. For example, you have a piano instrumental after one verse, and a short guitar riff after another, and these appear to be identical both in terms of their melodic composition, and in terms of their placement in the arrangement.'

'Yes, I see,' Piers continues. 'And are you able to say whether that selection of instruments – piano, guitar, and so on – is the selection used by the Joe Kingsley Sextet generally in their performances and recordings?'

Understandably, Chivers hesitates. 'I believe so, yes. It was certainly the selection used in this album.'

Given that there is no longer any member of the Joe Kingsley Sextet capable of giving evidence, we're in danger of straying into the world of unsubstantiated hearsay, and I'm half expecting Julian to object. I know Julian enough to know that the point will not have escaped him. But he is sitting back contentedly chewing on his pen, giving every indication that the selection of instruments is not something he's too concerned about. But with Exhibit one having the same instruments and potentially the same arrangements as Exhibit two, in addition to the same sixteen tracks, I must admit I'm a bit curious about what Bert Coggins's defence is going to be.

Chivers ventures a few further details of the apparently overwhelming similarity of the two recordings, but I must say they are a bit on the technical side, and as Piers doesn't ask to play the track again to illustrate them, I don't find them particularly helpful. We then go through exactly the same procedure with 'Just One of Those Things', 'You Do Something to Me', and 'Night and Day'. In these cases, too, the poor quality of the Bert Coggins album makes it hard for the musically challenged, such as myself, to make a comparison; though by now, even I am hearing, or think I'm hearing, the same selection of instruments in each track. By the time Mr Chivers has enlightened us about all four tracks the afternoon is well advanced, and I'm only too well aware that I still have Meredith to deal with. For some reason – probably to ensure that I remain aware of that fact – she has been sitting in court all day, even though there hasn't been any question of anyone pleading guilty to anything since about eleven o'clock this morning. That's as far as we will go with Bert Coggins today, and 'Night and Day' seems an appropriate enough title with which to sign off until tomorrow. The Reverend Mrs Walden and I exchange a signal meaning, 'see you at home later' and I make my way back to chambers.

Carol has provided us with tea and biscuits and I notice, as Meredith takes a seat in front of my desk, that she has come prepared. Apparently she has engaged in a veritable orgy of note-taking during the day, the evidence of which, comprising two large notebooks, she arranges ominously in front of her.

'Thank you for seeing me, Judge. I know you've had a long day, and I don't want to keep you. I'm sure you're aware of our concerns.'

'Yes, of course,' I reply. 'You're concerned that allowing people charged with criminal offences to have their day in court is an old-fashioned luxury the taxpayer can no longer afford in this age of austerity.'

All right, that was a bit strong, but as Meredith said herself, I've had a long day and if there's one thing guaranteed to wind me up, it's hearing that what we do at Bermondsey doesn't represent good value for the taxpayer. In my opinion, we're cheap at the price. Actually, if the truth be known, what really winds me up isn't even that: it's the thought that what it costs the taxpayer should even come into it. Still, my reaction was strong, and I do my best to remind myself that she's only doing her job, and that it's her job I resent, not her.

'We would prefer to see it as making sure that we can afford to give those who have a valid defence their day in court,' she replies, somewhat frostily.

I take a deep breath.

'But that's the whole point, isn't it, Meredith? We don't know who has a valid defence and who doesn't until a jury hears the case and returns a verdict.'

'Yes, but experienced judges and lawyers have a good sense of what's going on in any given case, don't they?'

Meredith consults her notes, flicking over the pages between sips of her tea.

'For example, that case of Jolly in your list this morning…'

'The domestic assault.'

'Yes. I read the CPS file, and it's open and shut. He gets upset because she's cooked something he doesn't like for supper. He throws the food all over the place and punches her in the face several times, dislodging one of her front teeth, all this with the children looking on. How does he have a valid defence?' she asks indignantly.

There are times when you just don't know where to begin.

'I'm not saying he does,' I reply eventually. 'That's the whole point. I don't know.'

'But if he doesn't, we don't need to spend two or three days of Crown Court trial time on him, do we?'

'So, you're judging Mr Jolly by what's in the CPS file?'

'That's going to be the evidence at trial, isn't it?

'I don't know, Meredith, and neither do you.'

'But –'

'And in any case, that's only the prosecution's version of events, based on the investigation. What if the wife recants, or changes her story, or refuses to give evidence? They often do, you know. And what does the defendant say about it all? What if she was the one who threw the food on the floor because he was late getting home for supper? What if she went for him with a kitchen knife and he had to punch her to defend himself?'

'With all due respect, Judge, that's all very far-fetched,' Meredith says primly.

'Really?' I reply. 'I offer those examples because I've tried cases in which that kind of thing happened.'

'It's still highly improbable.'

'Of course it is,' I agree, 'and a jury will almost certainly see it the same way and convict him. But that's how we do things in the Crown Court. We ask a jury to decide based on all the evidence. We don't ask the court manager to decide after looking at the CPS file.'

'That doesn't mean that a judge can't point out to Mr Jolly which way the jury is likely to go, and at least encourage him to plead out.'

'Yes, it does mean that, actually,' I reply. 'Mr Jolly is represented by highly competent solicitors and a highly competent barrister, and between them they will leave Mr Jolly in no doubt about what a jury is likely to decide. But that's their job, not mine.'

I'm exaggerating slightly. I could push a defendant to some extent if I chose to, and you can't always guarantee that solicitors will be as frank with their clients as they should be. But in this case, the solicitors have briefed Susan Worthington and I'd be very surprised if Mr Jolly emerges from his first conference with Susan ignorant of the facts of life. I don't think he's going to hold out until the trial. It's just that Susan hasn't had time to get him there today. But I sense that's not going to get me off the hook this afternoon.

'There's only so much a judge can legally do,' I add for good measure. 'I'm allowed to point out to the defendant that he gets one third off any prison sentence for pleading guilty at the earliest opportunity. Actually, he knows that already without my having to tell him. It's one of the first things any solicitor tells a client. All the same, it reinforces the message if I repeat the information, which, as you will recall, I did this morning.'

'It didn't make him plead out, though, Judge, did it?'

'He didn't plead out today. That's all we know. He may still plead guilty before trial. I don't know. What I do know is that I'm not going to pressure him to plead guilty.'

Meredith consults her notes again.

'Well, all I can say, Judge, is that the minister needs judges to be aware of the cost of jury trials to the public.'

'I have no intention of being aware of any such thing,' I reply, rather tartly, I'm sure. 'That's not my job. If the minister wishes to be aware of the cost, that's all well and good, and if he thinks the cost is too great, he can introduce legislation to change the system. Good luck with that though, Meredith. When it comes right down to it, the great British public are rather fond of juries, and they won't give jury trial up without a fight.'

She nods. 'I'm not saying we should get rid of jury trial, and neither is the minister. All we're saying is that there must be more we can do to make sure that cases don't go to trial unless they should.'

'And all I'm saying is that we're already doing all we can; and at the end of the day, it's not something we can control unless we're prepared to risk pressuring defendants who may be innocent into pleading guilty because of fear of the consequences. As it is, there are probably cases where that happens.'

'In the West Country – ' she begins.

'In the West Country, they've got the early guilty plea rate up to eighty per cent,' I interrupt. 'I know. I've read the statistics.'

'Eighty-two point four, actually. How do you think they're doing that?' she asks, with a false air of innocence.

'I don't know,' I reply, 'and I'm not sure I want to know. But however they're doing it, it's not going to happen at Bermondsey. Not on my watch.'

There is a long, uncomfortable silence, during which I begin to foresee a long week ahead. Meredith isn't going away; on the other hand, neither am I. Eventually, she gathers up her notes and shakes her head.

'I mean, just look at that case you've got going on now,' she says. 'Coggins. Surely, that should never have gone to trial?'

'You think he's guilty, then, do you?'

'Don't you, Judge, really?'

'On the evidence so far, it's looking that way,' I agree. 'But we haven't even finished the prosecution's case yet, and we have the defence case to come. And anyway, what I think doesn't matter. It's what the jury thinks that counts.'

She doesn't respond to that, but mutters a sceptical goodnight as she leaves.

* * *

Monday evening

Tonight the Reverend Mrs Walden is preparing her delicious fettuccine with clams and garlic bread, and I've raided our small remaining collection of Lidl's Founder's Reserve Chianti to wash it down. I can't resist asking what she thought of the afternoon's proceedings. I hand her a glass and stand at a respectful distance as she works at the kitchen counter.

'It was very interesting,' she replies. 'You can't hear too well from the back of the court, but from where I was sitting the two recordings sounded very similar. Was that your impression?'

'Yes, I thought so, but given how little I know about music, I'm not sure my impression is very helpful.'

'Most of your jury will be having the same thoughts,' the Reverend observes, 'and what the prosecutor has to explain to them is that you don't have to be a musical expert to tell if two recordings sound alike.'

'What does defence counsel have to explain to them? At the moment, I'm not sure where he's going.'

'The defence has to avoid falling into a trap.'

'Oh? What trap would that be?'

'The trap of trying to tell the jury that there are different shades of "alike".'

'Explain, please.'

'Charlie, "alike" isn't enough. What the prosecution has to prove is that the two are *identical*. They're saying that the bootlegged album was copied from HMV's original, so "alike" doesn't cut it.'

'Well, I'm certainly not sure my ear is good enough to hear that,' I say.

'That's the point the defence has to make. The best evidence would be for someone from the Joe Kingsley band to say, "Yes, that's our work", but apparently that can't happen, so all the prosecution has is some debatable circumstantial evidence about how similar the two albums are.'

'It doesn't strike me as such a weak case,' I reply, 'when you think about the fact that they have the same sixteen tracks in exactly the same order.'

'I'm not necessarily saying it's a weak case,' she replies. 'I'm just not sure it's as strong as the prosecutor thinks it is.'

We sit down together on the sofa with our wine to wait for the fettuccine to cook.

'Have you ever heard of either of these two bands?'

She shakes her head. 'The name Joe Kingsley strikes a distant chord, but I can't remember having heard anything by them. Arthur Swivell I've heard of, but only because he's a local boy. My older parishioners mention him occasionally when they're reminiscing about the old days and their Saturday nights at the Palais de Danse. I'm sure he must have retired years ago; in fact I was quite surprised to hear he was still alive. He must not be quite as old as I'd assumed.'

The conversation turns to other things, but over coffee after dinner, she brings up Arthur Swivell again.

'It will be interesting to see him,' she says. 'I must admit I'm curious about what he's going to say.'

I sit up and take notice.

'You think he will be called to give evidence?' I ask. 'By whom?'

'The defence, I should think,' she replies. 'But surely someone has to? He's the only person who can tell the jury whether the album is bootlegged or not, isn't he?'

* * *

Tuesday morning

The case's connection to Bermondsey and Arthur Swivell has attracted the attention of the *Standard* overnight, so it's no surprise that this morning I'm interrogated about it by two of Bermondsey's older residents.

'It's such a shame they knocked down the old Palais de Danse, sir,' Elsie laments after a general inquiry about the case. 'That's where we went on Saturday nights when we were young, wasn't it, Jeanie?'

'Always,' Jeanie agrees. 'You could have a good night out for five bob in those days, meet some boys, have a couple of drinks and a good dance. It was good, harmless fun. They can't leave anything alone, can they? And what have they put in its place? More of those cheap-looking flats. There's nowhere for the young people to go anymore, not to hear live music and dance like we did.'

'So you would have heard the Arthur Swivell band, then?' I surmise.

'Oh, yes,' Elsie replies. 'Arthur was there at least two Saturday nights a month. He was very good. He played all the good tunes, didn't he, Jeanie? George Gershwin, Irving Berlin.'

'Cole Porter?' I ask on impulse.

'Oh, yes,' she replies, and to my surprise, she treats us to a rather good verse of 'Anything Goes'. Elsie and I give her a round of applause, and she takes a bow, smiling.

'Couldn't you have them done for it, sir?' Jeanie asks a minute or two later, handing me my latte and my lunchtime ham and cheese bap.

'Have who done for what?' I ask.

'That developer, for knocking down the old Palais and putting up that monstrosity of a block of flats.'

'I'm afraid not,' I reply, with an attempt at sounding sad. 'I'm sure they had planning permission, so there's nothing we can do now. Anyway, you couldn't rebuild the Palais now, could you? Not like it was. It wouldn't be the same.'

'That's the truth, sir,' Jeanie replies. 'But they'll take anything away these days if it saves somebody some money – or makes some money for somebody – won't they?'

I reflect briefly on the Grey Smoothies and on Senior Inspector Thwaites and on their respective preoccupations with the same subject.

'It certainly appears so,' I agree.

Julian asked me to let him think overnight about whether he wanted to ask Chivers any questions, and in a tricky case like this I'm not going to rush him. It may also have saved some time. For Julian, he is unusually brief and direct in coming to the point.

'Mr Chivers,' he begins, 'you never heard the Joe Kingsley Sextet play yourself, did you?'

'No, sir.'

'A bit before your time?'

'Yes, I'm afraid so.'

'So when you told the jury yesterday that the line-up on the vinyl recording, Exhibit two, which we all agree to be a Kingsley recording, was: piano, guitar, clarinet, bass, and drums – plus vocals of course – you must either have been relying on what someone told you, or what you heard on the recording yourself. Which is it?'

Chivers considers for some time. 'Both, actually. Our retired employee, who worked with the Kingsley Sextet, confirmed it to me, but I've listened to enough music in my time to know my instruments.'

'You know an instrument, for example the clarinet, when you hear it?'

'Yes, sir. I sure do.'

'Thank you,' Julian smiles, resuming his seat.

The prosecution case won't take much longer. Piers is obviously convinced that his demonstration yesterday afternoon is going to prove sufficient to persuade the jury that *Arthur Swivell Sings Cole Porter* is a direct rip-off of the HMV recording of the Joe Kingsley Sextet. He reminds the jury that, when they are considering their verdict, they will have both albums available to them in the jury room, with the equipment necessary to listen to them as many times as they like. They will be free to compare all sixteen tracks if they wish, and they will find that each track on the album Bert Coggins had for sale is indistinguishable from the HMV original. With that assurance, he concludes by calling DC Watson, the officer in the case, to deal with the investigation in general.

There's not much the officer can add to what the jury already know. He worked with Inspector Thwaites in an effort to trace the origins of the bootlegged album, but in the end, felt compelled to join in the general conclusion that the evidence pointed to Hong Kong, but not to any person or place that could be identified. When cross-examined by Julian, like Inspector Thwaites, he is strangely unable to explain why no one in the investigation thought to talk to Arthur Swivell, and I am reminded of the Reverend's observation at the end of dinner, which now seems eminently sensible, if not prophetic.

The only other contribution DC Watson can make is to give evidence about his interview of Bert Coggins under caution, which, as foreshadowed in Piers's opening speech, doesn't take the case much further. Bert was forthcoming and open about his intention of selling all one hundred albums he had, if possible, but was unwilling to name his supplier; not, he emphasised repeatedly, because there was anything shady about it, but because it just wasn't good business to expose your suppliers to the risk of inquiries by the Old Bill, however ill-founded those inquiries might be. On which note, Piers closes his case and hands over to Julian.

'How old a man are you, Mr Coggins?' Julian asks, once Bert has taken the oath and given us his full name.

'I'm sixty-eight.'

'Have you ever been convicted of any criminal offence?'

'No, I have not. I've never even been nicked until this mess happened.'

'How long have you been a trader in the Bermondsey market?'

'I've traded on my own account for about thirty five years. It was my old man's business originally, and I helped him on the stall every Saturday from when I was old enough to reach the top of the stall, come rain or shine; and when he died I took it over.'

'Has the stall always had more or less the same kinds of merchandise for sale?'

'More or less, yeah. My old man was the first trader to deal much in electrical goods. Of course, in his day, it was those little gramophones and such, wasn't it? That, and the old vinyl records, either music or for learning foreign languages, which was quite popular for a while, as I'm sure you remember. But of course, now, you've got all the more modern stuff, DVD players, and even phones and tablets and what have you.'

Julian is smiling, and I think I know what's coming next. I'm right.

'Now, in his opening speech, my learned friend Mr Drayford told the jury that you have the same line of banter as Del Boy in *Only Fools and Horses.* What do you say about that?'

The jury are already smiling, as is the witness, and already Piers is regretting the jibe.

'Well, yeah, of course,' Bert agrees immediately. 'You have to put on a bit of a show for the punters, don't you? They expect it.

That's what makes them come back to my stall, to have a bit of a laugh, and that's what makes them buy things. My old man had his routine that he did in his day. His was all those old radio shows: *Hancock's Half Hour*; *Round the Horne*; *The Billy Cotton Band Show*. He could do all the voices for you. So could I after hearing them for so many years, but nobody remembers that old stuff now. But they all know Del Boy. Everybody loves Del Boy in Bermondsey.'

He's absolutely right. There are parts of London where items that fall off the backs of lorries are an important part of the local economy, and where the offence of handling stolen goods is regarded as a technical infraction, comparable to running a red light, and certainly not one carrying any moral opprobrium. Del Boy lends the art of fencing dodgy goods a respectability many Londoners think it deserves, and any comparison between Bert and Del Boy is only leading in one direction with this jury. It's apparently something Piers has still to learn, and I wonder if this will be the case in which the light will dawn.

'Now, let me ask you about these albums you had on sale when the Inspectors called,' Julian continues. 'Your Honour, if the witness may please have Exhibit one?' Dawn swiftly obliges.

'Mr Coggins, is this one of the albums you were offering for sale?'

'Yes, that's one of them.'

'We've heard that you had one hundred of them in all: is that right?'

'That's right.'

'When you were interviewed by the police, you were unwilling to tell them where you got these albums: are you still unwilling to do that today?'

'That's correct.'

'Would you explain to the jury why?'

'Because I do a lot of business with that supplier, and I have no reason to think that there's anything dodgy about him. I've bought lots of stuff from him over the years, and my old man did before me, and we never had a question asked by anyone. And if I go grassing him up to the Old Bill now, that's the last I'll see of him. He doesn't need that kind of aggravation, with the Old Bill sniffing round asking questions.'

Julian nods. 'In relation to these particular albums, including Exhibit one, was there any reason for you to suspect that they were bootlegged? How much did you pay for them?'

'I paid five quid, and I was going to sell them on for nine ninety-nine. That's not unusual for albums from abroad.'

'From abroad?

'Yeah. People are always looking for ways of getting their hands on cheap music, aren't they? I mean, for years, people were just downloading albums for free using the internet – illegally of course – but it took the recording companies forever to even try to put a stop to it, didn't it? But before there was any of that, we've always had cheap records from abroad. All right, how they got here is one thing, but it doesn't mean they're bootlegged, does it? It just means they're cheaper than if you buy them on the High Street. And people like my supplier have contacts in Hong Kong and other places who can supply these cheaper albums, and they sell some of them on to my supplier, and he sells them on to me, and everybody makes a few bob and everybody's happy.'

'Yes,' Julian says, 'but what may interest the jury is this: if you look at Exhibit one, it has no date, and the only details of the recording company seem to be false. Doesn't that make a trader with your experience a bit suspicious about what your supplier is offering you?'

'No, not really. I mean, I don't only sell stuff with the HMV logo on the cover, do I? There are lots of start-up companies producing albums these days, and I can't check on them all to see if they're genuine or not, can I? I don't have the tools. Why should I, anyway? That's the Old Bill's job, not mine. If my supplier, who's always been reliable, comes to me with a product that looks all right, and I want to buy it, that's what I do. It's not like the price he was asking was dodgy. Actually, it was a bit on the high side. In fact, if it hadn't been for the local connection, I might not have bothered, to be truthful. American jazz from the 1960s doesn't exactly fly off a stall in Bermondsey market, if you take my meaning.'

'Yes,' Julian says, 'I was going to ask you about the local connection. You noticed the title of the album, of course. Was the name of Arthur Swivell familiar to you?'

Bert laughs. 'Of course, it was,' he replies. 'I've known Arthur for years. I used to go to hear his band down the Palais de Danse in the old days. Of course, it's not there any more, like Mr Thwaites said. But I've known Arthur ever since. I don't see a lot of him, but he comes by the stall every now and then and we have a chat. He likes to see what I've got. It's not his cup of tea, most of the time. These days, it's more likely to be rap or punk rock and what have you, but I do get the odd piece of jazz or classical, and he sometimes finds something he likes.'

'Was that what made you buy this album?'

'Yeah. I thought it would sell well with the more elderly local people once word got round. A lot of people like Arthur, and I thought it would bring back happy memories of Bermondsey in the good old days.'

'Let me ask you this,' Julian continues. 'Did you ever get the chance to speak to Arthur about this album before you were arrested?'

'No,' Bert replies immediately. 'I'd only just taken delivery of them when I got nicked, hadn't I? It was the first time I had them out for sale. To be perfectly honest, I didn't know Arthur had ever made a record. He never mentioned anything about it to me. I'm sure it would have been big local news if he had – you know, we would have all rushed out and bought it, wouldn't we, all us older folk in Bermondsey? So it came as a bit of a surprise, and I was going to ask him about it when I next saw him.'

'Did you see Mr Swivell subsequently, after you'd been arrested?'

'Yeah. The police gave me bail the same day, once I'd been interviewed, so I was back on the stall the next day. Arthur had heard I'd got nicked, and he wanted to find out what was going on, and he came round to the stall to see me and I asked him about it. He told me –'

But before Bert can answer, Piers is on his feet.

'Your Honour, I must object to that. Any answer the witness may give would be hearsay.'

'Why can't I say what he told me?' the witness demands. 'It's important.'

I jump in. I'm sure Julian has explained it to him more than once, but hearsay is a strange rule as far as most people are concerned, and naturally enough, Bert is dying to tell us what Arthur told him. But we have rules of evidence, and strange or not, hearsay often has to be excluded.

'That's a matter of law for me to decide, Mr Coggins,' I reply.

'But –'

Technically, Piers may well be right. But I conclude that it can't do any harm to let Bert repeat to the jury what Arthur said to him. If Julian calls Arthur to give evidence, he will either confirm it, or not; and if he doesn't call Arthur, the jury probably won't give too much credence to Bert's account of the conversation. I rule accordingly.

'Much obliged, your Honour. You can answer the question, Mr Coggins,' Julian beams.

Bert nods vigorously in my direction, with a look that says, 'So I should bloody well hope'.

'Arthur told me that he and his band made that recording,' he replies, to an audible gasp from the jury. 'He was intending to have it made into a record and released. But apparently, he had a bent agent who took the original recording because he was claiming that Arthur owed him commission or some such thing. They were arguing about it, but then the agent disappeared before the album could be sold to be produced. So Arthur thought the recording was gone forever, and he'd never see it again. But it had turned up on my stall on Bermondsey market. He was so happy to see it, he was almost crying. "That's all very well, Arthur," I say to him. "But I've bloody well been nicked on account of it, haven't I?" "Don't you worry about that, Bert," he says. "I'll take care of that for you." And that was it. That's what Arthur told me.'

Wisely, Julian wants to end on that flourish, with the great revelation ringing in the jury's ears, and after a few more questions he concludes his examination in chief. We're not too far away from lunch by now, and in deference to Bert's age I agree to postpone cross-examination until two o'clock.

* * *

Tuesday afternoon

'Mr Coggins,' Piers begins, 'what steps do you take to make sure you're not selling bootlegged albums on your stall in Bermondsey market?'

'Steps? I'm not sure what you mean?'

'Well, you don't want to be selling dodgy stuff do you, not after all the years you and your father have been running an honest business?'

'No, of course I don't.'

'So when you're offered an album like our Exhibit one, what do you do to satisfy yourself that it's not dodgy?'

Bert has to think about it.

'Well, there's not much you can do, really. Like I said, there are so many companies putting out recordings now and I don't know one from the other. In my old man's day, you just had a handful didn't you: HMV, Decca, EMI and so on? But now they spring up overnight. So I have to rely on my supplier. He's never let us down yet.'

'You don't follow up on the website given on the cover, for example?'

'Follow up on the website? I don't even listen to the albums. I'm not a great music fan, to be honest. I listened to this one, obviously, because it had Arthur's name on it, and Arthur is somebody I know; but I wouldn't even do that usually. I'm a trader. I buy and sell, and that's it.'

'But you did listen to this album, did you, Mr Coggins?' Piers probes, sensing an opening.

'Yes, I did.'

'And did you recognise Arthur's voice on it?'

Again, Bert has to think about it, and this time it takes him a bit longer.

'Well, I assumed it was Arthur,' he replies eventually. 'I didn't have any reason to think otherwise, did I?'

'But you didn't recognise the voice?'

'Well, no, not if you put it like that. But I hadn't heard Arthur sing for more than twenty years, had I? And I didn't hear anything to make me think it wasn't Arthur.'

'You could have waited until you saw Arthur, couldn't you? You could have put your supplier on hold until you asked Arthur if he had made an album?'

'I suppose I could have. But you never know when Arthur's going to show up. He doesn't come to the market every week, and my supplier wanted an answer. He has other places to sell things on to if I'm not interested. But, like I said, I was interested. I thought this would sell well in Bermondsey.'

'But in behaving in that way, Mr Coggins, you never inquired into whether this album might have been the work of someone else, such as the Joe Kingsley Sextet?'

Bert flings his arms wide out to his sides in exasperation.

'I'd never even heard of the Joe Kingsley Sextet until this case started. Why would I inquire into whether they did anything?'

'The point is, Mr Coggins, that you didn't ask whether it could be anyone other than Arthur Swivell, whether it was Joe Kingsley or anyone else. You saw the chance to make a few bob and you took it, asking no questions?'

'Yeah. It looked all right, and it was from a reputable supplier, so yeah, I bought it and I was going to make a few bob off of it. What's wrong with that?'

'Did you think Arthur Swivell was going to make a few bob out of it too, Mr Coggins?'

Again, some hesitation.

'I don't know, do I? I don't know what goes on with that. From what I understand, he would have been paid for the recording, and he would be getting, what do you call them, royalties for it, yeah.'

'But if it was a bootlegged recording, your friend Arthur wouldn't be getting anything, would he? He'd be the victim of a fraud, wouldn't he?'

'I don't deal in bootlegged albums,' Bert protests.

'But you have this time, haven't you, Mr Coggins?'

'Not as far as I know, no. Not according to Arthur.'

'You've heard the evidence of Mr Chivers, haven't you, and you've seen the vinyl record we have, Exhibit two? Are you telling this jury that you still think this album you bought, Exhibit one, is by Arthur Swivell?'

'That's what Arthur told me, and you can ask him yourself when he comes to give evidence, can't you? He'll tell you himself.'

Further audible gasps from the jury and even a look of surprise from Piers. I don't understand the prosecution's lack of concern with Arthur Swivell. Are the Reverend Mrs Walden and I the only ones who think he may have something useful to say in this case? Even now, Piers doesn't react.

'Yes, I see, Mr Coggins. Thank you. I have nothing further, your Honour.'

Bert Coggins returns to the dock. Julian rises to his feet.

'Your Honour, I wonder if the jury might like a break? I would like to address your Honour in their absence about the remainder of the defence case, and this would be the appropriate moment.'

'Yes, very well,' I agree. 'Tea break, members of the jury. I'm sure we won't be too long.' They duly troop out.

'Your Honour, the reason why I asked that the jury retire,' Julian begins, 'is that this is rather an unusual case, and I propose to call some rather unusual evidence to deal with it.'

'Well, we've already gathered that you will be calling Mr Swivell to give evidence, Mr Blanquette,' I reply. 'But I don't see anything particularly unusual in that.'

'Not in that, your Honour, no. But it is Mr Coggins's case, not only that he had no reason to believe that these albums were bootlegged – and indeed had every reason to believe them to be genuine – but that Exhibit one is in fact the work of the Arthur Swivell Sextet.'

'And I assume that Mr Swivell is being called to confirm that?'

'Indeed, your Honour, yes. But in the light of Mr Chivers's evidence, which invites the jury to compare the two albums in great detail, I take the view that Mr Swivell's evidence alone may not be enough. I have other evidence available and I propose to call it before the jury, but as I've said, it will take a somewhat unusual form.'

'The court is all ears, Mr Blanquette.'

'Your Honour, the members of the Arthur Swivell Sextet are, on average, about a decade younger than the members of the Joe Kingsley Sextet, all of whom, your Honour will recall, are, sadly, either deceased or suffering from dementia. The members of the Arthur Swivell Sextet, on the other hand, are alive and well – relatively speaking, that is – and most importantly, are still able to play together. Indeed, your Honour, that's what they are doing at this precise moment at my request – rehearsing four numbers in particular from their repertoire; because tomorrow, I propose, with the court's leave, to bring them together for that purpose.'

He pauses to allow us to digest this.

'I'm not sure I've understood you correctly, Mr Blanquette,' I say after some time. 'Are you saying that you propose to ask the Arthur Swivell Sextet to perform live in my courtroom?'

'Indeed I am, your Honour.'

Piers is on his feet now, having recovered from the initial shock.

'Your Honour –'

I signal to Piers to let me deal with it for now. I'm sure he has a couple of points to make also, but it's my courtroom Julian wants to turn into a reincarnation of the late, lamented Bermondsey Palais de Danse, and I want to make my own points first.

'I'm not at all sure that I can allow that, Mr Blanquette,' I protest. 'First of all, how can it possibly be relevant?'

'It's relevant for two reasons, your Honour,' Julian replies, apparently unperturbed by the role he has undertaken as an impresario promoting a jazz concert in the Crown Court. 'First, it will provide compelling evidence that the Arthur Swivell Sextet did in fact make the recording we know as Exhibit one.'

'Even so many years on?' I ask. 'You don't dispute, do you, that the HMV recording of the Joe Kingsley Sextet, Exhibit two, was made in 1962?'

'I don't dispute that, your Honour.'

'And aren't the jury entitled to find, on hearing Exhibit one, that it is a copy of the same recording? Because if so, I can't see how allowing Arthur Swivell to perform these songs now, all these years later, can really be of help to the jury? Surely the sextet's sound is bound to be quite different after so long.'

'That might be true of Mr Swivell's vocals, your Honour, but the sound of the instruments doesn't change, and it's the instrumentation I'm concerned with.'

'I'm not sure I follow.'

'Your Honour, Mr Chivers made a number of points about the technical similarities between the two recordings, the arrangements of the songs and the instrumentation employed. If the sextet is allowed to play, I will be in a position to prove that Mr Chivers is wrong on at least one very important point. I can't do that without allowing the jury to hear the difference.'

I'm really not sure how to respond. I turn to Piers for backup.

'In addition to the points your Honour has made,' he protests, 'there is the question of whether Mr Swivell would be well advised to give evidence, either in musical form or otherwise, and I wonder whether my learned friend has advised him of that?'

'In what way might it be inadvisable?' I ask.

'Well, for one thing, your Honour, if he were to admit to having recorded an album that follows the Kingsley original bar for bar, note for note, track for track, in its arrangements, he would be admitting to very serious breaches of copyright. Your Honour would have to warn him of his right not to answer any questions that might incriminate him. He would be facing civil liability, of course, as well as criminal.'

So that's why the prosecution weren't worried about Arthur Swivell. From day one, they've been assuming that Arthur wouldn't dare to own up to plagiarising Kingsley's copyrighted work, when in addition to the damage to his reputation, it could expose him to a multitude of expensive legal problems.

'I have given Mr Swivell advice about that,' Julian replies smoothly, 'and I've given the same advice to the other members of his sextet; and their view is what's done is done, and if the CPS or HMV choose to hunt them down after so many years, then so be it. What they don't want to see is Mr Coggins being convicted of an offence he didn't commit.'

I ponder this for some time.

'In addition,' Piers adds in the subdued tone of an advocate who has just had to listen to his best point being demolished, 'I respectfully agree with the points your Honour made. It can't possibly be relevant, and in addition, it would be unseemly to stage such a performance in court when we're supposed to be conducting a trial.'

'Not as unseemly as it would be for the court to refuse to hear evidence that may prevent a miscarriage of justice,' Julian replies quietly.

And suddenly, I'm finding myself agreeing with him. But before I can say anything more, Carol stands and hands me a note. I'd seen Dawn approaching her clutching something in her hand, but I hadn't seen what it was or where it came from. It's a note for me from Meredith, who has once again been in attendance throughout the day.

'Judge, if you're seriously considering this,' the note reads,

'I need to speak with you in chambers before you decide.'

At first, I'm disposed to ignore it as an uninvited interference in matters that don't concern her. It's up to me how I run my courtroom, not the Grey Smoothies. But Meredith is making my life a misery this week, and I don't want to aggravate things further. Discretion, after all, is the better part of valour. The case involving her presumptive brother will be in my list tomorrow morning, and I don't want too much drama happening all at once.

'Bring her into chambers,' I whisper to Carol. She nods. I announce that I'm rising for some time to consider what counsel have said.

'We can't have musical recitals in the courtroom,' she insists once we're settled in our seats in chambers.

'I must admit, that was my first reaction too,' I agree, 'but what Mr Blanquette is saying is that it would be evidence, rather than a recital. He's not promoting a concert; he's just trying to present his case to the jury.'

'It's still a recital.'

'Well, perhaps it is, and I can see how in the old days a judge might get upset by the idea of musicians performing in court – not consistent with the court's dignity and all that kind of thing. But things have moved on, Meredith. Judges today –'

'It's not the court's dignity I'm worried about, Judge,' she replies. 'It's the legal problems we might have.'

'What legal problems? If I order –'

'The court doesn't have an entertainment licence, Judge. You'd be sponsoring a public musical performance in unlicensed premises.'

For some moments, I'm speechless. But eventually I reflect that it's reassuring, in a rather perverse way. Of course, the Grey Smoothies wouldn't be concerned about the dignity of the court. What was I thinking? Of course, their preoccupation would be with the endless list of bureaucratic objections to Julian's planned recital, rather than with abstract considerations such as the dignity of the court, or preventing miscarriages of justice.

'Quite apart from the expense to the taxpayer,' Meredith is saying, 'you couldn't get a licence by tomorrow. Even on an emergency basis it's bound to take several days. And that's before you consider that it would set a precedent.'

'A precedent?'

'We don't want courts thinking they can apply for entertainment licences for their Christmas parties, and the like, do we? We couldn't possibly support that.'

'Meredith,' I reply after a lengthy silence, 'I really don't see why a court would need an entertainment licence to take evidence. We're not setting out to entertain people, we're conducting a trial, and it's not as though we're selling tickets.'

'I don't think whether you're charging for admission is the real point, Judge. I'd have to check that, but even if it's free I think there's a problem. Members of the public would be entitled to be present, wouldn't they?'

'Yes, of course, but that's because we're conducting a trial. The public come to court to hear a trial, not to attend a concert. It's not like you're going to have an influx of young people holding their phones or cigarette lighters in the air to light up the room.'

She looks at me rather strangely.

'I'm not sure that makes any difference,' she insists.

My instinct as a lawyer and a judge is that this is all nonsense – this cannot be a world in which a judge has to deny a jury evidence for want of an entertainment licence. But I'm now in the universe of the Grey Smoothies, and in that universe, my instinct isn't going to prevail – certainly not this afternoon. Perhaps the only way is to allow Meredith time to check her facts. You never know: her universe is bizarre enough for her to be right. If so, we'll have to find a solution. If not, perhaps I will be able to get on with my trial tomorrow.

'Let's go back into court,' I suggest. 'I will tell counsel what the concerns are, and they can look up the law and think about it overnight. We can't go any further today. The sextet can't perform until Arthur Swivell has given evidence, so we don't have to decide immediately.'

Meredith assents to this proposal, and even offers to discuss the matter with counsel, if it would help. I'm not sure it will, but I make encouraging noises in the interests of diplomacy. With impeccable timing, Carol knocks on the door and comes in to see if we're ready to return to court. We confirm that we are.

'Judge, there is one thing that's worrying me about Mr Blanquette's application,' she says.

'Oh, yes,' I reply wearily. 'What's that?'

'How on earth are they going to get a piano into court?'

Meredith and I look at her, blankly at first. But it doesn't take us long to work out that she's put her finger on a highly practical problem that hadn't occurred to either of us.

'Well, the piano is one of the instruments on the recordings, isn't it, Judge? We don't have one at court, and they do tend to be rather on the large side, don't they? I'm not sure the courtroom doors would be big enough to get a piano into court one, even if they could get it into the building and up the stairs. I suppose you could hold court downstairs in the foyer; then they'd only have to get it through the main doors. But even then, how would they manoeuvre it around the security apparatus? And if you did hold court in the foyer, we'd have to close the building – otherwise you'd have people milling around all over the place...'

She pauses. 'I'm just not sure how we would handle it.'

I smile. 'Let's go and ask counsel.'

* * *

Tuesday evening

'How on earth would they get a piano into your courtroom?' the Reverend Mrs Walden asks, before I've even had a chance to mention Carol's inquiry to that effect. We are talking about the day's events over dinner, my signature spaghetti bolognese washed down by a bottle of Sainsbury's industrial Merlot.

'Apparently, they have a firm of specialist piano movers and a very small upright piano,' I reply. 'Defence counsel, Mr Blanquette, seems to have it all under control. But even if he can manage the piano, the Grey Smoothies are threatening to close us down for promoting an illegal concert. They seem to be worried that the pensioners of Bermondsey will invade the court in their thousands with their phones and cigarette lighters and get up to whatever antisocial behaviour they got up to in the old days at the Palais de Danse.'

She laughs. 'Now that, I would like to see.'

'So would I,' I admit.

'But there's another problem, isn't there?' she asks after a pause.

'Is there?' I had thought we'd exhausted the list of possible disasters by now.

'You can't move a piano just like that, Charlie, and expect it to be ready to play.'

'Oh?'

'You'd have to have it tuned. And that has to be done at least a day before the recital, to allow the strings time to adjust to the piano's new environment.'

I pause, a forkful of pasta suspended in the air, halfway between plate and mouth. So there are musical problems to add to the logistical and bureaucratic ones we have already identified?

'Really? Are they that sensitive?'

'Oh, yes. I mean, if it was just for fun – for a sing-along at a party or something – it might not matter; but if you need to be as precise as you do in this case, it could make a real difference. Added to which, the other instruments have to tune to the piano, so if it's out of tune, it could throw them off, too. And piano tuners are few and far between these days. You could find one, but you'd have to make an appointment, and it could take some time. You wouldn't be holding your illegal concert tomorrow, and probably not this week.'

I put my fork down and take a long draught of the Merlot. In a way, I'm relieved. I would like to allow Julian to stage his recreation of the recording of Exhibit one. For one thing, I'm intrigued to hear the Arthur Swivell Sextet in their dotage, and I have a feeling that it might be decisive. I and the jury had some difficulty in following Chivers's technical analysis just by listening to the recordings; but if Piers plays us the Kingsley original just after we hear the Swivell Sextet live, it will probably conclude the matter one way or the other. It's also occurred to me that Julian must be very sure of his ground. If anything at all goes wrong, from his point of view, the results may be catastrophic. In fact, he may be about to take one of the biggest gambles in legal history. But now, I don't see how I can let him do it. I'm on the brink of concluding that I may have to pull the plug on the idea, when the Reverend comes up with a remarkable suggestion.

'Why don't you use the church hall?'

'What?'

'Well, why not? You can't get into trouble for playing music in the church hall, provided the priest-in-charge approves it, which I do. And we have a very serviceable piano in place, which was tuned just last month, so there would be no need for Mr Blanquette to bring one with him. I can even get Ian and

Shelley to record it for you. They record music in the church and the hall all the time, and I bet the acoustics in the hall are much better than in that huge courtroom.'

'You might have lots of members of the public crowding in to see the show,' I point out.

'That would make a nice change,' she replies.

* * *

Wednesday morning

I've been waiting for Meredith to mention the name of Stanley Everett, and the fact that she hasn't has persuaded me that Marjorie's theory about his being her brother must be wrong. She seems completely oblivious to the fact that her supposed brother is due to appear for his preliminary hearing this morning at Bermondsey Crown Court, where she is currently looking into the mystery of why more defendants don't plead guilty at this stage of the proceedings. Perhaps she just hasn't bothered to check the list for the whole week. Or perhaps she thinks the name is just a coincidence. After all, if this is the Stanley Everett she grew up with, surely he would have told her about such a major development in his life. I know families are not always as good at communicating as they should be, but if you've been charged with a number of serious frauds, and you're due to appear before a Crown Court for which your sister is administratively responsible, you would expect the subject to come up at some point, wouldn't you? It's not a conversation you would look forward to, but surely you would eventually realise it's not one you could avoid indefinitely. But not a word from anyone.

That is about to change. When the case of Stanley Everett is called on, it becomes clear that the defendant has at last brought himself to mention this detail of his family tree to his legal advisers, even if he hasn't breathed a word to his sister. Susan Worthington is representing him, and she has wisely alerted the prosecution, represented by Piers Drayford. They are all ready to explain the situation to me and make the inevitable request for the case to be transferred to a distant circuit. Meredith, on the other hand, is obviously hearing this for the first time. Sitting towards the back of the public gallery with a clear view of the dock, she looks as if she might faint when Stanley makes his appearance, being brought up from the cells by a dock officer. Her face turns ashen and she slumps back into her seat. I actually feel a bit sorry for her, but this is no time for sentiment. Our statistical reputation is at stake.

'Your Honour,' Susan begins, once Stanley has been duly identified, 'there has been a development in this case, of which I became aware only this morning, and which I immediately communicated to my learned friend Mr Drayford. It appears that the defendant, Mr Everett, is the brother of Meredith Everett, the cluster manager for the group of Crown Courts that includes Bermondsey, who, I'm told, is in court today.'

'Really?' I reply, feigning innocence. 'What an extraordinary thing. I must say, this seems highly unsatisfactory, Miss Worthington. Miss Everett has been with us at court every day this week, so far. We've been working together on some statistical issues. I'm extremely surprised that I haven't heard anything about this before now, either from Miss Everett or from the defendant's advisers.'

'I quite understand your Honour's surprise,' Susan replies, 'and indeed I share it. I'm forced to admit that the defendant Mr Everett himself is entirely to blame for this situation. He instructs me that he was so embarrassed about being charged with these offences, when he has a sister in a high position in the court service, that he didn't know how to tell her. Of course, he didn't know that she would be at court today, but it was inevitable that it would come to Miss Everett's attention before long. He realises now that he has acted stupidly. But, be that as it may, your Honour may feel that there is only one course of action open to the court: that is to transfer the case to another circuit, to avoid any appearance of a conflict of interest. I haven't had a chance to speak to Miss Everett, but I'm sure she would agree with my proposal, as does my learned friend Mr Drayford.'

Piers confirms this at once. I glance in Meredith's direction and see that she has recovered enough to agree wholeheartedly, which she is indicating by means of vigorous nods of her head.

'Well,' I reply, after pretending to think about it for a few seconds. 'I think that must be right. I'm sure we can find a place for it down in the West Country somewhere. I'm told they're rather short of work down there because of the remarkable incidence of early guilty pleas in that circuit. I will ask the list officer to contact the cluster manager in Devon or Cornwall.'

'I'm much obliged, your Honour,' Susan says.

'On the other hand,' I continue, 'I see no reason not to explore the possibility of an early guilty plea first. There's no point in wasting the taxpayer's money by sending a case all the way down to the West Country just for an early plea, when we could just as well take an early plea here.'

Susan seems rather taken aback by this suggestion. All counsel who appear at Bermondsey regularly are aware of the relaxed, civilised approach the judges here take to the subject of early pleas, and she would have been expecting me to whisk this case out of the door without further ado, except perhaps to hear a bail application.

'Your Honour, there is no possibility of a guilty plea in this case, early or otherwise,' she replies. 'Mr Everett strenuously denies the charges against him, and intends to fight them all the way at trial.'

'Have you advised Mr Everett,' I ask, 'of the advantages that would accrue to him if he were to plead guilty at an early stage? If, and only if, he is guilty, of course. But if he should be guilty of one or more offences, and if he were to save the time of the court and the expense of a long trial by admitting his guilt now, he would be entitled in law to a significant reduction in the length of any prison sentence that might be imposed on him.'

'I have advised him of that, your Honour,' Susan replies, a touch frostily, 'but as I said before, Mr Everett denies the charges and will be contesting them at trial.'

'I'm surprised to hear that, Miss Worthington,' I say. 'As it happens, I had an opportunity to review the CPS file before coming into court this morning, and on the face of it, it's difficult to see what defence he could possibly have. Selling timeshares that don't exist, or that can't be used, is a very serious matter, which might well attract a substantial sentence –'

'Your Honour –'

'I would be very happy to put the matter back until later in the day to allow Mr Everett further time to reflect and to allow you further time to advise him. It would be highly regrettable if he were to allow this occasion to slip anyway. After today, any reduction in sentence would be appreciably less, as you know.'

The frost has now turned to ice. 'That won't be necessary, your Honour. I have advised Mr Everett, and he has given me his instructions. This is a complicated case, and your Honour will not find the whole story in the CPS file. When the judge in Devon or Cornwell sees Mr Everett's defence statement in due course, he or she will see that Mr Everett has a clear defence, one which I am confident a jury will accept.'

Susan and Piers are both looking at me as if to ask who I am, and what I've done with Judge Charles Walden. Perhaps they suspect me of being a West Country spy infiltrating the court in disguise. Under any normal circumstances, of course, they would have expected me to back off as soon as Susan told me in no uncertain terms that this was a not guilty plea; and under any normal circumstances, that's exactly what I would have done. But these are not normal circumstances: Susan and Piers are not aware of the nature of the statistical work Meredith and I have been doing for the last couple of days. I hear a sudden commotion at the back of the courtroom, and looking up, I see Meredith walk hurriedly out of court clutching her files and handbag. Stanley seems ready to call out to her, but thinks better of it and watches her go forlornly.

'Yes, very well, Miss Worthington,' I say, resuming my customary demeanour. 'In those circumstances, I will order this case to be transferred to another circuit without taking any further action, except to hear any application for bail.'

I have two more preliminary hearings in my list. In violation of the Bermondsey statistical norm, both defendants offer pleas of guilty. I adjourn both cases for pre-sentence reports, and assure both defendants of the benefits that will accrue to them by reason of their public-spirited saving of the taxpayer's money. Now I'm ready to resume the trial of Bert Coggins.

'Mr Blanquette,' I begin, 'having thought about your application overnight, I am minded to grant it. I shall allow the Arthur Swivell Sextet to perform relevant songs for the jury. But I have certain logistical arrangements in mind, which I will announce in due course.'

'Yes, your Honour. I'm much obliged,' Julian replies. Piers doesn't seem obliged at all, nor does Mr Chivers, sitting behind him.

'But I think the appropriate course is for you to call Mr Swivell first, and then any other members of the sextet you wish to call. Even if you don't plan to call them all, it seems to me that they all ought to take the oath at some point, because they will in a sense be giving evidence when they play.'

'I respectfully agree, your Honour. In that case, I will call Mr Swivell now.'

Arthur Swivell is tall and thin and walks with the aid of a cane, leaning forward a bit, but it doesn't seem to slow him down very much. He strides briskly enough into the witness box. He's dressed in a light brown sports jacket and a blue open-necked shirt. He reads the oath from the card without any need for glasses.

'Mr Swivell,' Julian begins, 'what is your full name?'

'Arthur James Swivell.'

'If you don't mind my asking, how old a man are you?'

'I don't mind at all. I'm seventy-five.'

'And are you a musician, and have you been a musician throughout your working life?'

'Yes.'

'Are you the leader of a jazz ensemble known as the Arthur Swivell Sextet?'

'Yes.'

'For how long has your sextet been together as a working band?'

'We started out when we were just lads, in the mid-1960s.'

'The court has heard that you played for many years in the Palais de Danse here in Bermondsey, is that right?'

Arthur nods. 'We were the resident band there for donkey's years, from the sixties until the mid-nineties, when those fascist bastards knocked the Palais down to build those horrible flats. Absolute bloody disgrace.'

'Mr Swivell,' Julian intervenes quickly, 'please remember

where you are and try not to use that kind of language.'

Arthur turns towards me. 'Sorry, Judge,' he says. 'But it still hurts to think about it, even now. If you were from around here you'd understand. The people in Bermondsey loved the Palais. It was part of the community. They had nowhere to go when it closed, did they? And we already had plenty of flats. It was all about money. That's all it was.'

I see the jury nodding sympathetically.

'That's quite all right, Mr Swivell,' I reply. 'But take Mr Blanquette's advice from now on.'

'Yes, Judge.'

'Mr Swivell, so that we all know the cast of characters, please tell us the names of the members of the sextet, and what instruments they play.'

'Right. Well: there's Terry Mayhew, he's our pianist; Bill Fogarty, guitar; Lofty Harris on English horn, or oboe once in a while, as the mood takes him; Phil O'Grady on bass; Mitch Buller on drums; and myself doing the vocals.'

'Thank you.' Julian pauses – one of those significant pauses he does so well. 'Mr Swivell, who in your sextet plays clarinet?'

'No one. We've never had a clarinet.'

Glancing to my left behind Piers, I see Mr Chivers, the musical expert from HMV, freeze for some moments, and then start to scribble furiously in his notebook.

'Thank you. Now, I want to ask you about the recordings the jury has heard in this case. Have you been able to listen to them?'

'I've listened to ours, the one Bert had for sale on his stall. But I haven't been able to listen to the Joe Kingsley album again. My copy went missing years ago, and I wasn't allowed in court when it was played here.'

'But you're familiar with the Kingsley album from hearing it in the past?'

'Oh, yes, very much so. It was always one of my favourites. I must have played it hundreds of times.'

'All right. With the usher's assistance, if Mr Swivell might see Exhibit one?' Dawn takes only a few moments to rush Exhibit one to the witness box. 'Is this the album you referred to as "ours", the one Mr Coggins had for sale?'

'Yes, it is.'

'Tell us, please, why you refer to it as "ours". Tell us what you know of its history.'

Arthur pauses for some time, nodding.

'We made this album in the late 1970s at the old Elephant and Castle recording studio. It's gone now, of course, just like the Palais, but it was a decent studio in its day. We'd never made a recording before. We were busy playing the Palais and one or two other venues, but we'd never been signed to a label. At that time, we had an agent called Monty Rascall – I kid you not, that was his name, and never was a name more deserved. He was bent as a three pound note, was Monty.'

'You mean that Mr Rascall was dishonest?' Julian asks, rather unnecessarily.

'You can say that again. Monty was trying to convince us to make our own demo recording for him to play to record companies who might want to sign us to a contract. We were a bit reluctant, because we didn't have that much money and it wasn't a cheap thing to do. But Monty kept telling us it was the only way, so eventually we agreed. We put our money together, and we just about had enough to book the Elephant and Castle for two days – but no longer.'

'So time was of the essence?'

'Yes, we couldn't afford to overrun.'

'So, what did you decide to do? Mr Swivell, before you answer – and you and I have talked about this, haven't we? – can you confirm to His Honour and the jury that you understand you are under no obligation to answer any question you think may incriminate you?'

Arthur nods. 'I understand, Mr Blanquette. But it's water under the bridge now, and I can't watch Bert go down for something he hasn't done. Look, what we did was this: I had a copy of the Kingsley recording at that time. As I said, it was one of my favourites, and the same went for the other lads. We all loved it. So what we did, we listened to it over and over, until we could do those numbers in our sleep. We knew the arrangements and everything. In fact we'd played almost all those numbers at the Palais at one time or another. So we decided we would record the same numbers, exactly as they were on the Kingsley album. We knew we could do that in two days, no trouble. And that's what we did. It was a rip-off. I know that. But the Kingsley Sextet had disbanded by then, and you couldn't get that album in this country for love or money. It never sold very well over here, even in the early sixties, which was a shame because it was a great record. By the seventies it was as dead as the dodo.'

'All the same, you must have worked hard to get ready?'

'Oh, we did. We rehearsed night and day…'

'And all the other songs on the album,' Arthur and Julian add together – an outrageous set piece, but it has me and the jury laughing, and even Piers can't resist a smile.

'And did you in fact make a tape of the songs on the Kingsley album, in the same order, and using the same arrangements?'

'Yes, we did.'

'With one exception?'

'With the one exception, that there was no clarinet. Kingsley had a clarinettist, Miles Abrahams by name, but we didn't have one. We had Lofty on English horn, and he took the part Miles played on the Kingsley album.'

'Are those instruments similar enough to be interchangeable?'

'For our purposes, yes. In fact, I always thought the horn produced a nice deep tone that the clarinet doesn't always have. But you'd have to ask Lofty for the technical details. He knows far more about all that than I do. He actually played in a symphony orchestra. Jazz was a kind of hobby for Lofty, so he can fill you in on that.'

'We will ask him a little later,' Julian assures Arthur. 'What happened to the recording you made at Elephant and Castle?'

'Monty took it,' Arthur replies bitterly. 'He claimed he was holding it because we owed him money, which was total bollocks – excuse me, Judge, I mean it was complete nonsense. We didn't owe him anything. He owed us. He'd taken our money, and he was supposed to pay the Elephant and Castle for our sessions, but he only paid them half of it. Then he disappeared, taking the only copy of the tape with him, and because we hadn't paid, Elephant and Castle wouldn't let us have access to the master tape, or make any more copies for us. So we were well and truly stuffed. Then some time later, we found out that Monty had got done for fraud, and got sent down, and we never saw him or the tape again. By the time we'd scraped together the money, Elephant and Castle had got tired of us and erased the master, so all our work was gone.'

'And the next thing you knew…?'

'The next thing I knew was that Bert told me about these tapes he'd bought for his stall on the market, and told me that he'd got nicked because the inspectors thought they were rip-offs.'

'Is this album, Exhibit one, in fact a bootlegged copy of the recording you and your sextet made in the late 1970s at Elephant and Castle?'

'It is. You could have knocked me down with a feather when I heard it. I never thought I'd hear it again. Who made this CD, where and when, I have no idea. But whoever it was,

Monty must have sold the tape to them when he got out of the nick, and they've made a copy and sold it on through the markets.'

'Are you quite sure that Exhibit one is your work, and not the work of the Kingsley Sextet?'

'You're asking me if I can recognise my own voice, and the work of my sextet? Yes, I can, and so can they, and so can anyone who can tell an English horn from a clarinet.'

Mr Chivers is staring ahead, somewhere into the middle distance.

'That's all I have,' Julian says. 'Wait there, please, Mr Swivell.'

Piers rises slowly.

'Your Honour, if there's no objection, I would prefer to reserve my cross-examination of Mr Swivell and any members of the sextet who may be called until we have heard their performance.'

Julian stands at once. 'That is perfectly reasonable, your Honour,' he concedes. 'I have no objection.'

'Yes, very well,' I reply.

'In that case, your Honour, I will call Mr Lofty Harris. I may add, your Honour, that depending on the line taken in cross-examination with Mr Swivell and Mr Harris, I don't intend to call any of the other members of the sextet, but they will be available, should my learned friend wish to cross-examine them.'

Lofty Harris doesn't take long. He has enjoyed a long career playing the English horn – or the *cor anglais*, he insists, to give it its proper title – in the BBC Symphony Orchestra, and occasionally in other ensembles such as Arthur's sextet, to earn an extra couple of bob or two, or sometimes just for fun. He cheerfully admits to being party to the rip-off of the Kingsley album at the old Elephant and Castle recording studio, and insists that he played the *cor anglais* on that recording throughout. He has never picked up a clarinet in his life, and doesn't intend to start now.

And so to lunch, an oasis of calm in a desert of chaos.

'Just out of curiosity,' Marjorie asks mischievously, as I take my seat, 'what happened to the Everett case this morning? Did he plead guilty?'

'I'm afraid Mr Everett made no contribution to our statistical performance at all,' I reply. 'He insists on going to trial and pleading not guilty.'

'Didn't you try to persuade him otherwise, Charlie?' Legless grins.

'Of course, I did. I gave him almost the full West Country treatment, but Susan Worthington is representing him, and she wasn't having it.'

'What did Meredith think of that?' Legless asks? 'Was she disappointed not to see another one bite the dust?'

'I'm afraid history doesn't record her reaction to that,' I reply, 'but I rather doubt it. It seems that Mr Everett hadn't quite got round to telling her that he'd been nicked and was going to trial for fraud, so the first she knew about it was when they brought him up from the cells this morning.'

'Oh, dear,' Marjorie says.

'Yes. All very unfortunate. The last I saw of Meredith, she was leaving court rather abruptly, looking a bit put out.'

Marjorie grimaces. 'I imagine there'll be a few words exchanged between them when she goes to see him on remand.'

'She won't have to go to prison to see him,' I reply. 'I've given him bail pending trial, so they can argue to their hearts' content in the privacy of their own homes. He's not a flight risk, especially now Meredith knows all about it, and I don't know how long it will take to come to trial.'

'Are you sending it to the West Country?' Legless asks, with a grin.

'I've left that up to Stella,' I reply. 'She knows what our trade deficit or surplus is with the other circuits better than I do. It may go no farther than Leicester or Birmingham.'

'Do you think that's the end of this attack of the Grey Smoothies?'

I reflect for some time.

'One would hope so. Meredith has certainly retired hurt, but knowing the Grey Smoothies, I wouldn't be entirely surprised if they field a substitute. We shall see.'

* * *

Wednesday afternoon

'Now,' I begin after court has reassembled, without the jury for the time being, 'Mr Blanquette, if there's to be no further conventional evidence today, shall we turn to the arrangements for the musical evidence?'

'Yes, your Honour.'

'Your original proposal was that they should play here at court, but it seemed to me that there were some significant logistical, and perhaps even legal, problems with that proposal. So I have decided to accept a kind offer made to the court to take the sextet's evidence elsewhere.'

I see that I have everyone's full attention. I'm sure Julian is worrying about his specialist removal firm and their small upright piano.

'The priest-in-charge of the church of St Aethelburgh and all Angels in the Diocese of Southwark has generously placed her church hall at our disposal. It's not far from the court; it's modern and comfortable; it has better acoustics than the court; arrangements can be made to record the evidence, and perhaps most importantly, it has a very nice piano which has recently been tuned. I imagine that will come as something of a relief to Mr Terry Mayhew, compared to the proposal to shoehorn a piano into the court building.'

Terry isn't in court, but Arthur Swivell looks up at me with a smile and nods his thanks. Arthur approaches Julian and they whisper for a few moments.

'I'm much obliged to your Honour, and of course to the Reverend Mrs Walden,' Julian replies. 'That sounds like an excellent idea, if I may say so. Mr Swivell's only concern is to inspect the venue, and, if possible, to rehearse briefly before performing – or giving his evidence, perhaps I should say.'

The Reverend, with her understanding of musicians, presciently raised that very subject with me this morning. She even offered to provide tea and biscuits for the sextet during rehearsal, but given that she is my wife and that I'm trying the case as the judge, I insisted that she make a small charge for any refreshments, proceeds to go to the church fund. We don't want any suggestions that I'm showing partiality towards the defence witnesses, and in any case, the church fund can do with all the money it can get.

'We can't take the evidence this afternoon, in any event,' I point out. 'If Mr Swivell and his colleagues present themselves at the church hall at three o'clock, they can have until six-thirty to rehearse. It's needed for the youth club after that, I'm told. We will begin at the church hall at ten o'clock tomorrow morning.'

'Your Honour,' Piers inquires, 'would your Honour prefer to have cross-examination at the church hall, or back at court? If it's going to be at the church hall, I will have to arrange to have Exhibit one and Exhibit two brought to the church hall, so that they can be played there.'

'My learned friend should please bring them anyway,' Julian

replies. 'I would like the jury to hear them after the sextet has given evidence.'

'I agree,' I say, 'but we will return to court for cross-examination.'

'As your Honour pleases.'

'Let's not bother with robes tomorrow morning,' I say to counsel. 'Ordinary street clothes will do for the church hall. No need to draw more attention to ourselves than we have to.'

Both counsel agree immediately.

I have the jury brought down to court, and advise them that they are going to have the rare privilege of going on an expedition away from court. They seem pleased, but I have to explain the rules about events of this kind. They are not allowed to talk about the case to anyone, or ask any questions, while we are away from court. All they are allowed to do is watch and listen. They are to assemble at court at nine-fifteen tomorrow morning, so that Carol and Dawn can escort them to the church hall. They will be escorted back to court afterwards, and they are not to separate unless released for lunch. That about covers it. We adjourn for the day to allow Arthur Swivell and his sextet time to rehearse at 'the venue'.

I return to chambers, and call the Reverend Mrs Walden to warn her that the first part of the musical invasion is on its way. She assures me that all is prepared. Ian and Shelley have already set up their impressive recording equipment, and are standing by to test it out once the band arrives. All seems well.

With everything that's been going on this week, I haven't had much chance to work on my summing-up, and I'm not familiar with these trading offences – which are something of a rare breed at the Crown Court – so this seems a good moment to look at the law and write myself a few notes about what I'm going to say to the jury about it. After half an hour or so with

Archbold, it occurs to me that, entertaining as it is going to be to have this private performance by Bermondsey's most famous jazz band, in the end the case is going to come down to Bert Coggins's state of mind. If Arthur Swivell and his mates are in fact the authors of Exhibit one, that's the end of it. Bert Coggins was selling exactly what he claimed to be selling, and he must be not guilty. But even if the jury think otherwise, they have to ask themselves whether Bert had any reason to disbelieve what his supplier told him. If he had no reason to doubt that it was an Arthur Swivell recording, again he must be not guilty. Only if he knew all along that Exhibit one was a rip-off and deliberately took advantage of the misrepresentation made by those who created it, can he be convicted. It's all about his state of mind. And now it occurs to me that Julian could have dealt with Bert's state of mind without acting as impresario for the great Arthur Swivell Bermondsey revival. In fact, the whole performance may be no more than one colossal red herring. But you have to hand it to him. Even by Julian's theatrical standards, it's an extraordinary piece of wizardry, and he may have pulled off an ingenious sleight-of-hand. He's certainly put Piers and Mr Chivers on the back foot. They were looking pretty discouraged when we rose for the day.

My mind suddenly turns to the question of whether there is any chance of persuading Piers and Mr Chivers not to exact revenge on the now elderly members of the Arthur Swivell Sextet, who by their own admission were guilty of an egregious copyright violation in the late 1970s. True, they have nothing to do with the unexpected re-emergence of their recording in Bermondsey, and true, they have never made a penny from their crime – indeed, quite the opposite, it seems that it left them seriously out of pocket. But that wouldn't make any difference if HMV chose to use the legal system to flex its corporate muscles. I would like to discourage that if I can. But before I can explore this chain of thought any further, there is a quiet knock on the door, and Carol pokes her head around it.

'Meredith is here, Judge. She would like to see you for a moment if you have time.'

'Certainly, Carol. Show her in.'

'Would you like me to be here with the hand-held?'

I shake my head. 'No. No need.'

Meredith enters and sinks into a chair in front of me without a word. She looks mortified. No sign of any files or notebooks this afternoon.

'Meredith, I'm so sorry about your brother,' I say. 'If he'd said something about you to his solicitors earlier, they could have alerted the list officer, and she could have –'

'It's no one's fault except Stanley's, Judge,' she concedes at once. 'He is such a fool. The whole family warned him not to mess around with that kind of investment. He knows nothing about timeshares, or about doing business abroad at all, for that matter. But he wouldn't listen, and now he's embarrassed all of us – me in particular.'

'Well, it will all get sorted out,' I assure her. 'Stella is deciding where we ought to send the case, but wherever it is, it will be far enough away that there won't be any professional embarrassment to you.'

She looks down at her feet.

'To tell you truth, Judge,' she says quietly. 'I wish it could stay here. I know all the judges at Bermondsey, and at least I would know he was getting a fair trial.'

'I'm glad to hear you say that, Meredith,' I reply, quite genuinely. 'But there are fair judges everywhere. I know that because I've met most of them during my years on the bench. So do try not to worry unduly. But keeping it at Bermondsey is not an option, I'm afraid. It's all to do with appearances. I'm sure Sir Jeremy would agree.'

She nods. 'Sir Jeremy does agree. I've just come from a long meeting with him. He accepts that I didn't know, so I'm in the clear. But he agrees that the case has to be moved.'

She raises her eyes and finds mine.

'Sir Jeremy also agrees,' she said, 'that we should discontinue our inquiry into the statistics about early pleas of guilty at Bermondsey for the time being: certainly until Stanley's case has been concluded, and probably for some time after that – just to make sure that there is no possible connection to his case.'

I make a huge effort not to show the wave of relief and pleasure that suddenly invades and floods my mind.

'I quite understand that, Meredith,' I reply, 'and Sir Jeremy is absolutely right.'

There is an awkward silence.

'Would you like a cup of tea?' I ask. 'It's that time of day, isn't it? I'm sure Carol won't mind bringing us some.'

'No, thank you, Judge,' she replies, pushing herself to her feet. 'I must be off. I promised my parents I would let them know what's going on as soon as I could. Stanley didn't say anything to them either.'

'How dreadful for you all,' I say. 'In that case, don't let me keep you. I'll ask Stella to keep you up to date about where we're sending the case. I imagine she should have an answer for us tomorrow.'

'Thank you, Judge.' She offers her hand. I take it. She walks to the door and opens it, then suddenly turns back to face me.

'It was so horrible this morning,' she says.

'Well, of course. Seeing your brother being brought up from the cells like that: it must have been dreadful for you.'

'It was. But what was even worse was listening to you explaining to him why he should plead guilty –'

'Only if he is guilty,' I point out.

'Even so. Having to make that choice. It's a frightening thought.'

'Yes, it is,' I say out loud, once she is safely on the other side of the closed door. 'And so it bloody well should be.'

* * *

Thursday morning

It's surprising how odd it feels to sit without robes. The civil and family courts do it all the time, but in the criminal courts we still adhere to tradition – and take advantage of the disguise afforded by the wig and gown, which offers some modest, but welcome, protection against being recognised outside court. Apart from the rare event we're having today, we are also supposed to sit without robes when young children are giving evidence. It's supposed to make them relax and take their minds off the case, we're told. My experience is exactly the opposite. Children tend to find the sight of grown-up men and women wearing fancy dress in public rather funny, and if counsel and I join in the fun, it can help them to relax a little. Being exposed to normal adult dress isn't funny at all, and so doesn't seem to have any effect in terms of defusing the tension.

Early in my career, I asked a ten-year-old girl, newly arrived in this country from Iran, who had witnessed a serious assault, whether she would like counsel and myself to take off our wigs. 'Oh, no, Judge,' she replied with a giggle. 'Please don't. In Iran, everyone wears silly things on their heads – women, the mullahs, everybody. We always laughed at them, and if you don't mind, I'd like to laugh at you too.' I invited her to laugh at us as much as she wished, an offer of which she took full advantage. She was an excellent witness, and the defendant against whom she gave evidence went down like a lead balloon.

The new feeling of freedom in the absence of robes seems to

have infected Julian in particular. As soon as all the members of the sextet have taken the oath, he seems to appoint himself master of ceremonies for the occasion. Well, I suppose, having acted as impresario, it's the role he feels he should take on next. I must admit, Ian and Shelley have done a wonderful job with the 'venue'. They have made sure that the church hall conforms to the general shape of a courtroom, with tables and chairs for me, the defendant, counsel, and the jury, from which we can see everything. There is a small stage at the front of the hall, and by the time I arrive, all the instruments are already in place, including the recently tuned piano. Benches have been placed at the rear of the hall for members of the public. Mercifully, it's not too large a crowd. That's the one thing I had worried about. Our security officers are with us, but without their screening equipment they have to check all bags by hand, and it's taking longer than I would like. But it's necessary, and at least we haven't had a wholesale invasion of the elderly of Bermondsey – though the word has spread among the church community, and a good number of the Reverend's congregation have come to see the show. The Reverend herself is among them, needless to say. She wouldn't miss this for all the tea in China.

'And now, ladies and gentlemen,' Julian announces proudly, looking every inch the impresario/MC, 'the defence proudly presents the Arthur Swivell Sextet.'

The side door of the hall opens, and in walk the musicians. The members of the public present applaud, as one would at a concert. It takes me by surprise, and I feel embarrassed. Once a year all judges go for continuing education, and often the instructors devise odd courtroom situations and ask us how we would deal with them. But somehow, the situations we have to deal with in court always seem to be ones we've never encountered in class. It occurs to me belatedly that the situation we have now would be a good example for the instructors to use, and that I haven't given any thought to how to deal with it. I should probably have warned everyone present that there should be no applause. That's what I imagine most judges would do – the dignity of the court raising its head again. But after the jury has joined in the applause, and counsel and I have reluctantly followed suit, I have a second thought. Applause is part of a musician's professional environment. It's only fair that they should play under normal conditions, insofar as any of this can be made to appear normal. Counsel don't seem concerned. Let them have their applause. What would the instructors think of that, I wonder?

Arthur walks to the microphone provided by Ian and Shelley for the vocalist, and beams out over the audience.

'Good morning, ladies and gentlemen, we're the Arthur Swivell Sextet, Bermondsey's own jazz band, and we'd like to do a few numbers for you from our new album, *Arthur Swivell Sings Cole Porter.* We'd like to begin with one of his most popular songs, "Anything Goes".' He turns towards the band. 'Take it away, boys. One, two, three, four...'

The effect is extraordinary. Even a sextet can sound very loud in a small space, and once they're into it you can hardly hear yourself think. But you can hear – at least I think I can hear – a sound that reminds me unmistakeably of the sounds I heard on the two recordings at the beginning of the trial. I'm not musically adept enough to say whether every detail is the same. I'll have to wait for cross-examination for that, and I see Mr Chivers passing lots of notes to Piers. But the overall effect feels remarkable similar.

As soon as they finish, Piers and Julian jointly arrange for the same track to be played, first on Exhibit two, the HMV original, and then on Exhibit one, the CD Bert had for sale. I don't know what impression this makes on the jury, but it reinforces the feeling I have that the sextet can't be faking this. Before we go any further, Arthur introduces each member of the band to the audience individually, including 'Lofty Harris on English horn, or *cor anglais* as he prefers to call it', and each musician is suitably applauded. We then go through the same exercise with three other songs. Intriguingly, although Julian has followed the prosecution's example by starting with 'Anything Goes', the first track on the albums, he then takes the bold step of choosing two tracks the jury haven't heard before, 'Easy to Love', and 'Every Time we Say Goodbye'. He asks the band to conclude with 'Night and Day'. At the end, there is a prolonged ovation from both public and jury.

'Your Honour,' Julian says. 'If I may, there is just one question I'd like to ask Mr Harris, who is under oath.'

'By all means,' I reply.

'Mr Harris, would you please hold up the instrument you have been playing, so that the jury can see it, and would you please identify it for us?'

'Yes, sir,' Lofty replies, holding it proudly on high. 'This is a *cor anglais*, otherwise known as an English horn. I've had this instrument for many years. In fact it's the same horn I played on the recording at the Elephant and Castle all those years ago.'

'Thank you, Mr Harris,' Julian says. 'Your Honour, subject to cross-examination, that is all I have.'

The clock on the wall is indicating eleven-thirty, and we've probably done all we can in the church hall, but I can't be sure of that without allowing counsel time to reflect, and in any case, it's time for a break. The Reverend Mrs Walden's helpers have coffee and biscuits on hand at the very reasonable price of fifty pence per head. I declare a twenty-minute adjournment. It's slightly worrying from a security perspective. We are all mingling around the coffee bar together – we're not in the court building now, and there's no practical alternative. But despite Bert Coggins, jurors, the sextet, the officer in the case, and sundry members of the public buying their coffee and biscuits in close proximity, there is no sign whatsoever of anything untoward going on. I decide, with relief, not to worry about it.

I can't help noticing that Piers has been conferring in a corner for most of the break with Mr Chivers and a representative from the CPS. I am suddenly reminded of my thought that the sextet's evidence might in some way be decisive, and I start to experience a premonition. Judges have premonitions sometimes that a case is about to change direction; and sure enough, when we resume, Piers stands at once to make a historic announcement.

'Your Honour, I've had the opportunity of discussing the case further with those who instruct me, and as a result of that discussion, the prosecution offer no further evidence against Mr Coggins, and invite the court to direct the jury to return a verdict of not guilty.'

For a moment there is total silence. This is rapidly succeeded by an outburst of loud applause, led by the Arthur Swivell Sextet, who have taken seats in our makeshift public gallery. This time, I do call for order, and direct that there shall be no further interruptions.

'Mr Drayford,' I reply, 'this comes as rather a surprise.'

'Yes, your Honour.'

'The jury are listening, of course, and before I give them any direction, I'm sure they would be interested in knowing the reason for this rather abrupt change of heart. Are you in a position to oblige us?'

'Yes, your Honour. Mr Chivers has, very fairly, your Honour may think, told me that, having listened carefully to the music played here today, he cannot in all conscience exclude the possibility that the instrument used in Exhibit one might be an English horn.'

'Indeed?'

'Yes, your Honour. He tells me that the register of the English horn and the clarinet – in other words, the range of notes the two instruments are capable of – while not identical, are quite close, certainly close enough to account for the use of either in the arrangements of these songs. Their tones differ to some extent, as one would expect, but given the indifferent quality of the recording, while he remains open to a clarinet, he cannot exclude the English horn.'

'As you say, Mr Blanquette, that is conspicuously fair on Mr Chivers's part,' I acknowledge. Chivers nods briefly.

'In the light of that information, your Honour, I cannot properly challenge the evidence of Mr Harris; and I must accept that if the instrument played on Exhibit one may have been an English horn, and not a clarinet, the jury can't be sure that that recording is a bootleg of the HMV original, Exhibit two. In those circumstances, it is my view that I can no longer properly ask the jury to convict Mr Coggins of the offence charged.'

As I concluded during my brief preparation for the summing-up I now won't have to give, that is also my view. I give the jury the appropriate direction. They return a verdict of not guilty accordingly. I thank them for their service, and ask them to report to court tomorrow to see whether there is another case for them to try. I tell Mr Coggins that he is free to go.

'Can Del Boy have his CDs back?' he asks, looking at Piers.

'I'll ask Inspector Thwaites to return them without delay,' Piers replies.

'*Senior* Inspector Thwaites,' Del Boy corrects him, before turning his back and striding defiantly out of the church hall.

Once the throng has dispersed, and Ian and Shelley have started to restore the hall to its natural order, we are down to Piers, Julian, the Reverend Mrs Walden and myself. The Reverend asks whether the church fund, which has benefitted quite well from today's session of the court, may be allowed to offer judge and counsel a free cup of tea, now that the case is over. I rule in favour of the application, and we all sit around a small table out of Ian and Shelley's way.

'Thank you for the use of the church hall, Mrs Walden,' Julian says. 'I could get used to this – sitting in such a nice friendly place and not having to wear robes.'

'You're welcome,' the Reverend replies. 'It was something different for us too, and it gave Ian and Shelley the chance to show off what they can do in the recording world.'

'They're also the church's golden vocal duo,' I confide with a smile.

'Thanks from me too, Mrs Walden,' Piers adds. 'I don't know quite how to put this,' he adds rather wistfully, 'but listening to Arthur and his band play made me understand why everyone is so angry about the Palais de Danse being closed down. It must have been a great night out for everyone in those days. They sounded good to me today, and there's not one of them under seventy. They must have been really something back then, mustn't they?'

'They were,' the Reverend agrees. 'A bit before our time, but my older parishioners all remember them. For some reason, once the Palais went away, they couldn't find a good local venue to play on a consistent basis. It's such a shame. But they're still here, and still going strong, aren't they?'

'Piers,' I say after a pause. 'I'd hate to think of Mr Chivers going after Arthur and his merry men. I know they committed a serious breach of copyright, but…'

Piers smiles. 'It's interesting that you should mention that, Judge. As it happens, I've talked with Chivers about it, and I'm pretty sure you have nothing to worry about. Yes, they did commit a serious breach of copyright, but it was many years ago, and they've never made any profit from it. They're probably judgment-proof in any case. He tells me that HMV are ready to close the book on it.'

'I'm very glad to hear it,' I reply.

'And actually,' Piers adds, 'they might even go a bit further than just closing the book.'

'Oh?'

'Chivers liked what he heard today. He was really surprised that Arthur and his band were never picked up by a record company. He thinks it was probably because of their dishonest agent, the aptly named Monty Rascall.' He smiles again. 'If we were to go outside at this moment, Judge, we might well find Mr Chivers and Arthur deep in conversation. Chivers thinks that a really good jazz band made up of musicians over seventy might just be of interest to his colleagues back home. He told me he's thinking of bringing one or two HMV executives over to London to listen for themselves. We might need your church hall again, Mrs Walden.'

'I'm sure HMV would book them into a proper professional recording studio,' the Reverend smiles, 'but if they should need the hall, all they have to do is ask.'

* * *

Thursday evening

The Reverend and I settle down together after supper – her home-made lasagne washed down with a celebratory bottle of Aldi's Chianti Classico. She rummages through her extensive collection of CDs.

'How about some Cole Porter?' she suggests.

'Why not?' I agree. 'That sounds very appropriate.'

'I've got some by Ella.'

'Sounds perfect.'

'"Begin the Beguine", "Love for Sale", "You Do Something for me".' She laughs. 'What do you think would be Bert Coggins's favourite track tonight?'

I laugh too.

'I'm not sure Bert is a great Cole Porter fan,' I reply.

'Probably not, after his recent experience.'

'But if anything, he might fancy "It Was Just One of Those Things".'

'Coming up,' she says.

And within seconds, Ella's incomparable voice is filling the room, and washing the cares of the week away.

THE OWL AND THE PUSSYCAT

THE OWL AND THE PUSSYCAT

Monday morning

The Owl and the Pussycat went to sea in – well actually, in a nine-metre-long bright orange RHIB, a rigid hull inflatable boat, powered by two 175 horse-power outboard motors and capable of doing up to 40 knots in decent conditions. Whether or not they took some honey remains unclear. But they certainly took some money – rather a lot of money, in fact – and it was wrapped in something bigger than a five pound note: because although the Owl and the Pussycat were romantically involved, they weren't interested in buying a ring from a pig in a wood, or in being married by a turkey on a hill. What they *were* interested in is a subject of some dispute and will be for a jury to decide, as Susan Worthington is about to explain. But as far as the prosecution are concerned, the Owl and the Pussycat were up to no good: and unfortunately for them, unlike Edward Lear's characters, their voyage was not only of interest to the moon and the stars. It was also watched, with considerable interest, every nautical mile of the way, by a well-organised investigative team of Her Majesty's Revenue and Customs.

As I sip Jeanie's latte, I reflect that they haven't picked the best morning for the trial. Some cases had to draw the short straw, and this is one of them. Bermondsey Crown Court is in a state of disorder this week, and will be for several weeks to come. A month or so ago there was serious flooding in South

London in the wake of several violent storms. We thought at the time that we'd escaped without any damage beyond some limited water seepage. But now it turns out that the building's foundations may have been compromised, and we have a team of workmen digging large holes all over the place to ascertain the extent of the damage and determine what should be done about it. Mercifully, they've found a way to do most of the excavation some distance from the most critical parts of the building – the courtrooms and chambers, the barristers' robing room, and the canteen. In fact, most of it is taking place in the rear courtyard, which serves as a car park for those judges and staff who drive to court. They've had to find alternative parking, which has been inconvenient for them, but fortunately there are commercial car parks not too far away; and to my surprise, the Grey Smoothies have agreed to reimburse them for the cost. But, inevitably, the diggers have had to venture some distance inside the back door, to investigate the condition inside the building itself, so the rear part of the building is a mess, and the incessant barrage of drilling, hammering, and general building noise permeates every part of the court.

I did suggest to the Grey Smoothies that it might be best to close the court for a week or two, rather than have us trying to concentrate on trials with that racket going on. But, of course, closing the court wouldn't represent good value for the taxpayer – even if it would represent good value for those of us trying to do justice to prosecution and defence under such adverse conditions. So I always knew the answer I could expect, and sure enough, here we are.

I'm not even sure why we've got the Owl and the Pussycat, as opposed to some court on or near the south-east coast. It has no geographical connection to Bermondsey at all. I would like to think that it's another example of Bermondsey attracting work from afar because of our track record, and, as far as hiding from the press is concerned, our relative obscurity. We have had a number of such cases recently and it is a trend to be welcomed. It certainly broadens one's horizons. On the other hand, it could be because the defendants and most of the witnesses in this case seem to be based in the London area. Scanning the file this morning as I sip Jeanie's latte, I see that the case has a pronounced nautical flavour, including a range of unfamiliar terms I can only assume relate to navigation in some way. I'm sure counsel will explain it all to the jury and me as we go along.

'May it please the court, members of the jury, my name is Susan Worthington and I appear to prosecute in this case. The defendant Jules de Crecy, who sits on the left hand side in the dock, is represented by my learned friend Mr Kenneth Warnock.'

Well, this is going to be fun. On the rare occasions when Kenneth Warnock puts in an appearance at Bermondsey Crown Court, it's a guarantee of an interesting, and often, amusing trial. Warnock is known at Bermondsey for two things: his extraordinary flair for abstruse legal arguments that would never even occur to most lawyers; and his slightly manic air – a combination of his generally dishevelled appearance, his tattered wig, worn favouring the left hand side of his head, and the disconcerting smile that seems to be a permanent feature of his face whenever he is in court. The last time he was before me was also the last case we had with a maritime connection – the notorious Foggin Island case; and if that's anything to go by, we're in for a lively trial once again.

'The defendant Lucy Warrender, who sits on the right hand side of the dock, is represented by my learned friend Miss Emily Phipson.'

Emily Phipson is not at all dishevelled and will make sensible legal arguments that any lawyer would understand instantly. I have a feeling that she will be a welcome foil for Warnock, and provide some sense of balance in the trial. I certainly hope so; with Warnock on the rampage, some balance may be needed.

'Members of the jury, Professor de Crecy and Miss Warrender have a particular interest in naval history, and in particular the location and exploration of wrecks of historic naval warships in the waters surrounding Great Britain. Indeed, Professor de Crecy teaches naval history as a visiting lecturer at a number of academic institutions. He also gives lectures at the Royal Naval College at Dartmouth, and other venues. Which of those institutions conferred the title of professor on him, members of the jury, the prosecution doesn't know, but it's a title he seems to use quite freely. No doubt it is useful in a number of ways, including the development of the more commercial side of his work: because Professor de Crecy is also the chief operating officer of a company called De Crecy Naval Wreckers UK, a company he created, the stated purpose of which is locating and investigating wrecks for the purpose of salvaging valuable items and selling them on. I anticipate that you will hear more about that company as the trial proceeds.

'Miss Warrender is a graduate student in naval history, who studied under Professor de Crecy. But, members of the jury, their relationship progressed beyond that of professor and student. There will be no dispute that they are also romantic partners and live together in London. Miss Warrender is also the secretary of the company to which I referred a moment or two ago, and is very actively involved in its management.

'Members of the jury, some of the company's work involves navigating one's way to the suspected site of a wreck. Locating wrecks is not an exact science, and may take a considerable time, even with the many modern aids available for seeing underwater. Companies like Professor de Crecy's are often unable to afford luxuries like miniature submarines, and, therefore, have to rely on their knowledge and research and painstaking searches by means of diving. This means that Professor de Crecy and Miss Warrender are both expert pilots and divers. They have to be. Not only do they have to undertake long and difficult dives in areas where they suspect a wreck may be, but they have to do this in some of the world's busiest shipping lanes, for example, those in the English Channel. It's not only challenging work; it's also very dangerous if you don't know exactly what you're doing.

'But, members of the jury, Professor de Crecy and Miss Warrender are not before you today because of their diving activities. They are here today because the prosecution say they have used their wreck location business as a front. We say that they placed themselves, their RHIB – a rigid hull inflatable boat called the *Tiffany May* – and their navigational expertise at the disposal of a man called Edgar Rice. Mr Rice, members of the jury, is in a rather different business, the business of importing large quantities of cannabis resin – sometimes known as hashish – into this country from sources on the Continent. A relatively small, manoeuvrable craft, which can come and go across the Channel unnoticed, and which can leave and return to shore at almost any place it chooses, is a perfect vehicle for that purpose. The prosecution say that one Friday, about four months ago, these two defendants brought in a consignment of almost one hundred kilograms of cannabis resin from a location in Belgium on behalf of Mr Rice, landing at Folkestone harbour, from which they had left earlier that day.'

Susan, quite rightly, is cautious about how she puts this. I know from the file this is not the first occasion on which the Owl and the Pussycat have been suspected of being up to no good in cahoots with Edgar Rice in the English Channel; but the investigators have never before been in a position to prove anything, and both defendants are technically persons of previous good character. This is clearly a source of some irritation to HMRC, one they would dearly love to put an end to in the present case.

'Members of the jury, the prosecution are in a position to reconstruct the defendants' movements that day in considerable detail. That's because, three days before Professor de Crecy and Miss Warrender left from Folkestone harbour, Mr Rice had been arrested in connection with this matter. He subsequently pleaded guilty to the offence of importing cannabis resin – the offence with which these defendants are charged – and he will be sentenced at a later time. Members of the jury, Mr Rice will not be a witness in this case, and the rules of evidence don't allow me to tell you what he said to the police when he was interviewed after his arrest. Suffice it to say that at about nine o'clock on the morning of Friday the eighteenth of November of last year, when Professor de Crecy and Miss Warrender arrived at Folkestone harbour, investigating officers from Her Majesty's Revenue and Customs were observing, and indeed filming, their every move. They observed the pair driving a Jeep SUV, and towing the *Tiffany May* behind them. With the usher's assistance, I will hand out copies of a map of the Folkestone harbour area, one between two, please.'

Dawn quickly obliges.

'Your Honour, I'm told there is no objection. May this please be Exhibit one?' I assent.

'Members of the jury, the officers saw Professor de Crecy drive into the harbour, where there is a jetty, and unload the *Tiffany May* from the tow trailer into the water, tied up to the jetty. While Miss Warrender made the boat ready for departure, Professor de Crecy drove the Jeep to a car park a short distance away off the Old High Street. You can see those locations towards the bottom of the map. The officers continued to film as Professor de Crecy returned to the boat a few minutes after parking the

Jeep, and as the pair left Folkestone harbour at ten o'clock, with Miss Warrender piloting the craft. Not only that, members of the jury: using different technology, other HMRC officers were able to track Professor de Crecy and Miss Warrender at every stage of their voyage. They tracked the *Tiffany May* as it crossed the Channel, arriving at a seaside town called De Panne, in Belgium, just before twelve forty-five, almost three hours after leaving Folkestone. The boat remained stationary at De Panne for just over an hour, leaving for the return journey at just after one forty-five. They arrived back at Folkestone just before five o'clock, and their arrival was filmed. Miss Warrender was again piloting the boat during the return voyage.

'Members of the jury, after Miss Warrender had landed the boat at the jetty, Professor de Crecy made his way to the Old High Street car park to retrieve the Jeep, returning a few minutes later. In the back of the Jeep was a metal trolley, which Professor de Crecy used to unload five black canvas bags from the boat and deposit them on the ground near the Jeep. It was at that point, members of the jury, that the officers pounced.

'The defendants were arrested. Inside the black canvas bags, the investigators found a grand total of 98.4 kilograms of cannabis resin – a large, commercial quantity which has a street value in the region of three hundred and thirty to three hundred and thirty-five thousand pounds. Both defendants were cautioned on their arrest. They made no reply to the caution, and when later interviewed in the presence of their solicitors, both exercised their right to say nothing except "no comment" in reply to all the questions put to them. Members of the jury, the defendants were fully entitled not to answer any questions; they had no obligation whatsoever to do so. But that is a matter to which I shall return later in the trial.

'Lastly, members of the jury, this is one of those very unusual cases in which you will be able to watch the whole story unfold before your eyes on film. You will be given photographs of the black canvas bags and the cannabis, and indeed the officers will bring one bag into court for your inspection – although as you may well appreciate, it will not remain in court for very long because such a large quantity of the drug has a very strong odour, and if left in court for long enough, might even start to affect us – and I'm sure no one wants to be under the influence of cannabis.'

The grins on the faces of one or two jurors suggest a less than unanimous verdict on Susan's last statement. If she notices, she ignores it very well.

'But, members of the jury, despite what the Crown say is the overwhelming evidence in this case, you must bear in mind that it is for the Crown to prove the case against the defendants so that you are sure of their guilt – nothing less will do for a conviction. You must also consider the cases of the two defendants separately. The fact you may decide to convict one defendant – or acquit one defendant – does not mean that you must reach the same verdict in the case of the other. And now with His Honour's leave, I will call the first witness, Officer Anne Johnson.'

Officer Johnson is tall and elegantly dressed in a black two-piece suit, and somehow seems to epitomise the HMRC prosecution of which she is a part. Judges and prosecutors alike appreciate the high quality of preparation in all the cases brought by HMRC. It seems that, in contrast to most police prosecutions, money is not an issue – or, to the extent it is an issue, it is an issue that takes second place to the goal of presenting the evidence in the most professional and helpful way possible. The witness statements, photographs and other exhibits are placed sequentially in fully indexed binders, and it is not unusual to have, as we do in this case, crucial events fully recorded by means of high-quality cameras and tracking devices. It makes a nice change from the postcode lottery of whether CCTV footage is available, and if so, whether it is clear enough to be of any use, which is the story of most police prosecutions.

'Officer Johnson,' Susan begins, once the witness has taken the oath and identified herself, 'on the morning of the eighteenth of November last year, were you a member of a team of HMRC officers assigned to keep observation on certain suspects at Folkestone harbour on the Kent coast?'

'Yes, that's correct.'

'And please answer this question just yes or no. Were you there at that time because of information received by HMRC?'

'Yes.'

'Who were the suspects, the subjects of your surveillance?'

'They were the two defendants in the dock today: Professor Jules de Crecy and Miss Lucy Warrender.'

'How many officers were involved in the surveillance, and what were your roles?'

'There were eight of us altogether, under the command of Senior Officer Vaughan, all dressed casually. My particular assignment was to record certain events using a high-powered movie camera. Other officers were responsible for tracking the movements of the suspects on the ground in and around the harbour, and others for tracking the RHIB once it was launched and underway. All of us were in constant radio contact, and I was given instructions as to what to film as we went along.'

'And just so that everyone is clear, Officer Johnson, I think you have been instructed not to divulge details of your whereabouts or movements, or those of other officers during the surveillance unless ordered to do so by His Honour, so that your methods of surveillance are not compromised?'

'If it assists, your Honour,' Kenneth Warnock intervenes, giving me his invariable, slightly creepy smile, 'I have no interest in inquiring into those details, so Officer Johnson needn't worry about it.'

'Same here,' Emily Phipson adds.

'I'm much obliged to my learned friends. Then, Officer Johnson, did you on that day make a movie showing two phases of activity?'

'Yes.'

'The first phase being the movements of the two defendants in and around the harbour during the morning, before and at the time of their departure from Folkestone; and the second being the events occurring at the time of their return to Folkestone during the afternoon?'

'Yes, that's correct.'

'And do you now produce the film of the two phases? Exhibits two and three, please, your Honour.'

'Yes. They are set up, ready to play.'

If this were a police prosecution, we would be watching on big screens, one placed on the wall opposite the jury, one placed near the dock for the defendants, and one on the wall behind the bench to my left, for the general public. I have a small screen on the bench, but everyone else has to rely on being able to see often quite small details at some distance. But this is an HMRC prosecution, and small screens have been provided for the defendants in the dock, for each member of the jury individually, and for each counsel. The screens were installed overnight, after court had ended yesterday.

'Thank you. Then, Officer Johnson, would you play the first phase for us, please, and would you give us a running commentary, so to speak, on what we're watching?'

'Yes. May I leave the witness box, your Honour?'

'Yes, of course,' I reply. Officer Johnson positions herself alongside Susan, where the equipment has been set up. She pushes one or two buttons and the high-quality film springs to life on our screens. It's like watching a commercially produced movie. The opening screen tells us that it is an HMRC production and gives us the name of the case and the date of the events filmed. The film is so good that I'm almost expecting the next screen to identify the famous director and stars who have created it. As the film moves smoothly along, the time is recorded digitally in the top left hand corner of the screen. We begin at just after nine o'clock.

'What we are seeing here,' Officer Johnson observes, 'is a dark grey Jeep SUV, registration number NS58 00Y, being driven slowly on the A260 in a southerly direction towards the Folkestone harbour area… we then see the vehicle turn left on to The Stade. The vehicle is towing a trailer with an orange rigid hull inflatable boat named the *Tiffany May*. The driver is male, and there is a female passenger in the front passenger seat.'

Officer Johnson has to pause for some time, not only while we watch the slow progress of the Jeep, but also while we adjust to the series of dull thuds emanating from the excavation area at the back of the court building. Everyone knew this was coming at some point during the day, but it is disturbing when it actually begins. Periodically it stops for a short time, but we're always expecting it to resume before very long.

'What we're seeing now is that the Jeep is being driven very slowly through the entrance to the harbour and towards the jetty. We see the driver reach the water's edge. He makes a sharp right turn, away from the jetty, so that the trailer brings the RHIB up close to the jetty and parallel with it. The Jeep then stops and both the driver and passenger get out of the vehicle.'

Susan waits for them both to come into focus.

'Right, let's pause it there for a moment. Can we now see that the driver is Professor de Crecy and the passenger is Miss Warrender?'

'Yes, that's correct.'

'All right, let's start it again. What happens next?'

'We see Miss Warrender secure the RHIB to the jetty with a line. Professor de Crecy then uncouples the RHIB from the trailer, while Miss Warrender boards the craft and stands ready to control it. Professor de Crecy uses a winch to release the craft gradually from the trailer into the water. Once it is in the water, he pushes the craft forward slightly so that it is floating freely, subject to the line tethering it to the jetty. There is some conversation between the two of them.'

'Which we can't hear?'

'Yes, that's correct.'

'We see that Miss Warrender appears to be smoking a cigarette while this is going on?'

Officer Johnson laughs. 'She was smoking throughout the time I was filming her, including while she was piloting the craft. I don't think we see her without a cigarette for more than a minute or two at any point.'

'Then Professor de Crecy re-attaches the trailer to the Jeep?'

'Yes.'

'He gets into the vehicle, turns right again and makes his way slowly towards the harbour entrance?'

'Yes.'

We follow his progress to the accompaniment of the dull thuds for several minutes.

'He goes back along The Stade, up to the Old High Street, and parks the Jeep in the Old High Street car park?'

'Yes.'

Further minutes with dull thuds while we alternate between the Owl returning from the car park, and the *Tiffany May*, where the Pussycat appears to be stowing various items and generally preparing the boat for departure, her signature cigarette dangling from her lips.

'Professor de Crecy is walking back to join Miss Warrender in the *Tiffany May*?'

'Yes, that's correct.'

I think I hear a shout. I'm so involved with the film that for a few moments I think it must be coming from Folkestone harbour, but I remind myself that this is a silent movie and I conclude that it must have come from somewhere in or around the court, perhaps from the direction of the excavations. As if to suggest that I may be right, the dull thuds stop abruptly.

'Once Professor de Crecy is on board,' Officer Johnson resumes, 'the movement of the RHIB suggests that the motors have been started – you can see the forward section of the craft come up out of the water while the aft section goes lower in the water, and there's some lateral motion also.'

'Professor de Crecy unties the line holding her to the jetty?'

'Yes.'

'And away she goes?'

'And away she goes. The time is almost exactly ten o'clock. We follow the craft into the distance until it disappears from sight.'

'Which ends phase one?'

'Which ends phase one.'

'Your Honour,' Susan says, 'I've discussed this with my learned friends, and in order to present the case to the jury chronologically, the best course, it seems to us, would be to interrupt the evidence of Officer Johnson at this point, and bring her back later to deal with the return to Folkestone. In the meanwhile, I will interpose Officer Callaghan, who will give evidence about the tracking of the craft during the voyage. If your Honour agrees, then my learned friends will cross-examine Officer Johnson at the conclusion of her evidence.'

It's a sensible suggestion; Kenneth and Emily indicate their agreement.

'In that case,' I say, 'I'm sure the jury would welcome a break, after concentrating on the evidence with so much noise going on. I will rise for twenty minutes, which should give everyone time for coffee.'

It's one of the rare decisions I make of which everyone seems to approve.

Our court manager, Bob, is waiting for me in chambers. He's wearing a yellow hard hat and high visibility jacket. The contractors, represented on site by the crew foreman, Jake Moran, insist on these supposed safeguards for anyone who comes anywhere near the excavations. Quite why, I don't really understand. It's always seemed to me that hard hats are intended to protect you against heavy objects falling on your head, and that high-visibility jackets are intended to protect you from being run over by a lorry or a forklift truck that might not see you if you were wearing black. The only real danger with excavations, surely, is that you might fall into a large hole in the ground, and I'm not sure how either would protect you against that. But we're in Jake's jurisdiction now, and we have to follow Jake's rules. I have the same protective items of my own on one of my chairs, ready to trade for my robe and wig.

'I'm glad you've taken a break, Judge,' he says. 'I got a message from Jake a few minutes ago, asking if we could see him as soon as possible.'

'I noticed that the thuds have stopped,' I reply. 'Has that got anything to do with it?'

'I've no idea, Judge. All he said was he needed to see us as soon as possible.'

I see the prospect of coffee receding into the distance. I sigh, reaching for my protective gear. It's not the first time Jake has summoned us almost on a life or death basis, and so far any urgency has seemed rather illusory.

'All right. I suppose we should go and see what he wants.'

When we leave the building through the rear door, picking our way carefully past a rather large hole that has been roped off, we see that the entire crew is at a standstill. They are standing around drinking fizzy drinks out of bottles, and in one or two cases, smoking. Jake is smiling rather oddly. He's a rotund man in his early forties, and not much given to levity, in my experience. It doesn't seem to bode well.

'Ah, Mr Walden, thank you for coming, sir. We've run into a bit of a problem. We've had to shut the job down for a while.'

I look around. I can't see anything obviously wrong. No one seems to have been injured, and the digging equipment looks the same as it always does.

'So I see,' I reply.

'You'll have to step this way to see it, sir. You, too, Bob, if you like. Tread carefully. We don't want you falling in the trench, sir, do we?'

No, we don't. Bob and I dutifully follow Jake in single file alongside the trench and approach the far end.

'You've got to lean over a bit to see it, sir. Be careful. It's tucked in there at the back, just next to that small pile of earth and concrete. Do you see?'

He's pointing into the trench. At first I don't see anything; but then, suddenly, I do. It's a long, tapered, metallic item, all of seven or eight feet long, stained and covered with dirt.

'It looks almost like… like a cannon,' I say to Bob, 'a ship's cannon. What's something like that doing here?'

'That's just what I thought, sir,' Jake replies in Bob's stead, looking around like a man who has just been vindicated. 'I thought it had to be something like that.'

Bob is nodding. 'That's why you shut the job down?'

'We have to, sir. If we come across an item of – what d'you call it? – an item of possible archaeological interest, we have to shut the job down and make arrangements for it to be safely removed.'

'How do you do that?' Bob asks.

'Ah, well, that's a good question,' Jake concedes. 'I'll tell you the honest truth: I've got no idea. I've never had it happen on one of my jobs. Some of my mates have, mind you. One found a complete Roman bath – up at Shoreditch, that was; and another of my mates came across some theatrical items on a site Shakespeare might have used. He was telling me that –'

'Yes,' I interrupt, briefly remembering that I'm supposed to be on a short coffee break. 'Forgive me for interrupting, Jake. I'm sure you're right to shut the job down. Well spotted and well done. But the priority now is to find out what we have to do to extract this item of archaeological interest safely, and then get on with the job. Can you call your head office and ask them?'

'I could,' he replies. 'I'm not sure there will be anyone who knows, but I daresay they could ask around.'

I shake my head. I'm having a very strange sensation. I somehow feel that the arrival of this cannon at Bermondsey Crown Court is no accident. It belongs here. Already, I feel protective of this artefact, which I'm already calling, in the privacy of my mind, the Bermondsey Cannon. I'm seeing it in the foyer of the court, resting on a carriage shrouded by purple cloth, under protective glass. Where this is coming from, I haven't a clue. Is it some kind of strange spiritual awakening? I hope not. I must ask the Reverend Mrs Walden when I get home this evening.

'We can't take chances with this, Jake,' I say. 'We must find out what it is; and then we must find out exactly what equipment will be needed to haul it up safely and put it somewhere out of harm's way until we decide what to do with it.'

Bob takes a deep breath. 'I hesitate to suggest this, Judge, but...'

I take his arm and we turn away from Jake together.

'No, go ahead.'

He's still hesitating. 'Well… I was thinking, Judge… we do have an expert on this kind of thing with us at court at this precise moment, don't we?'

I stare at him, and it dawns on me. I think for some time.

'It would have to happen without my being on site,' I reply eventually. 'He's on trial in my court. I can't allow anything to get in the way of the trial, and I can't have him thinking he's doing us a favour, or that we owe him something. It can't come from me.'

'Of course, Judge. But he may find it of professional interest, and he may be prepared to help us regardless of the trial. He is on bail, isn't he, so there would be no problem…?'

'There's no problem in letting him back here, as long as you can get him a hat and jacket. But you'll have to speak to his counsel, Mr Warnock, and explain that the court is asking his help without prejudice to his trial – it can't have anything to do with the trial – and that if he has any doubts about that, he should say no, he prefers not to help us.'

'Yes, Judge. I suppose, even if he doesn't want to help us himself, he could suggest a name, someone we could talk to?'

'Yes, good idea.'

'And if he is willing to help?'

'He should come at lunchtime and take a look, and tell us what he thinks. But it's only for information. We can't let him undertake anything himself, you know, he can't make money from the court while he's on trial.'

'No, of course, Judge. In any case, we'll have to let the Grey Smoothies know, won't we? They'll have to authorise any expenditure, won't they?'

I nod. Bob is right, of course. We will have to let them know; and I see at once that they may pose a problem for my plans for the Bermondsey Cannon. But I've already decided that I'm not giving up without a fight. I glance at my watch.

'I'll adjourn for lunch now, even though it's a bit early. We've got to allow Professor de Crecy time before the trial resumes, and if he agrees to help us, I don't want to cut into his lunch hour.'

'Right you are, Judge,' Bob says. 'I'll tell your court they're adjourned, and I'll have a quiet word with Mr Warnock, shall I?'

'Very quiet,' I suggest.

And so to lunch, an oasis of calm in a desert of chaos.

With all the banging this morning, and the promise of at least two weeks more of it to come, we are all in a rather irritable mood, although in my case, the finding of the Bermondsey Cannon has cheered me up considerably. In the hope that it may have the same effect on my colleagues, I tell them all about it, including my vision for the cannon as the new image of the court, impressing court users with a sense of history as they enter the building.

'Good luck with that, Charlie,' Legless says. 'The Grey Smoothies are bound to whisk it away to some museum or other.'

'Not necessarily,' Marjorie replies. Of the three, she seems the most enthused by the idea of having our own cannon to adorn the foyer. 'If this is where it was found, why not leave it here? I don't think naval cannons are all that uncommon. There are probably any number of them in museums already. I think we can make a good case for keeping it.'

'I think it's a splendid idea,' Hubert adds. 'And once we've got it set up, I think that once a year, on the anniversary of Trafalgar, we should take it out of its case and fire it in the general direction of Bermondsey – just to remind the inhabitants to be on their best behaviour.'

'Really, Hubert?' Legless asks. 'And what about all the people we would kill?'

'We should display their heads on the north battlements,' Hubert replies, '*pour encourager les autres*.'

I return to chambers just before two o'clock to find Bob waiting for me, clutching several sheets of paper torn from a notebook. He seems quite excited.

'I spoke to Mr Warnock, as you asked, Judge, and Professor de Crecy was only too pleased to help. He says he understands that this is not connected to his trial in any way. He came and spent about half an hour with us on site, and he said…' Bob looks hurriedly through his sheets of notepaper. 'I wrote it down as he said it, Judge… right, here we go… you were absolutely right, Judge. It is a naval cannon dating from the mid-to-late eighteenth century. It appears to be complete and intact and in good condition, although we won't know that for sure until we bring it up and wipe all the mud and debris off it. Assuming that it is in perfect condition, Professor de Crecy thinks it will be quite valuable, and a definite museum piece.

'He's given me the name of a firm in London which specialises in moving items like this. They will need everyone out of the way, and they will need access to the site for their equipment – which shouldn't be a problem – and they will probably need half a day to lift the cannon out of the ground, clean and inspect it, and wrap it in protective material of some kind. They can store it at their premises, if we wish, until we – or the Grey Smoothies – decide what to do with it.'

'This is remarkable,' I say.

Bob smiles. 'Yes, Judge. Quite a turn-up for the book, isn't it?'

'Did Professor de Crecy have any ideas about how we come to have an eighteenth-century naval cannon in our back yard?'

Bob consults his notes again. 'He seemed quite mystified,

Judge. Apparently, most findings like this are made closer to Woolwich or Greenwich, wherever the Royal Dockyards were; although when you think about it, we're not really all that far away from Woolwich along the river. So he thinks the cannon may have been lost while being transported on the river for some reason; or it's possible that a warship got into trouble during a bad storm and drifted farther upstream than intended, and lost it somewhere near here. He says he can check to see whether there's a record of something like that happening. Alternatively, it could be that it was found somewhere else and dumped in this area sometime during the last two hundred years, for whatever reason – perhaps whoever found it didn't know what it was – and it found its way to the court through the silt over a long period of time. Apparently, such things do happen.'

'Remarkable,' I say again. 'Well, obviously we should contact this firm as soon as possible.'

Bob nods. 'I'm going to call the Grey Smoothies now, and ask for permission to go ahead with it. I'm sure it won't be a problem once I've explained that we've had to shut the job down until it's done, and in the meanwhile we're still paying the contractors.'

'Not to mention that they may have a valuable historical artefact on their hands,' I add, '"valuable" being the operative word.'

* * *

Monday afternoon

Officer Martin Callaghan is also tall and elegantly dressed.

'My assignment during the operation,' he says in reply to Susan, 'was to track the craft's course once it was underway.'

'Yes. Officer, please tell His Honour and the jury by what means you were able to track the voyage.'

'We use what we call an AIS system, an automatic

identification system. The AIS is a land-based tracking system which makes use of a satellite to keep a vessel under constant surveillance. The data appear on a screen at intervals of time – in this case, intervals of five minutes –'

'Sorry to interrupt, Officer, but why five minutes?'

'It was adequate for this particular observation where the vessel's progress was regular. We could have reduced the intervals if necessary – for example, if some irregularity of movement occurred – but there was no need in this case.'

'Thank you. Please continue.'

'This enables you to see the vessel's position in terms of latitude and longitude as of any given date and time, as well as its average speed between observation points.'

'Does the AIS system operate independently of any navigation equipment on board the vessel?'

'It can, to some extent, but the best results are obtained when the vessel is equipped with an AIS transceiver.'

'Do you know whether the *Tiffany May* was equipped in that way?'

'Yes. This craft was legally required to have a working transceiver because it was carrying passengers on the high seas, and it was clear from the results we obtained that the equipment was in place and functioning normally. In fact, I was able to check that personally after the vessel had docked again at Folkestone and the defendants had been arrested.'

'Thank you, Officer. Are you now able to show us the results of your tracking of the *Tiffany May's* voyage on the eighteenth of November of last year?'

'Yes, if I may leave the witness box, your Honour?'

'Yes, of course,' I say.

Officer Callaghan takes his place at Susan's side, and within seconds another pristine HMRC visual presentation springs to life on our screens. Its impact is not as immediate as the film, but it is just as precise. The *Tiffany May*'s movements are shown on the screen in the form of a digital image of a boat, progressing in a leisurely way across the English Channel. The boat's position is recorded at intervals of five minutes, and, as Officer Callaghan has promised, each position is given with reference to the date and time of the observation, and the latitude and longitude of the vessel's location.

'Officer, please talk us through the first screen, which His Honour and the jury can now see. What does this tell us?'

'The first observation is of the vessel apparently stationary in Folkestone harbour, at ten hundred hours, at latitude 51 degrees, 5 minutes north, longitude 1 degree, 11 minutes east.'

'North, of course, referring to a position north of the Equator, and east referring to…?'

'East referring to a position east of the international date line at Greenwich.'

'Yes. Thank you, Officer. What happens then?'

'The *Tiffany May* then departs Folkestone harbour and proceeds out to sea in a direct line away from the harbour until it is clear of the coast. It then makes a slight turn to the north-east and continues across the Channel towards the coast of Belgium, at an average speed of between twenty-five and thirty knots.'

'A knot being, in case the jury are not familiar with the term…?'

'A knot is a standard measurement of the speed of a vessel's travel over water. As with land-based measurements of speed, it is made with reference to the time taken to cover a given distance. One knot represents progress at the rate of one nautical mile per hour.'

Susan is going into so much detail partly because HMRC presentations are always very detailed, and that's the way they like their cases to be presented; but also because she has no real idea what the defence is going to be. As the defendants gave the police no explanation for their possession of a large commercial quantity of cannabis resin, and the defence statement is – to put it neutrally – rather vague, she has no basis for making any assumptions about what she has to deal with. She has no alternative but to nail down every aspect of the prosecution's evidence, and wait for the defendants to give her some clue, either through cross-examination, or during the defence case itself. Suspects and defendants have the right to remain silent, and they often think they're being clever by not saying a word to the police. But Susan has more than enough experience to know that she will probably make them regret it later in the trial.

'And do we see that the *Tiffany May* continues towards the Belgian coast until it finally appears to arrive at a destination at about twelve forty-five?'

'Yes, that's correct.'

'Crossing a number of very busy shipping lanes?'

'Yes, though that's not a problem here. This is a very quick, manoeuvrable and stable craft, the weather is reasonably good, and with a competent pilot such as Miss Warrender at the helm it's perfectly safe.'

'Is there any evidence that the *Tiffany May* stopped at any point en route to the Belgian coast, for example, long enough to examine a particular site for evidence of a wreck, if Professor de Crecy or Miss Warrender had been interested in doing that?'

'Yes, the vessel does appear to slow down and come to a stop at about five minutes past eleven, and remains stationary for about twenty minutes before proceeding again. When we come to the second screen, we will see that there is a corresponding stop for about fifteen minutes on the return trip beginning at three thirty-five. We don't know why, of course. There are other points where the vessel slows down, probably because of traffic or some choppiness in the water, but there's no evidence of the vessel coming to rest other than on those two occasions.'

'The vessel arrives, apparently at its destination, just after twelve forty-five. Where was that?'

'That was at the Belgian seaside town of De Panne, latitude 51 degrees, 6 minutes north, longitude 2 degrees, 35 minutes east.'

'What was the distance covered by the *Tiffany May* between Folkestone and De Panne?'

'Fifty-five to sixty nautical miles. De Panne is on the coast between Dunkerque and Oostende. Folkestone to Oostende is sixty-five nautical miles, so depending on exactly where the vessel was berthed, the distance I gave is about right.'

'We can't say, can we, exactly where, in or around De Panne, the *Tiffany May* was berthed after her arrival?'

'No, we can't tell. All we know is that the vessel came to rest at that general location.'

'Thank you, Officer. Turning now to the second screen, do we see the *Tiffany May* leaving De Panne at about one forty-five, about an hour after it arrived?'

'Yes, that's correct. The vessel then makes essentially the same voyage in reverse, with a similar average speed, arriving back at Folkestone at about five o'clock.'

'Stopping along the way, as you told us earlier, at about three thirty-five for about fifteen minutes?'

'Yes.'

'And was that the end of your involvement in the observation?'

'Effectively, yes. The AIS equipment I was using was located a short distance from the harbour itself, so I didn't play any part in the arrests. After the defendants had been arrested, as I said before, I did examine the vessel's navigational equipment, which was in good working order. But the defendants and the drugs had been removed by then.'

'Did you notice any other equipment on board, other than the navigational instruments?'

'Yes. Inside the wheelhouse I did observe some diving equipment – two dry suits and helmets, and two oxygen cylinders. All this equipment appeared to be dry and was wrapped up for protection. It showed no sign of recent use.'

'Thank you, Officer,' Susan says. 'Please return to the witness box and answer any further questions.'

'Officer, you've told us that the *Tiffany May* made two stops: one on the outward leg of the journey, and one on the return leg?' Kenneth begins.

'Yes, sir, that's correct.'

'And we know this because the AIS system shows the vessel making no forward progress at those times, for twenty minutes on the outward leg, fifteen minutes on the return leg? The latitude and longitude of the vessel's position don't change during those times, do they?'

'That's correct, sir.'

'And incidentally, the reason why you have such detailed coverage of the *Tiffany May*'s movements is that it had a working AIS transceiver. Yes?'

'It's not the only factor, but it certainly enabled us to make a more detailed record of the vessel's position and progress than would have been the case without it.'

'So nobody had disabled the transceiver, had they?'

'No, sir.'

'And as the jury can see, the two stops the *Tiffany May* made were in mid-Channel?'

'Yes.'

'In or adjacent to some of the busiest shipping lanes in the world?'

'Yes, I would agree.'

'That's something no experienced pilot would do without a good reason, wouldn't you agree?'

'I always assume that an experienced pilot has a good reason for everything he or she does, sir.'

'And the prosecution accepts, I think, that both Professor de Crecy and Miss Warrender are qualified and experienced pilots?'

'Yes, sir.'

'They are also qualified and experienced divers, aren't they?'

'Yes, sir.'

'And they have a company that specialises in locating and recovering historic wrecks?'

'Yes, sir.'

'Would you accept that work of that kind may involve stopping in waters that are believed to contain wrecks, and diving at those sites to determine whether they seem to merit further investigation?'

'I would accept that, sir; but I would question how useful diving is in waters of the depth you'd expect in the mid-channel shipping lanes. Closer to shore would be a different matter, but in that kind of depth, it strikes me as unusual.'

'Would you accept that Professor de Crecy may know rather more than you do about diving?'

'I'm not a qualified diver myself, sir. I accept that.'

'Thank you, Officer. And in any case, as you told the jury, while there was diving equipment in the boat, it appeared not to have been used recently: isn't that right?'

'Yes, that's correct.'

'Officer, is it within your knowledge that the stretch of the Belgian coast between Dunkerque and Oostende is known for having a large number of outlets selling cut-price cigarettes and tobacco?'

Susan and I both sit up and take notice at the same time.

Have we at last heard a hint of a possible defence? Susan turns behind her to whisper to Senior Officer Vaughan, who nods and leaves court.

'Yes, sir. It is a well-known destination for tourists shopping for cheap tobacco products.'

'And there's nothing wrong with buying cut-price cigarettes and tobacco in Belgium, and bringing them back into Great Britain, is there? There's no limit on the quantity you can bring back from Belgium, is there?'

'No, sir, as long as it's for your personal consumption or as a gift, and as long as the appropriate duty has been paid in Belgium. But you have to declare it to a customs officer, and if you bring back quantities above a certain amount you may well be asked questions to ascertain whether you're bringing in a commercial quantity with the intention of selling it. You can't do that legally unless you're a licensed importer.'

'What would the questionable amount be?'

'As a general rule, anything above eight hundred cigarettes or one kilo of loose tobacco.'

'Yes, thank you, Officer,' Kenneth says, 'I have nothing further.'

'I have no questions, your Honour,' Emily says.

Officer Johnson returns to the witness box.

'Officer,' Susan begins, 'you are still under oath. You understand?'

'Yes.'

'Thank you. Earlier you took us through the first phase of the film you took on 18 November. Was there also a second phase when the *Tiffany May* returned to Folkestone harbour?'

'Yes.'

'With His Honour's permission, would you please leave the witness box and take us through the second phase?'

Once again, a perfectly clear film appears on all our screens.

'Do we see the *Tiffany May* approaching the harbour at about four-fifty – she starts as little more than a speck on the horizon, but she gets bigger as she approaches?'

'Yes.'

'Right. Fast forward, please, Officer, to just before five. What do we see at that time?'

'We see the *Tiffany May* slow down as she approaches the jetty. We see Miss Warrender at the helm…'

'With her cigarette?'

'With her cigarette. She slows down and heaves to alongside the jetty. We see Professor de Crecy take a line, jump up on to the jetty, and tie the vessel up. To judge by the posture of the boat – the forward end goes down in the water, and there is no sign of motion except for the action of the water – Miss Warrender has shut down the outboard motors.'

'Fast forward again, do we see Professor de Crecy leave the jetty and disappear in the direction of the Old High Street?'

'Yes.'

'Fast forward again, and do we see the Jeep SUV, with Professor de Crecy at the wheel, towing the empty trailer, and approaching the jetty?'

'Yes, and we can see, by now it's just after five twenty-five.'

'Thank you, Officer. Then, what happens?'

'Professor de Crecy and Miss Warrender are on and off the boat a fair bit, apparently talking and removing some small personal items from the boat to the Jeep. Fast forward just over five minutes… and we see Professor de Crecy unloading a black canvas bag from the wheelhouse area of the boat, and placing it on the ground at the passenger's side of the Jeep. He repeats the process, until there are five such bags lined up together.'

'What is Miss Warrender doing during this time?'

The officer smiles. 'She appears to be watching him, leaning up against the jetty and smoking.'

'Then, what happens?'

'At this point, evidently, Senior Officer Vaughan has given the order to arrest them, and except for myself and Officer Callaghan, all the available officers descend on them. Obviously, I can't tell you what was said, but…'

'No, that's all right, Officer, we will get the sound track from Mr Vaughan. But do we see that both Professor de Crecy and Miss Warrender are stopped and detained, and they are both handcuffed?'

'Yes.'

'Despite which Miss Warrender appears to continue smoking the cigarette she has between her lips.'

Everyone, including the jury, has a short chuckle at the Pussycat's expense.

'Apparently so, yes.'

'What do we see next?'

'We see Senior Officer Vaughan take one of the black canvas bags and carry it back to the jetty, where the defendants are standing with the other officers. We see him open the bag and allow the other officers and the defendants to inspect the contents.'

'Yes. You can't get close enough with your camera to show us the contents in any detail on film, can you?'

'No. But at that stage, I left my position and joined the other officers with another camera, and took a large number of still photographs of the bags, their contents, and the wheelhouse area of the *Tiffany May*.'

'Exhibit four, your Honour, please. Usher, there are copies for the jury, please, one between two. Officer, does this album contain forty of the photographs you took?'

'Yes, it does.'

'And if we go through the first twenty quite quickly, are these pictures of the five black canvas bags and their contents?'

'Yes. They show that each of the canvas bags contains a large quantity of cannabis resin, wrapped up in several large heavy-duty plastic bags.'

'The remaining photographs are of the defendants and the interior of the *Tiffany May*, inside the wheelhouse, including the diving equipment, all wrapped up, which the jury have already heard about?'

'That's correct, yes.'

'Officer, while you were inside the wheelhouse taking these photographs, did you notice anything in particular?'

'Yes, I did. There was a very strong smell of cannabis. Actually, it was almost overpowering.'

Neither Kenneth nor Emily has any questions for Officer Johnson. She leaves court, and Susan calls Senior Officer Vaughan.

'Mr Vaughan, as the senior officer in this investigation, were you in overall charge of the operation on eighteenth of November last year?'

'Indeed I was.'

'We've already seen a good deal of what went on that day in Officer Johnson's film and the AIS surveillance record. But perhaps you can fill in a few details for us?'

'Yes.'

'Firstly, were you the officer who arrested Edgar Rice?'

'I had other officers with me, but I was in charge of the operation to arrest Mr Rice.'

'Is Mr Rice a man who has two previous convictions for importing or supplying cannabis resin?'

'Yes, that's correct.'

'Did you interview Mr Rice under caution, and was he

subsequently charged with importing cannabis resin, a controlled drug of class B – the same offence as these defendants are charged with in the indictment before the jury?'

'He was.'

'Did Mr Rice plead guilty to the charge, and is he awaiting sentencing?'

'Yes, that's correct.'

'Mr Vaughan, please don't tell us anything that was said, but was it as a result of your interview of Mr Rice that you decided to mount the operation to keep observation on these two defendants at Folkestone harbour, and to track any voyage they might make on the eighteenth of November?'

'Yes, that's correct.'

'Thank you. Let me come to the arrest of the defendants. We've already seen it all on the film, but supplying the soundtrack, as it were, what happened?'

'I and the other officers approached the defendants and detained them, as you saw. I cautioned them and they made no reply to the caution.'

'Mr Vaughan, please tell the jury the words of the caution.'

'Yes. The caution is: "You do not have to say anything. But it may harm your defence if you do not mention when questioned something which you later rely on in court. Anything you do say may be given in evidence".'

'Thank you. After the defendants had been arrested, did you have occasion to board the *Tiffany May* yourself?'

'I did, briefly. My officers were making a thorough search and I didn't want to get in their way. But I did have a quick look round.'

'Did you notice anything in particular?'

'Yes, indeed. In the enclosed area of the wheelhouse, there was a very powerful smell of cannabis.'

'When you say powerful…?'

'It was something you couldn't possibly miss if you had any sense of smell at all.'

'Finally, Mr Vaughan – and I see that Officer Jones has kindly brought it into court for us – do you produce one of the five black canvas bags, and does it contain the quantity of cannabis resin present at the time you seized it, wrapped in the same plastic bags?'

'Yes, it does.'

Susan grins up at me. 'Your Honour, so that the jury will understand, I'm not asking for any of the black canvas bags to be made exhibits. There's no question of them being allowed in the jury room.' This provokes a burst of good-natured laughter from the jury box, in which Susan joins. 'But of course, the jury will be able to see them all if they wish. I'm hoping this one will be enough, so that we don't have a large quantity in court.'

'I quite agree,' I smile back.

'In fact, your Honour, if Mr Vaughan may leave the witness box and stand in front of the jury box, I would like the jury to see it now.'

'Certainly.'

Senior Officer Vaughan collects the canvas bag, carries it over to the jury box, and opens it so that the jury can see – and no doubt, smell – the contents clearly.

'Thank you, Mr Vaughan. And now, your Honour, and I appreciate that this may be a bit unusual, but I have my reasons: I would like the jury to have the opportunity to pick the bag up and feel its weight. I will ask Mr Vaughan to zip the bag back up. May the jurors leave the jury box and pick the bag up in turn? Then I would like to invite your Honour, counsel, and the defendants to do the same.'

I look at Kenneth and Emily. For a moment, Kenneth seems poised to object, but I sense that he can't think of any coherent objection to make. Neither can I, and I'm pretty sure I know why Susan wants to lay on this particular demonstration. If I'm right, it's an ingenious move.

'Yes, very well,' I reply. 'One at a time, please, members of the jury.'

We wait patiently as the jurors form a queue and pick the bag up in turn. Several look surprised at how much it weighs, and one or two can hardly move it off the ground. Kenneth and Emily follow suit, not because they want to, but because they can hardly decline the invitation in the circumstances. Neither can I. Officer Jones kindly brings it up to the bench for me and I pick it up. It is certainly heavy – if the cannabis resin was evenly distributed, each of the five bags would have to weigh close to twenty kilos. You wouldn't want to carry it too far.

'Your Honour, if the defendants wish to feel the weight, would your Honour permit them to leave the dock?'

'Yes, of course,' I reply. 'Let's make sure we have the bag in a position where we can all see.'

The Owl agrees with some show of ill grace. He leaves the dock accompanied by the dock officer. Officer Jones has left the bag in front of the jury box. The Owl picks it up rather nonchalantly, as if to suggest that it doesn't weigh very much and he can't understand what all the fuss is about. But the jury and I know better, and we are beginning to understand what all the fuss is about. In the meanwhile, Emily has taken the opportunity to make her way to the dock to confer with the Pussycat.

'Miss Warrender does not wish to feel the bag's weight, your Honour,' she says once the Owl has returned to the dock. 'There is no evidence that she handled any of the bags, and we anticipate that there will be no such evidence. In those circumstances, there would be no point in her handling one now.'

'Thank you, Officer Jones,' Susan says. 'You may remove the bag from court for now. Mr Vaughan, please return to the witness box.' Unhurriedly, the officer makes his way back. 'I only have one or two further questions for you. Did the search of the *Tiffany May* reveal any quantity of either cigarettes or loose tobacco?'

'I recall that Miss Warrender had three packets of cigarettes on her when she was arrested, but other than that, no: we didn't find any cigarettes or tobacco.'

'And the three packets of cigarettes Miss Warrender had: can you say whether they were packets purchased abroad or in this country?'

'There were no foreign customs markings or stickers on the packets. They were packets purchased in the UK. They are outside court. I can produce them if required.'

'I don't need them,' Susan says. 'If my learned friends do, I'm sure they will ask. Wait there, please, Mr Vaughan.'

'Mr Vaughan,' Kenneth begins, 'I think this is clear from the film, but so that there is no doubt, you arrested the defendants immediately after Professor de Crecy had removed the five black canvas bags from the boat, didn't you?'

'Yes.'

'When you seized the bags, were they all zipped shut?'

'Yes, they were.'

'I ask because you opened them to display their contents. But it was you who opened them, or one of your colleagues. My point is that neither of these defendants opened any of the black canvas bags at all: isn't that right?'

'Certainly, they didn't open them at any time when I was watching, and as I say, the bags were all zipped shut when we seized them.'

'Thank you. Finally, is Professor de Crecy a man of previous good character? In other words, can you confirm that he has no previous convictions or cautions?'

'That is correct, sir,' Vaughan replies, with just the slightest hint of resentment. He would like to add, 'for now', if he could.

Kenneth resumes his seat.

'Same question from me,' Emily says, springing to her feet. 'Is Miss Warrender a woman of previous good character: no previous convictions or cautions recorded against her?'

Mr Vaughan concedes that such is the case.

After a few items of formal, agreed evidence to prove the weight of cannabis resin in each of the bags, the total weight, and its likely street value, Susan is ready to close her case. Even though the dull thuds have stopped for now, there is no appetite to go any further today, and I adjourn until tomorrow when we will begin the defence case, whatever it may turn out to be.

When I return to chambers, I find Bob waiting for me.

'I called the Grey Smoothies, Judge, about having the cannon brought up.'

'Oh, yes. Thank you. How was it?'

'Same as usual, Judge – like pulling teeth. First they put me through to Jack, who had no idea what I was talking about. He put me through to Meredith, but she didn't have the authority to agree, so she put me through to Sir Jeremy Bagnall. Sir Jeremy said he had to consult with goodness only knows who, so he put me on hold for a good fifteen minutes. But finally, in the end, after I'd explained several times about having to pay the contractor for not working, he agreed.'

'Excellent,' I reply. 'Did you contact the firm de Crecy recommended?'

'Yes, Judge. They're called Theydon Henderson, and they said they'll be here at eight thirty tomorrow morning, and they say they will have the cannon safely up by lunchtime. They want the area to themselves, so Jake will be on site to represent the contractor, but he's sent everyone else home.'

'Good,' I say. 'Very good.'

Bob is looking hesitant.

'Is there a problem?'

'Not about having the cannon brought up. But judging by what Sir Jeremy was saying, I don't think they're going to let us keep it at the court.'

'What? Why on earth not?'

'Well, Theydon Henderson don't exactly come cheap, Judge, and Sir Jeremy was explaining that he has to get the best possible value for money for the taxpayer...'

'Oh, yes, of course – the taxpayer. And how exactly does he propose to do that?'

'I'm not sure I got it all, Judge, but what I understood him to say was that the cannon is treasure trove, so it belongs to the Queen.'

'The Queen? What, you mean like swans and sturgeon?'

'Yes, Judge. Legally, he says, the Grey Smoothies have a duty to report the find to the coroner, who acts on behalf of the Queen, and to the British Museum, so that it can be disposed of to a museum, as the Queen or her ministers may direct. But then, since it was found on ministry property, the ministry might be entitled to a reward, which would enable them to pay Theydon Henderson, and make a couple of quid profit into the bargain.'

'Typical,' I comment. 'Absolutely bloody typical.'

'Sir Jeremy said to tell you that he'll explain it all to you tomorrow. They're coming at lunchtime to inspect the cannon.'

'This is outrageous,' I protest hopelessly.

Bob nods. 'I agree, Judge. But we can't keep it if it belongs to the Queen, can we?'

I wend my way sadly homewards, and not even the Reverend Mrs Walden's excellent home-made lasagne and a bottle of Sainsbury's Founder's Reserve can console me over the impending loss of the Bermondsey Cannon.

* * *

Tuesday morning

Kenneth announces that he will call the Owl to give evidence. The Owl is a short, thin man, as divers tend to be; and looks, as divers tend to look, older than he is, as if his profession and the water have worn him away to some extent. He is dressed tidily enough in a light blue suit and dark blue tie, but there is something about him, perhaps the length of the hair, tied up at the back, or the incipient beard and moustache, that doesn't quite fit the image of the shrewd businessman.

'Professor de Crecy, how old a man are you?' Kenneth asks.

'I'm forty-two.'

'Let me ask you this, first. We've been calling you "Professor" throughout the trial. My learned friend seemed to suggest in her opening speech that you're not entitled to describe yourself in that way. Can you clarify that for us?'

'I was given the title when I did some teaching for the University of Singapore, years ago,' the Owl explains, 'and I've kept it ever since. My level of expertise, and my teaching and research experience, are the equivalent of any professor in this country, so I'm not embarrassed about it.'

'Quite so,' Kenneth says, wisely moving on from what one hopes is not the strongest part of his client's evidence. 'Now, in addition to your teaching and research, the jury have heard that you have a company called De Crecy Naval Wreckers UK: is that right?'

'Yes. I started the company about twelve years ago. I'm the chief executive officer and the chief operating officer. Lucy – Miss Warrender – is the company secretary. But we both pilot the boat and do some diving.'

'Miss Warrender, we've heard, is also your partner; you live together, is that right?'

'Yes, it is.'

'You're both qualified as pilots and divers, we understand?'

'We are. Well, we have to be. We're the company. There isn't anyone else to do it.'

'Professor de Crecy, tell the jury in a little more detail what the company does.'

'We try to locate wrecks, almost exclusively wrecks of historic warships, off the coast of Great Britain. We're both naval historians by training, so we have some background knowledge of where to look. But it's not an exact science. The older records dealing with the loss of a vessel aren't always very helpful. They tell you where the vessel is said to have gone down, but you can't always take that at face value, and they don't take into account that she may have drifted, either before or after she went down, due to the currents and events on the ocean floor. So it involves a lot of searching. The record may tell you that the ship was lost off Spithead, but with drifting and so on, you may find her off Dungeness. You just never know. If you can afford things like miniature submarines, it makes life easier, but we can't afford that kind of thing. So we have to use our best judgement and try to establish an approximate location, and after that, we dive and try to confirm it. Once we confirm it we have to bring in the big boys to recover it, but we get our share of the recovery.'

'Of course, this is a commercial venture, isn't it? You hope to make some money from what you find?'

'Yes, obviously. But it's not a matter of just going and finding a wreck and looting it. You'd get in serious trouble for that. It's all regulated. You have to get permission to explore and recover a wreck, and you have to account for everything to the Receiver of Wreck. If you know what you're doing, and do it right – and if you have a bit of luck – you can make a decent return on your investment. The problem is that you don't find a wreck every day. Undiscovered wrecks are becoming rarer and rarer.'

Kenneth pauses. 'All right. Let me ask you about the *Tiffany*

May. Does it belong to you, or Miss Warrender, or the company?'

'She… I'm sorry, I know I'm supposed to call the boat "it" these days, but I'm old school and I just can't. A boat is "she" to me, and always will be.'

'I'm sure the jury won't hold it against you,' Kenneth assures him, to a chuckle from the jury box.

'She doesn't belong to us,' the Owl continues. 'She's on lease to the company. She isn't cheap, but she's exactly what we need. As the officers said, diving in the middle of a busy shipping lane, you really have to know what you're doing, and you need a fast boat. You could perform acrobatics in her and take on board tons of water, and the *Tiffany May* will stay upright and get you back to shore. She's ideal for what we do, which is: start, stop, dive; start, stop, dive; sometimes for hours on end, if we're homing in on an exact location.'

'At the time of your voyage on the eighteenth of November, were you interested in any particular exploration?'

'Yes. Lucy and I had been on the trail of a wreck for a few months. The ship was HMS *John of Gaunt*. She was a Royal Navy frigate, fourth class, with fifty-four guns, built by Phineas Pett at Ratcliffe and launched in 1653. She saw action at Porto Farina against the Barbary pirates in 1655, and during Blake's raid on Santa Cruz de Tenerife in 1657, among other engagements; and in 1688, in common with most of the rest of the Navy, she defected to William of Orange. But she went down on – well, using the modern calendar it would be the seventh of December, but according to older records that used the old calendar, on the twenty-sixth of November 1703 – during what was known as the "Great Storm". In modern terms, the Great Storm was a category two hurricane. It destroyed a large number of ships, as well as doing considerable damage all across the country.'

'I take it the wreck hasn't been recovered?'

'No,' the Owl replies. 'It's a perfect example of what I was saying. The official record says she went down off Spithead. But although the captain and most of the crew were lost, the ship's carpenter and three sailors survived, and they came to shore somewhere east of Hastings. So it's very likely that she was blown a long way off course before she sank, and today, she may be even further along the coast than she was then. It's anybody's guess, really.'

'And when you stopped twice during your voyage on the eighteenth of November, were you on the trail of the *John of Gaunt*?'

'Yes. We'd already made a number of dives over the past several weeks, and we were hoping to get a few more in before the weather turned too bad. It was a bit too deep for us where we stopped, but we were trying to work our way in towards the shore, opposite where we thought she might be.'

'But you didn't dive on that day?'

'No.'

'Why was that?'

'I just didn't fancy it. The forecast wasn't too bad, but the sea was pretty choppy, and I didn't like the look of the weather. Also, we were in a lane and there was quite a bit of heavy traffic. It was a combination of things. There are times when you just have to trust your instincts.'

'But you did go on to De Panne in Belgium?'

'Yes. We did.'

'Tell His Honour and the jury what that was about.'

The Owl takes a deep breath.

'I'd met this fellow called Edgar Rice. Of course, with what I know about him now, I wish I'd stayed clear of him. But I met him in the King's Oak at Epping Forest, which is where Lucy and I live. He seemed a pleasant enough fellow. We got talking and had a drink, and he mentioned that he had a retail outlet in Essex somewhere, and he was always interested in acquiring items that might sell well.'

'Did he say where this outlet was, exactly?'

'No. I don't think he did.'

'What kind of goods was he interested in?' Kenneth asks.

The Owl laughs. 'To hear him talk, almost anything,' he replies. 'I'd told him what I was doing, and at one point he was more or less asking me whether I could find him some items from a wreck. Obviously, I knocked that idea on the head. But then, he started asking me about the *Tiffany May*: how much did she cost to lease, how much did she cost to hop over to the Continent and back? And the third or fourth time we met, he came right out and asked me how far ten thousand pounds would go towards meeting my operating expenses.'

'What did you say to that?' Kenneth asks.

'At first I laughed at him. But he said he was serious, so eventually I asked him what I would have to do for ten thousand pounds.'

'What did he say?'

'He said he had a very large consignment of cigarettes and tobacco to bring over from Belgium, but he didn't have any way to do it, except by road, which would be quite hazardous.'

Kenneth pauses for some time.

'All right, Professor, you and I have talked about this, haven't we? I have to ask you what you mean when you say "hazardous", and I must ask you: do you understand that you may be about to admit to having committed a criminal offence?'

'Yes, I do understand that, and I understood at the time. He was suggesting that this was to be a smuggling operation. He didn't want to risk bringing the load in by road. I was to take the *Tiffany May* over to De Panne, where I would be met by two men, who would identify themselves as Jan and Piet. They would hand over the cigarettes and the tobacco in a number of heavy-duty canvas bags.'

'Did you agree to his suggestion?'

'I did. It seemed like easy money. Stupid, I know now. But at the time, things weren't great financially, and I wasn't sure how long we could go on unless we had a good find. This was a way to tide us over for a while until we found the *John of Gaunt*.'

'Did he pay you anything in advance?'

The Owl nods. 'Five hundred in cash, for expenses, fuel and so on.'

'What about the money to pay for the cigarettes and tobacco? Where did that come from?'

'Edgar gave me the money in a thick envelope. I was instructed not to open it, so I have no idea how much it was, but Jan and Piet seemed satisfied on the day – they took the envelope from me, opened it, and counted the money – and then they loaded the bags on to the boat for us. It only took a few minutes. Then Lucy and I found a café to have lunch, and then we turned round and came back. And that was it.'

'And why the choice of Folkestone harbour?'

'It's a fairly quiet harbour, but there's always something going on, so a boat like the *Tiffany May* probably wouldn't attract too much attention. It also meant that the goods would come into the country without going through customs, but if we did get caught, we could always claim that we assumed there would be customs officers at the harbour, and we were about to go in search of one.'

'Professor de Crecy, did you or Miss Warrender open any of the canvas bags at any time after Jan and Piet loaded them on to the *Tiffany May*?'

'No, we did not.'

'What did you think you were carrying back to Folkestone harbour?'

'A large consignment of cigarettes and tobacco.'

'Did you have any idea that you were carrying a large consignment of cannabis resin?'

'I had no idea at all, and I would never have done that.'

'Not even for ten thousand pounds?'

'Not for any sum of money.'

'According to the arrangement you had made with Mr Rice, what was supposed to happen when you arrived back at Folkestone?'

'Mr Rice was supposed to meet us, take possession of the load, and pay us the rest of our money.'

'But, for obvious reasons, he wasn't there?'

'No, he wasn't there.'

'You were arrested and cautioned, and is it correct, as the officers have told us, that you made no reply in response to the caution?'

'Yes, that is correct.'

'And similarly, when you were interviewed, you declined to answer any questions put to you by the officers. Please tell the jury why you wouldn't answer their questions.'

'My solicitor advised me not to answer questions. I'd never been arrested before; I didn't know what to do; so I followed her advice.'

'Professor de Crecy, when you made this arrangement with Mr Rice, was Miss Warrender present?'

'No, she wasn't, unfortunately.'

'Why do you say "unfortunately"?'

'Because she would never have let me do it. She would have dragged me off home before I had any chance to agree to the deal. She would have told me to forget about Edgar Rice and the ten thousand pounds, and I would have listened to her.'

'Did you tell Miss Warrender about the arrangement you'd made with Mr Rice?'

'Not until that morning, when we were driving down to Folkestone.'

'What did she say when you told her?'

'Your Honour,' Susan intervenes, jumping to her feet, 'that sounds like hearsay. If Miss Warrender decides to give evidence, she can tell us about what she said, but I'm not sure Professor de Crecy can.'

'It goes to her state of mind,' Kenneth says. 'But let me try it another way. Professor, as a result of what she said, what impression did you have of her reaction to what you had told her?'

'She was absolutely furious. She wanted to turn around and go home there and then. But I told her I didn't fancy letting Edgar down – not when he was involved in a deal where he could afford to pay us ten grand just for the transport. I mean, it was a huge deal, and if it went bad, it would have been our fault. So she didn't speak to me for the rest of the way, but we did carry on.'

He looks fondly towards the Pussycat in the dock. 'Lucy would never have agreed to carry cannabis resin, never in a million years. She knew nothing until that morning. If she'd known beforehand, she wouldn't even have agreed to smuggle tobacco. She would have whacked me in the head just for suggesting it.'

How sweet: he's doing his best to row her out; and they say chivalry is dead.

'Finally, Professor, when was the first time you realised you had transported a load of cannabis resin, and not a load of cigarettes and tobacco?'

'When Officer Vaughan unzipped the first bag and showed us what was in it.'

'Wait there, please, Professor, and answer any further questions.'

Emily stands briefly and says she has no questions for the Owl. That's a wise decision, and one a less experienced advocate might not have had the nerve to make. It must have been hugely tempting to offer the Owl the chance to say more nice things about the Pussycat, and go back over how little she knew and how furious she was when she knew it. But it's unnecessary: she couldn't really improve on what he's said already, and like all unnecessary evidence, repetition can be dangerous. She doesn't want to take the risk that he might say something stupid and leave Susan an easy target in cross examination.

'Your Honour,' Susan begins after a whispered conversation with Officer Vaughan, 'I may be able to assist Professor de Crecy to this extent: the prosecution accepts that two men met the *Tiffany May* on the beach at De Panne, and that they loaded the five black canvas bags on to the boat and accepted the money from Professor de Crecy. They were Dutch, not Belgian, and I'm sure it won't surprise anyone to learn that Jan and Piet are not their real names. But we do accept that those men were there and played their part in the transaction, and I can also tell the court that they were arrested later that afternoon by Belgian police.'

'I'm much obliged to my learned friend,' Kenneth says. I suspect it's going to be some time, if ever in this case, before he can say that again.

'Why didn't you tell the police that this was just a case of cigarette smuggling?' Susan begins.

'My solicitor advised me to say nothing.'

'Assuming that to be true, you were cautioned by the officers at least twice, weren't you?'

'I was cautioned, yes.'

'So you knew that it might harm your defence – *your* defence, Professor, not your solicitor's – if you failed to mention when questioned something you rely on in court. So, why didn't you just tell them: "Look, there's been a misunderstanding: Jan and Piet were supposed to give us cigarettes and tobacco, not cannabis resin. They're the ones you should be arresting"? Wouldn't that have been the sensible thing to do?'

'With the benefit of hindsight…'

'You were caught red-handed, importing a large, commercial quantity of cannabis resin into this country weren't you, Professor?'

'Yes, but…'

'You couldn't think of anything to say that would make any sense, so very sensibly, you bought yourself some time. You refused to answer questions to buy yourself time to invent a story you thought had some chance of pulling the wool over a jury's eyes. That's what happened, isn't it?'

'No. I…'

'And this desperate story of smuggling cigarettes and tobacco is the best you could come up with, even with all the time you bought?'

'No. It's not a story. It's true.'

'Did you think that the tobacco was coming from one of the many cut-price tobacco outlets on the stretch of the Belgian coast around De Panne?'

'I don't know.'

'Well, your learned counsel Mr Warnock, in his cross-examination of Officer Callaghan on your behalf, established that there are many such outlets in that area. Do you remember that? Is that because you assumed that's where the tobacco came from?'

'Well, yes, I suppose I must have.'

'Yes. There's nothing unreasonable about that, is there? But in that case, given that you were being paid ten thousand pounds, why didn't Mr Rice just ask you to collect the load from the outlet yourself, rather than pay two more men to meet you with it on the beach?'

'I have no idea what Mr Rice was thinking. Perhaps he didn't trust me with so much money.'

'How much money didn't he trust you with, Professor?'

'Well, I don't know. But obviously, a lot.'

'Obviously, a lot. Did you ever ask yourself how much money must have been involved in this deal, if he could afford to pay you ten thousand pounds just for the transportation?'

'I didn't think about it.'

'Did you not, Professor? All right. Professor, you told the jury that the first time you realised what was in the black canvas bags was after you'd been arrested, when Officer Vaughan opened the bags and showed you: is that right?'

'Yes.'

'You'd been in the boat with almost one hundred kilos of cannabis resin for over three hours, hadn't you, by the time you arrived back in Folkestone harbour?'

'Yes'.

'With the cannabis resin stashed away in the small space in the wheelhouse, where you and Miss Warrender would have spent the entire voyage, or almost the entire voyage: yes?'

'Yes.'

'And do you remember what the officers who inspected the boat said? They told the jury that the smell of cannabis was powerful, almost overpowering – even after all the bags had been removed. You're not going to tell the jury you didn't notice it, are you, at any time during that three-hour voyage?'

No reply.

'The jury are waiting, Professor.'

He nods. 'I did notice at some point, yes.'

Susan also nods. 'Thank you. So, can we take it then, that at some point in the voyage, you knew that Mr Rice hadn't told you the truth; you knew he'd set you up with the importation of a large quantity of cannabis resin, a controlled drug?'

'Yes. I think it was after we'd stopped to look at the possibility of a dive. I'd been outside the wheelhouse for some time, looking at the weather and the traffic, and I came back inside. I thought before then that there was a bit of an odd smell, but when I came back inside it really hit me.'

'Did you say anything to Miss Warrender about it?'

'I didn't have to, did I? She was giving me that look of hers.'

'So, why didn't you do something about it?'

'Like what?'

'Like dropping it overboard with a marker so that customs officers could recover it later?'

'What, and go back to Folkestone and tell Edgar Rice I'd thrown his drugs over the side, but could I please have my ten grand anyway? You must be joking.'

'All right, then: why not divert to another port and deliver it to customs officers there? If you did that, Mr Rice would be arrested, and you would be safe, wouldn't you?'

No reply.

'Now, if Officer Jones is outside court?' She turns to Officer Vaughan, who leaves court and returns a few seconds later carrying a black canvas bag, accompanied by Officer Jones, carrying a second black canvas bag.

'Your Honour, with the court's leave, Officer Jones has with him the black canvas bag containing cannabis resin that the jury and your Honour, counsel and Professor de Crecy, picked up yesterday in order to feel its weight. Officer Vaughan has a second black canvas bag, the contents of which I will disclose in due course. But I would now like to ask the jury, your Honour, and Professor de Crecy, to pick up the two bags, one at a time, to compare their weights.'

The bags are placed side by side in front of the jury box, and the jurors test them one by one. No one says anything, but there is a very obvious and universal reaction, one of surprise, on picking up the second bag. Counsel are too experienced to give anything away, but I know what I'm going to find before Officer Jones brings them up to the bench for me. Compared to the first bag, the second weighs very little. The difference is dramatic. Lastly, the Owl makes his way rather slowly over to the jury box and makes the comparison himself.

Susan then asks Officer Jones to open the second bag and show us all what's in it. It contains cartons of cigarettes and packets of loose tobacco.

'Officer Vaughan kindly borrowed some contraband from the HMRC warehouse,' she explains. 'I think I'm right in saying that, in place of the original cannabis resin, this bag now contains cartons totalling two thousand cigarettes and fifty packets of loose tobacco. Did you notice any difference in weight, as between the two bags, Professor?' she asks.

'The second bag is a lot lighter,' the witness concedes.

'Yes, it is, isn't it? Professor, why didn't you tell the jury that you knew you were carrying cannabis resin, at least for the last hour or so of your voyage, when you were being examined by your own counsel? Why did I have drag it out of you in cross-examination?'

'Your Honour…' Kenneth protests.

'I'll move on. You told the jury that your title of Professor was conferred on you by the University of Singapore. I have here a printout of a list of the faculty, including visiting faculty, of that university, and I can't find your name mentioned at all. Would you like to see it?'

'No,' the Owl replies. 'I'll take your word for it. I was only out there once, for about two weeks, but that's what the students called me then. I suppose it's a kind of honorific title.'

'I suppose it must be,' Susan says, resuming her seat.

Emily indicates that she would like further time to confer with the Pussycat, and asks me to adjourn until two o'clock. As it happens, I'd been planning that in any case. Legless has sent a message asking me to sentence a prolific fencer of stolen goods. He's at a critical stage of his trial, and doesn't want to interrupt it. The sentence occupies me until just before one o'clock.

And so to lunch, though today, not likely to be an oasis of calm in a desert of chaos.

When Bob and I arrive, suitably attired, on site, Jake introduces us to a Mr Henderson, who is supervising the extraction, as the term apparently is, on behalf of Theydon Henderson. Also present are the Grey Smoothies, in the persons of Sir Jeremy Bagnall and our cluster manager, Meredith, who have somehow managed to find hard hats and high-visibility jackets. I find myself wondering where they got them. Do they keep them hanging up in the office in case someone unearths a cannon on court premises? Mr Henderson proudly escorts us to the rear of the trench, where, resting on what appears to be a large and very thick mattress, is the Bermondsey Cannon. Two of Mr Henderson's men are gently removing debris using small, soft brushes. They have some way to go, but already it looks very impressive. It also looks fully intact.

'It's magnificent, Charles,' Jeremy says, 'don't you agree?'

'I certainly do,' I reply.

'What are you going to do with it next?' he asks Henderson.

'Well, sir, with your permission we'd like to take it to our premises. We can keep it there until you decide where it's going to end up. It will be perfectly safe and well looked after, I can assure you. This is what we do. We've already cleaned it up a bit, as you can see, but there's a lot more we can do. But for that, we need to have her indoors and under the lights at our place. By the time it goes on display, it will look incredible, I can promise you. We may even be able to bring out some of the shine or gloss of the original metal. It's in remarkably good condition. Goodness knows how it got here without sustaining any damage, but it's absolutely pristine.'

'Sounds like a plan to me,' Jeremy says.

After congratulating all concerned on the successful extraction, Bob and I retire to my chambers with Jeremy and Meredith. Stella has arranged for sandwiches, crisps, and soft drinks. There is an awkward silence for some time. Eventually, I decide I might as well jump in with both feet.

'I was rather hoping,' I begin, 'that we might be allowed to keep the cannon here. We would place it in the foyer in a suitable case. It would add a real lustre to the court, as well as in a sense celebrating the history of Bermondsey as a community close to the River, and celebrating its long maritime tradition.'

Bob gives me a look, but he needn't have bothered. I don't sound convincing even to myself. Usually, when I'm negotiating with the Grey Smoothies, it's purely on behalf of the court. It doesn't mean I don't care about the outcome; I care very much. But in this case, for some reason I still can't explain to myself, I have an unaccountable personal interest. I'm too close to it.

'I do understand that, Charles,' Jeremy assures me with his best civil service purr. 'But unfortunately, our hands our tied.'

'Oh?'

'Yes. As I was explaining to Bob yesterday, an archaeological find like this is treasure trove. It belongs to the Crown, and the Crown has to decide what to do with it.'

'But surely the Crown would delegate that decision to your minister?' I ask.

'Yes, probably so,' he agrees. 'But there's a procedure we have to go through. First, we have to notify the coroner within fourteen days of the find. It's an offence not to report it. The coroner decides whether there are any possible claimants other than the Crown – which there aren't in this case. The coroner also has to notify the British Museum, so that they can decide what recommendation to make to the minister.'

He exchanges a look with Meredith.

'But what we're hoping for, in this case, is that the minister will argue that we should be entitled to a reward for finding the cannon. There's a power to pay a reward up to the market value of the artefact, which in this case will be quite substantial. You see, Charles, we're incurring quite a bit of expense. Theydon Henderson will charge us several thousand pounds for what they're doing. We've lost two days of work here, for which we will have to pay the contractor. So we have a duty to the taxpayer to recoup as much as we can.'

He smiles.

'Don't look so glum, Charles. Bermondsey might well benefit from the find, as it should. There will probably be some money left over after we've paid the bills, and we might just give the place a new coat of paint. It looks in need of one, doesn't it? I don't see why we couldn't manage that. Don't you think, Meredith?'

'Absolutely,' Meredith agrees.

'Forgive me for pointing this out, Sir Jeremy,' Bob says after a few seconds of pregnant silence. 'But the ministry isn't actually the finder in this case.'

'What?' Jeremy asks, sounding surprised. 'Well, who is, for goodness sake?'

'Jake.'

'Jake? Who on earth is Jake?' he asks, getting a bit exasperated now, one feels.

'The site foreman,' Meredith reminds him. 'We met him outside.'

Jeremy's jaw drops. You can sense the promise of the reward fading away in his mind.

'But the find was made on ministry premises...' he manages eventually.

'But if Jake found it,' Bob adds, 'he was working for the contractor at the time, so it may be their find, technically.'

This doesn't appear to comfort Jeremy very much.

'I'm just saying,' Bob replies. 'It would be up to the coroner to decide, I suppose.'

'Well,' I say, 'I still see no reason why we can't keep the cannon at Bermondsey. If the ministry gets a reward, so much the better. But it's a very logical place for it, and we could make the argument to the British Museum. As I understand it, naval cannons are ten a penny anyway, and the museums may not need another one.'

Again, not the best of arguments, but I'm not sure Jeremy is even listening.

'I'll have to get on to the Government Legal Department,' he says fussily to Meredith. 'We may need some legal advice. We may even need to take counsel's opinion.'

'Absolutely,' she says again.

'We'll come back tomorrow, after court,' he promises.

'Be sure to tell the Government Legal Department about our proposal, won't you, Jeremy?' I say as they are leaving. 'I'd be interested to know whether there's really any legal impediment to it.'

* * *

Tuesday afternoon

The Pussycat gives evidence, a touch reluctantly, it seems to me, and very tearfully; even though Emily has undoubtedly explained to her, in no uncertain terms, that continuing to remain silent is not a viable option when you're caught with 98.4 kilos of cannabis resin stashed away in a boat you've just piloted, cigarette dangling nonchalantly from lips, into Folkestone harbour.

She dutifully follows the party line. She knew nothing about the proposal to import cigarettes and tobacco for Edgar Rice in return for ten thousand pounds until the Owl dropped it on her while they were driving to Folkestone on the fateful morning. At first, she screamed and shouted and demanded to be taken straight home, but once the Owl had enlightened her as to the possible consequences of letting a major drug dealer like Edgar Rice down, she reluctantly agreed that there was no real choice but to go ahead. She was a bit surprised by the arrival of Jan and Piet on De Panne beach. She was even more surprised, she reveals – having learned from the Owl's fiasco the wisdom of volunteering this not insignificant detail, rather than waiting for it to be dragged out in cross-examination – when, as they stopped at their possible dive site on the return journey, she detected the distinctive smell of cannabis. She was standing right over the bags in the wheelhouse while she was piloting the boat, so it was in her face, she explains, both figuratively and literally. She recognised the smell from being around people smoking cannabis at student parties when she was younger, though of course, she has never indulged herself.

By the time she realised what she was dealing with, she didn't see any way out except to complete the voyage. She acknowledges that she intended to smuggle cigarettes and tobacco into the country, although only because she was afraid of what Edgar Rice might do if they failed to deliver. But she is horrified by the suggestion that she would knowingly play any part in importing controlled drugs, and assures the jury that she would never have begun the return voyage with the canvas bags on board if she had known what was in them. She would have dumped the bags on the beach, she replies at first when Emily asks her what she would have done instead; though with some encouragement, she clarifies that what she meant was, she would have handed them over to the Belgian police.

She makes a token effort to return the Owl's chivalry, and insists that he would never have agreed to import cannabis resin any more than she would. It doesn't sound terribly convincing. I get the impression that she hasn't forgiven the Owl for, as she sees it, landing her in her present predicament, and I have the feeling that in the long run the Owl may find himself searching for HMS *John of Gaunt* without further assistance from her.

The Pussycat has assembled no less than thirty-five letters from friends and associates attesting to her hitherto excellent character. That's quite a good total. You rarely see more than three or four, and they're mostly from parents and other relatives who don't really have much choice when approached to write a good character letter. Emily provides the jury with copies of them all, and reads the best four aloud, leaving the jury to read the rest whenever they get the chance.

Emily then calls the Pussycat's vicar as a live character witness. Fortunately, I don't know him. I meet quite a lot of vicars through my good lady wife, and I would prefer to avoid the embarrassment of having one turn up as a witness in my court if I've partaken of a glass or two of sherry with them at some church reception the week before. Besides, with all due deference to the Reverend Mrs Walden, it's been my experience that for a defendant to call his or her vicar as a character witness is dicing with death. Quite often, it turns out that the vicar's knowledge of the defendant is pretty tenuous, and that the defendant's only connection with the parish is living in it; and so, when the vicar goes overboard about what a good person the defendant is, and how it must have been a transitory error of judgment that drove him or her to commit the offence, one totally out of character, it can all sound a bit hollow. Not so in this case. The Pussycat has apparently attended church, not exactly regularly, but fairly often, and has helped out with cleaning and supplying flowers for the church from time to time. The vicar has got to know her, and regards her as basically honest and trustworthy. Well, I reflect, at least she hasn't been using the title of professor, which is an improvement on her co-defendant.

We agree that we have time for the prosecution's closing speech, but that it would be best to defer the defence speeches until tomorrow morning. Susan is excellent: short and to the point. She pours scorn on the idea that the Owl could possibly have thought he was being paid ten thousand pounds to smuggle cigarettes and tobacco. It must have been obvious from the outset that he was being asked to deal in controlled drugs, and even if he didn't know that the drug concerned was cannabis resin, in law, if he intended to import a controlled drug, the result is the same. But it must have been obvious, she insists, from the weight of the bags and the smell they gave off – we only had one bag containing cannabis resin for a few minutes, she reminds the jury, and already there was something of a smell in court. She's right, there was: even up here on the bench it was noticeable; the jury had the bag right in front of them. The Owl may well have been afraid of Edgar Rice, she acknowledges, and with good reason. But he had a clear alternative open to him. He could have opted out by diverting to another port and surrendering the drugs to the authorities. He had no way of knowing that Rice had already been arrested, but that makes no difference; Rice would have been arrested in short order once the Owl had grassed him up.

Even if he didn't take that way out, Susan adds, why didn't he tell the officers what was going on when he was arrested? By that stage it was clear that he was in a hopeless situation, and prevaricating could only make it worse. His refusal to answer questions had nothing to do with his solicitor, she tells the jury. He didn't even have a solicitor when he was arrested; he could have told his side of the story then. No, she concludes, the reason he refused to answer the officers' questions is that he had no answer to give; certainly no answer that made any sense. He needed time to think up some desperate story to tell, and the jury has heard that desperate story today. The defendant himself admitted that he was in financial difficulties, and he fell into temptation when offered a quick fix by a drug dealer.

Susan is much more low-key when she comes to the Pussycat. She acknowledges the weight of the character evidence; and the evidence that the Pussycat didn't know anything was amiss until the morning of the eighteenth of November; and even then, that she didn't know what she was dealing with until the smell started to permeate the *Tiffany May*'s wheelhouse. Susan bases the prosecution's case squarely on the proposition that the Owl must have confided fully in his partner from the start. How could it have been otherwise? He needed her to pilot the boat. How could he suddenly confront her with five canvas bags on a beach in Belgium and ask her to pilot the boat back to Folkestone? She knew all along, Susan suggests. Besides, she adds, just look at her in the film. There's no hint of fear, or nervousness, is there? She's taking control of the *Tiffany May* with a jaunty, confident air, cigarette in mouth, preparing the vessel for departure, and then taking the helm for both legs of the voyage. The Owl's financial problems were the Pussycat's too, she reminds the jury. There is no immediate prospect, if any prospect at all, of finding the *John of Gaunt*. They were in trouble. Ten thousand pounds would have been a lifesaver, and she jumped at it just as quickly as her partner.

There are some problems of law worrying me, in relation to knowledge and intention, and I'm going to have to give the jury some very clear directions about what's required in those areas before there can be a conviction for importing controlled drugs. It's a discussion we will have to have on the record in open court tomorrow, but it will save time if I can make some progress with it this afternoon. As it's been a long day for all of us, I invite counsel into chambers for tea, and we spend a happy thirty to forty minutes with *Archbold*, sorting it all out, and it's all quite helpful. Then, just as they are about to leave, the subject changes.

'How are things going with the cannon, Judge?' Kenneth asks. 'It's the talk of the court today, and I felt I had to let counsel in on the secret of the modest role my client played in it all.'

'Yes, what an amazing thing,' Emily says.

'Well, they've brought it up unscathed,' I reply. 'It's in very good condition, apparently, and the people who extracted it are going to clean it up and look after it until someone decides what to do with it.'

'I heard a rumour that you want to keep it here at the court, Judge,' Emily says. 'I think that's a great idea. It would really give the foyer a boost, wouldn't it?'

'It certainly would,' Susan adds. 'God only knows, this building could do with brightening up.'

'Yes, well, that was my idea,' I say. 'But sadly, it seems the Grey… I mean, the civil servants may have put paid to it.'

'Oh, no,' Emily exclaims. 'How? Why?'

So, I find myself rehashing the Grey Smoothie doctrine of treasure trove; and the suggestion that the cannon belongs to the Queen; and the role of the coroner and the British Museum; and how the whole point of it all seems to be getting their hands on as much money as they can by way of reward, without any concern about the cannon or Bermondsey Crown Court.

'That's terrible,' Susan says quietly.

But Kenneth has been sitting, listening closely, with his usual strange smile, and without warning he suddenly breaks into a fit of loud, slightly manic laughter.

'I'm glad you find it amusing, Kenneth,' I say.

'No, no, Judge,' he replies, doing his best to compose himself. 'It's not your idea I'm laughing at. It's the civil servants. Did they really give you that line about treasure trove and the coroner and all the rest of it?'

'Well, yes, they did,' I admit.

'Unbelievable,' he says.

'Don't tell us you know all about treasure trove, Kenneth,' Susan grins. 'I know you're an expert in some fairly arcane areas of law, but…'

'I can attest to that,' I say, to general merriment.

'Actually, I do happen to know a bit about it, Judge,' Kenneth insists. 'Not because of a case: I have a twelve-year-old son who's fascinated by metal-detecting. We bought him a detector last Christmas, and he's been at it ever since. He didn't find much until one Saturday this summer, when he suddenly turned up a collection of Victorian farthings. He hoped they might be Roman or Saxon coins, which are the holy grail for detectors. No such luck, but it turned out they were worth a bit. So I did look into the law, just to see if he was entitled to the find.'

'And what did you discover?' I ask.

'More than enough to see off your civil servants, Judge,' he grins. 'I'd be happy to act *pro bono* if you would like to appoint me as honorary counsel for Bermondsey Crown Court.'

'I can't ask you to do that *pro bono*,' I protest.

'Yes, you can, Judge,' he replies. 'I've always had a soft spot for Bermondsey. Besides, their argument doesn't hold any water at all.'

'Pray tell,' I say.

'Well,' he begins, 'in the first place, we don't use the term "treasure trove" any more. That was the common law term, but the common law was superseded by the Treasure Act 1996. It's now simply called "treasure", and...'

Kenneth continues in this vein for about ten minutes, during which time he holds us all spellbound – particularly me, because by the time he's finished, I have to agree with him. Wherever Sir Jeremy or Meredith came up with the Grey Smoothie treasure trove doctrine, their source is apparently more than twenty years out of date. If they've taken advice from the Government Legal Department this afternoon, they will already know this; if they haven't, they're in for quite a surprise tomorrow. Either way, the proposal to keep the Bermondsey Cannon here at court is not quite as dead as I'd feared. There is one further, non-legal area of uncertainty, and I will ask Bob to look into it as soon as counsel have gone. But I feel considerably cheered. We're still in with a chance.

'The civil servants are coming back tomorrow, after court,' I say.

'I'll be here, Judge,' Kenneth assures me.

* * *

Wednesday morning

Unsurprisingly, Kenneth's closing speech takes as its text the old French adage, *Les absents ont toujours tort*. It's all going to be Edgar Rice's fault – which, in fairness, much of it is. It was the siren Edgar Rice who lured this innocent, unsuspecting naval historian of previous good character on to the perilous rocks of the drug trade. The Owl intended no more than a flirtation with tobacco smuggling, to keep himself and his company afloat until the much-drifted *John of Gaunt* revealed itself, or herself, as he would say. By the time he realised the truth, it was too late. It's all very well for the prosecution, with the benefit of hindsight, to suggest strategies like diverting to another port to surrender the black canvas bags to the nearest customs officer. But if you're halfway across the English Channel in an RHIB, and you've never been in trouble before, and you're starting to panic because you suddenly realise that you're on the hook for importing a commercial quantity of cannabis resin, it would take an unusual degree of composure to come up with something like that. You're more likely to contemplate leaving the boat in the nearest harbour and making a run for it.

Kenneth does it very well, as one would expect, but there are three things that just won't go away: his client's reluctance to admit that he knew what he was dealing with before he arrived back in Folkestone harbour; the weight of the bags; and the princely sum of ten thousand pounds. He struggles valiantly, reminding the jury that there is no evidence that the Owl handled the bags until he unloaded them after docking in Folkestone harbour, and that a man of previous good character would have no reason to know that ten thousand pounds might be a bit on the high side for a routine smuggling expedition for cigarettes and tobacco from Belgium. But the sinking feeling remains.

Emily is, as always, commendably brief and to the point. There is no evidence that the Pussycat knew about the smuggling proposal before she and the Owl were well on the way to Folkestone. At that point, it was not unreasonable for her to assume that she had no real alternative but to go ahead. The jury should disregard Susan's mocking comments about her cigarettes and jaunty manner, as depicted on film, which have nothing to do with the case and offer the jury no assistance when it comes to the serious business of deciding where the truth lies. There is no evidence that she ever handled the black canvas bags, and, therefore, the prosecution's laboured theatrical production, having everyone except the clerk and the usher compare the weight of two canvas bags, is meaningless and irrelevant in her case. Finally, Emily dwells at some length on the burden and standard of proof, reminding the jury that they may convict only if they are sure of her guilt, and that even if they conclude that the Owl is guilty, that doesn't mean that the Pussycat must be guilty. They must consider her case separately.

Then it's my turn. It's a tricky summing-up. In law, it's not entirely clear that these defendants can escape liability for importing controlled drugs, even if they didn't realise what they were carrying in the *Tiffany May* until they were halfway across the Channel. But it's a legal question that can be fudged, and most judges encourage the jury to give defendants the benefit of the doubt if there's a realistic basis for thinking that they were deceived into importing the contents of a closed bag. I send the jury out just before lunch, and arrange for them to have access to the prosecution's film and digital tracking of the boat, and the photographs.

* * *

Wednesday afternoon

They return to court just after three thirty. It's not a long retirement for a case of this kind, and it seems likely that they have made their minds up at a relatively early stage of the trial. That happens sometimes, and not always in the cases in which you would expect it. The foreman is a young man wearing a dark blue jacket and an open-necked shirt.

'Members of the jury,' Carol begins, having asked the defendants and the foreman to stand, 'please answer my first question just yes or no. Has the jury reached a verdict on which you are all agreed with respect to both defendants?'

'Yes,' the foreman replies.

'On the sole count of this indictment, charging the defendants with being concerned in the unlawful importation of cannabis resin, a controlled drug of class B, do you find the defendant Jules de Crecy guilty or not guilty?'

'We find the defendant guilty.'

'You find the defendant Jules de Crecy guilty, and is that the verdict of you all?'

'Yes, it is.'

'Do you find the defendant Lucy Warrender guilty or not guilty?'

'We find Miss Warrender not guilty.'

'You find the defendant Lucy Warrender not guilty, and is that the verdict of you all?'

'Yes.'

I can't say I'm surprised. It's probably a sympathy verdict. I'm sure the jury were reluctant to blame her for the Owl's stupidity, and I can't find it in me to criticise them for it. I thank the jury for their service and order that the Pussycat may be discharged. Before she leaves the dock, the Owl and the Pussycat engage in a tearful embrace, but I doubt that the Ghost of Christmas Present will find them together again any time soon. The Pussycat knows she's had a close call and she may decide that she's learned her lesson. In any case, the Owl's not going to be around for a while. Although Edgar Rice is eligible for the lion's share of the sentences I'm going to pass in a month or so, when I have the pre-sentence reports, I will be surprised if I can justify to myself giving the Owl less than five or six years. I try my best not to impose immediate prison sentences for cannabis offences. It's legal in so many places now that it just doesn't feel right. In terms of inspiring criminal conduct, cannabis is considerably less dangerous than alcohol, and treating possession as a criminal issue is starting to have a very archaic feel about it. In most cases, I'm glad to say, I can avoid immediate incarceration; but not for importation – especially importation of such a large quantity with such a significant street value. In this case, my hands are tied, and if I don't give him five or six years, the Court of Appeal will. I remand the Owl in custody for sentence on the same occasion as Edgar Rice.

Stella has provided us with tea and biscuits. Sir Jeremy and Meredith arrive just after four o'clock, unaccompanied by anyone from the office of the Government Legal Department. I have Stella, Bob, and Kenneth Warnock, honorary *pro bono* counsel to the Bermondsey Crown Court.

'Jeremy,' I begin, once we're all comfortably settled, 'I've been thinking a good deal about what you said yesterday, and as luck would have it, I've had Kenneth in front of me, and it so happens that he's something of an expert on the law of treasure. It was his client Professor de Crecy, incidentally, who first identified the cannon.'

'Is the Professor going to join us as well?' Jeremy asks, rather defensively.

'No, I'm afraid he's rather tied up at the moment,' I reply. 'But I thought it might be useful to hear what Kenneth has to say, because… well, frankly, he's given us a rather different interpretation of the law, and I'd like to get your reaction to it.'

Jeremy raises his hands, as if to invite Kenneth to speak. He doesn't need a second invitation.

'Thank you, Judge. Well, to start at the beginning, we no longer use the term "treasure trove". That's the term used in the old days of the common law. The common law was superseded by the Treasure Act 1996, which came into effect on the twenty-fourth of September 1997. Essentially, in order to qualify as "treasure" under the Act, an artefact must usually be at least three hundred years old, and a significant proportion of its content must consist of precious metals – gold or silver. It was much the same at common law, as a matter of fact. Treasure has always referred mostly to things like coins, jewellery, and other items like goblets and plates made of precious metals.'

'Are you saying that the cannon isn't treasure?' Meredith asks, aghast.

'Not under the Act, and for that matter, not at common law,' Kenneth replies. I see that his disconcerting smile is in place, and it appears to be having an effect. 'This means that it doesn't belong to the Crown, and there's no obligation to inform the coroner or the British Museum. In fact, there's no reason why the finder of the cannon shouldn't decide what should be done with it.'

'But it was found on ministry premises,' Jeremy protests.

'True, Sir Jeremy,' Kenneth replies, 'and as I read the Act, you could challenge the finder in court, but it's unlikely that you would get very far. The law seems to favour the principle that the finder can keep and dispose of the artefact.'

'There's no duty to report the find at all?'

'There is what's called the Voluntary Portable Antiquities Scheme. A finder of an artefact that isn't treasure can report the find to the Finds Liaison Officer; and it can be worth doing because they can give you all kinds of good advice about what an artefact is worth and what you might consider doing with it. But it's a purely voluntary scheme, and as a matter of fact, the cannon probably doesn't even qualify because it's not more than three hundred years old – unless you can find someone to disagree with Professor de Crecy's evaluation of it.'

Jeremy and Meredith exchange looks.

'And we think the finder is the contractor, do we?' Jeremy asks eventually. 'It was found by their foreman… what was his name?'

'Jake,' Meredith reminds him.

'Jake. So we have to deal with the contractor about this?'

'Well, actually, Sir Jeremy,' Bob breaks in tentatively, 'it may not be quite as simple as we thought.'

It's the turn of Bob and myself to exchange looks now. No one else in the room suspects it, but this is a critical moment. I know that Bob and Jake had a conversation late yesterday afternoon at my suggestion, but I don't know exactly what the outcome was. Bob nods briefly to reassure me.

'In fact,' Bob continues, 'it may be a good idea to hear from Jake himself. I asked him to wait outside. May I bring him in?'

Jeremy nods his assent. Bob leaves the room, returning a moment or two later with Jake, wearing his yellow high-visibility jacket and gripping his hard hat nervously in both hands.

'Now, don't be worried, Jake,' he says. 'Just tell these ladies and gentlemen what you told me yesterday afternoon about finding the cannon.'

'Yes, sir,' Jake replies, maintaining what looks like a death grip on the hat. He's not sure who he should be speaking to, so he focuses on Jeremy. 'Well, after I found the cannon, I called two or three members of my crew to look at it, and then we called the office to report it, because we had to shut the job down.' He stops abruptly.

'It's all right, Jake,' Bob half whispers encouragingly. 'Go on.'

'Yes, sir. Well, I know the company has a rule that anything you find while you're working on a job belongs to the company, not to you, so I reminded the office of that in case they wanted to send someone down to the site to inspect it. But they were asking me all kinds of questions, what it was and when exactly I'd found it, and so on, and I told them the truth – that I'd found it during my break. The lads on the crew would back me up on that. We were all on break and drinking our coffee at the time, weren't we? So, Bill in the office laughs, and says, "Blimey, Jake, it's your lucky day, mate, innit?" I have no idea what he's talking about, do I? So I ask him, and he explains to me that if you find something on your own time, it's yours. It only belongs to the company if you find it when you're working. Well, I had witnesses to back me up, didn't I? So they couldn't really argue about it, and now they've told me officially that it's mine to keep.'

Kenneth is staring at me. He's not privy to all the discussions that have taken place, so understandably, he's treading warily.

'In that case, Judge,' he says, 'on the face of it, it's up to Jake to decide what should be done with the cannon.'

'Unless we contest the find based on the fact that it was found on our premises,' Jeremy points out.

'Well, as I said before, Sir Jeremy,' Kenneth replies, 'the ministry is entitled to go to court and contest it. But of course, if you were to be unsuccessful, as I think you would be, you would end up paying Jake's legal costs – or, I suppose, to be strictly accurate, the taxpayer would end up paying Jake's costs, which could be substantial in a case like this. You may want to talk to the Government Legal Department about it, although I'm pretty sure they would give you the same advice.'

Silence reigns for some time. Jeremy and Meredith are looking a bit shell-shocked. Jake is standing, motionless, hat in both hands, looking around from face to face for guidance about what, if anything, he should do next.

'Jake,' Bob says, after a very brief glance in my direction, 'I know this must all seem rather new and strange to you, but have you given any thought to what you might want to do with the cannon?'

Jake appears to consider the question seriously for some time.

'Well, the wife wouldn't have it in the house,' he replies. 'Not that we'd have room for it, anyway. I mean, we're in a flat on the fifth floor, aren't we? I'm not even sure how we'd get it in through the door. So I'd have to give it to someone who'd look after it, wouldn't I? I could ask around, but from what I understand, the people here want it to stay at the court, and that's only fair, isn't it, if it was found here at the court?'

He turns to me.

'Mr Walden, if you kept it here at the court, is it possible that you could put up a notice of some kind, saying that it was me that found it during my break?'

'A plaque? Yes, I'm sure we could,' I reply. 'We would house the cannon in the foyer downstairs, by the main entrance, where everyone coming to the court can see it; so yes, I'm sure we could put a plaque on the wall nearby, to tell everyone who found it.'

'And of course, sir, if there was any question of a reward for finding it...?'

'It appears that you would be entitled to it,' I reply. 'Needless to say,' I add, smiling in Jeremy's direction, 'the plaque would also include our thanks to the minister for allowing us to display it at the court.'

'You're welcome,' Jeremy replies glumly, indicating, I sense, that the Government Legal Department may well already have given him much the same advice as Kenneth.

* * *

Wednesday evening

'Are you really going to call it the "Bermondsey Cannon"?' the Reverend Mrs Walden asks, as she chops up lettuce for our salad.

In a celebratory mood, I pour two large glasses of a fine Sainsbury's red table wine.

'Yes, I don't see why not. After all, it went to a lot of trouble to find its way through the silt as far as Bermondsey. I think it would be churlish to call it anything else.'

'What about "Jake's Cannon"?' she asks mischievously.

'Certainly not. Jake's part in history will be recorded, of course, but the cannon is owned by no one.' I take a draught of my wine, briefly imagining what the Bermondsey Cannon might have looked like sailing into battle aboard HMS *John of Gaunt*. That thought leads me to another. 'I must confess that I do feel rather sorry that the Owl won't be able to see it in place for some time.'

She nods. 'Yes,' she replies. 'But it's his own fault, isn't it? He should have taken the Pussycat to buy a ring from the pig, shouldn't he, instead of messing around with drugs?'

'Yes. They could have been married by the turkey, and then they could have looked up at the moon and stars together.'

'And he could have serenaded her, and told her what a beautiful pussycat she was. Much better idea, all round.'

MORTIFYING THE FLESH

MORTIFYING THE FLESH

Sunday morning

'Historians tell us,' the Reverend Mrs Walden begins, 'that the flagellant movement started in the city of Perugia, in Northern Italy, in the early fourteenth century. It spread rapidly across Italy and gradually across Europe generally. There were even some outbreaks of activity here in England. The flagellants were men and women who whipped themselves severely as they paraded through the streets of a town or village, and demanded that the inhabitants follow them and imitate them. In those days, apparently, the flagellants thought of what they did as a penance, a religious observance designed to divert the wrath of God from their communities, or to curry favour with Him. In today's more secular society, and even within the church, many would call such deliberate infliction of pain self-harm. So we must ask: what was it that led these men and women to parade themselves through the streets, whipping themselves until the blood ran; and what is it that leads men and women to do similar things today? I wish I could answer those questions for you, but I can't.'

I've often pondered the strange correlation that seems to exist between the Reverend Mrs Walden's sermons and the cases I try at Bermondsey Crown Court. It could be sheer coincidence, but it's amazing how many times the two coincide. It's something of a chicken-and-egg conundrum, I suppose.

Sometimes her choice of subject reflects what she knows is going on at court. Sometimes I gain inspiration from her sermon when a certain case comes my way later. But, chicken or egg, there's no mistaking the connection between today's sermon and the case I have to try this week. The connection is clear from the fact that she is delivering her sermon, not at her home church of St Aethelburgh and All Angels in the Diocese of Southwark, but at the nearby church of St Mortimer-in-the-Fields. At the request of her bishop, the Reverend Mrs Walden has taken over an additional role as acting priest-in-charge of St Mortimer's until further notice. Her assignment is to pour such oil as she can on the troubled waters caused by one of the defendants I'm about to try. The penitential predilections of the Reverend Mr Joshua Canning, the recently suspended vicar of St Mortimer's, have achieved notoriety, not only throughout London, but throughout the country, and far beyond. The church needed to speak out, and speak out without delay. The Reverend felt that a strong sermon was a necessary first step, and this morning she is duly delivering it.

'Naturally enough,' she continues, 'in mediaeval times people across Europe saw the judgment of God in the many wars and disasters that afflicted them. For example, there were virulent outbreaks of the practice of self-flagellation coinciding with outbreaks of the Plague, the Black Death. It is understandable that people felt that some penance was required to avert this judgment of God. But it's easy for that kind of practice to get out of hand, and even to take on sexual connotations, and unfortunately, that's what happened. The flagellants tried to dominate the people of the communities through which they passed. They acted as if they, rather than the church, were now the source of salvation, and accordingly entitled to exercise power over other believers. They demanded that all other believers join them, and if anyone refused to join them in whipping themselves into a frenzy in the street, that person must be obstructing the attempt to deflect God's judgment, and so must be a disciple of the Devil. They often took it upon themselves to impose punishment on those individuals. They became a law unto themselves. As a result, successive Popes condemned and banned the flagellant movement. But, as tends to happen when activities are banned, they don't go away; they simply go underground.

'Even today, we see the practice of self-flagellation and other self-harming penitential activities in the church. Today, it doesn't take the form of men and women whipping themselves in the street. Today, it's all done more discreetly, behind closed doors. But it's none the less real for that. Those of you who've read Dan Brown's book *The Da Vinci Code* may recall the *cilice*, the painful suspender-like device worn around the thigh. Now, all right, Dan Brown may have exaggerated the effects of the *cilice*, and the activities of the Roman Catholic *Opus Dei* movement, for dramatic effect. He was writing a novel, after all. But there is a kernel of truth in his writing, which should concern and alarm us – especially when it shows up on our doorstep in Bermondsey, as it has recently. I want to make it clear that the church is not opposed to penance as such. But it does not and cannot condone acts of self-harm.'

It is a powerful and well-balanced sermon, and I sense that it is having a reassuring effect on the unusually large congregation gathered in St Mortimer's. But now, I'm about to take over where the Reverend Mrs Walden is leaving off; a judicial inquiry into the recent events involving St Mortimer's and the Reverend Mr Joshua Canning is about to begin under the watchful eye of the nation's media. It's a sensational enough case, and inevitably the Grey Smoothies will be watching too, hovering in the background, as is their wont. But on this occasion, I'm not too worried about them. Sensational as it all is, there is nothing particularly complicated about it. It's all stuff I've done many times before.

The Reverend Mr Canning is charged with one specimen count of theft relating to the questionable financing of his adventures with a professional dominatrix who works under the name of Madam Rosita. The only slightly odd thing – given that the penitential Mr Canning gave his full consent to whatever went on – is that the prosecution have dragged Madam Rosita in too. They have charged her with assault occasioning actual bodily harm. Interestingly, there's no charge of sexual assault, even though there is an unmistakable whiff of sexual motive in the air. It's almost impossible to deny when you have voluntary sado-masochistic activity going on. But, as usual in this kind of case, nothing in the file suggests any sexual contact between Madam Rosita and the Reverend Mr Canning; the only sexual activity involved would have been taking place in the mind of Mr Canning. Based on my limited understanding of such matters, that's always the case with a professional dominatrix. No professional dominatrix wants to be suspected of running a brothel: it's the only sure way of having the police take an interest in her. The client can indulge himself in whatever fantasies he likes as the lashes rain down on his back, but fantasy is all it's going to be.

***

Monday morning

'May it please your Honour,' Roderick Lofthouse begins, with a distinct theatrical flourish, 'I appear on behalf of the prosecution in this case. My learned friend Miss Cathy Writtle appears on behalf of the first defendant, Rosie O'Mahoney – or Madam Rosita, to use her professional name, which I understand she prefers. My learned friend Mr Aubrey Brooks appears on behalf of the second defendant, the Reverend Mr Joshua Canning, the currently suspended vicar of the church of St Mortimer-in-the-Fields in the Diocese of Southwark.'

I can't blame Roderick for playing to the gallery. The doyen of the Bermondsey Bar is in his element in a high-profile case, and this morning the press and public are going to be hanging on his every word. Roderick is a reassuring presence with his many years of experience and low-key approach. Aubrey Brooks in the role of defender of church and clergy is also comforting. His urbane manner and understated presentation may be the perfect sequel to the Reverend's calming sermon. Cathy Writtle on behalf of Madam Rosita, on the other hand, is not necessarily such a comforting prospect. Cathy is a first-rate advocate, but there's nothing remotely low key about her. She's the forensic equivalent of an attack drone, and in contrast to Aubrey, her instinct will be to muddy the waters rather than pour oil on them. Still, one way or another, there will be more than enough for the legion of hungry reporters to feast on.

'Yes, Mr Lofthouse,' I reply. 'Are we ready for the jury panel?'

All three counsel agree that we are. This morning's panel will have had an interesting introduction to jury service in the form of a discreet, but direct, interrogation. In every case, we ask prospective jurors a few questions, simply to make sure that we don't end up with anyone on the jury who knows the defendant or an important witness, or anyone who is a bit too familiar with a venue that features in the case. Ordinarily, I would ask these questions when the panel is brought downstairs to court. But in the present instance, the inquiries we have to make are rather more delicate than usual, and I have asked the panel to answer in writing in a confidential questionnaire before they are brought down. The questionnaire begins innocently enough by asking them whether they know either of the defendants, or attend St Mortimer's church. But it quickly moves on to ask whether they have ever patronised Madam Rosita's 'House of Pain and Submission'. The questionnaire then canvasses their religious affiliations, if any (response voluntary) and their views on flagellation and similar acts in the context of religious observance (not voluntary). This is a new batch of jurors beginning their two weeks of service this morning, and God only knows what they make of it all. They might be forgiven for thinking they have unwittingly stepped into some strange alternate universe. There are days at court when I feel that way myself, so there would be nothing remarkable about jurors forming that impression. The court staff are very good at reassuring jurors who feel anxious about what awaits them, but I'm fairly sure they had their work cut out this morning.

While we are waiting for the jurors to make their way downstairs to court, I peruse the results of the questionnaire, which Carol has just received from Dawn and passed up to me on the bench. Their answers don't shed much light on the sixteen good citizens of Bermondsey who have found themselves appointed to this particular panel. That may not be too surprising. To judge by their names, the panel is predominantly female and predominantly unlikely to be even nominally Christian. The main surprise is that not one of them has requested to be transferred to another case. Such requests are not unusual when there's a suggestion of sex, and I'd fully expected two or three to have an attack of the vapours, but apparently no one is too concerned. There is one odd response, asking if Madam Rosita has any connection to a Madam Audrey of Barking. The author, male, doesn't elaborate. I quietly ask Carol to relegate his name card to sixteenth position in the pile, just in case. But other than that, there doesn't seem to be any cause for concern. I inform counsel that we have no obvious problems with the panel, and despite my misgivings we empanel a jury without any difficulty, and away we go.

'Members of the jury,' Roderick begins after introducing himself and his two opponents, 'on a Friday evening about six weeks ago, an ambulance was called to an address in Toulmin Street SE1, not very far from this court. The ambulance crew had received a report over the radio from the dispatcher that a male had received potentially serious injuries. But no further details were provided. Although the ambulance crew were veterans of all kinds of situations – well used to accident and crime scenes – they will tell you that they were not prepared for what they found at the address to which they had been dispatched. They will tell you that they were met at the door by a woman dressed in a most unusual way. She was dressed in a garment bearing some relationship to a one-piece swimsuit, a garment with stripes designed, in terms of appearance and colour, to be reminiscent of those of a tiger. Her hair was held back by a black band and she was wearing high black boots over black tights. The woman led the ambulance crew down two flights of stairs into the basement, where a sign over a door proclaimed the entrance to "Madam Rosita's House of Pain and Submission".

'Members of the jury, the woman who escorted the ambulance crew to the basement was the defendant Rosie O'Mahoney. You will hear, members of the jury, and there will be no dispute about it, that Miss O'Mahoney is what is called a dominatrix, and that she works under the name of Madam Rosita. You may or may not know, members of the jury, that a dominatrix is a woman who is paid to inflict pain in one form or another on masochistic clients who derive sexual or other satisfaction from the administration of pain. It may surprise you to know that this form of activity is by no means uncommon in London.'

If the jury are surprised by this revelation, they're not showing it. Cathy and Aubrey are listening impassively, but with just the faintest suggestion of a smile. It is rather funny. Roderick has a way of creating the impression that he is shocked and horrified by the dreadful details he is obliged to present to the jury, when all of us who know him know that he would sound exactly the same if called upon to announce the day's cricket scores.

'The ambulance crew, members of the jury, were even more surprised by the scene that awaited them when they entered the House of Pain and Submission. The House itself appeared to be nothing less than a fully equipped torture chamber. They found a naked man lying on the floor, obviously in a good deal of pain. When they examined the man, the crew found wounds on his back consistent with his having been whipped quite severely. The skin was red, there were a number of raised welts, and in some places blood had been drawn. Members of the jury, there was no mystery about how those injuries had been caused. The crew noticed no less than three whips of different kinds lying nearby, and there were others in a rack against the wall. The crew also noticed a large, man-size St Andrew's cross made of wood, which had what appeared to be cuffs attached to it at hand and foot level. The cross was lying on the floor.

'Members of the jury, Miss O'Mahoney explained to the ambulance crew that the cross had been standing, apparently safely, up against the wall, but had somehow become unbalanced while she was using her whip, with the result that it had collapsed and fallen to the ground, with the man still attached to it by means of restraints around his wrists and ankles. When she removed the restraints Miss O'Mahoney observed that the man had sustained what appeared to be a broken right wrist, in addition to his other injuries. At that point, Miss O'Mahoney had decided that she had no alternative but to call for an ambulance. The man involved in this incident, members of the jury, was the defendant Joshua Canning, the vicar of St Mortimer-in-the-Fields, in the Diocese of Southwark.

'The ambulance crew administered first aid before taking Mr

Canning to Guy's Hospital so that he could be kept overnight for observation, and so that doctors could offer further treatment and medication as required. They also called the police. The crew, members of the jury, believed that one or more criminal offences might have been committed. The prosecution agree. With the usher's assistance, I will now provide you with copies of the indictment, one between two, please.'

Dawn, as ever, is eager to assist, and positively bounds across the courtroom to distribute the copies to the jury.

'Miss O'Mahoney is charged in count one with one of assault occasioning actual bodily harm. Actual bodily harm means any physical injury, however slight, and we say that the whipping she administered to Mr Canning resulted in physical injury that required treatment in hospital. The defence will suggest to you, I anticipate, that Mr Canning consented to being whipped, and that his consent provides Miss O'Mahoney with a defence. The prosecution disagree, for reasons which will become clear as we go along. We say that a conviction is clearly called for on the facts of this case, which, I anticipate, will not be disputed as far as Miss O'Mahoney is concerned.'

Roderick pauses to turn over several pages of his notebook.

'Members of the jury, count two of the indictment charges Mr Canning with theft. It is what we call a specimen count, meaning that it covers a large number of dishonest transactions over a period of time, in this case a period of almost two years. After Mr Canning had been taken to hospital, the police made inquiries which led them to believe that Mr Canning had been visiting Madam Rosita at her House of Pain and Submission once every two weeks for the past two years or thereabouts. Madam Rosita's charges, members of the jury, are quite substantial – never less than one hundred to one hundred and fifty pounds for each session – and naturally enough, the officers asked themselves how Mr Canning was able to afford that level of expenditure on his salary as a vicar. They were anxious to ask Mr Canning about that, and once he had recovered sufficiently from his injuries, they interviewed him under caution at the police station in the presence of his solicitor. Members of the jury, it is right to say that Mr Canning attended the interview voluntarily; he was not under arrest at that time; and although he was under no obligation to do so, he answered all the officers' questions. He gave them an explanation of where the money came from. But members of the jury, it is an explanation you may think is extraordinary; it is an explanation the prosecution say is obviously false and dishonest.

'Mr Canning told the officers that he had taken the money from three of the several bank accounts held by his church, to which, as vicar, he had an access that allowed him to sign cheques or make withdrawals of up to five hundred pounds without a second signature. Evidently, St Mortimer's is a well endowed parish which has several sources of income as well as many outgoings – so much so that even relatively large sums of money going missing from the accounts might not be noticed unless there was a detailed audit. The officers adjourned the interview for two weeks, during which time they obtained copies of the relevant accounts and conducted an audit of their own. It soon became clear that there was a pattern of withdrawals of sums of up to two hundred pounds from three separate accounts, and that those withdrawals corresponded with the dates of Mr Canning's visits to Madam Rosita.

'When the interview was resumed, Mr Canning did not deny any of that. But he explained to the officers that his visits to Madam Rosita were in the interests of doing penance, mortifying the flesh, which as a Christian minister he was obliged to do; that this practice was essential to his ministry; and that accordingly, the payments made to Madam Rosita represented a legitimate church expense, for which he was entitled to reimburse himself from the church's bank accounts.

'Members of the jury, the prosecution are unkind enough to suggest that Mr Canning's explanation of his expenditure of his church's money is obviously false and dishonest. We say that his visits to Madam Rosita had nothing whatsoever to do with penance, or indeed with religious observance of any kind. We are unkind enough to suggest that, like Madam Rosita's many other clients, his interest in receiving whippings had nothing to do with mortifying the flesh: on the contrary, he was indulging the flesh in the form of sexual gratification. But members of the jury, be that as it may, you will hear that at no time did Mr Canning disclose to anyone that he was using church funds for that purpose. If he had been acting honestly, would he not have told his parochial church council, or, if he preferred to keep it confidential within the church, perhaps the church's outside auditors? Would he not have asked advice of someone, just to make sure that what he was doing was above board? But he never told a soul, members of the jury. Those concerned with the church's finances remained in ignorance of his withdrawals until the police alerted them after Mr Canning had been arrested. This isn't a case of legitimate church expenditure, members of the jury. It is a case of good old-fashioned theft.

'With your Honour's leave, I will call the first witness.'

The first witness, Edie Morgan, is petite with big blonde hair. She's a member of the ambulance crew. She is so slightly built that you find yourself worrying about the idea of her having to lift a patient, even one her own size. But she carries herself in such a way as to suggest that she would make light of it. She seems remarkably cheerful for someone who is about to give evidence in the Crown Court, and takes the oath with an obvious good humour. But it soon becomes clear that the cheerfulness is a façade which is about to fall away. She is desperately fighting off the urge to giggle, and once she catches sight of Madam Rosita in the dock – demurely dressed as she is for her court appearance – it's a fight she starts to lose. She turns away from the dock and focuses on Roderick instead of Madam Rosita, which seems to do the trick for the moment.

'Miss Morgan,' Roderick begins, 'please tell the jury what you do for a living.'

'I'm an emergency services technician, a paramedic. I'm one of the two members of an ambulance crew which responds to emergency calls.'

'You and your partner are called out to medical emergencies, you render first aid, and you take the patient to hospital if necessary?'

'Yes, exactly.'

'Thank you, Miss Morgan. Your Honour, I've been told that Miss Morgan's evidence is not in dispute, and so I will lead her to some extent.'

Both Cathy and Aubrey confirm this by nods of the head. It's a point that the jury don't need to worry about, but I need to know about as the judge. Leading questions – questions such as the one Roderick is about to ask, that tell the witness in so many words the answer the questioner expects – are not permitted when the evidence is challenged; but when the evidence is not disputed they can save a lot of time.

'I think it's right that on the occasion in question, a Friday evening, the sixteenth of April, you and your partner, Mr Jeffrey Ackroyd, were on duty at about seven thirty, is that right?'

'Yes.'

'And you received a call from the dispatcher advising you that an ambulance was needed at an address in Toulmin Street SE1, because a male had suffered injuries at that address, is that right?'

'Yes, it is.'

'You proceeded to the address as quickly as you could, and you were met by a female, is that also right?'

'Yes.'

'Is that female in court today?'

Miss Morgan looks around dutifully. That's all it takes.

'Yes. She is in the – what d'you call it? – the dock, at the back of the court.' She just about gets the answer out before collapsing in a gale of laughter.

Roderick pauses. He's obviously not quite sure how to rescue the situation. Waiting for the witness to recover her composure is one way, but her laughter is infectious, and the jury are starting to giggle in sympathy. Of course, the case has its funny side. Many cases do, and once in a while laughter breaks out in court and everyone joins in. Usually it's a momentary outburst which dies away as quickly as it erupts. But occasionally you get a virus you can't control. Once or twice in the past I've had to adjourn for a few minutes to restore order – most recently in a case in which a witness, for no apparent reason, favoured the court with a lengthy lament about his dead parrot – and I'm thinking I may have to do the same again. But before I can intervene, Roderick decides to take charge himself.

'Forgive me, Miss Morgan, but this is a serious matter, and I must ask you to concentrate on your evidence.'

Edie makes a visible effort to recover, apparently successfully.

'Yes, I'm sorry.'

'I should think so, too,' a female voice adds from the dock.

'That will do, Miss O'Mahoney,' I say.

She mutters something I don't quite catch. Probably just as well. I let it go.

'Thank you,' Roderick continues. 'You've identified the female who met you at the address as the defendant Miss O'Mahoney. On the occasion in question, was Miss O'Mahoney dressed in a kind of one-piece outfit with tiger stripes, and... I'm not quite sure of the proper way of describing it...?'

I can't imagine what Roderick is thinking. Of all the questions he could ask at this juncture, he's picked not only the most unnecessary, but also the question most calculated to overwhelm Edie's efforts to stop laughing. She does her best, but the memory of Madam Rosita's working outfit is obviously a vivid one. She has to bite her tongue and pause for several seconds before replying, desperately keeping her eyes away from the dock.

'The only way I can describe it is that she was dressed in your typical dominatrix outfit, straight out of central casting, complete with the black tights and boots, and...' she manages before collapsing again in fits of laughter. Naturally, the jury join in.

'She is *so* rude,' Madam Rosita comments.

Now Roderick really doesn't know what to do.

'Would you like a break, Miss Morgan?' I offer. 'I know it's difficult to stop laughing once you start, but Mr Lofthouse is right – this is a serious matter.'

She has to punch the edge of the witness box a few times, but she eventually seems to pull herself back together.

'No, I'm fine, your Honour. Thank you. I'm really sorry, but you know, in my job you always think you've seen it all, but then something like this happens...'

'I do understand,' I assure her. 'I often feel the same way in my line of work.'

She does seem to have got over it now, at least for the time being.

'I'm much obliged, your Honour,' Roderick says, and I think he means it. 'Miss Morgan, when you entered the address, where did Miss O'Mahoney lead you?'

'She led us down two quite steep flights of stairs. I remember that, because that's the kind of thing you have to be aware of as a paramedic. You're always thinking, what would we have to do to lift a patient up to street level to the ambulance?'

'Yes, quite. On your way downstairs, did you observe a sign that said you were entering Madam Rosita's House of Pain and Submission?'

'Yes. I do remember that. Jeff and I had a bit of a giggle about it.'

She's about to have a bit of a giggle again now, but she bites her lip and just about keeps it at bay.

'When you entered the House of Pain itself, what did you see?'

'Well, the first thing we saw was the patient. He was naked, lying on the floor, not moving very much. We made our way over to him. He was conscious and responsive, but he was obviously in pain. We asked him if he was able to answer our questions and he said he was.'

'Do you see that man in court today?'

'Yes, he is the man in the dock.'

'Mr Canning. Thank you. Did you examine him?'

'Yes. We examined Mr Canning as gently as we could. We saw that the skin on his back was red, he had a number of raised welts, and he had been bleeding.'

'Did you notice any possible cause of those injuries?'

'Yes. Well, actually, the cause was pretty obvious. The injuries appeared to be the result of Mr Canning having been whipped, and we saw three whips of different kinds lying on the floor.'

'What else did you notice?'

'We noticed a large, man-size St Andrew's cross made of wood. There were cuffs – restraints – attached to it for the hands and feet, and we concluded that Mr Canning had at some stage been attached to the cross by means of those restraints. There were some marks on his wrists and ankles which confirmed that. But the cross was lying on the floor, suggesting that it had fallen over with the man still attached to it.'

'Did you make any inquiries about that?'

'Yes, we questioned Miss O'Mahoney, and she told us that she had attached Mr Canning to the cross before whipping him. The cross at that stage was upright, standing up against the wall, but, as we suspected, it had somehow fallen over with him still attached to it. Miss O'Mahoney couldn't explain how that had happened; she said it had always been safe in that position. But she saw that Mr Canning was in pain and might have been injured, so she undid the cuffs and pulled the cross off him and called 999 for the ambulance.'

'Did you find any further injuries that might have resulted from the fall?'

'Yes. We found that Mr Canning had broken his right wrist, which had probably been trapped under one limb of the cross when it fell. He also had a number of bruises and abrasions resulting from the fall.'

'Did you decide to take Mr Canning to hospital?'

'Yes. We administered some first aid to stop any bleeding, but he was going to need to go to hospital to have his injuries treated. Apart from the visible injuries, we couldn't rule out possible internal injuries or the effects of shock or concussion. So we got him dressed and explained to him that we would take him in the ambulance. Fortunately, he'd recovered a bit by then and he was able to walk upstairs on his own, and we took him to Guy's Hospital.'

Roderick pauses to consult his notes.

'What else, if anything, did you notice about the House of Pain and Submission?'

'It was done out like a torture chamber. The lighting was subdued. There was a rack containing a number of whips and canes and a few other nasty-looking things – I don't even want to speculate what they were for. There was what appeared to be another kind of rack, if you know what I mean, the kind for stretching people. There were several sets of hooks in the wall with restraints attached to them. I'm sure there were other things as well, but our attention was mainly on Mr Canning as the patient.'

'Yes, of course. But as a result of what you saw, did you call the police?'

'Yes, we did. We felt that it was possible that a criminal offence might have been committed. That wasn't for us to say, obviously, but we did feel it was a situation that called for the police to be informed, so once we'd got Mr Canning safely into hospital we called it in.'

'Thank you, Miss Morgan. Please wait there in case there are any further questions.'

'Miss Morgan,' Cathy begins, 'is it fair to say that Miss O'Mahoney was completely frank with you about what had happened on that evening?'

'Yes, as far as we could tell, she was. She gave us information that explained Mr Canning's injuries, and she was quite up front about it, quite matter-of-fact.'

'She told you that she was a dominatrix – which was pretty obvious in the circumstances – and that Mr Canning was one of her clients?'

'Yes.'

'She told you that she had tied Mr Canning to the St Andrew's cross, and had whipped him while he was tied up in that way?'

'Yes.'

'And was it clear to you from what she said and from what Mr Canning said that Mr Canning had consented to being whipped in that way?'

Edie hesitates. 'I think that's something I assumed, given the circumstances. I didn't ask either of them about it specifically.'

'But is it right to say that Mr Canning made no complaint of having been forced to submit to being tied up and whipped?'

'No. There was no suggestion of anything like that.'

'And Miss O'Mahoney was completely frank with you about the cross falling over and Mr Canning sustaining injuries because of the fall?'

'Yes. As far as I could tell, she didn't try to keep any information from us. She volunteered information and answered all the questions we put to her.'

'And it was Miss O'Mahoney who called for an ambulance to attend?'

'Yes. That's correct.'

'So, when you told the jury that you and your partner decided to report the matter to the police, it wasn't because you thought that unlawful force might have been used against Mr Canning, was it?'

'No. We're trained to call the police if we think that there are any possibly suspicious circumstances, but in this case it might have been no more than a health and safety issue. We are trained not to try to draw conclusions. If we think there is any reason to report the incident, we report it. That doesn't mean that an offence has been committed. Often we do it just to be on the safe side, for example in cases of possible domestic or child abuse.'

'Thank you, Miss Morgan. I have nothing further, your Honour.'

'Your Honour,' Roderick says, 'I have Mr Ackroyd available. I'm quite prepared to call him and tender him for cross-examination if my learned friends wish me to.'

Cathy and Aubrey whisper for a moment or two.

'I don't need him, your Honour,' Cathy replies.

'Neither do I,' Aubrey adds.

'In that case' Roderick says, 'this may be a convenient moment to read the medical evidence to the jury.'

There is no dispute about the medical evidence, so the doctors' reports are read to the jury. There is nothing surprising in them. When the Reverend Mr Canning arrived at Guy's Hospital, the staff quickly confirmed the ambulance crew's diagnosis of a fractured right wrist. The wrist was placed in a cast. Mr Canning was treated appropriately for his other injuries, and because of a suspicion of concussion he was kept overnight for observation, and released the following day with analgesics and instructions to report back if he felt in any way unwell.

'I will call my next witness, Archdeacon Duncan Winston-Smith,' Roderick announces.

The archdeacon is a stout man in his late fifties, wearing a cassock and clerical collar and sporting a large gold cross around his neck. He takes his time making his ponderous way to the witness box, almost as if he is carrying the whole weight of the church's burdens on his shoulders.

'Archdeacon, are you based at Lincoln Cathedral, and have you been asked to give evidence in this case because you are from a diocese outside Mr Canning's home diocese of Southwark, and because you have no prior knowledge of Mr Canning?'

'Yes, that's correct.'

'For how long have you been in holy orders?'

'For just over thirty years.'

'And in addition to the usual theological training necessary to become a priest, do you hold a doctorate in theology from Cambridge University?'

'Yes.'

'What was the subject of the thesis for which you were awarded that doctorate?'

'My immediate subject was the so-called Flagellant

Movement in the mediaeval church. But it wasn't just a historical review. I also dealt with the wider issue of penance in the life of the church, at that time and at later times, leading up the present.'

'Thank you. Archdeacon, when we speak of the Flagellant Movement, what do we mean?'

The archdeacon nods several times and fixes the jury in his gaze.

'The word "flagellation" means whipping. Flagellants were men and women who believed that it was necessary, or at least appropriate, to perform a penance in the form of self-flagellation in order to placate God or to divert some perceived judgment of God away from them or their community.'

'Was this self-flagellation carried out publicly?'

'In mediaeval times, very much so. They would usually process through the streets, whipping themselves and encouraging others to join them. But, of course, the practice was also not uncommon in monasteries and convents, in which case it was a more private matter, except for other members of the community who might be encouraged to watch as an inducement to their own good behaviour. In the monastic context, it was not unusual for members of the community to carry out the flagellation on each other, so it was not strictly a case of self-flagellation. But the principle is the same.'

'Archdeacon, I don't think we need to dwell on this, but I understand from your thesis that the papacy on several occasions condemned the practice of the flagellants, not so much because of what they were doing to themselves, but because they were actively coercing others to join them whether they wanted to or not.'

I'm impressed. These days Roderick doesn't do as much reading for his cases as he used to, and the idea of his tackling a whole theological thesis for one expert witness sounds like rather a lot of work. Perhaps he finds this an unusually interesting case.

'Yes, that's quite correct. The flagellants were overstepping the mark, and in many ways claiming some of the powers of the papacy itself.'

'Let's move on to the present day, if we may, Archdeacon. To what extent does penance such as self-flagellation still occur within the church?'

The archdeacon is nodding again.

'That's a very difficult question to answer. For one thing, in the pre-Reformation period, there was only the Roman Church to consider, and they have always been the main proponents of penance in that sense. I'm not saying there hasn't been some interest in the Lutheran and Anglican communities, because there has. But less so than in the Roman Church, and the incidence of such interest in the non-conformist churches has been very rare.'

'Well, let's confine ourselves to the churches in which such practices were once common. Are they still common today?'

'Again, that's a difficult question, simply because, to the extent it goes on at all, it goes on behind closed doors – certainly in this country. There are some countries, such as the Philippines and Mexico, in which flagellant processions are by no means unknown. Indeed, in the Philippines, as you may know, they even stage partial crucifixions at Easter time, which is an even more extreme form of penance or devotion. But in most countries today, such public displays would be disapproved of, and would very likely be suppressed by the authorities.'

'Well, perhaps I can come at this in another way,' Roderick suggests. 'What attitude is taken today by the church to the idea of penance?'

The archdeacon ponders his reply for some time.

'If you mean penance in the broad sense, I think the idea is widely accepted. Roman Catholic priests often impose penances after pronouncing absolution in the light of what the penitent has said during confession, although those penances are nothing like self-flagellation – they usually involve saying a number of set prayers, or making amends to someone you have wronged, and so on. And I think in the church generally, penances in that sense are regarded as appropriate acts of devotion which should be encouraged. But beyond that, I think we're all aware today of the dangers of self-harm, and that has inhibited any conduct that might be construed in that way.'

'Inhibited, or driven it underground?' Roderick asks with a smile.

'Another good question. It's anybody's guess, but if you ask me – as you have – I would say, driven underground. We know that there are those in religious communities, whether religious communities or lay communities such as *Opus Dei*, in which painful penances are still practised, with at least the tacit consent of the church. But the church generally is aware that it's an area in which you have to be very careful.'

'For what reason?'

'For at least two good reasons: firstly, there are undoubtedly individuals who are interested in painful penances for sado-masochistic reasons, which introduces a sexual element into it; and secondly, and closely related to the first reason, it is easy, even inadvertently, to put pressure on vulnerable people, people who may not be able to exercise a free and informed choice about whether to participate. We must remember how overbearing that kind of pressure can be, especially when it comes from a priest, or any religious adviser, for that matter.'

'Thank you, Archdeacon,' Roderick continues. 'Now, turning to the case at hand, have you been made aware of the circumstances surrounding Mr Canning's appearance in court today?'

'Yes. I understand that he visited a dominatrix in order to have himself whipped, and when questioned about it by the police, stated that it was a form of penance, a devotion necessary or desirable for his ministry at St Mortimer's. There is also a financial question...'

'Yes, let's leave the money on one side for a moment,' Roderick suggests.

'Yes, very well.'

'As far as Mr Canning's visits to Miss O'Mahoney are concerned, as such, what view do you take of that as a senior member of the same church?'

Aubrey is on his feet in a flash.

'Your Honour, I fail to see the relevance of my learned friend's question. He has already established from this witness that penance, carried out in private, remains a feature of church life. Even if the archdeacon disapproves of it, that doesn't mean that Mr Canning has to share his opinion, and it certainly doesn't mean that Mr Canning isn't free to follow his own beliefs.'

'The question,' Roderick replies, 'also relates to the circumstances in which Mr Canning carried out this so-called penance, which goes directly to the question of whether the defendant's use of church money for that purpose was justified. Mr Canning isn't on trial for having himself whipped; he's on trial for theft – for appropriating church money to pay for it. I know I haven't asked the witness about the money yet, but we are getting there.'

I nod. 'I agree,' I reply. 'You'll have your chance to cross-examine, Mr Brooks.'

'As your Honour pleases,' Aubrey says, resuming his seat. I'm sure he didn't expect me to agree with him, but he's achieved his main goal – he's made his point to the jury.

'I don't necessarily disapprove of such a penance in the case of a priest,' the archdeacon replies. 'I don't say that there may not be occasions when it is appropriate. I think those occasions would be few and far between, but I don't exclude the possibility. What disturbs me is the fact that Mr Canning went to a professional dominatrix, and that he did so on such a regular basis.'

'Why do those matters disturb you?' Roderick asks.

'Because they inevitably raise the spectre of a sexual motivation,' the witness replies, 'especially the regularity of his visits. If Mr Canning was doing this for the purpose of sexual gratification, that would not be consistent with the idea of doing penance. On the contrary, he should consider doing penance for his visits to the dominatrix, not claiming the visits as penance.'

'Then, let's come now to the matter of the money,' Roderick says. 'Are you aware that, when challenged by the police about the amounts of money he had withdrawn from church accounts to pay Madam Rosita, Mr Canning said that the object was to improve his ministry in some way, and so was a legitimate expenditure of church money?'

'Yes, I have been made aware of that.'

'What is your opinion about Mr Canning's position?'

'My opinion is that it is entirely misconceived,' the archdeacon replies at once.

'For what reason?'

'In the first place, if there is any hint of sexual motivation, it could have no positive effect on his ministry at all, only negative effects. But even without that, the idea that Mr Canning needed to practice flagellation at regular intervals of two weeks in order to maintain his ministry is absurd. And even if he did, it would be his own responsibility to make suitable arrangements.'

'What kind of arrangements?' Roderick asks. It's one of those obvious questions advocates often ask automatically, without considering whether it's necessary. I suspect Roderick was having second thoughts about it as soon as the words were out of his mouth. The archdeacon seems uncomfortable with the question.

'Well,' he suggests after a significant pause, 'he could have practised self-flagellation without incurring any expense at all. Or he could have appealed to some member of a religious order to help him. In my mind, the danger was that, if he couldn't do it any other way, he might have tried to persuade a member of his congregation to help him, which could have given rise to some very undesirable situations. In any case, the idea that it could be a legitimate expenditure of church funds to pay a professional dominatrix is ridiculous.'

'In your opinion, would expenditure of that kind by a priest be regarded as honest or dishonest?'

'Your Honour, my learned friend knows better than that,' Aubrey protests. 'That's the very question the jury will have to decide.'

Roderick holds up his hands. He was trying to get away with one, but with Aubrey on the other side, the chances of that were very slim indeed.

'I won't pursue it, your Honour. Thank you, Archdeacon. I have no further questions.'

It's slightly early, but Carol is asking me to rise. Cross-examination of the archdeacon will have to wait until two o'clock.

And so to lunch, an oasis of calm in a desert of chaos. Or so I've been hoping, but today, calm is going to be the last adjective you'd apply to lunchtime.

I arrive back in my chambers to find Bob and Stella waiting for me, with a woman I've never seen before.

'Judge, we're sorry to disturb your lunch hour,' Bob begins, 'but something rather serious has come up.'

'Oh?'

'This is DI Derbyshire of the Judicial Protection Unit.'

DI Derbyshire stands and extends her hand. She looks to be about forty to forty-five, slim and tall with short black hair, smartly dressed in a dark grey two-piece suit and flat black shoes.

'The Judicial…?' I stammer, taking her hand.

'The Judicial Protection Unit,' she confirms. 'We become involved if there's a credible threat to the life or safety of a judge.'

I release her hand and sit down behind my desk. They tell you about officers like DI Derbyshire when you become an RJ. Somewhere in my desk I have the number of an emergency help line in case one of my judges should ever receive a serious and credible threat to their well-being. But like most RJs, I suspect, I've never seriously considered the possibility of anything like that actually happening at my court: it's the kind of thing that happens elsewhere. DI Derbyshire sits down in an armchair opposite me, while Bob and Stella remain standing, leaning against my book case. I do my best to make light of the moment.

'I can't imagine anyone wanting to threaten any of the four of us at Bermondsey. We don't do anything serious enough to attract that kind of attention.' I look appealingly in the direction of Bob and Stella. 'Do we?' DI Derbyshire reaches across my desk and hands me a document consisting of several pages.

'This was delivered to the court this morning,' she says. 'As your court manager, Bob took it upon himself to alert me – quite rightly – and I came as soon as I could.' She smiles. 'There's no reason why you would have noticed, Judge, because we're vey discreet about it, but you've had an armed officer in your court since about eleven o'clock.'

'An armed…? In *my* court?' I ask.

'The staff on the door are aware, Judge,' Bob reassures me. 'I've told them to let armed officers through security on production of their warrant cards, and to keep quiet about it.'

'Why don't you read this, Judge?' DI Derbyshire suggests, 'and then I'll tell you what I think we're dealing with.'

I examine the front page. It appears to have been composed using an old-fashioned typewriter, and to judge from the quality, an old-fashioned typewriter with a dodgy ribbon. Corrections have been made here and there with the aid of a white-out fluid, and all in all the front page looks a bit of a mess. Despite my rapidly growing anxiety, I find myself experiencing a feeling of nostalgia for my early days at the Bar when we prepared pleadings and opinions for solicitors in the same way. We didn't even have a typist in chambers when I started, so I became something of an expert on handling white-out and carbon paper, and on the whole inky-fingered process of producing documents. Since those days I've assumed that typewriters, carbon paper and the rest of it are to be found only in museums of antiquated technology, and it gives me a warm glow to think that someone somewhere is still keeping the craft alive. But the glow doesn't last long.

THE ORDER OF ORIGINAL AND RETROGRADE ENGLISH MEN

The Order of Original and Retrograde English Men, being a Society of those free men who demand their birth right as free English Men, who demand the rights invested in them by the Great Charter as well as by the laws of this Realm from time immemorial, and who refuse to accept the rule of those self-styled officers of state who now falsely claim to be the government and the judges of this country, and under cover of these falsely claimed offices deprive free English men of their rights: we now accuse the following of unlawfully conspiring to impose their rule on free English men in violation of the Great Charter and of the laws of this Realm from time immemorial –

The self-styled Pope, also known as the Bishop of Rome

The self-styled Monarch of the United Kingdom

The self-styled Prime Minister of the United Kingdom

The self-styled Parliament of the United Kingdom and the members thereof

The self-styled European Union and the self-styled officers thereof

The self-styled Lord Chief Justice of England and the self-styled judges under his control

The self-styled Archbishop of Canterbury

The self-styled Commissioner of Metropolitan Police and self-styled officers under her control

The self-styled British Broadcasting Corporation and the self-styled officers thereof

The said conspiracy being as follows: by means of unlawful self-styled parliamentary elections purporting to give them standing as officers of government, whereas no election is necessary to enforce the Great Charter and our ancient laws; and by means of so-called Acts of Parliament and court judgments: to deprive free English men of their rights by falsely claiming to declare certain acts to be crimes, arrogating to themselves the right to arrest free English men for such so-called crimes, arrogating to themselves the right to grant bail to those arrested, who under ancient law are already free men without any need for so-called bail, arrogating to themselves the right to bring free English men before false courts consisting of self-styled judges and jurors, and arrogating to themselves the right to punish free English men falsely adjudged to be guilty of such so-called crimes.

It goes on for another three pages in much the same vein – all very interesting in its own weird way, especially the passages that explain the involvement of the Bishop of Rome and the Monarch. But what really gets my attention is page five, which DI Derbyshire has helpfully flagged up with a paper clip. Page five contains a fuller list of the leading conspirators. This includes a list of false self-styled judges, who are marked out as the main judicial perpetrators of the conspiracy to deprive the Original and Retrograde English Men of their rights under the Great Charter and the laws of the Realm from time immemorial. This list, in addition to the Lord Chief Justice, contains the names of two High Court judges and four circuit judges, with yours truly in second place behind a judge of the Old Bailey. All of us, the writer adds, are deemed worthy of death for our treason in participating in the conspiracy. Fame at last, I reflect ruefully.

'I hope you see now why we felt we had to take immediate action, Judge,' DI Derbyshire says. 'We've put in place a coordinated security plan for all the judges named in this document. In fact, I have to be off to the Old Bailey as soon as I've finished here.'

'You're taking this nonsense seriously?' I ask.

She nods vigorously. 'Very much so, Judge.'

I shake my head. 'But whoever wrote this must be…'

'Mentally disturbed in some way. Yes, I agree. We have some experience with groups of this kind, and for the most part, yes, they do tend to be harmless nutters. I'm not aware of any case in which the Free English Men have been involved in serious violence. But that doesn't mean we don't take it seriously – there's always a first time.'

'Judge, I talk with managers at other Crown Courts all the time,' Bob says. 'I know quite a few of them have had members of this group charged with some offence or other in their courts, and they've had letters like this delivered. But nothing has happened beyond that. I didn't know we'd had any at Bermondsey, to be honest, but apparently we must have.'

'We're familiar with this kind of letter,' DI Derbyshire confirms. 'We don't always treat them as an immediate threat. Usually they go off on a rant but don't actually make any specific threat against anyone. This one is different, obviously, because it names names and makes a specific death threat. In all probability it's just another rant and the writer is just trying to stir it up, but we can't take chances.'

She pauses.

'Judge, I don't want to alarm you, but we've already taken the precaution of advising your wife about what's going on, and two of my technical officers are installing panic alarms in the vicarage as we speak. There will be one in your kitchen and one in your bedroom. Once they are activated, if you trigger the alarm you will have armed officers with you in a matter of a few minutes. Again, I'm very optimistic that nothing will happen, but as I say, we're not taking any chances. You might want to call Mrs Walden just to touch base, but my officer reported that she took it all in her stride.'

I smile. 'She would,' I reply.

'DI Derbyshire has asked us to review all the cases we've had over the last six months,' Stella says, 'to see if we can identify any likely suspects.'

'They tend to come up on firearms and cannabis charges,' the DI adds. 'They tend to assume that free English men have the right to bear arms to resist the false self-styled government, even though we don't have a Second Amendment; and of course, no one can tell a free English man that he can't consume a plant capable of growing naturally on English soil.'

'You should probably look at any file that has a psychiatric report in it,' I suggest. I'm feeling a bit weak at the knees, and I'm not sure how much sense I'm making. Not much, apparently.

'That's not a real indicator,' DI Derbyshire replies. 'The kind of people who write rants like this can appear quite normal in other circumstances. For instance, the lady who accepted this letter at your front desk this morning says that the man who delivered it looked perfectly normal and was very polite.'

'Did she get a description?'

'A rather vague one. I'm not sure how helpful it's going to be, but I'm going to hook her up with a sketch artist just in case, and of course, we've dusted the document and the envelope for prints. Let's hope we get lucky. But in the meanwhile, we will take every precaution. We will ferry you to and from court in a police car until we're sure it's safe.'

'Is that really necessary?' I ask, somehow thinking, despite the circumstances, how much I will miss my walks and my daily visits to Jeanie and Elsie, and George.

'It's the easiest way,' she replies. 'I could have an officer follow you, but there's no guarantee he could react in time if anything kicks off, so a car is the best option.'

She stands.

'Judge, I have to be off to the Bailey soon, but I would like you to take me to the lunch room so that I can explain what's going on to the other judges, and answer any concerns they may have.'

'Yes, of course,' I say helplessly.

Like me, the others are at first too taken aback to have much in the way of sensible concerns. DI Derbyshire reassures them that I'm the only judge of the court to appear in the list of the leading conspirators, but fails to mention the denunciation of all judges under the self-styled Lord Chief's control, thereby, it seems to me, painting a slightly misleading picture; though in fairness, given the number of judges in the country – several hundred circuit judges alone, before you count the High Court, district judges, and so on – there's no basis for assuming any enhanced risk at Bermondsey.

'There's no reason to think you're in danger,' she assures them. 'I just wanted to make sure you know what's going on.'

Legless points out, reasonably enough, that if they come after me with a bomb, everyone at court will be in danger. The DI replies that bombs aren't the kind of weapon you would expect from people like this, though she doesn't elaborate about the kind of weapon you *would* expect.

Marjorie asks whether an officer could alert the school and keep half an eye on Simon and Samantha. DI Derbyshire assures her that this will be done.

Hubert expresses concern for the Garrick Club and volunteers to alert the secretary, so that the staff can be put on heightened awareness of the Club's security without putting any additional strain on police resources, for which the DI expresses her appreciation.

She concludes by inviting all of us to call the police immediately if we feel in any way uneasy during the short time before the matter is resolved.

I call the Reverend Mrs Walden, who, as DI Derbyshire observed, sounds considerably more in control than I feel. She has provided tea and biscuits for the officers who installed the panic alarms, she tells me, and they have just left. She's checked that all the doors and windows are secure; she's just off to meet with the parochial church council, and she intends to keep calm and carry on. She suggests that I do the same, which for the first time brings me some feeling of confidence.

* * *

Monday afternoon

It's hard not to stare into the public gallery in an attempt to identify the armed officer assigned to guard me. There are two possible suspects, one male, one female, both dressed in that semi-formal way police officers often resort to when attending court. For the life of me I can't remember whether either of them was in court during the morning. It's impossible to tell. I don't want to cause whoever it is any concern and I deliberately turn my gaze elsewhere.

Cathy has no questions for the archdeacon, so it's Aubrey's turn.

'Archdeacon,' he begins, 'I'm not entirely sure, but it seemed to me that when you were answering questions put by my learned friend Mr Lofthouse, you acknowledged that flagellation might be a legitimate penance, even in this day and age. Is that right?'

Even with the lunch hour to anticipate cross-examination, the archdeacon still doesn't seem particularly comfortable with this subject.

'I believe what I said was that I could conceive of occasions when it might be appropriate, but not as a regular practice, and certainly not under the circumstances in which Mr Canning indulged in it.'

'Well, I'll come to Mr Canning in a moment. But first, let's think about this from the point of view of general principle, shall we?'

'If you wish.'

'Thank you. Assume with me, then, that a priest considers that he ought to do penance in the form of flagellation. Would you agree that he ought to do so in private, rather than the kind of public display the mediaeval flagellants indulged in?'

'Of course.'

'If that's true, Archdeacon, you would agree, wouldn't you, that he must make arrangements of some kind for the flagellation to take place?'

'Arrangements?'

'That was the word you used when my learned friend was asking you questions, wasn't it? To put it simply, either he has to find a way to whip himself, or he has to find someone to whip him: wouldn't you agree?'

'I suppose so.'

'Well, that's what you told my learned friend earlier, Archdeacon. Next, let me ask you this. Can you imagine a situation in which a priest feels that he ought to undergo the penance of flagellation, but can't quite bring himself to inflict it on himself?'

'Can't bring himself to do it?'

'Yes. He's squeamish about doing it to himself for some reason, but he thinks he would be all right if someone else tied him up and administered the whipping. Can you imagine that situation?'

The archdeacon gives the impression of never having considered such a scenario.

'It never occurred to you when you were doing the obviously extensive research you did for your thesis?' Aubrey presses him. 'Well, indulge me for a moment,' he continues after waiting in vain for some time for an answer. 'Assume that we have a priest who finds himself in that situation.'

'If you wish.'

'Thank you. Does it not follow that the priest has to find someone willing to administer the whipping?'

'If he really wishes to go through with it, then yes. I would have expected him to think twice about it if he couldn't bring himself to do it.'

'No doubt there are those who would think twice,' Aubrey agrees urbanely. 'But our priest really wants to do it. Who should he approach? A member of a religious community? You suggested that to my learned friend, didn't you? That might work, but it would have to be embarrassing, wouldn't it, trailing around monasteries and convents trying to find a fellow-flagellant who wouldn't mind lending a hand, as it were?'

'Not convents, I would sincerely hope,' the archdeacon protests. 'Monasteries, perhaps.'

'Oh?' Aubrey asks, feigning surprise. 'Why not convents? Is that because of sex raising its ugly head again?'

'Obviously.'

'Obviously? You're assuming the priest to be heterosexual, Archdeacon, are you?'

No reply.

'And of course, you might find a monk or nun willing to help out occasionally, but if it were to become a regular thing, their superior might start asking questions, wouldn't you think? Not an ideal scenario, is it?'

'Nothing about what the priest is doing is ideal,' the archdeacon observes.

'No. So the next possibility is that the priest asks a member of his congregation to assist. When you were answering questions from my learned friend, I got the impression that you disapproved of that option?'

'In the strongest possible terms.'

'Please explain.'

The archdeacon shakes his head vigorously. 'It would be bound to lead to difficulties. A priest is not on level terms with the members of his congregation. He is their minister, their spiritual adviser. Even in the case of a strong and mature person, if he were to approach them about something like this, it would be bound to invoke very strong feelings. If you had a person with any vulnerability at all, the sexual element would be almost certain to arise. And that's before you consider the high probability that what the priest was doing would become public knowledge within his church and potentially beyond.'

Aubrey pauses and turns towards the jury.

'Given all those difficulties, Archdeacon, would you not

agree that a professional dominatrix is the obvious, and by far the most satisfactory, solution to the priest's dilemma?'

'I most certainly would not agree,' the witness splutters loudly, after considering this apparently outrageous suggestion in a furious silence for some time.

'Really?' Aubrey continues, unabashed. 'Even though the dominatrix would offer privacy and discretion; would be available when needed; would be the answer to the priest's unwillingness to whip himself; and would be competent to monitor the whipping to ensure that it doesn't go too far?'

I glance over at the jury. When Aubrey started this line of inquiry, I must admit that I couldn't see it going very far. But now, I'm not so sure he doesn't have a good point, and to judge from the jury's reaction, they don't seem to be dismissing it out of hand.

'I cannot agree to that suggestion,' the archdeacon replies with an air of finality. This doesn't deflect Aubrey in the slightest.

'Well, it will be a point for the jury to consider,' he continues. 'Now, I concede of course, Archdeacon, that using a dominatrix does have one drawback, and that is the cost.'

'Exactly,' the witness replies at once, apparently grateful for this opportunity to escape to safer ground. 'That's one very sound objection.'

'But what is it you object to, specifically?' Aubrey asks. 'Do you object to his paying for the service under any circumstances, or only if church funds are used?'

'Mr Canning did use church funds,' the archdeacon points out.

'Yes. But again, you see, I'm trying to deal with the matter on the basis of general principle. What if the priest had sufficient private means to allow him to visit the dominatrix as often as he wished? Is that still a problem for you?'

'Yes, it certainly is.'

'Because of the sexual implications?'

'Yes.'

'Are you aware that Miss O'Mahoney has not been charged with sexual assault in this case?'

'I'm not an expert on the law, so…'

'Very well. Are you aware that a dominatrix is someone who engages in role play with her client, but who does not engage in sexual activity with the client?'

'I'm not personally familiar with the work of the dominatrix,' the witness replies, 'so I have no basis for answering your question.'

'You should try it sometime, darling,' I'm almost sure I hear in a stage whisper from the dock.

'Did you say something, Miss O'Mahoney?' I ask as sternly as I can manage.

'No, your Honour,' she replies with an air of injured innocence.

The jury chuckle, and you can feel their imaginations clicking into high gear as they picture the archdeacon getting together with Madam Rosita.

'But you are familiar with the evidence in this case, Archdeacon, aren't you, and you are aware that there is no evidence of sexual contact of any kind between Miss O'Mahoney and Mr Canning?'

'That appears to have been the case on the occasion in question,' the archdeacon concedes. He thinks he's being clever with the implication that it might have been different on other occasions, but Aubrey and Cathy between them are going to dismantle that implication as the trial goes on. Just in case, Madam Rosita lends a hand.

'That's always how it is,' she protests. 'No sex – that's the rule.'

'That will do, Miss O'Mahoney,' I admonish her.

'Well, I'm sorry, Judge, but he shouldn't be saying these things.'

Cathy has turned around and is doing her best to signal to her to be quiet.

'That will *do,* Miss O'Mahoney,' I repeat. 'No more.'

'Thank you, Archdeacon,' Aubrey says. 'I have no further questions, your Honour.'

It's a good place to stop. There remains, of course, the use of church funds, but Aubrey himself prevented the archdeacon from commenting on the honesty and dishonesty of that when Roderick asked him to, and he is very wise to leave it alone now. Only Mr Canning can explain to the jury how that expenditure could have been honest, and he's not going to get any help from the archdeacon.

The remainder of the afternoon is devoted to the evidence of a Mr Dwyer, one of the auditors for St Mortimer's, who is clearly rather embarrassed – as he should be – that monies totalling more than seven thousand pounds disappeared from the church's accounts in the direction of Madam Rosita on his watch, over the course of two years or so; even if the withdrawals were withdrawals Mr Canning was authorised to make. Questions, it seems, were not asked if the vicar was the one spending the money. Nonetheless, Mr Dwyer is at pains to emphasise that he would not have approved of this use of church funds, and would have questioned the vicar on the subject if he had been aware of it. As he takes us through the church's various accounts, Roderick helpfully marries up the dates of the regular withdrawals of one hundred or one hundred and fifty pounds, and sometimes more, with entries in Madam Rosita's professional diary recording appointments with 'Rev Josh C'. The picture is compelling. There is no time for cross-examination this afternoon, and we gratefully adjourn until tomorrow.

***

Monday evening

The police car, driven by an amiable uniformed sergeant called Stevens, drops me off at the vicarage. It's a relief to be home, but as I insert my key into the lock I have a momentary feeling of panic, imagining that I am about to activate some deafening alarm that will bring a carful of officers carrying sub-machine guns to the door. I remind myself that the panic alarms have to be triggered from within the house. To make sure the Reverend Mrs Walden is not tempted to trigger one, I call out loudly as soon as I've opened the door.

'Clara, it's me. I'm home.'

'In the kitchen,' she calls back.

Relieved by the continuing silence, I walk into the kitchen. She is wearing an apron and is holding a knife, with which she has been cutting up vegetables for dinner, but she walks over to me and we exchange a long hug.

'Are you all right?' she asks.

'Yes, right as rain,' I exaggerate slightly. 'They brought me home in a police car driven by a very nice sergeant, and they'll take me in to court in the police car in the mornings until it's sorted out. How are you?'

'I'm all right now,' she replies. She walks back to her work space and pours me a glass of Chianti from the bottle she has open in front of her. 'It was a bit scary this morning when the police suddenly turned up and announced that they were installing panic alarms. I tried to reach you, but you were in court. But they were very professional, and they said it was nothing to worry about. So I made myself calm down.'

We clink glasses in a toast to our joint well-being.

'Do they have any idea who's behind this?' she asks.

'Not really, but there are one or two clues. Whoever wrote the letter has forgotten whatever they taught him in school about punctuation, but at least he's literate.'

'Oh?'

'Well, he's familiar with the verb "to arrogate", which isn't one you come across every day.'

She gives me a look.

'Oh, well, that's a relief. I'm sure we'll feel better if we can talk literature with him when he breaks into the house wielding a large knife.'

'I'm joking,' I assure her. 'Look, there are these shadowy groups of people calling themselves Free English Men. Some of them have form, so they may have a particular grudge against judges, but they seem to have some grudge or other against everyone, from the Pope downwards. Apparently they write letters like this all the time, but they don't usually make threats, and the police say they've never been involved in serious violence. In any case, the threat in the letter seems to refer to a number of judges: I'm not the only one.'

'That's not going to be much consolation if something happens to you,' she observes.

'I'm sure everything will be all right,' I reply as reassuringly as I can. 'What's the word from St Mortimer's?'

'It's beginning to calm down. Several parishioners have asked to see me, and I've arranged to meet them during the week, but the church council has been working hard and they're asking everyone to be patient. They know that nothing will be decided until the trial is over. How is it going?'

I pour more wine for both of us.

'Quite quickly. Apparently, there's no dispute that Canning was injured during a session with Madam Rosita, so the first question is going to be whether what he was doing was a legitimate penance, or just something for his own enjoyment. But, of course, even if it was a penance, there's also the question of how he persuaded himself that it was proper to pay Madam Rosita out of church funds.'

'There are all kinds of rumours flying around about that,' the Reverend says. 'How much is involved?'

'The auditor says, a bit north of seven thousand pounds over a two-year period.'

She takes a deep breath and exhales forcefully.

'Not only that,' I add. 'He never told anyone what he was doing, and he covered his tracks by withdrawing money from three separate accounts. Apparently St Mortimer's has a lot of money coming in and going out, and the auditors missed it.'

'Or *say* they missed it,' she suggests quietly.

'You don't buy it?'

'I'm not sure I do, Charlie. The only reason a vicar has access to an account is to deal with routine church expenditure. All right, St Mortimer's is much better endowed than St Aethelburgh, so yes, perhaps the accounts are more complicated, but I can't see my parochial church council overlooking such a long series of withdrawals by the vicar. And even if they didn't spot it, the auditors certainly would.'

I retire to a comfortable armchair to contemplate that answer. Later, after a delicious vegetarian lasagne and several glasses of Chianti we have both relaxed a little; no literate person has tried to break into the house, with or without a huge knife, and the cares of the day have receded to some extent.

'So tell me,' I say, 'have you ever been tempted to do penance like Mr Canning?'

'Flagellation?' she laughs. '*Moi*? No, never.'

'You never had a flirtation with anything like that?'

She thinks for a while.

'Not with flagellation,' she replies. 'But now that I think about it, I suppose I was seduced into a penance once. It was before we met. I'd just graduated and I was thinking of theological college, but I wasn't a hundred per cent sure it was what I wanted, and a group of us who were all contemplating our futures decided to make a pilgrimage to Glastonbury in the hope of receiving some guidance.'

'A pilgrimage on foot?'

'Yes. We started out at Wells Cathedral, where one of my friends worked with the choir, so it wasn't a huge distance, and we had plenty of time. But I was told it was a tradition that pilgrims should walk the last mile – or the last two miles, if you were really serious – barefoot. Of course I didn't want to look like a wimp, so when the time came I abandoned my shoes and socks and did the whole two miles in my bare feet, like everybody else.'

'Ouch,' I said. 'Did that experience make you feel any closer to God?'

'Quite the opposite, Charlie. It put me right off Him for several days. Eventually my feet started to recover, but until then I felt distinctly irritated with Him. But I did go to theological college, so I must have forgiven Him at some point. Since then, I've never felt the urge to repeat the experience; and trust me, flagellation is right out of the question.'

* * *

Tuesday morning

I've talked Sergeant Stevens into stopping along the way so that I can grab a latte and a sandwich from Jeanie and Elsie, and my copy of the *Times* from George. Free English Men or not, life has to go on, and I've shamelessly bribed the sergeant with the offer of a latte for himself.

'That's a shocking case you've got, sir, isn't it?' Elsie says as she puts the finishing touches to my ham and cheese bap. 'I was reading all about it in the *Standard*. You don't expect that with vicars, do you?'

'I don't know about that,' Jeanie replies, putting the lids on our lattes. 'I always thought our vicar, growing up, was a bit strange.'

'Strange in what way?' Sergeant Stevens asks.

'Well,' she replies confidentially, 'whenever you walked past the vicarage you could see him through the window, and he wasn't wearing many clothes, if any at all. It was difficult to tell, but he wasn't wearing much, I can tell you that.'

'But hopefully he wasn't being whipped,' the sergeant suggests cheerfully.

'Who knows?' Jeanie replies. 'But I'll tell you this for nothing: Hattie Buscombe was there with him most of the time. The story was that she was his housekeeper, but he wouldn't be parading round without his clothes in front of his housekeeper, would he? So I reckon there was something going on. Even if she wasn't whipping him, she was up to something.'

'There's all sorts of stories about priests, isn't there?' Elsie joins in. 'That's why we've got to have that big public inquiry that keeps stopping and starting, with all those judges who keep leaving, isn't it? But if you ask me, they're all at it. I don't know why we need a public inquiry to tell us that.'

George offers me the *Sun* and the *Mirror*, both of which seem to have reported every moment of the trial, but this morning I can't bring myself to worry about the field day the tabloids are having with the salacious goings on at St Mortimer's. If the Grey Smoothies are worried about anything the papers have reported, they are welcome to deal with it. I've got more than enough to keep me occupied.

Cathy has one question for Mr Dwyer, which has to do with the fact that Canning always paid Madam Rosita in cash, the implication being that she had no reason to know where the funding for her services came from. Aubrey is also very brief.

He seems content to establish that every withdrawal Canning made was within his authority as the vicar, and that the vicar had an absolute discretion about how his withdrawals up to five hundred pounds should be spent. He stays well away from the question of how the auditors missed this pattern of activity for such a long time. I suppose it couldn't do his case any good to turn over that particular rock, but I find myself wishing that someone would.

Roderick calls the officer in the case, DI Fraser, who takes us through the investigation, and the interviews of both defendants under caution at the police station. Unusually, both defendants were forthcoming, answering all the questions put to them, and giving a clear, if not always convincing, explanation of events. The Reverend Mr Canning told them all about his desire to do penance and about his sincere conviction that it was quite proper for him to use church funds to pay for services that would so obviously enhance his ministry to the benefit of his entire congregation. Madam Rosita told them that she is a professional dominatrix, and acted as such towards Mr Canning. She tied him to the St Andrew's cross and whipped him with his full consent, and indeed at his request, as she had on the many other occasions on which he had visited her for professional purposes. She emphasised that no sexual activity ever took place on her premises. It would be professional suicide, she said, if there were any suggestion that she was running a brothel – something she had never done and had no inclination to do.

Shortly after that, the jury having been told that both defendants are persons of previous good character, Roderick closes the prosecution case. Cathy asks for the jury to retire so that she can mention a matter of law, and I send them away for a coffee break. I've been expecting this, and I have a shrewd idea that it's going to involve me in one of those situations all trial judges dread – having to emerge from the jurisprudential shadows into the sights of the predatory snipers who lurk in the Court of Appeal.

'In law, Miss O'Mahoney has no case to answer,' Cathy begins. 'Your Honour can't possibly leave her case to the jury.'

'The consent question,' I observe.

'Yes. As your Honour knows, any case of assault requires proof that the victim didn't consent to what the defendant did. In this case, everyone agrees that there was consent. The prosecution accepts that Mr Canning consented to being whipped, as does Mr Canning himself. Mr Canning is an adult, and he is free to consent or withhold his consent as he chooses.'

'I'm not sure he consented to the broken wrist,' I suggest tentatively for the sake of completeness, even though I know Cathy is poised to shoot that argument down almost before it becomes airborne.

'Miss O'Mahoney didn't cause the injury to his wrist, at least not intentionally,' she points out immediately. 'That injury was caused when his right hand became trapped under the cross, as Miss Morgan told us. No one suggests that the cross falling down was anything other than an unfortunate accident.'

She resumes her seat and Roderick rises to his feet.

'Your Honour, my learned friend overlooks the decision of the House of Lords in the case of *Brown*. In that case the House clearly held that consent does not provide a defence to the infliction of harm at or above the level of actual bodily harm – in other words, where there's any physical injury. The effects of the whipping clearly amounted to actual bodily harm. My learned friend must be submissive to decisions of the House of Lords. It was, after all, our highest court before we invented the Supreme Court.'

'Your Honour,' Cathy retorts at once, '*Brown* was decided in

1994. Since then, the Court of Appeal has suggested repeatedly that we no longer need to be in bondage to *Brown*. In *Wilson*, for example, in 1996, where a husband branded his wife's initials on her buttocks at her request, the Court held that no assault was involved because there was no hostile intent. The husband was simply assisting the wife in an act she wished to have performed, presumably for her own pleasure and satisfaction, even though it obviously involved some pain and even though the branding would have amounted to actual bodily harm.'

There is a silence for some seconds as everyone in court either tries, or tries not, to imagine the scene. It is certainly a vivid example.

'But even if the Court of Appeal did take that view, Miss Writtle,' I reply, 'surely my hands are tied if I'm dealing with a decision of the House of Lords?'

'Your Honour, even decisions of the House of Lords can be overtaken by social change,' Cathy replies. 'So I submit that your Honour is free to throw off his restraints. Even in 1994 *Brown* was a majority decision – two members of the House dissented. We've moved on from that kind of outdated Victorian attitude: that Society can't condone consensual sado-masochism because it's all too awful to contemplate. Today, adult men and women are free to do whatever they find pleasurable, as long as it's consensual – even if it involves a certain amount of pain.'

'I'm not at all sure that we've moved on as far as my learned friend seems to think,' Roderick says with a smile. 'I'm not sure we give people *carte blanche* to inflict *any* kind of injury on each other, however serious, even in this day and age.'

'I didn't say that,' Cathy insists. 'But even in *Brown*, Lord Mustill, one of the dissenters, said that the case should have been dealt with as a case about consensual sexual activity, not a case of assault – and in *Brown* the injuries were horrific, far more serious than in this case.'

'That's a question of degree,' Roderick points out. 'Where would my learned friend draw the line?'

'I would draw it where the dissenting Lords in *Brown* said it should be drawn,' Cathy replies at once, 'at the level of GBH, really serious bodily harm.'

'Well, that's the same as the length of a piece of string, isn't it?' Roderick retorts. 'If that's the test, no one would ever know where they stand. It's rather tortured reasoning.'

'It's nothing of the kind,' Cathy protests. 'It's about protecting conduct many people indulge in for pleasure. Assault must involve hostile intent. There's no hostile intent where two people engage in role play – which is essentially what a dominatrix and her client do. There was certainly no hostile intent in this case.'

Roderick doesn't reply at once, so Cathy takes the opportunity to press harder.

'I would ask your Honour to consider the consequences of the view my learned friend is urging on the court. If he's right, the profession of dominatrix is doomed. Everything Miss O'Mahoney does would suddenly become illegal.'

'Perhaps it would,' Roderick concedes with another smile. 'But not suddenly, surely – we've all known about *Brown* since 1994. If Parliament thinks the law is out of date, then it's up to Parliament to change it. So far, they've shown no inclination to do so.'

'It's the thin end of the wedge,' Cathy persists. 'Think of the other things you would have to ban using the same logic – boxing's gone, for a start, and perhaps wrestling, and some martial arts, and some contact sports. And what about a couple who like to play this kind of game in the privacy of their own bedroom? Would my learned friend want to send the storm troopers into their bedroom to catch them at it and haul them in front of the court?'

Roderick isn't going to be drawn on that one.

'All right,' I say, 'I've got the point.'

There's no way I'm going to rule on this off the cuff – not when I'm being invited to ignore a decision of the House of Lords, even if it is a majority decision from 1994. I announce that I'm adjourning until two o'clock to consider the matter.

I find Stella waiting for me in chambers.

'Does the name Elias Shakespeare mean anything to you?' she asks.

'Stella, is this a trick question?'

'No, Judge. DI Derbyshire called this morning and asked me to check it. His name came up on a list of possible members of the Order of the Original what's-its. The information goes back several years, but guess what?'

'We've had Elias Shakespeare here?' I speculate.

'Yes, Judge. It was about four years ago. He was charged with supplying class A drugs, cocaine mostly. He came in front of Judge Dunblane; he was convicted, and Judge Dunblane sent him down for three and a half years.'

'So he's out by now?'

'Yes, Judge, he's been out for some time.'

'I'm sure I would have remembered the name if I'd dealt with him,' I reply. 'But this is outrageous. Judge Dunblane sentences him, but I'm the one receiving death threats? How is that fair?'

Stella nods. 'I know, Judge, but at least we're making some progress. DI Derbyshire has officers out looking for him. He seems to have gone to ground in the last few months, but she thinks they'll track him down before long.'

'Elias Shakespeare?' I muse, as much to myself as to Stella. 'Well, I suppose he does sound like the literate type, doesn't he?'

'Judge?'

'Oh, nothing,' I reply, pulling myself together. 'Thanks, Stella. I'll go and tell Judge Dunblane how lucky he is.'

And so to lunch, an oasis of calm in a desert of chaos.

Legless is annoyingly amused by his lucky escape from the clutches of Elias Shakespeare, and shows not the slightest sympathy for me as the vicarious recipient of a threat that should have been going in his direction – which I think is a bit much. But taking the high ground, as one has to as part of the price of high command, I decide not to berate him, and instead ask whether anyone has had any cause for concern.

'No, I'm pleased to report that I spent a peaceful and undisturbed night,' Legless replies cheerily. I ignore him.

'Simon and Samantha enjoyed it enormously,' Marjorie says, 'having a police officer come to school just to make sure they were all right. It made them both feel like celebrities, terribly important. I hope it doesn't go on for too long, though. I don't want them getting too many ideas above their station. Nigel offered to come home early from Brussels, but I told him there was no need.'

'The security of the Garrick Club remains intact,' Hubert says, 'thanks to the vigilance of the members, principally myself, and the staff.'

'I'm particularly relieved to hear that, Hubert,' I say.

Once I've got that responsibility out of the way, I tell them all about Cathy Writtle's submission of no case to answer, and her invitation to me to ignore a decision of the House of Lords.

'If ever there was a case where the Court of Appeal is likely to drop me on my head from a great height,' I complain, 'this is it. And I daren't even imagine what will happen if it goes up to the Supreme Court. I'm sure I'll be gathering up what remains of my pension and sitting for my memorial portrait in the very near future.'

Marjorie shakes her head. 'I don't think so, Charlie. I think Cathy's right. We have moved on since 1994, and if you have a decision of the Court of Appeal to hide behind, they may disagree with you, but they can't be too hard on you.'

'Never underestimate the Court of Appeal,' I reply.

'I don't. But there's been a lot of academic criticism of *Brown* too, much of which was mentioned in the Court of Appeal decisions since 1994. I think you're on solid ground. Actually, I think they would applaud you. *Brown* has to go eventually, but there's no sign of Parliament stepping in; so it has to start somewhere and somewhere means with a judge in the Crown Court. This is your big chance to write your name into the books.'

'If you're allowed to brand your wife's initials on her buttocks,' Legless says, 'how can they object to a little whipping?'

'The senior judiciary can object to almost anything if they put their minds to it,' I reply.

'Charlie,' Legless retorts, 'I guarantee you that there are members of the senior judiciary who enjoy being tied up and having things done to them, either by their wives or by someone like Madam Rosita. And this is a perfect case for them to stand up without being counted. They're not going to give you a hard time. They will probably agree with you.'

'I'm not convinced,' I reply.

Hubert looks up from the vegetarian chili, the dish of the day.

'Are you familiar with the wanker test, Charlie?' he asks.

'The wanker test?'

'Yes. It's by far the best test for deciding whether or not to take the risk of being appealed.'

I glance at Legless and Marjorie, both of whom seem as mystified as I am.

'I must have missed that lecture when I was a law student,' I reply.

'It's a test based on common sense,' Hubert explains, 'far more effective than looking at it from the point of view of the law. If you look at it as a legal problem, you can make a case for almost any argument, and then it's difficult to decide; and when it's difficult to decide, that's when you're most likely to end up in the Court of Appeal's bad books.'

'So, how does this test work, Hubert?' Marjorie asks.

'Simple,' Hubert replies. 'You imagine members of your club reading the *Times* in the lounge over a drink before dinner, and you imagine that the *Times* has given them a fair report of your decision and the decision of the Court of Appeal. And then you ask yourself: are my friends going to say, "How could Hubert have made a decision like that? What a wanker!" or are they going to say, "How could the Court of Appeal have reversed Hubert like that? What a bunch of wankers!" And according to how you answer that question, you decide what to do. It's got nothing to do with the law. The question is: who's going to come out of this looking like a wanker – you or the Court of Appeal?'

* * *

Tuesday afternoon

After due reflection, I conclude that Hubert makes a good point, even if couched in unorthodox legal language. If the judges of the Court of Appeal rule that no one can safely go to a dominatrix, or even ask his partner to tie him up and spank him at home, without incurring the risk of a criminal prosecution, surely in any reasonable universe they are the ones who are going to look like wankers. I'm going to come out of it as the voice of progressive social change, and I calculate that there's only a limited chance that I'm making a rod for my own back, so to speak. Accordingly, when I return to court I rule in favour of Cathy's submission of no case to answer, though of course, I base my reasoning on the legal arguments she has presented, rather than trying to articulate the wanker test.

I hope I'm right, because if not, my discomfiture will not be long delayed. Roderick is entitled to appeal against my decision, and to have the trial delayed for a day or two while he asks the Court of Appeal to reverse it. If he succeeds, we will continue with the trial with Madam Rosita still in the dock. If not, we will continue with Mr Canning alone. But from his demeanour, I sense that Roderick may be just as familiar with the wanker test as Hubert. After only a few seconds of apparent reflection, he announces that the prosecution will not appeal. The apparent reflection was for my benefit, I feel sure. This wasn't an off-the-cuff decision. Roderick has been doing this too long to leave a decision like this until the last minute. He would have run this scenario past someone at a high level in the CPS some time ago, and a decision not to appeal would have been taken before the trial even started. Apparently neither Roderick nor the Director of Public Prosecutions has any appetite for defending *Brown* in the Court of Appeal and looking in consequence like a wanker.

There is a flurry of activity in the press seats, and there can be no doubt that this will be a major headline this evening and tomorrow. So if I am going to be seen as a wanker, it starts now. But I feel some confidence that Hubert has given me sound advice. We bring the jury down. I explain the situation and direct them to return a verdict of not guilty in Madam Rosita's case, which they duly do. I have the distinct impression that the outcome is not unexpected. I direct that Madam Rosita should be discharged. Touchingly, she kisses Mr Canning on the cheek before leaving the dock. Far from rushing from court to celebrate her new-found freedom, I note, she takes a seat in the public gallery with a certain flourish and a glance in the direction of the press. I daresay she's interested in the Reverend Mr Canning's case as well as her own, but I suspect she may be even more interested in the possibility of some publicity for her professional activities. I see one or two reporters passing her surreptitious notes, which suggests that there may be interviews in her future. Cathy bows towards the bench with a happy smile, and leaves court, no doubt to prepare for her next case.

Aubrey announces that he will call the Reverend Mr Canning to give evidence.

Throughout the trial he has been wearing a grey jacket and slacks with a black shirt and clerical collar. In the circumstances, the clerical collar is a bold move, one which not every defendant in his position would make. No doubt Aubrey has encouraged him to act as though the trial is no more than an inconvenient temporary disruption, and that he stands ready to resume his ministry as soon as the jury are sensible enough to return a verdict of not guilty. But even so, it must take a certain amount of nerve with the country's press looking on.

'I swear by Almighty God that the evidence I shall give shall be the truth, the whole truth and nothing but the truth.'

'Is your full name Joshua Foster Canning?' Aubrey asks.

'It is.'

'How old are you?'

'I'm forty-four.'

'For how long have you been a Church of England minister?'

'For just over eighteen years.'

'Mr Canning, it may be that the jury are not familiar with the process of becoming a vicar. Please tell them briefly what it involves.'

'Well, first, you have to be recommended by your bishop as a suitable person for the ministry. So you have to be well regarded in your home church, and –'

'Yes, I'm sorry to interrupt you, Mr Canning, but while we're on that subject, does any part of that process involve an inquiry into your character?'

'Very much so, yes. They will check for any previous

convictions, they will question your teachers, friends, family; they're quite serious about it, believe me.'

'And did your bishop recommend you for the ministry after an inquiry of that kind had been carried out?'

'Yes, he did.'

'Mr Canning, have you ever been convicted of any criminal offence?'

'No, I have not.'

'Had you ever been arrested before this case?'

'No.'

'What preparation or training do you need after the bishop has recommended you?'

'Typically, you go to university, get a degree, and then go to theological college, though I don't think a degree is strictly necessary. Then, once you've completed your studies you can be ordained. There's some on-the-job training too. You start out as a curate, working under the vicar in one or two bigger parishes, before they give you your own living as a vicar.'

'And in your case, Mr Canning, did you eventually become vicar of St Mortimer-in-the-Fields in the diocese of Southwark?'

'Yes. I've been vicar of St Mortimer's for about six years now.'

'Are you exercising your ministry there currently?'

'No. Obviously, when I was charged with this offence the bishop suspended me pending the conclusion of the trial. It goes without saying that I fully expect to resume my ministry in the very near future.'

Judging from his first reaction, this was an answer Aubrey has discouraged Canning from giving. It's never a good idea for a defendant to show undue confidence in the outcome – with some juries it can be a source of real temptation to bring him swiftly back down to earth. But with some defendants, it's a temptation they just can't resist offering the jury, however much you try to discourage it. The rueful smile that crosses Aubrey's face suggests that this is one such case; but he recovers quickly.

'Well, in the light of that,' he continues, with the air of one who is following up on an answer he was expecting and welcomes, 'let me ask you this. You are charged with theft from your church in the amount of more than seven thousand pounds over a period of some two years. Mr Canning, are you guilty of stealing from your church? Have you ever acted dishonestly in relation to church funds?'

'Categorically not.'

'Then let me come to the subject of penance and flagellation in particular. For how long has that practice been part of your own private devotions?'

That, of course, is rather the like classic question, 'When did you stop beating your wife?' I wonder whether Roderick will object. If he does, it will be somewhat *pro forma*: Aubrey can easily correct the situation by asking whether flagellation has ever been part of his devotions, and then, for how long; so it's a pretty pointless objection. But as I look over to Roderick's side of the court, I see that objecting is the last thing on his mind. Something very interesting is taking place. DI Derbyshire has made her way quietly into court and is in muted conversation with the officer in the case, DI Fraser. This is happening in the row behind Roderick, but he has turned his head halfway round towards them, clearly hoping to overhear. Then, abruptly, he nods and DI Derbyshire leaves the courtroom with DI Fraser close behind her. It's now too late for Roderick to object, even if he had considered it.

'Ever since my first year of theological college,' Canning replies. 'At least, that's when I came to believe that it had great value in one's spiritual practice. But I can't say I have really practised it until the last two years.'

'Why is that?' Aubrey asks.

'I couldn't bring myself to inflict the pain on myself,' Canning replies quietly. 'I wanted to, and it seemed easy enough in theory, but every time I bought myself a whip of some kind and actually tried, I couldn't do it – at least not to the degree required.'

'What is the degree required?' Aubrey inquires.

'Well, ideally to the point where you draw blood,' Canning replies in an oddly matter-of-fact way, 'or at least to the point where you raise welts and you are going to feel it for several days. I couldn't get to that point.'

'Did it occur to you to ask someone to help you?'

'Not really. I have no idea who it would have been. It's all very well for the archdeacon to go on about people in monasteries, but he and I must move in different circles, because I don't know anyone in a monastery, or a convent, for that matter. And I wasn't going to approach anyone in my congregation, for exactly the reasons the archdeacon gave. It wouldn't have been appropriate, and the chances are it would have been all over the *Standard* within a week – your average Anglican congregation is a hotbed of gossip, and St Mortimer's is no exception.'

'But in due course, a little more than two years ago, did a solution suggest itself?'

'Yes. I'd been reading a novel in which one of the characters was going to a dominatrix. To be honest, I wasn't even sure such people really existed. But I did an internet search, and I found that not only did they exist, but there were any number of them in London. Madam Rosita had her... studio... in Toulmin Street, not too far from my church, so one day I plucked up my courage and went to introduce myself to her.'

'What was your reaction to Madam Rosita?'

'It was very positive. She explained that what she did was to engage in role play, and she was very clear that she didn't judge her clients at all – and that she didn't engage in any sexual activity with them.'

'Since you mention that, Mr Canning,' Aubrey asks, 'is penance in general, or flagellation in particular, a sexual issue for you? Do you derive any sexual pleasure from it at all?'

'From the thought of it, yes,' Canning replies, with what seems to me to be a remarkable degree of candour. 'I think anyone who seriously intends to be involved with penance on this level must experience some kind of sexual satisfaction. In my case, the sexual interest is only in the thinking: the anticipation can be very arousing. But the physical reality of being tied up and whipped isn't erotic at all. There may be those who experience it differently, but for me the pain itself doesn't provide me with any satisfaction.'

'Did you explain what you wanted to Madam Rosita?'

'Yes. I explained to her about penance, and that I was doing this to enrich my private devotions, and so make myself a more effective minister in my church.'

'What did she say to that?'

'To be honest, I don't think she cared whether I actually was a vicar looking to improve my ministry, or whether that was just a role I was acting out. She explained to me that all her clients had some fantasy or other: whether it was as a member of the French Resistance being tortured by the Gestapo; or as a warrior captured in battle in ancient Persia who had to become a personal slave to the sadistic victorious princess. I was just the same. She treated me just like any other client. Whether my story was real or not didn't matter to her.'

'That's right,' I hear from a female voice from the public gallery. 'It's my job to make it *feel* real.'

'Miss O'Mahoney,' I say, 'if you interrupt again, I will have you removed from court. Do you understand?' I can't stop her reaching out to the press for some publicity, but I'm determined that she's not going to get it from the court.

'Yes, your Honour,' she says, with a mischievous look in the direction of the jury. 'Sorry.'

The mischievous look is almost enough for me to throw her out without waiting for another outburst, but as I'm contemplating that possibility I am once again distracted by activity on the prosecution's side of the court. DI Fraser has entered court with a sense of urgency, and hands Roderick a file with a few muttered words. Roderick opens the file and appears to turn over a number of pages in quick succession before handing a document from his own file to DI Fraser, who once again disappears from court. There is no further sign of DI Derbyshire, and I can't help wondering what is going on.

'And taking it shortly,' Aubrey is saying, 'did you, as the evidence suggests, visit Madam Rosita on average every two weeks for almost two years, and on the occasion of those visits did she tie you naked to the St Andrew's cross and whip you to a degree satisfactory for the purposes of penance?'

'Yes, that's correct.'

'On the evening when the cross collapsed and you sustained a broken wrist, do you accept that the collapse of the cross was an accident?'

'Yes. Everything seemed the same as usual and I'd been tied to the cross for a good twenty minutes. Then suddenly, it collapsed to the floor and I was trapped under it. Madam Rosita acted quickly to undo my restraints and called the ambulance, but of course my wrist was broken by then and I had some cuts and bruises. But it was an accident.'

'Before that evening, had you ever needed medical treatment for injuries caused by the whipping?'

'No, not at all. Madam Rosita knows when to stop because she knows her clients.'

I sense another comment coming, but seeing me looking at her, the sensitive dominatrix contents herself with a brief nod of the head.

'Did she ever do anything to you other than whipping you when you were tied to the cross?'

'On one occasion she proposed tying me to a table, lying on my back and whipping the soles of my feet. I think she brought that up because my back was still sore from the previous occasion. I agreed to try it, but it was too much for me, and we had to stop.'

'All right, Mr Canning. Now, let me come to the question of money,' Aubrey says. 'I understand that Madam Rosita's charges were one hundred and fifty pounds for an hour, is that right?'

'Yes, I didn't always have a full hour – if it was getting too much for me before the hour was up we would stop – and in that case she had a minimum charge of one hundred pounds.'

'Could you have afforded that on your salary as a vicar?'

'No. I would have been able to go on an occasional basis, but not regularly, and I believed that I needed to go regularly.'

'In fact, what you did was to pay Madam Rosita from monies you withdrew from the St Mortimer's bank accounts. Is that right?'

'Yes. As priest-in-charge I was authorised to withdraw up to five hundred pounds at any time for any purpose, at my discretion.'

Aubrey thinks for a moment or two.

'Yes, but Mr Canning, was it not your understanding that the purpose should be a purpose related to the church? You wouldn't have been allowed to use it to swan off to Bermuda for a couple of weeks' holiday, would you?'

'No, of course not. But as far as I was concerned, this was a purpose closely related to the church.'

'In what way?'

'Because regular penance enhanced my private devotions, and thereby made me a better minister to my flock.'

'Did you intend to act dishonestly in any way?'

'No, certainly not. I honestly believed that I was perfectly entitled to do as I did, and I believe that to this day.'

'Yes. Wait there, please Mr Canning. You will be asked some further questions.'

But not, as it happens, this afternoon. Roderick is still in conversation with DI Fraser, and before he can get to his feet, Carol stands and turns towards me.

'Judge, there's been a security incident in court three,' she says quietly, 'and given the current situation, Judge Dunblane would like you to deal with it. He's waiting for you in your chambers.'

I explain that I have to rise to deal with another matter, and release everyone for half an hour. I have no idea whether half an hour will cover it, but it will give everyone time for a tea or coffee break. Roderick stands.

'Your Honour, in fact, I was going to ask whether I might cross-examine Mr Canning tomorrow morning? DI Fraser has brought certain matters to my attention which I would like to inquire into, and I wouldn't be ready to begin this afternoon, certainly not without keeping the jury unduly late.'

Aubrey is looking rather uneasy, though he can't really oppose Roderick's application. I certainly don't object. There's something going on involving DI Derbyshire, and I'm anxious to know what it is. My best chance is to give Roderick all the time he needs.

'Yes, very well, Mr Lofthouse,' I reply. I release everyone until tomorrow morning.

'It may be nothing at all, Charlie,' Legless begins. 'But better safe than sorry.' Bob and Stella are waiting for me with him.

'Absolutely,' I agree. 'What seems to be the problem?'

Bob takes the initiative. 'Judge Dunblane rose this afternoon for a break before dealing with a case in his list called Ian Caulfield,' he explains. 'During the break, a man we have identified as Caulfield's father entered the courtroom and started taking pictures of the dock on his mobile. He thought he was alone and unobserved, but fortunately Trevor, Judge Dunblane's dock officer, was just behind the door and he was watching through the small glass panel in the door. He called security and they detained Mr Caulfield. He's in the cells now, and Judge Dunblane was going to deal with him for contempt, but he thought perhaps you should handle it.'

'What's Ian Caulfield's case about?' I ask.

'Nothing serious,' Legless replies. 'He was about to plead guilty to two counts of non-residential burglary. The proceeds are only a couple of hundred quid, and his only form is one previous for common assault and one for simple possession of cannabis, both in the Magistrates' Court.'

'But the father's not charged with anything?'

'Not today: not unless we deal with him for contempt', Legless replies. 'As far as I know, his only reason for being at court today is to be with his son.'

'But the father does have some significant form,' Bob interjects. 'The officer in the case ran a check on him. A couple of assaults and several convictions for robbery, the two most recent being quite serious. The last time he got seven years at the Old Bailey for holding up a sub-post office with an imitation firearm – though admittedly, that was ten years ago now.'

'We have a strict rule against taking photographs in court,' Stella points out. 'All Crown Courts do, to my knowledge, and given the present situation, Bob and I agreed with Judge Dunblane that it is potentially serious, and that you should deal with it.'

'Bob and Stella think the letter you received may be a decoy,' Legless says.

'A decoy? What do you mean?'

'I'm the one who dealt with Elias Shakespeare, Charlie,' Legless explains. 'We both thought it was odd that the threat would be against you rather than me, didn't we? Perhaps it was to hide their real intentions. Perhaps they intend to do something in court three rather than court one.'

'Where is DI Derbyshire?' I ask. 'I saw her going in and out of court earlier in the afternoon.'

'She was here, Judge,' Stella confirms, 'but she had to go to the High Court.'

'All right,' I say after some thought. 'I will deal with it: in court one. But I want the court closed to the public, including any other members of the Caulfield family; I want security there; and I want my armed officer there.'

'No problem, Judge', Bob says. 'Give me ten minutes.'

I go into court under what look like siege conditions. Two security guards are standing by the public entrance, which has been locked. My armed officer – female, as it turns out, I realise now – is sitting in the back row of the public gallery, and we have the officer in Ian Caulfield's case, a PC Patterson, for good measure. The father, Ben Caulfield, is brought up from the cells, escorted by two burly prison officers. Emily Phipson, who is prosecuting in Ian's case, has been co-opted to assist the court with the proceedings involving his father. Carol asks Ben Caulfield to identify himself by name, which he does without any hesitation.

'Mr Caulfield,' I say. 'Do you know why you've been detained and brought before me? Do you understand that you are in danger of being held in contempt of court and either fined or imprisoned? Don't answer yet. Before you answer, I must advise you that you are entitled to seek advice from a solicitor at no charge to yourself, and if you wish to see a solicitor before answering any questions, I will adjourn for a while and ask the court staff to find one for you.'

'That won't be necessary, your Honour,' Caulfield replies politely. 'I can explain everything.'

'Well, we shall see,' I say. 'Sit down please, Mr Caulfield, and I will hear more about what's happened and decide whether I need to take further action. If I do decide to take further action, I will assign you a solicitor to offer advice. Whether or not you take that advice is up to you, but you should understand that you may be in serious trouble.'

'All I did was take a few pictures,' Caulfield protests, again quite politely.

'Mr Caulfield, I strongly advise you to say nothing further at this stage. Just listen to what is said. Miss Phipson, can you assist?'

'Yes, your Honour,' Emily replies. 'Mr Caulfield is at court today to support his son, who was due to appear before Judge Dunblane this afternoon. But he was observed taking photographs in court three, which of course is prohibited, and I should add that there are numerous signs in and around the courtrooms drawing attention to that fact. I have Mr Caulfield's phone, which was seized by security, and I've set it to play a series of twenty photographs and moving images. Perhaps your Honour would wish to look at them now?'

'Yes, I would,' I reply. Dawn collects the phone from Emily, and it makes its way up to the bench via Carol. The twenty pictures are quite disturbing. Most are of the dock, seen from various angles, and include the area between the dock and the public entrance to the court. Several others feature the bench, and two of these show the location of the judge's entrance leading into the judicial corridor: in other words, they provide everything someone interested in an escape from the courtroom after some violent episode would need for planning purposes.

'As your Honour will see,' Emily says after allowing me ample time to peruse them, 'these photographs do give rise to security concerns. They are exactly the kind of photographs that might be useful to someone planning an attack of some kind in court three. In my submission, your Honour has more than enough evidence either to hold Mr Caulfield in contempt of court, or – preferably, I would submit – to place the matter in the hands of the police to allow a proper investigation of the incident to be made. I understand that PC Patterson is prepared to refer the case to a CID officer at his station.'

PC Patterson confirms that such is the case, and I find myself agreeing with Emily that it is the best option. There's no point in holding Caulfield in contempt if he is part of a wider plot, possibly including the Order of Original and Retrograde English Men. We need to find out what's going on, and that's a matter for the police.

'Gordon Bennett!' I hear, *sotto voce*, from the dock.

'Do you wish to say something, Mr Caulfield?' I ask. 'Bear in mind what I've said: you would be well advised to say nothing until you have seen a solicitor.'

Caulfield stands. 'Judge, this has got nothing to do with any security matters, or what have you. Look, I learned my lesson when I got sent down at the Old Bailey ten years ago. I don't have any truck with any kind of violence now, and I've raised my boy the same way. I'm not involved in any threat to the security of the court. On my mother's grave…'

'Mr Caulfield…'

'Judge, please. I'd like to show you something.' He reaches down for his black rucksack, which is lying by his side on the floor of the dock. One of the prison officers grabs it before Caulfield can. 'If the officer would assist,' Caulfield continues, apparently oblivious to any concerns we might have about the possible contents of the rucksack, 'he will find an album of photographs inside. I'd like you to look at it, Judge, if you wouldn't mind.'

I hesitate. It sounds a bit odd, but I can't really deny Caulfield the chance to explain himself. I've offered him a solicitor, but if he wants to tell me what's going on without the benefit of legal advice, he's fully entitled to.

'Yes, very well. If you would, Officer, please.'

The officer rummages around in the rucksack for some seconds and extracts a rather nice-looking silver-coloured album. I see, even from a distance, that it has the name Ian in large capital letters in black ink on the front cover. When Carol hands it to me and I inspect it up close, I see that the full legend is: 'Ian: Youth Court, Magistrates' Court'. The album is full of prohibited photographs showing the insides of courtrooms, described in handwritten captions as those of a Youth Court and a Magistrates' Court. They are intermingled with shots of a young man I take to be Ian, standing with his father outside the court. I surmise that the Youth Court photographs refer to some juvenile transgressions that involved referral orders, and which have since been expunged from his record. The Magistrates' Court shots would refer to the common assault and the possession of cannabis.

'It's like a family album, you see, Judge,' Caulfield explains. 'It goes all the way back to when he was just starting out in the Youth Court. My old lady and I wanted to make sure we had something for him to remember it all by later. She's the one who arranges the pictures and does the captions, because you'd never be able to read my handwriting. Then he moved up to the Magistrates' Court, and… and today… well, today, Judge, it's his first time in the Crown Court, and you only get one first time, don't you? So it's a special day for him, and my old lady is waiting at home with a new album for these pictures I took today.'

A silence descends on court one.

'So, this is a pictorial celebration of Ian's first time in the Crown Court? Is that what you're saying?'

'It was going to be,' Caulfield replies. 'I understand now that it was the wrong thing to do, and I suppose you'll delete them all. But honestly, Judge, it was just a matter of family pride, you know, the boy following in his old man's footsteps. I apologise if I've caused any inconvenience. As I say, you can ask Ian. He'll tell you: that's all it was.'

I close my eyes for a few seconds.

'Mr Caulfield,' I say, 'I don't find it necessary to take any action, except to find you in contempt of court and to fine you two hundred pounds, payable within seven days. If you wish to have a hearing and contest that decision, you may, and you may be legally represented; I will assign you a solicitor; or you can accept my decision and that will be the end of it.'

'I accept the decision, Judge,' he replies immediately. 'I suppose it's no more than I deserve for being so stupid.'

I exchange glances with Emily, who is smiling and shaking her head.

'Miss Phipson,' I say, 'please arrange for an officer to delete all these photographs and check to make sure they haven't been uploaded or emailed to anyone. If there's no problem, Mr Caulfield may have his phone back.'

'Yes, your Honour.'

'And I'm sorry to interfere with your family memories, Mr Caulfield, but I'm ordering the forfeiture and destruction of the album you've produced, on the ground that it contains a large number of unlawful photographs likely to prove useful to anyone planning an attack on the courts depicted.'

I see him nod sadly. 'Yes, Judge.'

'Carol, please tell Judge Dunblane that he's now free to proceed with the case of Ian Caulfield.'

'Right you are, Judge,' Carol smiles.

* * *

Tuesday evening
It's only the second night of our curfew, but the Reverend Mrs Walden and I are already feeling as though we're under house arrest. We're feeling the need to escape for a couple of hours. At her instigation, we creep surreptitiously out of the house at about eight o'clock, and she drives us to the Delights of the Raj for our regular samosas, chicken Madras, chapattis and a couple of Cobras.

'We're being followed,' she observes as we approach the first set of traffic lights after pulling out into the main road.

'Hostile?' I ask

'Negative, Captain,' she replies. 'That's the car that was sitting outside the house after Sergeant Stevens left. Do you want me to lose them?'

We both laugh. 'Negative,' I reply. 'But let's keep them in our sights.'

'Roger that, Captain.'

We ask our host, Rajiv, to find us a quiet corner table away from the throng, which he is good enough to do. After about five minutes, the two plain clothes officers enter the restaurant and take seats near the door. Once we've ordered, I send Rajiv to their table with two Cobras, with our compliments and my assurance that nothing will be said about drinking on duty, which they acknowledge with raised glasses.

'What did Joshua have to say for himself?' the Reverend asks.

I relate to her the sad tale of the man who would love to do penance, but can't quite bring himself to do it without help, and who enters the world of the dominatrix as a solution to this profound spiritual problem. 'He thought it was a legitimate expenditure of church funds,' I add in conclusion. 'The expenditure was for the improvement of his ministry.'

'Surely the jury aren't going to buy that,' she asks, 'are they?'

'I wouldn't have thought so, though they obviously thought I was right to let the dominatrix, Madam Rosita, out at half time. And Aubrey Brooks did well with his evidence; so you never know.'

She shakes her head. 'Well, at least that means I won't have to run two churches at the same time for long.'

'Oh?'

'Even if he's acquitted, the bishop will want to move him on, probably to another diocese. Joshua may have had what he thought were good reasons for going to see Madam Rosita, but the church isn't going to see it that way. He'll disappear for a while, and then surface again in Gloucester or Durham or somewhere after a suitable interval. That's what we do in cases of serious misconduct.' She pauses. 'Of course, on the other hand, if he's convicted he'll be defrocked. Will he go to prison as well?'

'He might have to,' I reply. 'It's a serious beach of trust, and a substantial amount of money.'

We tuck into the chicken Madras in silence for some time.

'He also said that the thought of the penance gave him a kind of sexual thrill,' I say, 'but not the reality of actually doing the penance. Apparently, the anticipation turned him on, but the whipping was just pain and nothing more.'

'My experience exactly,' the Reverend says, 'when I was walking to Glastonbury.'

'Really?' I reply.

'Yes. The walking was pure pain, but I was having multiple orgasms while I was taking off my shoes and socks.'

'But surely...' I begin. But I see the grin behind her hand and what remains of a chapatti.

I nod. 'Right.'

* * *

Wednesday morning
'They're calling him the "whipper-vicar" in the papers today,' Elsie giggles as she puts the finishing touches to our lattes. 'The *Sun* has a picture of him all dressed up in his, what d'you call them, his robes and that.'

'They always come up with a good line in the *Sun*, don't they?' I reply.

'Surely, he can't have much of a defence now, can he, sir?' Jeanie asks. 'Not now he's admitted it was all about sex? Not that we didn't know that all along, but still…'

'Mr Canning is actually charged with theft,' I point out. 'The case is about the money he took from church funds to pay for what he was doing.'

'But it's the sex the papers are interested in, isn't it, sir?' Elsie insists. 'It always is.'

'Well, I should think so,' Jeanie replies. 'Would you want your children going to church with a man like that in charge? Personally, I wouldn't care whether he was taking money from the church or whether he'd won the lottery. It's the children that would bother me.'

George is interested in why Sergeant Stevens is accompanying me on my morning journeys to court.

'If it's top secret, Sergeant,' he says confidentially, 'the secret's safe with me. My old man was in intelligence during the war, wasn't he? He knew all about keeping secrets, and he passed it on to me. And you have to have a certain discretion in my line of work, don't you, guv, with some of the clients I have?'

'It's nothing to worry about, George,' I assure him, paying for my copy of the *Times*, plus the *Sun* and one or two other titles. By now I'm intrigued to see what exactly they're reporting – even if the Grey Smoothies are following it, I'm ready to take a look myself. 'It's just a precaution for a few days.'

'Quite right, guv,' he replies. 'With all this crime and

terrorism going on, you can't be too careful, can you?'

Sergeant Stevens leans in towards George quietly. 'It's the whipper-vicar mafia we're worried about, sir. You never know with them; they're totally ruthless.'

'I never knew there was such a thing,' George says, aghast.

'No, well not many people do,' the sergeant replies. 'Mind how you go, sir, won't you?'

We walk back to the car with George staring after us.

I arrive at court to find Stella and Carol waiting for me.

'Counsel have asked to see you in chambers, Judge,' Stella says. 'They say it's a matter of, and I quote, great sensitivity. I've asked Carol to make a record with the hand-held.'

'Yes, all right,' I reply. 'They didn't happen to say what they want to talk about, did they?'

Stella shakes her head. 'They were very tight-lipped about it, Judge. Oh, but they did say they'd asked DI Derbyshire to come with them.'

Roderick and Aubrey are shown in five minutes later, DI Derbyshire bringing up the rear. Carol starts the hand-held, puts the name of the case, the date and time, and the names of those attending, on tape and hands over to Roderick.

'Judge,' he begins, 'Aubrey and I thought we ought to see you in chambers before the trial proceeds any further. In fairness, I've only been able to put Aubrey in the picture this morning, but he is up to date now. I'm going to ask DI Derbyshire to start things off. Of course, she's had nothing to do with this case until now, but for reasons which will become clear, she is very much involved now.'

He turns to the DI.

'When we last talked, Judge,' she begins, 'we were looking for Elias Shakespeare, and we were keeping a number of judges at different courts under our protection. Our inquiries at the other courts didn't produce any new names. There were two other individuals associated with the Original and Retrograde English Men who were dealt with at two of the other courts under threat; but they're both still inside doing time for serious firearms offences, so the only live name we have is Elias Shakespeare. He's been making himself scarce for some time, but yesterday morning we got lucky. We'd obtained a search warrant to turn over his house in North Kensington, and he was at home when my officers arrived. We had the house under surveillance, and how he got in without my officers noticing, God only knows. But anyway, he was nicked. The officers duly searched the house, and there was some paperwork in lever-arch files in the bedroom. Among the papers the officers found evidence of payments made to Shakespeare from a bank account belonging to the church of St Mortimer-in-the-Fields.'

There is silence for some time.

'What evidence?' I ask.

'Stamped paying-in slips, suggesting that these payments were made by cheque.'

'DI Derbyshire spoke to the officer in our case, DI Fraser,' Roderick says. 'DI Fraser has all the bank records at court, and he was able to match the payments to three cheques signed by Mr Canning, totalling just over five hundred pounds in all.'

'Was there any evidence of what these payments were for?'

'Not that we've found yet,' DI Derbyshire replies, 'although there's quite a lot of paperwork, and the officers are still going through it. Shakespeare was already at the nick by then, being interviewed, and when this information came to light he was asked to explain the payments. He told the interviewing officers that Canning is a member of the Original and Retrogrades, but he wouldn't say what the payments were for, except that they related to what he called "expenses of the Order".'

'I see,' I mutter, feeling very much taken aback.

'It gets better,' DI Derbyshire continues. 'Of course, the interviewing officers also confronted Shakespeare with the letter threatening the judges, and strongly suggested to him that he had written it. I can assure you, they came on pretty strong, pointing out that because of him we were having to protect judges at several courts at great expense to the public – not to mention that writing a letter like that could be construed as an act of terrorism.'

'What did he say about that?'

'Well, according to the interviewing officers, that really put the wind up him. But he denied it vehemently, and he told the officers he thought Joshua Canning had written it.'

I sit back in my chair. 'What?'

'When I heard about that,' the DI continues, 'I spoke to DI Fraser again. He told me that he remembered searching Canning's vicarage and seeing a clapped-out old manual typewriter. He kindly sent an officer round to the vicarage to retrieve it, and by yesterday afternoon we had tried it out and produced a template. It will have to go to a forensic expert, but to the naked eye the letter was definitely typed on that machine. There are irregularities in the results of keystrokes for several letters of the alphabet that recur both in the letter and the template, as well as the condition of the ribbon being much the same. So we don't have the evidence quite nailed down yet, but we will.'

'All of which,' Roderick resumes, 'leaves us in the following position. As far as the prosecution are concerned, the payments Canning made to Shakespeare fall within the period of the indictment and are covered by the charge of theft, just like the payments to Madam Rosita. I propose to ask him about them in cross-examination and to introduce my own evidence to prove them.'

'I can't object to that,' Aubrey says. 'I can't talk to Mr Canning while he's giving evidence, so I don't know what he says about it, but I agree that my learned friend is entitled to ask him about it.'

'Not only that,' Roderick continues, 'but once we have formal evidence that Canning typed the letter, the prosecution will say that it amounts to a threat to kill and possibly an attempt to pervert the course of justice. Ideally, I would like to introduce the letter into evidence and show it to the jury.' He pauses. 'The only problem with that is –'

'The only problem with that,' I interrupt quietly, 'is, in that event, I would become a potential witness. I would have to recuse myself, discharge the jury, and order a retrial before a different judge – indeed a retrial away from this court.'

'That's our view, too, Judge,' Roderick confirms. Aubrey nods his agreement. 'And in those circumstances, I think that will have to await a separate prosecution.'

'Well, there we are, then,' I say. 'Are we ready to continue?'

Aubrey seems rather uncomfortable in his chair.

'Judge,' he says, 'I'm wondering whether you'd be prepared to give me an indication of what the likely sentence would be on the charge of theft if Mr Canning is convicted? In particular, I'm wondering whether an immediate custodial sentence would be inevitable?'

I reflect for some time.

'Well,' I reply eventually, 'of course, it was a very serious breach of trust, and the amount of money involved is fairly substantial, even for a well-endowed church like St Mortimer's. On the other hand, perhaps the real punishment is that he is bound to be defrocked, which I suspect will be a very heavy blow to him, and one from which there is no way back.' I pause again. 'I think on balance that, if he is prepared to plead guilty, and if he makes a reasonable offer to repay as much as he can of the money over a period of time, I would be inclined to consider a suspended sentence.'

Roderick is trying to get my attention.

'The only thing I do need to point out, Judge,' he says, 'is that we would still be left with the matter of the threatening letter, which has caused a number of judges, including yourself, a great deal of anxiety and inconvenience, and has resulted in considerable expenditure of police time and public funds. I would have to speak to the CPS, of course, but I'm fairly sure they would want to charge Mr Canning and proceed against him. And, of course, that's not a matter you could deal with – it would have to go before another judge.'

'True,' I reply. 'And presumably, you would say that I should leave it to the judge who hears the new case to sentence for both matters at the same time?'

'If you don't,' Roderick points out, 'you're effectively tying the new judge's hands. If you give Mr Canning a suspended sentence now for the theft, the new judge may feel he can't give him an immediate prison sentence for the letter.'

'I'm afraid Roderick may be right, Aubrey,' I say.

'I'm afraid he may, Judge,' Aubrey agrees.

There is silence for some time.

'If I may, Judge?' DI Derbyshire says tentatively.

'Yes, Inspector.'

'From a police point of view, if Mr Canning were to cooperate with us, it might be a very important step forward in our fight against this kind of offence.'

'In what way?' I ask.

'Mr Canning knows people in the Original and Retrograde group, and possibly other similar groups. I suspect there is a great deal of information he could give us. If he's willing to cooperate fully and name names, it might lead us to understand who these people are and how they are organised. That would be like gold dust. If we could get our hands on information like that, it might make a decisive difference in our ability to deal with this group and other groups of the same kind.'

She pauses and looks around the room.

'It would be the kind of information that would entitle a defendant to a very significant discount on whatever sentence the court might impose. We would protect his identity at all times, and I would be very happy to set up a confidential debriefing for Mr Canning if he's interested.'

Aubrey has been nodding.

'I will have a very serious conversation with him about that, Detective Inspector,' he replies, 'once we've finished this trial.'

'I suppose,' I say, 'when you think about this case, it's a shame I don't have the sentencing powers I would have had in the nineteenth century and earlier.'

'What power did you have in mind, Judge?' Aubrey asks. 'Transportation to the colonies?'

'No. The power to order him, in addition to any other sentence, to be privately whipped,' I reply. 'We could have arranged for him to do penance at the same time as being sentenced, and it wouldn't have cost the church a penny.'

Roderick seems to enjoy this thought; Aubrey less so.

'Mr Canning,' Roderick begins, 'as I understand it, you don't dispute that you used church funds to pay Madam Rosita; but it's your position that it was a legitimate expenditure, is that right?'

'Yes. That's right.'

'But you never checked with anyone to make sure it was legitimate, did you?'

'Checked with anyone?'

'Yes, your bishop, for example, or a more senior clergyman you trust. Why didn't you ask them what they thought?'

'It never occurred to me.'

'Really? Even though Mr Dwyer or his colleagues would be going through the accounts in due course, and might well ask you about them? Wouldn't it have been sensible to get advice, so that if there was any question, you could say that someone higher up agreed with you?'

'I didn't think there was anything wrong with it, so it never occurred to me.'

'I see,' Roderick says. He pauses for a few moments. 'And what about the payments to Elias Shakespeare? Were they also legitimate?'

The Reverend Mr Canning is visibly shocked. He turns rather pale and starts rocking back and forth in the witness box.

'Who…? What…?'

'I'm going to show you three cheques drawn on one of the St Mortimer bank accounts,' Roderick continues, handing them to Dawn, 'totalling about five hundred pounds, drawn in favour of someone called Elias Shakespeare. Please look at them and tell me whether that is your signature on them?'

Canning takes the cheques and stares at them like a man who has seen a ghost. Time goes by.

'The jury are waiting, Mr Canning,' Roderick says. 'It's a simple question. Is that your signature or not?'

Canning still doesn't respond, but just as Roderick is turning to me for help in persuading him to answer, he blurts out –

'Your Honour, I'd like to change my plea to guilty.'

Aubrey looks at me, raising his hands. I nod.

'Mr Lofthouse, I'm going to give Mr Canning the opportunity of conferring with Mr Brooks before we continue.'

'Of course, your Honour,' Roderick replies contentedly.

'Members of the jury,' I say, 'in the circumstances, we will take a short break. Don't jump to any conclusions from what you've just heard. Mr Canning is entitled to receive legal advice, and at the present time his plea remains one of not guilty. We still have a trial to finish, and it would be quite wrong to hold what you've heard against him before you know whether he meant what he said seriously. Keep an open mind for now.'

The jury nod, though obviously, they can't ignore what they've heard, and if Canning doesn't plead now, I'm going to have a problem. It may be that I can find something to say during the summing-up that will alleviate the prejudice the defendant has brought on himself; but if I don't feel I can, I will have to discharge the jury and order a retrial. I know that's what's going through Aubrey's mind.

Just after twelve thirty, I receive a message via Carol that both counsel are deep in conference with DI Derbyshire and DI Fraser. They are asking if I will give them until two o'clock. I send a message back to the effect that they can have as long as they need.

And so to lunch, an oasis of calm in a desert of chaos.

I impart the glad news that the threat from the Order of Original and Retrograde Free English Men has been averted, and that the author or authors of the threat have been identified. The court, its Judges and their families, and the Garrick Club are all safe once again. Everyone reacts with apparent *sang-froid*, as if it was a foregone conclusion, it was all a storm in a tea cup, and they were never worried in the first place. I don't buy it, but I'm not about to stir anything up, especially with Legless, sentencer of the infamous Elias Shakespeare. We eat our lunches quietly for some time.

'I gather you defied the House of Lords, Charlie,' Marjorie says eventually, 'and stopped the case against Madam whatever-her-name-was. Good for you.'

'Yes,' I reply, 'and the remarkable thing is that Roderick didn't appeal. In fact, he didn't even ask for time to think about it. He just threw his hand in. He must have arranged that with the

Director of Public Prosecutions before we even started.'

'I'm sure he did,' Marjorie says. 'Roderick has been around long enough to know a losing argument when he hears one. He didn't want to get up in front of the Court of Appeal and argue in favour of putting the clock back.'

'He didn't want to look like a wanker,' Hubert says, pausing in his attack on the dish of the day, billed as a Greek salad with tomato soup and garlic bread, 'any more than you did. And that's what would have happened if he'd appealed. I told you that was the test to use. Never fails.'

'How right you were, Hubert,' I concede.

* * *

Wednesday afternoon

When we resume, with the jury in place, Aubrey asks for the indictment to be put again. Carol duly reads the count of theft to the Reverend Mr Canning, and asks him how he pleads. He pleads guilty. I ask him to confirm that he has received legal advice and understands the consequences of his change of plea. He assures me that such is the case. I explain to the jury that it is their duty to return a verdict and they have to decide what verdict to return, but I also make clear that, having heard what amounts to an admission of guilt from a man who has just received legal advice, the only proper verdict to return must be one of guilty. They agree, and duly return that verdict. I thank them on behalf of the court for their service, and I mean it – this hasn't been an easy case, particularly in view of the questionnaire I made them complete before they even started; and in recognition of this, I exempt them from further jury service for three years.

After the jury have gone, Roderick asks me to sit in chambers, asking any members of the public to leave court. There are one or two disgruntled reporters and random spectators who look a bit miffed, but they have no choice but to allow Dawn to usher them outside, promising that they will be able to return once I'm sitting in open court again.

'Your Honour,' he continues, 'my learned friend and I are grateful for the time you gave us to discuss where we go from here, and I'm glad to say that we have reached an understanding. During the lunch hour, DI Derbyshire charged Mr Canning with making a threat to kill. I understand from my learned friend that he is prepared to plead guilty to that charge…'

'That's correct, your Honour,' Aubrey confirms at once.

'So, if your Honour would pretend with us for a moment that we are in a Magistrates' Court and would transform himself into a district judge for a short time, we will ask for the case to be sent to the Crown Court for trial, as it were. If your Honour would then change himself back into a circuit judge, Mr Canning can be arraigned on the charge of threat to kill and will plead guilty. I have provided your learned clerk with a draft indictment, and again, I don't think there is any objection.'

'No objection at all,' Aubrey agrees.

In case you think Roderick is inviting me to perform some act of wizardry taken from a Harry Potter film, I should explain that no physical transformation is called for. It's a convenient feature of being a circuit judge that I am also entitled to act as a district judge, a professional magistrate, so we don't have to waste time sending the new case to the Magistrates' Court and then receiving it back a week or so later. I will be able to deal with it all in a few minutes without even leaving my seat, or changing my appearance in any way.

'Before we go back into open court to allow those steps to be taken,' Roderick continues, 'my learned friend and I are agreed that there is now no objection to your Honour sentencing Mr Canning on both charges, and I believe that would be my learned friend's preference.'

'Quite correct,' Aubrey agrees again.

'But I understand also that Mr Canning has a considerable quantity of information to provide to DI Derbyshire about the Order of Original and Retrograde Free English Men, and that, of course, is bound to affect the sentence your Honour will impose. In those circumstances, we invite your Honour, once Mr Canning has been arraigned and pleaded guilty to the new charge of threat to kill, to remand him in custody for sentencing on both charges. He will be kept at a safe location while DI Derbyshire and her colleagues debrief him, and he will be produced for sentence as soon as possible. I would invite your Honour to adjourn sentence for two weeks, but if we can produce him again more quickly, of course, we will.'

Aubrey rises to his feet.

'Your Honour, I don't want to anticipate everything I will be saying to your Honour in mitigation when Mr Canning is sentenced. But I do want to indicate that I have taken instructions about the three cheques written by Mr Canning in favour of Mr Shakespeare, and I am instructed that they were written as a result of Mr Canning being blackmailed.'

'Blackmailed?' I ask, with what I'm sure must have been an obvious raising of the eyebrows.

'Yes, your Honour. Unfortunately, Mr Canning got himself entangled with the English Free Men a number of years ago, when he was in his first parish as a curate. Mr Shakespeare and others were active in that area, and they persuaded Mr Canning to help them, initially by storing materials and money in his church for them, and other such services. But more recently, Shakespeare found out about Mr Canning's visits to Madam Rosita, and demanded money in return for not making those visits public knowledge within his church. For the same reason, Mr Canning agreed to type the letter which was delivered to your Honour and other judges, containing the threat to kill.

He asks me to assure your Honour that the letter was in no way connected to this case, and that he never had any intention of carrying out any act of violence. However, he does have a good deal of information, and he will be passing it on to DI Derbyshire.'

I return to open court, and Dawn readmits the miffed reporters and members of the public. She calls on the new case which I have duly sent, sitting as a district judge in an imaginary Magistrates' Court, to myself, sitting as a circuit judge in a real Crown Court. The Reverend Mr Canning is duly arraigned on a new one-count indictment charging him with making a threat to kill. He pleads guilty, and is remanded in custody for two weeks for sentence. Nothing further is said.

* * *

Wednesday evening

The Reverend Mrs Walden and I celebrate our new freedom with a visit to La Bella Napoli, and this evening no one follows us. In a carefree mood, we order the best the house has to offer: a salad with buffalo mozzarella and sun-dried tomatoes; spaghetti *aglio e olio*; a wonderful sea bass baked in salt; a home-made tiramisu; and a bottle of an excellent Valpolicella to wash it all down.

'I just can't believe it,' the Reverend says at last, as our waiter clears away the remains of the salad. We have avoided the subject up to this point, but I know she must have endless questions about the day's events. 'So, Joshua changed his plea to guilty?'

I nod. 'He did; and in addition, he pleaded guilty to an additional charge of making a threat to kill – the letter he sent to me and the other judges.'

The Reverend shakes her head sadly. 'I'd reconciled myself to Joshua being convicted of theft,' she says. 'At the end of the day,

I just couldn't see how anyone in a position of responsibility in a church could think he was entitled to spend church money in the way he did. But writing such a crazy, hate-filled letter…'

'It's pretty clear that he'd fallen under the influence of Elias Shakespeare a long time ago,' I offer, 'and for what it's worth, I don't think he would ever have tried to carry out the threats in the letter.'

'But Elias Shakespeare might have,' she points out, not unreasonably, 'and Joshua must have decided to get mixed up in all that horrible stuff.'

'Yes. But we won't know the whole story until he comes up for sentencing,' I say. I refill our glasses. 'Did you ever see anything in him to suggest an interest in groups like the Free English Men?'

'Never,' she replies. 'I suppose it goes to show that you never really know someone. I didn't see him that often, and when I did, it was always in the context of work. Even so, I'm usually a reasonable judge of character, and I didn't see this coming.'

We drink in silence.

'How long will it take them to find a replacement to take over at St Mortimer's?' I ask.

'They already have,' she replies.

'Really? That was quick.'

'I spoke to the bishop this morning. He'd already had the same thought I had – that Joshua had to go, regardless of the outcome of the trial. They're bringing in a new priest-in-charge from Durham – a woman, I'm pleased to say. She's a canon at the cathedral, so it will take her a week or two to hand over her responsibilities there. But after that I can get back to dealing with just one church – mine.'

'May I make a suggestion you might throw out to St Mortimer's before you leave?'

'Of course.'

'You might suggest that they take away the vicar's power to withdraw amounts up to five hundred pounds without a second signature.'

She shakes her head. 'That's a useful power, Charlie,' she replies. 'There are times when you need money and you can't find a second signatory. I wouldn't want to make the incoming vicar's life more difficult because of the sins of her predecessor.'

'Well, perhaps they could at least require the vicar to give the parochial church council a written report, once a month or whatever, explaining what the withdrawals were for?'

'Yes, that's not a bad idea,' she concedes. 'I'll suggest it to them. But the one thing I do want to make sure of is that I finish my sermons on penance. I want to lay this ghost before the new vicar arrives, if I can.'

'How will you do that?'

'I'm not entirely sure, but I think I'm developing a new theory that I'm calling "responsible penance".'

'Is that like responsible gambling?' I ask. 'When the fun stops – stop.'

She laughs. 'Something like that. I want to channel their thinking about penance away from Joshua Canning's ideas on the subject and into more constructive directions.'

'That's a lot to achieve in a couple of weeks,' I say. 'How are you going to do it?'

She shrugs. 'I'll think of something. Perhaps we'll all walk barefoot to Westminster Abbey.'

L'ENTENTE CORDIALE

L'ENTENTE CORDIALE

Monday morning

We have a distinguished guest with us at Bermondsey Crown Court this week. To most people, the idea of welcoming a distinguished guest probably sounds rather agreeable, and in the case of this week's guest, I have every confidence that it will be. But to an RJ, the words 'distinguished guest' conjure up certain feelings of foreboding. Guests, distinguished or otherwise, can be something of a mixed blessing – as I know only too well from my experience at home. It's not unusual for the Reverend Mrs Walden to have a guest at the vicarage, someone billeted on us by the bishop as often as not, a visiting minister or a missionary home on furlough. I can't really complain about having to put up with them for a day or two. I do live in a vicarage after all, and technically I'm living there at the pleasure of the incumbent. So I know my place and I join in as enthusiastically as I can. But with the best will in the world, there's a limit to the number of stories from the missionary wild frontier I can take without a glass of something in hand; and I'm not the only one – when it's finally time for them to leave, even the Reverend's protestations of wishing they could stay longer are beginning to ring a bit false. In most cases, we're hoisting a glass of a decent red together to mark their departure even as their car disappears from sight at the end of the driveway.

In my case, it's the presiding High Court judges or the Grey

Smoothies that send the guests, rather than the bishop, but the principle's the same – they will be descending on the court as our guests and we have to entertain them. In the old days, I'm told, High Court judges on circuit away from London would often invite their wives to sit on the bench with them. Why any judge would want to put himself through that, I can't even begin to imagine. All right, those were different times, and circuit visitations were important social occasions when wives were expected to put in an appearance; but still, it must have put a terrible crimp in the judge's style, and God only knows what inquisitions he had to endure after dinner in the judicial lodgings. I love the Reverend Mrs Walden dearly, but I can't imagine having her on the bench with me. In my early days as RJ, I did once propose in jest that she might act as the court chaplain and process into court before me carrying a bouquet of posies, but it didn't go down well and neither of us has broached the subject again.

We do have one advantage over the vicarage, of course: our guests don't stay the night, so at least we get a break from them. Even so, they're always a distraction. We are trying to run a court, after all. They're going to follow me around the building, sit on the bench with me in court, and demand my full attention for at least half a day. I'm going to be entertaining them to coffee before court when I should be reading my papers; and at lunch when I need to talk to the other judges; and I'm going to be explaining things that happen in court that a ten-year-old would understand without having to ask. Having them with me on the bench is the worst thing. It's not that I begrudge them the feeling of what it's like to be there. It's just that running a criminal trial is a job that demands your total concentration, and you don't want to spend all day answering whispered questions when you're trying to listen to the evidence; or worrying about whether your guest is comfortable, or interested in the proceedings; or needs a break to go to the loo; or is running late for their next appointment.

In fairness, we don't have many visitors at Bermondsey. Most of the entertaining of dignitaries in London goes on at the Old Bailey, where there are always bigwigs from the City of London eager to enjoy a morning's forensic action before a good lunch, so we get off fairly lightly. And for once, they've sent a guest we're all genuinely pleased to welcome.

Jean-Claude Maubert is a judge of the *Cour d'Appel de Paris.* He sits as a member of the court's *Chambre Civile* in the magnificent Palais de Justice on the Ile de la Cité – a far cry, architecturally and in every other respect – from the grimy, down-at-heel courthouse he's about to visit in Bermondsey. He's here by way of reciprocity. Last year, Marjorie went over to Paris for a two-week-long official visit to Jean-Claude's court. When the presiding judges contacted me and asked me to select a representative from Bermondsey, Marjorie was the obvious choice. Why they wanted a judge from a criminal trial court to visit the *Chambre Civile* of a *Cour d'Appel* they didn't make clear, but obviously I wasn't about to turn down an expenses-paid jaunt to Paris for a couple of weeks.

Much as I would have liked to go myself, it wouldn't have been right. Hubert, Legless and I are hopelessly linguistically challenged, except that Legless is reasonably fluent in Glaswegian; whereas Marjorie is effectively trilingual, her other two languages being French and Italian. That, by the way, makes her the slow one in her family – hubby Nigel is fluent additionally in German, Spanish and Arabic, and accordingly, is very highly placed in our nation's banking industry. But within the Bermondsey family she's a superstar, and she was on her way to Paris. Now it's time for the home fixture, and I only hope we can find something to interest Jean-Claude while he is with us. The Reverend Mrs Walden and I met him at a welcome dinner at Marjorie and Nigel's on Saturday evening, and he proved to be altogether delightful, a charming, urbane and cultured man. His English is excellent; he has a strong accent, of course, but this only seems to add to his charm.

Stella has arranged for him to sit with me today, because coincidentally my first case has a French connection. An Algerian gentleman called Hafiz Memmeri, ordinarily a resident of France, entered the United Kingdom recently using what the prosecution claim to be a false French driving licence. If he is convicted of this offence after a trial, I will give him six months inside and he will be deported in short order to France or Algeria, whichever agrees to take him – or whichever has no choice about it.

Most cases of this kind plead out quickly. There is almost never any possible defence. The Border Agency has a formidable battery of scientific tests available to root out false documents, and they almost always nail them in a jiffy, whereupon the defendant avails himself of the one-third reduction in time available to him for an early plea. Ominously, however, notwithstanding the Border Agency's findings, Mr Memmeri did not take the usual course at his plea and case management hearing. Stella assumed it was a case of denial, and that it was only a matter of time before he faced up to the inevitable, and so she listed the case for trial this morning, hoping it would have the desired effect. Apparently she's miscalculated. Chummy seems to think he has a defence, and proposes to go the distance. That's a bit of a nuisance, because we were planning on my starting the far more serious – not to mention far more interesting – case of Jack Verity as soon as I'd dealt with Mr Memmeri, and now we may have to do some urgent rethinking. But that's how it goes in the roulette wheel world of the listing officer: you can't win them all.

Roderick Lofthouse, the doyen of the Bermondsey Bar, is prosecuting. Rising ponderously, he reminds the jury – an assortment of typical Bermondsey citizens whose historic ethnic composition includes India, Bangladesh, Poland, and Lithuania – of the importance of keeping our borders secure, and protecting them against foreigners up to no good. This strikes me as a bit over the top. Roderick knows I'm entertaining a French judge. I introduced Jean-Claude to the court and explained why he's here at the beginning of the trial, so that counsel and jurors wouldn't spend the whole day wondering who he is. So in deference to our French guest – if not to the jury – surely Roderick could have opened his case without the full Brexit speech. I decide to give him the benefit of the doubt. He's here mainly to prosecute in the Verity case, and he's probably had Memmeri dropped on him at the last moment by the CPS; so in fairness, he probably hasn't had much time to meditate on any possible diplomatic implications. I glance across at Jean-Claude, who, to my relief, is smiling amiably and showing no sign of being in any way perturbed.

The rest of the opening is short and clear. When interviewed, Chummy offered a pathetic explanation of having had the licence issued to him by an officer of the *Préfecture du Rhône* in the city of Lyon. He filled in a form and paid the fee demanded of him, it all seemed above board, and if it's not, how could he possibly be to blame? The officer in question must have been corrupt, to take his money and issue him with a false licence, he suggests: everyone knows how corrupt public officials are in France – a suggestion, Roderick adds, smiling up towards Jean-Claude, that the prosecution naturally rejects in the strongest terms. The Border Agency submitted the driving licence to a veritable battery of scientific tests, all of which concur in the view that the document is a fake. He will call several experts to prove all this. He asks me whether I could rise for a few minutes so that he can line them up in the order he needs them. Of course, I can. He's had a busy morning.

I take Jean-Claude back to chambers and Carol brings us a welcome cup of coffee. I am about to apologise to him and express the hope that he hasn't been too offended by Roderick's remarks about controlling immigration, when he turns to me.

'Charles, may I see this false driving licence?'

'Of course,' I reply.

'I'll get it, Judge,' Carol volunteers.

She's back from court in less than a minute. She hands the licence to Jean-Claude, who stands and walks up and down for a few moments, scanning it. Then he resumes his seat and, to my surprise, starts to laugh.

'What is it?' I ask.

'Charles, don't any British children learn foreign languages in school?'

'Some of them do,' I reply. 'I think it depends on the school. I don't think it's required these days. We're not very good at languages in this country, I'm afraid.'

He shakes his head. 'I suppose it's because you assume that everyone speaks English.'

'I suppose so,' I agree.

'Do you think the lawyers in this case speak any French?'

'I have no idea,' I reply. 'They have access to interpreters. We use them at court all the time. The defendant obviously hasn't asked for one, or the interpreter would be in the dock with him. Why do you ask?'

He laughs again. 'Because, my dear Charles, if they spoke a few words of French, or if they had taken the simple step of showing this document to an interpreter, the Border Agency would not have needed all those scientific tests. Come, see.'

Carol and I walk over to stand behind his chair and position ourselves so that we can see over his shoulder. He points.

'This word should be "*Préfecture*" with an acute accent over the first "e". What do you notice about it?'

'There's no accent,' Carol replies at once

I stare at the document. She's right. The accent is missing.

'Yes.' He points again. 'Then here, they've run together the words "*du Rhône*", meaning simply "of the Rhône", so that it's become all one word, "*duRhône*", which is meaningless.' He looks up at us over his shoulder. 'It's absurd. No official document could be issued in France with such obvious errors. I'm sure this is true in England also.'

'So, it's an obvious fake, before you even start on the ultraviolet and all the rest of it?' I ask.

'Of course. I'm sure that if we look, we will find other errors also.' He starts to run his finger down the page, and laughs again. 'As I thought. This is unbelievable. Look. Here we have the phrase "*du police*," intended to mean, "of the police".'

'But "*du*" does mean "of the", doesn't it? As in "*du Rhône*",' I point out.

'Yes, but "*du*" is used only with masculine nouns. "*Police*" is feminine, so the correct form would be "*de la Police*".'

This fragment of knowledge somehow returns to me from the ashes of my long-abandoned school French. I nod.

'No, it's absurd,' Jean-Claude concludes. 'Not even a schoolchild in France would make such a mistake.'

I smile to myself. The gods are smiling on us today: a guest who is not only charming but is also making himself very useful is a real boon. We may have another spin of the roulette wheel. We may be able to reach the case of Jack Verity after all.

'Carol, would you please find out whether we have a French interpreter at court today?' I ask. 'If so, we're going to need them for this case in addition to whatever else they're doing.'

'Yes, Judge.'

'Oh, and hold the jury for a while. I want to have a word with counsel before we bring them back down.'

Carol smiles. '*Mais oui*, Judge,' she says, making cheerfully for the door.

'I wanted to ask,' I begin, 'purely out of interest, whether either of you speaks French at all?'

'Well, one has a smattering, of course,' Roderick replies, with a smarmy grin towards Jean-Claude. 'Holidays in Provence, long weekends in Paris, that kind of thing. I think I can claim to be moderately proficient.'

'But having been dropped into the case at short notice, you haven't had much chance to look at the document in question, I suppose?' I ask, trying to let him off the hook, since his 'smattering' obviously doesn't extend to rumbling the schoolboy errors Jean-Claude identified in a matter of seconds.

'That's true, your Honour. I'm afraid the experts have taken up all my time.'

'Miss Writtle?'

'Not really, your Honour,' Cathy Writtle replies. Cathy is defending Jack Verity as well, and quite fortuitously has had Memmeri come into the list on the same day. 'I did two or three school trips to France years ago, and I took my GCSE, but I'm afraid I can't really claim to speak French.'

'Well,' I say, 'as you know, we have the advantage of having Judge Jean-Claude Maubert with us today, and he tells me that he speaks excellent French. Judge Maubert took the opportunity of perusing the licence in my chambers, and he has drawn my attention to one or two grammatical curiosities, which lead me to believe that if we had the services of an interpreter, we might be able to shorten this case quite substantially.'

Cathy looks at me doubtfully. The phrase 'shorten the case' doesn't always bode well for the defendant.

'I haven't needed an interpreter,' she replies cautiously. 'Mr Memmeri speaks quite good English.'

'All the same,' I insist, 'I think it might save some time. And when I say it may save time, let me add that, contrary to the general practice, if it did have that effect, I would offer Mr Memmeri the appropriate reduction for an early plea, even if it is a bit late in the day for it to be early in the strict sense of the term.'

All right, I admit it: it's a shameless piece of bribery, but if there's any chance of making this case go away, I'm going to jump at it. Cathy stares at me for some seconds.

'I would be happy to take instructions if new evidence were to come to light,' she replies.

Carol stands and turns around to speak to me. 'I've made inquiries, your Honour. We don't have a French interpreter in the building this morning, but the agency says they can have one here by one o'clock.'

'In that case,' I say, 'I propose to adjourn and send the jury away until two o'clock. I would like both of you to confer with the interpreter before we resume, and, Miss Writtle, you can have such time as you need to take instructions in the light of that. Send word via the clerk when we're ready to continue.'

And so – at least for Jean-Claude – to lunch, an oasis of calm in a desert of chaos. Not for me, I regret to say. I have the Grey Smoothies waiting to see me. And ominously, they haven't been willing to say why in advance. Something is up.

As always on serious occasions, they are out in force, led by Sir Jeremy Bagnall of the Grey Smoothie *Politburo*, assisted by our cluster manager Meredith, and her sidekick, Jack. Meredith is wearing an unusually restrained outfit today, a dark grey suit with a black scarf. Even Jack, wearing his trademark ill-fitting suit, has chosen a sombre dark blue tie, though reassuringly, it is hopelessly scrunched up under his collar, so there is some semblance of normality.

Jeremy seems to be finding it difficult to begin. The canteen sandwiches would actually provide a more than sufficient excuse for that predicament, but somehow, I don't think it's due to a gastronomic problem today.

'As you know, Charles,' he begins in his most ingratiating tone, 'the minister has a duty to review the court structure from time to time, to make sure that we have it set up in a way which provides the taxpayer with the best value for money.'

'Of course,' I reply, with an entirely false show of sincerity.

'One of the things the minister has been looking at is the structure of the London Crown Courts, which represent a significant percentage of the overall budget. In London, you have the larger court centres such as Snaresbrook, and then you have the smaller centres such as Bermondsey. The minister has concluded that the larger court centres are a more efficient model, economically speaking, and he has asked me to make some proposals about how we might reorganise the London courts so as to make London lean more towards the larger centre model.'

It's immediately obvious where we're going, and I suddenly feel cold.

'What you mean,' I reply, 'is that you're looking at closing the smaller courts.'

He hesitates. 'I'm afraid that some closures may be inevitable.'

'Including Bermondsey?'

'No decisions have been taken yet, Charles.'

'You wouldn't be here otherwise, would you?'

He nods, conceding my point, but apparently can't quite bring himself to utter the fateful words.

'I'm not going to take any decisions without giving ample time for consultation, and your opinion, of course, will be taken very seriously indeed. That's why we're here today, very early in the process, to make sure you have as much time as possible to reflect, to consult with your colleagues, and to provide me with your advice.'

'How very kind of you, Jeremy,' I reply gloomily.

Although Jeremy has not said so out loud, we both know that the proposed 'reorganisation' is not just about preferring one 'economic model' to another. It's also about an infusion of capital into the ministry's coffers. Bermondsey, like other small London court centres, occupies a valuable piece of real estate in central London, the sale of which would be extremely profitable, and I'm sure the minister has had his eye on it for some time.

The meeting doesn't last much longer. There's not much to say, and the sandwiches don't provide any incentive for continuing. I have at least half an hour before court looms, and I sit silently at my desk. We have a happy little set-up at Bermondsey. We get on well, judges and staff, and we do a good job of dispensing justice in a fair and reasonably expeditious manner. None of that matters to the Grey Smoothies. If the court closes, the staff, who are devoted to the court, will have to move on. That means they will be offered work at another court, which on the face of it sounds reasonable enough. But long experience has taught me the truth about that. The offer of work may be at a lower pay grade, and it may be at a court too far away for them to travel to, in the light of their family circumstances. That means we will lose people like Stella and Carol, who have years of experience and know the job inside out. In a rational world, you would think that the ministry would be concerned about losing such a valuable and irreplaceable resource. Not a bit of it. As Meredith once confided in me in one of her rare unguarded moments, it's the kind of loss they welcome. They can always replace them with newcomers who enter at a far lower pay grade and who are offered no more than minimal training. After that, it's up to the court, of course. It's our problem. The Grey Smoothies have done their job. They've saved the taxpayer some money.

As far as the judges are concerned, I daresay my colleagues will come out of it well enough. Travel to a new court isn't likely to be a problem. We've all sat at several courts in the past, and we are adaptable creatures. Even Hubert will fit in as long as he can get from court to the Garrick in a reasonable time. I could move to another court without too much trouble, of course, but I would be facing a longer journey, and I might not be able to make my comfortable start to the day *chez* Elsie and Jeanie, and George.

Just before two o'clock, a dark thought enters my mind. I have the goods on Sir Jeremy Bagnall. I could raise a memory in his mind that might well induce him to spare Bermondsey from inclusion on the list of small court centre closures. Back in the days when he was still plain Mr Jeremy Bagnall CBE his name showed up in a 'black book', said to be a list of clients of a brothel tucked away above a restaurant and bar called Jordan's, here in Bermondsey. I emphasise the 'said to be' because we only have the word of Dimitry Valkov to go on, and Valkov is not exactly a stellar source. He was convicted in front of me of running the brothel, was sent down by me for a couple of years, and was subsequently deported back to his native Russia, to the general advantage. But during the trial, once word of the black book hit the street via the media, I was inundated for information about whose names appeared or didn't appear in the book. Jeremy's name was one of them, and he appeared in my chambers, pleading for help: with good reason; his family life and career were both under threat.

But I can't use it. I called in my debt at the time. The Grey Smoothies were threatening to close down the court cafeteria. I persuaded Jeremy to reverse the decision; not, I hasten to add, because of any reverence for the food, but because it's the only safe place for jurors, witnesses and other court users to have lunch within an hour without the risk of them running into a defendant without protection. In return, I assured Jeremy that I would destroy the black book if I could: and once the time for appeal had passed and the memory of the case had faded from public view, that's what I did. I did it quietly, at home, in the fireplace of the vicarage living room, on one cool winter evening, so that I could savour the thought that Dimitry Valkov had unknowingly contributed to keeping myself and the Reverend Mrs Walden warm for a few minutes.

So now the evidence is gone, and even if I still had the book, I wouldn't hold it over his head again. The thought came into my mind only when I began to ponder the consequences for Stella and Carol and the rest of our loyal and brilliant staff. At that moment, I admit, I was briefly tempted.

* * *

Monday afternoon

When we return to court, I see an elegantly dressed lady I know to be one of our regular French interpreters sitting with DC Bramwell, the officer in the case, behind Roderick. All three of them are smiling happily.

Cathy Writtle is not smiling, happily or at all; on the contrary, she rises rather glumly.

'I'm grateful for the opportunity to consult with the interpreter, your Honour,' she says. 'And of course,' she adds, slightly acerbically, 'for Judge Maubert's kind assistance. I have taken further instructions and given Mr Memmeri certain advice, as a result of which he would like to have the indictment put again.'

'Certainly, Miss Writtle,' I agree.

I call for the jury to be brought down, because now that the trial has started they must be called on to return a verdict, and for that purpose they have to hear his change of plea. The indictment is put to Chummy again, and he duly pleads guilty. I explain to the jury that in the light of the full confession of guilt he has just made, they have no alternative but to convict, which they proceed to do. I weigh him off for the promised four months and make noises encouraging the authorities to deport him as soon as reasonably possible. The jury, of course, had been looking forward to some action and are a bit disappointed about the abrupt end of the trial, but I'm able to assure them that they will probably be back in court soon as part of a fresh jury panel, so they will get a second bite at the cherry. This proves to be true, as we are now in position to move on to the case of Jack Verity, and in fact eight out of the twelve jurors we had in Mr Memmeri's case are called on to serve in Mr Verity's. I'll let Roderick tell you what the Verity case is all about.

'May it please your Honour, members of the jury, my name is Roderick Lofthouse and I appear to prosecute in this case. My learned friend Miss Cathy Writtle appears for the defendant, the gentleman in the dock, Jack Verity. Members of the jury, Mr Verity is charged with a single count of blackmail. I'm going to ask the usher to distribute copies of the indictment to you.'

He waits for Dawn to carry the copies over to the jury box and hand them out, one between two.

'As you see, the count with which Mr Verity is charged alleges that he made an unwarranted demand to a woman called Angie Simmons with menaces, namely by threatening to upload to the internet and social media a large number of images showing Angie Simmons naked and in sexually compromising positions, unless she agreed to continue a sexual relationship she had begun with Mr Verity.

'At a later stage of the trial the learned judge will explain the law to you in detail, and you must take the law from His Honour, and not from me. But I think I can safely tell you this much. The offence of blackmail is committed when the defendant makes an unwarranted demand of another person with menaces; with a view to gain for himself, or with the intent to cause loss to the other person; and a demand is unwarranted unless the defendant believes that he has reasonable grounds for making the demand, and that the use of menaces is a proper means of reinforcing the demand. Now, that's a bit of a mouthful, but you will be hearing about it throughout the trial, and I suspect that it will all become clear if I tell you what it is the prosecution say Mr Verity did in this case.

'As you will have gathered from the indictment, Mr Verity and Miss Simmons had been having an affair for some six months before the offence was committed. They met at work. Both Mr Verity and Miss Simmons have responsible jobs in the City of London, Mr Verity as an investment banker and Miss Simmons as a junior executive in the same bank. You will hear that they started to go out together socially, and the affair developed from there. Miss Simmons was then and is now unmarried. Mr Verity was then and is now married, but his wife, Megan, did not know of the affair at the time.

'At the heart of this case, members of the jury, is the fact that Mr Verity and Miss Simmons were unequal partners in their relationship. He was older – forty-four as compared to her thirty-one; he was her superior at work; and he earned very substantially more than she did. You will hear that Mr Verity was a domineering man, one who knew how to use his influence at work, his greater age, and his greater spending power to control his younger and less experienced lover.

'One of the things these two people had in common is that they both liked to spend their money on expensive restaurants, alcohol and drugs. Members of the jury, it's important that

I make this clear to you: this is not a case about drugs. The defendant is not charged with any offence related to drugs and you are not being asked to return any verdict in respect of a drugs offence. You're hearing about drugs only because they form an important part of the background to this case. It is important for you to put aside any feelings you may have about drugs, and to make sure that you don't hold drug use against either of them, and especially the defendant Mr Verity, in any way.

'As you will also have gleaned from the indictment, it is clear that the relationship between Mr Verity and Miss Simmons had broken down by the time this offence was committed. You will hear two versions of the history of the break-up. Miss Simmons's account of it is very simple. She had grown tired of the relationship and wanted to end it. She will tell you that she was tired of Mr Verity's domineering manner and his efforts to control her. She was also tired of something else. During their relationship, Mr Verity, while under the influence of alcohol or cocaine, took a large number of pictures of Miss Simmons naked and in an explicitly sexual context, using his phone. I very much regret that you will have to look at some of these images during the trial, because they are central to the prosecution's case.'

I glance over in the direction of the jury, and detect no evidence that they share Roderick's feelings of regret. Quite the contrary: they are looking at Dawn as if anticipating that the images are already on their way. Eight of them are grateful that Mr Hafiz Memmeri pleaded out. This promises to be far more interesting.

'Members of the jury, once you have seen these pictures, you may have little doubt that they would have caused huge damage if they were made public. There were a substantial number of pictures of Miss Simmons naked and engaged in various sexual activities, and it is not hard to imagine that her employers would not have taken kindly to them. Then, of course, there was the embarrassment she would suffer if her family and friends were made aware of them. Mr Verity told Miss Simmons that if she did not continue with their relationship, he would make sure that she suffered those consequences. He threatened to upload these pictures to social media and the internet. Miss Simmons felt that she was caught in a trap: either continue a relationship that had become abhorrent to her or have those images spread abroad. She chose a third course. She went to the police, showed them the pictures Mr Verity had sent from his phone to hers, and made a complaint. Mr Verity was arrested.

'When interviewed under caution, Mr Verity gave the police a very different account of how the relationship ended. He told them that Miss Simmons had been threatening to tell his wife about the affair because she thought he was not providing her with enough money. He told the police that, despite her own not insignificant earnings, she expected him to make a contribution to the rent of her expensive flat in Canary Wharf, and to provide her with two or three hundred pounds a week to feed her cocaine habit. He told the police that he complied with her demands for some time, but there came a time when he was no longer prepared to do so. Her reaction was to threaten to expose the affair to his wife.

'He told the police that he understood the effect they would have, but that he felt he had no alternative but to threaten to upload images of her, as a means of ensuring that she did not tell his wife about the affair. Mr Verity told the police that he believed he was fully entitled to act as he did. But the prosecution say that a man of his intelligence knew perfectly well that he had no reasonable ground to make that threat, and that it was not a proper way of reinforcing his demand.

'The prosecution say, members of the jury, that Mr Verity's

threat to upload the pictures was an unwarranted menace, for which he has no excuse at all, and it is on that basis that we say that the evidence will make you sure of his guilt of the offence of blackmail.'

It has been a good opening: short, clear and to the point. Finally, Roderick deals briskly with the burden and standard of proof, emphasising that it is for the Crown to prove the case so that the jury are sure of guilt, and that Mr Verity is not obliged to prove his innocence, or indeed to prove anything at all. He then announces his intention of calling Angie Simmons to give evidence.

Whichever way it goes, I reflect, the lives of these two people are lying in ruins on the courtroom floor, and there is nothing anyone can do about that. I turn to Jean-Claude.

'What did you think of the opening?' I ask quietly.

He gives me a thoroughly Gallic shrug.

'I will never understand you British,' he whispers discreetly, albeit with the trace of a smile. ''Why is everyone so obsessed with sex in this country?'

I feel momentarily taken aback. 'What do you mean?'

'To bring him before the court, just for this? It's hard for us to understand.'

'Are you saying this wouldn't come to court in France?'

'Why should this concern the court?' he asks. 'These two people have a good time together; they take some pictures. What is – how you say – the big deal?'

'The big deal is that he was going to make the pictures public,' I point out, trying my best to keep my voice down.

'So what if he does? She would then disclose other pictures in retaliation, and the only interesting question would be whose pictures are better. They would both be showing them off and boasting about them to their friends, and eventually the matter would die a natural death. Why does it concern the court?'

I can't help staring at him for a moment or two. He shakes his head sadly.

'You English are, how you say, so uptight about these things, Charles. In France, it's a purely private matter.' He pauses. 'Of course,' he adds, 'Verity might be in trouble with his wife, you know? It might cost him some jewellery, or a mink coat, or whatever else she might ask for.'

'But surely she wouldn't allow herself to be bought off with jewellery and furs for something like this?' I insist, trying my best to convey some sense of outrage. 'Surely she would divorce him?'

'It all depends,' Jean-Claude replies with another shrug.

'Depends on what?' I ask.

'On what she's been getting up to herself, of course.'

'I swear by Almighty God that the evidence I shall give shall be the truth, the whole truth, and nothing but the truth.'

I have to say, I can see why Jack Verity was tempted. Angie Simmons is a gorgeous redhead wearing a smart light grey business suit with black high heels and a pretty orange scarf, and looks altogether the model of the attractive young executive. I glance surreptitiously to my left and see Jean-Claude running a hand through his hair and straightening his tie.

'Miss Simmons,' Roderick begins, 'Please give the jury your full name.'

'Angeline Mary Simmons.'

'And are you employed as an executive by a bank in the City of London? I don't think there's any need to name the bank, unless my learned friend wishes me to.'

'No need as far as I'm concerned, your Honour,' Cathy says.

'Not any more,' Angie replies. 'I lost my job.'

'Was that as a result of the events in this case?'

'Yes. My employers said they didn't think I was sending the right message to their clients.' She turns towards me. 'Your Honour, my solicitor told me I shouldn't say any more about that. I'm suing them for wrongful dismissal.'

I see Jean-Claude nodding approvingly.

'Well, let's see where the evidence leads us,' I say. I'm sure her solicitor would prefer not to have too much said about the dismissal, but a defendant is on trial for a serious offence, and I don't think Cathy Writtle is going to let that aspect of the case pass without comment.

'I'm much obliged,' Roderick continues. 'Miss Simmons, tell the jury how you first came to meet Jack Verity.'

'We worked together. Jack was already with the firm as an investment banker when I joined as a junior executive.'

'Was Mr Verity your boss?'

'I didn't report to him directly, but he was above me in the hierarchy, of course.'

'Yes. Did there come a time when you started seeing each other away from the workplace?'

'Yes, he asked me out for a drink. I agreed to go, and after that it became a regular thing.'

'Where would you go?'

'We usually went to the Blue Lagoon.'

'The Blue Lagoon is a nightclub here in Bermondsey, is that right?'

'Yes. It's got quite popular with the City crowd. It's not hard to get to, but it's far enough away from work, if you know what I mean.'

Roderick nods knowingly, giving the impression that he knows exactly what she means. I have to say, I'm a bit taken aback myself – not at the mention of the Blue Lagoon, which is a perennial point of reference in cases at Bermondsey Crown Court – but at the implication that it's attracting an influx of well-heeled

City types. Until now, we've thought of it as a bit downmarket, the scene of your typical Saturday night South London sexual encounters and drug deals. But we may have to revise our image. The Lagoon must be moving up in the world, and I'm wondering whether we might start to get a better class of work as a result. A few glamorous City cases wouldn't go amiss.

'When was it you first went out together?' Roderick is asking.

'Just over a year ago now. We went out one Friday evening, and it went from there.'

'Yes.' Roderick pauses. 'When you say, "it went from there", can you tell the jury what you mean by that?'

'We found a space together at the bar and had a few drinks. We were talking. We were attracted to each other, and well… as I say, it went from there.'

'Yes. That's what I'm trying to explore with you,' Roderick persists patiently, 'what you mean when you say "it went from there". Let me ask you this. In addition to the drinks, what else did you do?'

Angie hesitates momentarily – but given what she's about to say, she doesn't hesitate for long. It's become a strange feature of trials today that, as long as they're not actually charged with it, witnesses cheerfully volunteer all kinds of admissions about their use of illegal drugs. The fact that they're coughing up to a criminal offence doesn't seem to bother them in the least. It's become such an everyday piece of background to cases of all kinds that we're all starting to take it for granted. Jurors don't seem to turn a hair, and neither do the police. There seems to be a tacit understanding that the police aren't going to investigate or charge anyone, however much they confess to while under oath; so we've reached the bizarre position that the court has become a safe space for sharing one's predilection for recreational drugs.

'We did some coke in the ladies,' Angie replies.

'And after that?'

'I took him home to my place.'

'And, taking it shortly,' Roderick says, apparently tiring of waiting for her to volunteer it, 'because I don't think there's any dispute about this, did you have sex that night, and did a sexual relationship thereafter develop between you and Mr Verity?'

'Yes.'

'Were you aware on that first evening that Mr Verity was married?'

'No. Not that evening, but I found out before too long.'

'Miss Simmons, once your relationship was underway, where did you and Mr Verity meet?'

'He came to my place, always. Well, we could hardly go to his house, could we?'

'No, of course. You have a flat in Canary Wharf, is that right?'

'Yes.'

'And how often would Mr Verity come to your flat?'

'Two or three times a week, after work. We got into a routine. It was a regular thing if he wasn't having dinner with clients or what have you.'

'And did these evenings follow the same pattern?'

'Yes. Jack would bring champagne and coke and we would tear each other's clothes off and carry on until the early hours, by which time we were both pretty much out of it, at which point he would leave. He had a limo service he always called to take him home.'

'"Out of it" meaning that you were both somewhat drunk and under the influence of drugs?'

'"Out of it" meaning that we were both completely wasted.'

'Quite so. I want to ask you about the champagne and drugs, Miss Simmons. Would it be fair to say that Mr Verity was earning more than you?'

'A lot more.'

'Because he's a banker and has commissions, whereas…'

'I was on a salary, yes. I wasn't doing badly, but I couldn't have afforded to live the way he did.'

'So, when you had the champagne and cocaine, who would pay for it?'

'Jack would get it for us. I'm not saying I didn't have some of my own, you know... but whenever he came to see me, he would bring enough for the night.'

Roderick pauses.

'Miss Simmons, did there come a time when Mr Verity started to do something you felt uncomfortable about?'

'Yes.'

'Please tell the jury what that was.'

'He started taking pictures of me on his phone while we were having sex.'

'So, these would be pictures taken while you were naked?'

'Yes.'

'And while you were engaged in sexual activity of one kind or another, is that right?'

'Yes.'

'Would he show the pictures to you?'

'Yes. He seemed to think that I was just as keen on taking photos as he was; and he would send them to my phone while he was on his way home in his limo.'

'Miss Simmons, why were you uncomfortable about that?'

'Because I had no control over the pictures. If he had them on his phone, there was nothing to stop him sending them to whoever he wanted to send them to, or uploading them on to his Facebook or whatever. They might even have ended up on the internet for everyone to see.'

'Did you express that concern to him?'

'Yes, I did. Many times.'

'And how did he respond?'

'He told me they were just for fun, and he would delete them.'

Roderick turns behind him to DC Featherstone, the officer in the case, who hands him a thick black folder. He summons our usher, Dawn.

'Miss Simmons, please look at what the usher is going to hand you. Can you tell the jury what this is?'

Angie takes her time, turning over the pages for some time before finally closing the folder with something of a bang.

'These are the pictures I still had on my phone when I went to the police.'

'Pictures Mr Verity had sent you from his phone?'

'Yes. I deleted most of them, but I still had these.'

'Just over seventy in all?'

'Yes.'

'Your Honour, if this might be Exhibit one, please?' Roderick asks. I assent. 'There are copies for the jury.' Dawn sets out for the jury box. 'Your Honour, perhaps we might give the jury a minute or two to have a look and get the flavour of this material before I move on?'

It doesn't take Jean-Claude and myself long to get the flavour of the material, and I'm sure the same is true of the jury. But to my surprise, they don't seem to react very much. I'm almost picking up some disappointment. They seem to be flicking the pages over quickly, with the briefest of glances at the contents, as if they were scanning a mail order catalogue. Is it possible that they see this kind of stuff every day? Perhaps it's like the drugs. Nothing shocks anyone much any more. It's all become part of the landscape. Nonetheless, Roderick allows the jury a fair time to work their way through the pictures before continuing.

'This may be an obvious question, Miss Simmons, but what concerns would you have had about these pictures, and others like them, being sent to others, or made public in some way?'

'They would have affected my reputation,' she replies simply, 'and put my employment at risk. As indeed they did.'

'Did there come a time,' Roderick continues, 'when you took a decision about your relationship with Mr Verity?'

'Yes.'

'Tell the jury about that, please.'

'I decided to end the relationship.'

'Why did you take that decision?'

Angie appears to think for some time.

'It was exciting at first, but as time went on he became more and more controlling. He had to say when we went out, and where we went, and when we had sex, and when we did coke, and when he would take photos. It was as if I had no say in it at all. And, of course, he was above me at the bank, and there was always the threat hanging over my head if I didn't do exactly what he wanted.'

'Did he make that threat explicit?'

'He implied it, and it was very obvious.'

'And did there come a time, about six months ago, when you told Mr Verity that you wanted to end the relationship?'

'Yes. I told him one evening, just as he was leaving my flat.'

'How did he respond?'

'He'd taken a number of photos of me that evening. He sent them to my phone, and he told me that if I tried to dump him, they would find their way on to social media and the internet.'

'How did you react to that threat?'

'I didn't react at the time. I was speechless. I didn't know what to say or do. He just laughed and left to go to his limo, and I'm sure he felt that I would cave in and let him keep doing what he was doing. But I thought about it that night and for several days afterwards, and I decided that I couldn't allow him to get away with it.'

'What did you do?'

'I went to the police and told them what had happened, and asked them to do something about it.'

'You were interviewed by DC Featherstone, who is now the officer in the case, and who sits behind me in court today?'

'Yes.'

'And you gave her such pictures as you found on your phone, which we now have in Exhibit one?'

'Yes.'

Roderick pauses.

'Miss Simmons, I have to ask you this. Did you consider what the consequences of going to the police were? I mean, in terms of having all of this become public, and perhaps having publicity given to the pictures?'

'Yes, I did. I didn't see that I had anything to lose. Jack spent half his life off his head on coke, and even if he didn't upload them deliberately, the pictures weren't safe with him. But the chances were that he would upload them deliberately if I pissed him off at all, even slightly; and it wasn't difficult to piss him off when he was wasted, which was most of the time he was with me. I couldn't live with that hanging over my head. I thought, if I went to the police, at least that ought to mean that they would stop him.'

'And, in fact, as far as you know, did Mr Verity ever upload the pictures?'

'No, not as far as I know. But word got around that they existed, and that was enough for the bank to fire me.'

Roderick looks up at me.

'Your Honour, that's all I have for the time being. But my learned friend and I wonder whether we could leave it there for the day. We would like to get the remaining evidence in order before my learned friend cross-examines. We're having the usual problems with the CPS photocopier and…'

I agree readily. The fragile state of the CPS photocopier is an accepted euphemism at the Bar for needing more time to get things organised, and this afternoon, I'm more than happy to oblige. I extend Jack Verity's bail for the duration of the trial and warn Angie Simmons not to discuss her evidence with anyone overnight.

* * *

Monday evening

The reason why I was happy to get out of court a bit early is my anxiety about the evening that lies ahead. Tonight, it's the turn of the Reverend Mrs Walden and myself to entertain Jean-Claude to dinner, and we are nervous about it.

Entertaining a guest to dinner may not seem like a cause for undue anxiety, and probably wouldn't be if we didn't feel ourselves being propelled unwillingly into some kind of nightmare gastronomic competition. If we had hosted the welcoming dinner on Saturday, there would have been no problem: but we didn't – Marjorie and Nigel did, and as I should have anticipated, they set the bar impossibly high. We sensed it the moment we set foot in their house on Saturday evening. I'm sure they didn't intend it – they were just being Marjorie and Nigel, and I'm sure they do this kind of thing all the time for Nigel's banking clients – but everything about the evening seemed calculated to ensure that any subsequent meal would look meagre by comparison. It was as if entertaining had become a new Olympic sport and Marjorie and Nigel already had the gold medal in the bag. Dinner was catered in, from La Maison in Covent Garden, and Nigel had raided his cellar to unearth several bottles of a vintage Châteauneuf du Pape, not to mention a bottle of Taylor's 1963 vintage port to go with the cheese. Jean-Claude would have been hard put to it to match it in Paris. Everything was a perfect ten from all the judges. As we were leaving, we were wondering whether we could even aspire to the bronze.

To make matters worse, I'm pretty sure that neither Hubert nor Legless, whose turns come later in the week, is experiencing any anxiety at all. Both of them fondly imagine that the evenings they have planned for Jean-Claude represent the height of London sophistication and couldn't possibly be improved on. Hubert is taking him to dinner at the Garrick, which in his mind is the ultimate exercise in civilised dining. Legless is taking him to some Scottish dining and folk singing establishment in the King's Road, which is his idea of a good night out on the town. Astonishingly, I don't think either of them has any sense of languishing behind Marjorie and Nigel at all.

After much soul searching, the Reverend Mrs Walden and I have taken a bold decision. We have concluded that we cannot possibly compete with Marjorie and Nigel on their own terms, and that it would be a huge mistake even to try. This means that we must steer clear of anything French, and go for something as different as possible – something Jean-Claude is unlikely to come across every day in Paris. We have finally opted for the Delights of the Raj – a selection of fine curries washed down with a few bottles of Cobra. We acknowledge the possibility that it could go wrong – well, let's be honest, the evening could turn into a total disaster – but we're out of ideas, and at least we can't be accused of not being different. Also, as regular patrons, we have the ear of Rajiv, the owner of the Delights. I've explained the situation to him, and he's promised to pull out all the stops; but whatever he means by that, it could go either way.

Late in the evening the verdict is in, and to our huge delight and relief, it seems to have worked. After dinner, a beautifully prepared and served sumptuous repast of samosas, lamb korma, prawn biryani, rice, garlic naan, and copious quantities of Cobra, Jean-Claude leans forward confidentially, and says –

'Charles, Clara, this is wonderful. I can't tell you how much I've enjoyed it.'

The Reverend Mrs Walden and I share a happy sigh.

'We weren't sure whether you would like it,' I confess, 'but we didn't feel we could compete with Saturday night.'

Jean-Claude holds up his hands.

'I'm glad you didn't try,' he replies at once. 'Saturday was delightful, of course, but it was just like being in Paris. Tonight you are giving me something quite different – something quintessentially British – the Indian dinner and the beer. The food is wonderful, the service is perfection, and the ambience is so relaxing. It's just what I needed. Truly, it couldn't be better.'

Suddenly the cares of the day begin to recede. I sense the same in the Reverend Mrs Walden, who gives our guest a playful smile.

'Charlie was telling me that you have a far more relaxed attitude to sexual indiscretions in France then we do here, Jean-Claude,' she suggests with a hint of Cobra-induced naughtiness.

He shrugs and smiles. 'But, of course, Clara. We are a nation of sexual indiscretions. It is expected of us.'

'Well, yes, but what if it involves a woman being exploited?'

'You mean the young woman in Charles's case?' He smiles. 'I don't think so. I can't quite see her as the victim of exploitation. Can you, Charles?'

'I'm not sure,' I admit. 'I'm waiting for Cathy Writtle's cross-examination.'

'Well, we shall see. But in any case, Clara, you are right. We do think differently about such things in France. We wouldn't call such things "indiscretions". I think "adventures" might be the word we would use.'

'That sounds like a very male point of view,' the Reverend Mrs Walden replies. 'It all sounds very macho. I'd be interested to hear the female side of it.'

Jean-Claude shrugs again.

'Of course. But that's the way things are with us. You must understand that this is France, a country in which a man cannot be taken seriously as a politician unless he has a mistress in addition to his wife. If he wishes to become President of the Republic, it is essential. If he doesn't have a mistress, people are not convinced that he is man enough for the job.'

We laugh. He continues confidentially.

'Do you know how Nixon smuggled Henry Kissinger into Paris for the first talks with China without drawing any attention to him – which was essential to maintain the secrecy?'

'I have no idea,' I admit.

'He sent Kissinger to West Germany by military transport and then hired a private pilot with a light aircraft to fly him across the border into France without filing a flight plan.'

'And that didn't attract attention?' I ask.

'No. Because when the West German Secret Service interviewed the pilot the next day to ask him why he had made this flight, he replied, "I can tell you only that the matter concerns the President of France and a woman". That was all he had to say, but it was enough. It was a complete explanation. The matter went no further.'

We laugh loudly, and I order another round of Cobras.

'I heard that from the presidential aide who arranged it,' Jean-Claude adds. The Cobras arrive and we share a toast. 'Charles,' he says, 'it may be the beer affecting me, but may I ask you something?'

'Yes, of course.'

'I was talking to Marjorie before we left court. Of course, we like to chat away in French, as you know. She told me that you were all worried that the Bermondsey court may be closed down. Is that true?'

I feel myself sober up.

'It's true,' I reply. 'Nothing has been decided officially, but I'd be very surprised if we survive. We're the smallest court centre in London. We don't fit the approved economic model.'

'And it's not enough that you're doing a good job?'

'Apparently not.'

'Well, that's very sad.' He hesitates for a few moments. 'You know, before I came to England, I made certain inquiries about the court – simply out of interest, you understand, to inform myself about what I could expect to find – and I learned something quite interesting.'

'Oh, yes?' I banter. 'You must tell me, Jean-Claude. I didn't know anything interesting went on at Bermondsey.'

'You are too modest, Charles, but you can't keep it from me.' His voice takes on a more confidential tone. 'You see, I have certain contacts in France, including some at the Quai d'Orsay – our foreign service.'

'Ah, so that's how you come to hear things from presidential aides,' the Reverend Mrs Walden observes, smiling.

He nods with a smile. 'I hear things from time to time. And in this case, I heard that it was at Bermondsey that the court – presided over by none other than His Honour Judge Charles Walden – decided in favour of France in the matter of L'Ile des Fougains. My friend was unsure of the details, but it all sounded very interesting. Perhaps you can tell me more?'

I look inquiringly at Jean-Claude. This is a well-informed man, and something tells me that he's not relying solely on my memory for the detail of the case of Walter Freedland Orlick. But why is he asking about it?

'I tried a man called Orlick,' I recall, with a quick refreshing mouthful of Cobra. 'He was guilty of several serious frauds and money-laundering. In an effort to avoid prosecution, he pleaded sovereign immunity, claiming to be the king of a small island – well, no more than a large piece of rock really – in the English Channel. He claimed that he had "conquered" or "occupied" the island with his two accomplices, and he was entitled to be recognised, not only as king, but as the island's lawful government. Its English name is Foggin Island.'

Jean-Claude claps his hands together. 'Yes, but in French, L'Ile des Fougains.'

'Yes. Orlick claimed that he was entitled to claim sovereignty over the island under international law because Great Britain had never occupied it, and it was virgin territory. But unfortunately for him, it transpired that England had claimed sovereignty, and had then ceded Foggin Island to France as part of the Treaty of Calais 1360. I invited the French Government to intervene, and once Chummy realised that he wasn't the king of anywhere, and was in danger of being sent to France to be tried there, he caved in and pleaded.'

'*Oui, c'est ça,*' Jean-Claude says. 'And so in France we suddenly realised that we own a piece of rock very close to the English coast. In earlier times, this would have been a very important asset, militarily speaking.'

'You're not going to use it as a base to invade us, are you, Jean-Claude?' the Reverend asks, 'taking your revenge on us for Agincourt?'

He laughs. 'No, no, Clara, I assure you. No. In fact, my friend was aware of some negotiations between France and Great Britain about the use of the island. I don't know the details, but I feel confident that L'Ile des Fougains will not be the cause of renewing the Hundred Years War.'

He raises his glass and we drink a silent toast – presumably to the Hundred Years War not being renewed.

'You may think nothing interesting ever happens at Bermondsey, Charles. But as a Frenchman, I find this case of considerable interest.' He drains his glass with the air of a man who has just made a decision. 'In fact, I propose to bring it to the attention of our ambassador.'

'The French Ambassador?'

'Yes. Her name is Valérie Bernard. She's an old friend, and it so happens that I shall be seeing her at a reception at the embassy tomorrow evening. Charles,' he continues before I can inquire further, 'it has been a delightful evening at the Delights of the Raj. Truly, the highlight of my visit to London. But it's getting late and we have work tomorrow. Shall we adjourn?'

* * *

Tuesday morning

'So, Jack was domineering, was he, Miss Simmons?' Cathy Writtle begins. 'He was older; he was above you in the company; he earned more money, and he tried to use all that to control you?'

'That's correct.'

'And you were powerless to resist?'

'That's how it felt to me.'

'Yes. Please remind the jury of how old you are.'

'I'm thirty-one.'

'And remind them of what you do for a living.'

'I'm an executive of the bank.'

'You're in good health, physically?'

'Yes.'

'And all this controlling behaviour took place in your home, didn't it?'

'That's correct.'

'So you were entitled to ask him to leave at any time. Correct?'

'Theoretically.'

'Theoretically? Was he ever violent to you?'

'No.'

'Was there ever an occasion when you asked him to leave and he refused?'

'No.'

'And when you tried to end the relationship, you say he threatened to upload all those pictures to social media or the internet, yes?'

'Yes.'

'Let me make it clear to you, Miss Simmons, there's no dispute about it. Mr Verity agrees that he did make that threat.'

'Thank you.'

'Well, don't thank me, because Mr Verity says he did so in circumstances very different from those you describe. I'll come back to that. Let's stay with the threat for now. You say it horrified you because of the potential consequences for you at work?'

'They weren't potential; they were real consequences.'

'Well, let's think this through for a moment. If Mr Verity had carried out his threat – and we agree that he never did upload any pictures, yes?'

'Yes.'

'If Mr Verity had carried out his threat, the consequences would have been just as real for him, wouldn't they? More so, in a way, since he was higher up and earned more? He had more to lose than you, didn't he?'

'Mr Verity isn't in any of the pictures. He was very careful about that. It's just me.'

'Yes, but if Mr Verity uploaded them, it wouldn't take long for someone to work out whose phone they came from, would it?

It would be obvious that these were pictures he took, wouldn't it?'

'Yes, I suppose so.'

'Mr Verity hasn't lost his position at the bank, has he?'

'I don't know.'

'Will you take it from me that he hasn't?'

'Yes, if you say so.'

'Thank you. Is it possible at all that your dismissal had more to do with your last end-of-year performance review?'

'No… I…'

'I have it here. I can show it to you, if you like; or I can read it to the jury. It's not very flattering about your performance, is it?'

'That's just an excuse. My solicitor says the report doesn't come close to being grounds for dismissal. They told me I was being fired because of the pictures.'

'"They" being who?'

'The directors and senior management.'

'But if Mr Verity never uploaded the pictures, how did the directors and senior management find out about them?'

'They found out when I went to the police, obviously. I had to tell them. I'd accused one of their bankers of taking the pictures. He was about to be arrested. I couldn't keep it a secret.'

'So, was it you who showed them the pictures?'

'Yes.'

'And they fired you – but not Mr Verity – without even waiting for the outcome of these proceedings?'

'That's correct.'

Cathy pauses for a few moments.

'Now, you told the jury yesterday that you were uncomfortable about Mr Verity taking explicit pictures of this kind, is that right – pictures showing you naked and engaged in sexual activity?'

'I was very uncomfortable.'

'Well, let's see how you look when you're uncomfortable, shall we?' She turns to the jury. 'Let's turn to Exhibit one.' The jury need no encouragement.

'There are seventy-two pictures in our folder, and if I understand correctly, they are just a fraction of the total number he took over a period of several months, most of which you deleted from your phone. Correct?'

'Correct.'

'So you permitted Mr Verity to take hundreds of such pictures of you?'

'I didn't think of myself as permitting it.'

'They were taken in your home, weren't they?'

'Yes.'

'And we've already agreed that you could have asked him to leave your home at any time. You could also have told him to stop taking pictures, couldn't you?'

'That's easy for you to say,' Angie protests.

Cathy spreads her arms out wide. 'If I'm being unfair to you, please explain and I'll apologise. It's not my intention to take advantage.'

'He was controlling me.'

'Really? Well, let's look at one or two examples of you being controlled by Mr Verity, shall we? Don't worry. I'm not going to go through all of them. The jury will be able to do that for themselves and form their own impression. But let's just look at one or two. Please turn to page four. Is that you in the picture at top left on page four?'

'Yes.'

'You seem to be naked, is that right?'

'Obviously.'

'Obviously. And how would you describe what you're doing when this picture was taken?'

'That's also obvious.'

'I'm sure it's obvious to you, but for the jury's benefit, perhaps you would describe what you're doing?'

'I'm in the process of performing oral sex on Mr Verity.'

'Yes, and you've paused to look up towards his phone, haven't you, looking right into the camera? How would you describe your facial expression?'

She shrugs. 'I don't know.'

'It's quite suggestive, isn't it? Seductive? Sexy? Would any of those words describe it?'

'Whatever you say.'

'I'm interested in what *you* say, Miss Simmons. I'm asking you to help the jury to understand what's going on in this picture. Let me ask you directly, then: is that the look of a woman who's being controlled?'

Finally, Roderick rises to his feet. I'm surprised he didn't weigh in some time ago, though so far, Cathy's cross has been a *tour de force*, and she's hardly paused for breath, so perhaps he couldn't find a way in.

'Your Honour, it's not proper for my learned friend to ask the witness to express an opinion on that. The jury will make up their own minds what the picture shows, if it shows anything.'

'I think that must be right, Miss Writtle,' I say. 'It is a matter for the jury to draw conclusions, isn't it?'

'Very well, your Honour. Please look at page six, Miss Simmons, middle picture, top line. Would you please describe for the jury what's going on in that picture?'

'He's having sexual intercourse with me from behind.'

'Yes, with you on your knees, looking backwards into the camera. How would you describe the expression on your face in that picture?'

No reply.

'Well, it's not the expression of a woman being controlled by the man she's with, is it, Miss Simmons?'

Roderick is on his feet in a flash.

'Again, your Honour –'

'I'll move on,' Cathy replies without waiting for me to intervene.

'Miss Simmons, did Mr Verity give you money during your relationship?'

'I don't understand.'

'It's a simple question. Did Mr Verity give you money during your relationship?'

'Yes, he gave me money sometimes.'

'For what purpose?'

She hesitates.

'Was it to buy cocaine for yourself?'

'Yes, sometimes.'

'You couldn't afford to keep up with his lifestyle on your salary, could you?'

'No,' she concedes. 'He led a fast life. I couldn't have kept up, and I'm not sure I would have wanted to.'

'But you did keep up, with the help of his money, didn't you?'

'Look, he would pay when we went out to dinner or when we went to a nightclub, that kind of thing, and if I needed drugs he would sometimes buy them for me – but not always; I'd been using cocaine long before I was with Mr Verity, and I had my own dealer.'

'How much were you spending just on cocaine during the period you were together?'

'Somewhere in the region of two hundred, three hundred pounds a week.'

I glance over at the jury and see some eyebrows being raised, eyes being opened wide.

'But he benefitted from that, too,' she added quickly. 'It was a joint supply to some extent.'

'You also asked Mr Verity for money towards the rent of your flat, Miss Simmons, didn't you?'

'No, I did not. Why would I do that?'

'Well, it's fairly expensive, isn't it, living in Canary Wharf? And now that you'd found yourself a sugar daddy –'

'He was *not* my sugar daddy. I resent that suggestion.'

'He was subsidising your coke habit, not to mention taking you out for dinners and drinks, and in return he was having sex with you. What would *you* call it?'

'The sex wasn't "in return for" anything. We had sex because we were two consenting adults, who enjoyed it.'

'Yes, so we can see from the pictures in Exhibit one.'

'Your Honour –' Roderick growls, half standing up, not conceding the commitment of a full stance.

'Miss Writtle...' I say.

'Yes, your Honour. Miss Simmons, what happened was this, wasn't it? You were making ever-increasing demands for money from him, to feed your coke habit and pay your rent?'

'No.'

'It got up to two or three hundred pounds a week, and still you wanted more and more because you saw him as your sugar daddy?'

'No. He wasn't –'

'And the time came when he said, "No. Enough is enough. I'm not giving you any more money". You persisted in your demands, and that was when he told you that he wanted to end the relationship?'

'I was the one who ended it.'

'I put it to you that he was the one who ended it, and that when he told you that, you threatened to tell his wife Megan all about the affair?'

'No.'

'And it was for that reason and no other, to prevent your

telling his wife, that Mr Verity threatened to upload the pictures he had taken of you. It was to stop you telling his wife, wasn't it?'

'That's not true.'

Cathy glances up at me. 'I have nothing further, your Honour.'

It's a trick many advocates use – to pretend to have finished and then leap back up with an important question they almost omitted 'inadvertently' – but few are as good at it as Cathy. I've seen her do it many times, and the effect is very dramatic.

'Oh, I'm sorry, your Honour, there is one more thing, if I may… Miss Simmons, from what you've told the jury, there could be no possible question of your distributing the pictures we have in Exhibit one to anyone else yourself? That's totally out of the question, isn't it?'

'For me to distribute them? No, of course not. It would be totally out of the question. I'd have to be mad to do that. I was desperately trying to suppress them.'

'Of course you were.' Cathy reaches behind her and takes a document from her instructing solicitor. 'Your Honour, I've shown this to my learned friend, and I will have evidence to authenticate it during the defence case. I'll ask for it to be made an exhibit at that stage. With the usher's assistance…' She waits for Dawn to take the document to the witness box.

'It follows from what you say, Miss Simmons, that you would have no idea where this document could have come from?'

Miss Simmons is flicking through the document, and seems to be going a bit white around the gills.

'I've never seen this before. I don't know where it could have come from.'

'Very well,' Cathy says, resuming her seat. She really has finished now.

That's as far as we're going before lunch. Stella needs me to take a sentence. Marjorie was supposed to do it, but she's reached a critical point in her trial and can't make time. Chummy is a habitual residential burglar, who has admitted to thirty-six such offences in the six months since he was released from the mandatory minimum three-year stretch he was given for his already dreadful record for residential burglary. I have no alternative but to send him inside again, this time for five years. Let's see if that makes a difference in curbing his pattern of recidivism. You never know, but the cynical part of me thinks we will probably see him back at Bermondsey six months or so after his release.

And so to lunch, an oasis of calm in a desert of chaos.

'What do you think of Miss Simmons now?' I ask Jean-Claude as we stroll from chambers to the judicial mess. 'Are you beginning to doubt her?'

He smiles. 'I don't know yet. I think this new document may be interesting. I'm looking forward to learning more about it.'

'So am I,' I agree.

With Jean-Claude at the table as well as the rest of us, lunch is even more intimate than usual in our small space, taken up as it is by our massive dining table, free to us, regardless of utility, from another government department. Jean-Claude has ordered a salad. He looked a bit shell-shocked after lunch yesterday. As I was busy with the Grey Smoothies, I wasn't able to look out for him, and Hubert talked him into the dish of the day, some kind of cheesy, creamy pasta. I'm sure that came as a nasty shock to his Parisian taste buds, and it's not going to happen again on my watch. I have my ham and cheese bap from Elsie and Jeanie. We are the last to arrive. Jean-Claude and Marjorie chat away in French for a minute or two before she turns to me.

'Thanks for taking my sentence, Charlie. What did you give him?'

'Five years.'

She nods. 'Exactly what I had in mind,' she agrees.

'Should have been more like seven,' Hubert mutters, looking up briefly from his fish cakes and new potatoes.

'I didn't know this case was one of yours, Hubert,' I say.

'It's not,' he replies. 'Just saw it in the list. Three strikes burglar coming back for more. You can't be too hard on people like that. Cause people no end of misery. I may be too low. Perhaps nine would be closer.'

'So how did it go with the Grey Smoothies?' Legless asks me, a welcome relief from the prospect of another seminar on Raj-era sentencing from Hubert. 'Is there any hope for us?'

'I'm afraid not,' I reply. 'They're dead set against the outdated model of the small court centre, and we're the smallest of the small. I'm afraid we're for the chop. Have you all thought about where you'd like to go? I think Bagnall will listen to me and do what he can. Let me know what your preferences are, and I will pass them on to him.'

Legless smiles. 'I think Marjorie should go and sit in Paris, shouldn't she, Jean-Claude? You could find a use for her, couldn't you?'

Marjorie laughs out loud.

'But of course,' Jean-Claude replies. 'She would make a most distinguished French judge.'

'Actually, Marjorie,' Legless says, more seriously, 'I think you should apply for the High Court next time there's a competition. You're wasted on us plebs in the Crown Court. You're more than qualified. You're a real lawyer. I think you ought to consider it.'

Marjorie doesn't reply, but she's obviously pleased by the compliment.

'I'm sorry you think so little of your other colleagues, Legless,' I remark. 'Plebs, are we?'

He laughs. 'Just a figure of speech,' he replies. He pauses. 'Actually, Charlie, I have the same thought about you. I think you could try for the High Court, or if not, certainly the Old Bailey.'

For whatever reason, this really takes me aback, and it's some time before I feel able to respond. As a circuit judge you do get those thoughts running through your head in your more imaginative moments. But eventually, you programme yourself to dismiss them as unrealistic as soon as they arise. The Grey Smoothie propaganda about the intellectual superiority of the High Court bench rubs off on us: much as we often find it to be unsupported by the evidence, and much as we sense that there are strong High Court judges and weak High Court judges, just as there are strong circuit judges and weak circuit judges – or dentists, or architects, or insurance brokers, or bus drivers. After some time, you begin to feel that there's a line you can't cross; that you've risen as high as you ever will, and as being a circuit judge is on the whole a rather enjoyable job, you relax back into it.

'That's very kind of you, Legless, but I hardly think that's on the cards.'

'Of course it is,' Marjorie chimes in.

'Of course it is,' Legless insists. 'You've done some big cases. What about that case you tried a year or so ago – you know, the one about that island in the Channel, where Chummy was claiming to be king and pleading sovereign immunity?'

I see Jean-Claude's eyes light up, and he flashes me a smile.

'The Foggin Island case,' I reply.

'That's the one,' Legless says, 'and they sent that ornament of the High Court bench Steven Gulivant to try it, and he had to recuse himself. You ended up trying it, and you did a far better job than he could ever have done. The man had no idea how to try a criminal case. You had to lead him by the hand through a simple offensive weapon case you gave him to keep his mind occupied for the rest of the week.'

'True,' I agree, 'but in fairness, he did start to get the idea eventually. In the end, the jury even sent a note saying how helpful his summing-up had been. Besides, he was very helpful to me over Foggin Island. It was some research he'd commissioned that opened my eyes to the solution – that the Island was actually French territory.'

'L'Ile des Fougains,' Jean-Claude intervenes.

'Yes. Once he realised that we were likely to ship him off to France for trial, he abandoned his plea of sovereign immunity and pleaded to the indictment quicker than you could say "extradition".'

Jean-Claude is smiling at me again.

'It's quite a coincidence that you should bring Foggin Island up,' I say. 'Jean-Claude was asking me about that case over dinner only yesterday evening. I don't know why it's raising its head like this all of a sudden, but apparently it's been the subject of discussion at the Quai d'Orsay, no less.'

'Really?' Legless asks. 'You knew about that case?'

Jean-Claude sits forward in his chair.

'Certainly. Perhaps here in Bermondsey, the case of L'Ile des Fougains is just another criminal case which has come and gone. But to France, it has some lasting importance. The end of the case at Bermondsey was only the beginning of an intense round of negotiations between France and Great Britain. It was quite a serious matter, actually. Here we had an island very close to the English coast under French sovereignty, because England had ceded it to us in 1360. In earlier days, it could have been the cause for war at any time. Today, that possibility is obviously extremely remote, but still, both sides were somewhat embarrassed that L'Ile des Fougains had found its way into the Treaty of Calais.'

'Great Britain more so than France, I imagine,' I suggest.

He laughs. 'Yes, I agree. But France was anxious to reach

an accommodation. We gave Great Britain assurances that we would not use the island for any purpose without prior notice, and in any case not for any purpose that could conceivably hurt British interests. In effect, we gave you a power of veto over any French activity on the island. In return, Great Britain made certain concessions to France on other fronts. I don't know the details of those concessions, which are diplomatic secrets, but I have friends at the Quai d'Orsay who were involved in the negotiations, and they assure me that these concessions are of the greatest importance to France.'

'So much so that Jean-Claude is going to brief his ambassador about the case at a reception this evening, he tells me,' I say with a smile.

'Certainly,' he replies, returning the smile. 'An ambassador can never be too well informed.'

'I almost made it up to the High Court once,' Hubert says, from nowhere, after a silence. All eyes turn to him.

'Really?' I ask, hoping that I'm not making the idea sound as improbable as it seems.

'Oh, yes. I was having dinner in Lincoln's Inn one evening, with old Monty Carstairs. He was one of the Lord Chancellor's right hand men when it came to appointments then. This was when I'd only been appointed for seven years or so. Monty was a bencher, you see, and he picked me out of the crowd in the bar and invited me to dine with him on the high table. Well, I was very flattered, of course. So he takes me into the benchers' room for the pre-dinner drinks, and then we go in to dinner, and we're getting as pissed as newts, I don't mind telling you. We'd started with the bubbly before dinner, white and red wine with dinner, and a dessert wine too, if I remember rightly. So we were well away, Monty even more than myself; and at the end of dinner, over the coffee and port, he suddenly leans across the table to whisper in my ear. Very confidential: you'd have thought he was about to reveal the plans for the atom bomb. And bugger me, if he doesn't say, "I've heard some very good reports about you, very good indeed. If I were to recommend you to the Lord Chancellor for higher preferment" – I remember those words specifically, because it's bloody difficult to say "higher preferment" when you're as pissed as Monty was, and it took him about three goes. Anyway, "If I were to recommend you to the Lord Chancellor for higher preferment," he says, "would you be minded to accept?" Well, he didn't mention the High Court as such, but when you're a circuit judge, what else could "higher preferment" mean? So, of course, I said I would definitely be minded to accept, and shortly after that dinner ended, and we had to process out of hall, the head porter giving us some welcome assistance because we were wobbling a bit by then, and I'm sure the students must have been noticing.'

Hubert stops, as if the story has reached its logical ending.

'But what happened, Hubert?' Marjorie asks. 'Why didn't they make you up to the High Court?'

Legless laughs. 'Old Monty was probably so pissed that the next day he couldn't even remember what he'd said the night before,' he suggests.

'No, not at all,' Hubert replies. 'He remembered perfectly well. The problem was, it was a case of mistaken identity. He thought he'd been having dinner with Clarence Darcy. I can't think why. Clarence and I don't look much alike, and if he wasn't sure he could have asked, couldn't he? Anyway, there it was; nothing I could do about it. And sure enough, they appointed Clarence about three months later.'

'That's terrible, Hubert,' Marjorie says.

'Oh, not really,' Hubert replies. 'Dog's life, being a High Court judge, according to everything I hear. You're away from home much of the year; you work all the hours there are; you're in court or writing judgments most of the day; and after that you have paperwork to do; and after that you have to go to interminable dinners with local dignitaries and the like. Wouldn't suit me at all. I'd never have time for the Garrick. Much better here.'

* * *

Tuesday afternoon

This afternoon is excruciatingly dull. Roderick, apparently spooked by the sudden appearance of document two, has decided to prove the transmission of the pictures from the defendant's phone to Angie Simmons's phone the hard way. Proving anything to do with mobile phones the hard way is always time consuming and usually terminally boring. Often the prosecution tries to prove where somebody was at a given time by proving where their phone was at that time. There are times when this works well, but not always. Even when it does, the court is inundated with charts and data showing signals bouncing off towers, and it can take hours for an expert to explain all this to a jury. It's much the same with our case. Here, it's not a question of signals bouncing off towers: it's a question of the 'interrogation' of both phones. But it still takes page after page of coded language, and we still need an expert witness to make sense of it all.

I had thought that both sides had agreed what had happened in this case, and that if we needed this kind of evidence, it could be reduced to a series of simple admissions of fact that both I and the jury could understand without the help of experts. It seems that document two has changed the landscape, and Roderick now feels the need to fortify his case against an unexpected attack; though as neither I nor the jury have yet seen it, we have no idea why. No doubt all will become clear in time.

Once we've finished with that, Roderick calls DC Featherstone, as the officer in the case. They begin with Jack Verity's police interview under caution. It's extremely long, and with Roderick and DC Featherstone reading questions and answers aloud – not always accurately and not always with any great indication of interest – you can see the jury beginning to nod off, even though they have copies of the transcript to follow. It's a process that always takes me back to the English play-reading society in the sixth form. We were an all-boys school, and the play-reading society was popular because our liberal English teacher made a deal with his counterpart at the local girls' grammar school to have some of their sixth-formers visit us to read the female characters. But even with that incentive, sleep never felt far away.

Roderick then deals with the investigation generally. DC Featherstone comes across as competent and thorough, and Cathy has no questions for her. By now it's after three thirty, and no one has the heart to go on. Besides, Roderick is ready to close his case, and we would all prefer to have the jury awake when Cathy opens the defence case. There's far more chance of that tomorrow morning than there is this afternoon, and to the general relief, I agree to adjourn the case until then.

* * *

Tuesday evening

Later, at home, over the Reverend Mrs Walden's fettucine con pesto, I tell her about the discussion in the mess at lunchtime.

'It's quite a coincidence, the Foggin Island case coming up again like that,' I say.

'But didn't you say that it was Legless who brought it up today?'

'It was. But Jean-Claude jumped right in, and he's still talking about briefing his ambassador. Why is he so keen to make sure the ambassador knows about Foggin Island? I can't put my finger on it, but I have the strangest feeling that there's something going on.'

'That's what I thought when he asked you about it last night,' she replies.

'You didn't say anything.'

'I didn't have anything useful to say. It might have been my imagination – or the quantity of Cobra we got through.'

'What do you think now?'

'I think it's possible that, in some strange way, he's made a connection between your case and the plan to close down the court.'

We are silent for some time.

'What connection?' I ask. 'What could the case possibly have to do with closing the court?'

'Your guess is as good as mine,' she replies. 'But I think there's a connection in Jean-Claude's mind. Actually, I think he has some idea that he can assist in your cause.'

'My cause? What, you mean keeping the court open?'

'Exactly.'

'How on earth could he do that?'

'I have no idea. But that's my feeling.'

I reflect for some time.

'Well, even if you're right, he won't get anywhere with it,' I say pessimistically, swirling the last of my Sainsbury's Special Reserve Chianti around forlornly in the bottom of my glass.

'I'm not so sure,' she replies.

'He doesn't know what he's up against, Clara,' I insist. 'He's never been up against the Grey Smoothies.'

We are quiet again for a moment or two.

'How do you say "Grey Smoothies" in French?' she asks suddenly.

We laugh.

'I have no idea. I'll ask Jean-Claude tomorrow.'

'Well, that's my point, Charlie. He'll know how to say it because, whatever they call them, they have Grey Smoothies in France too. My point about Jean-Claude is that he's obviously a man who is very well connected. Men like that don't pick fights they don't think they can win. Don't underestimate him, Charlie.'

* * *

Wednesday morning

This morning I pick Jean-Claude up at his hotel by appointment. I want him to walk to court with me so that we can call in to see Elsie and Jeanie. He didn't seem to enjoy his salad very much yesterday, and I can't have him being exposed to the dish of the day again: so a sandwich *chez* Elsie and Jeanie may be the best solution. Elsie and Jeanie are in a good mood today. When I introduce Jean-Claude, Elsie comes up with '*bonjour*', while Jeanie even manages an '*enchantée, Monsieur*'. Jean-Claude is visibly impressed. He's even more impressed when we go next door and George presents him with a choice of *Le Monde* or *Le Figaro*. He takes both, which I think is very classy, because I have little doubt that he has already scanned both in his hotel over his morning croissant and coffee.

'Clara was asking me last night how you would translate "Grey Smoothies" into French,' I say, as we stroll along to court with our sandwiches and lattes. 'Of course, I had no idea, but I said I would ask you.'

Jean-Claude laughs.

'That's a good question.' He thinks for some time. 'It's not a translation, but at my court we call them "*Les éminences gris*". So the element of greyness is present in French also. You understand, we use the word "*éminence*" in an ironic sense.'

'So you do have Grey Smoothies in France?'

'But of course. Smoothies, *éminences,* whatever you call them, the Grey Smoothies are everywhere, aren't they? We have an old saying in France, Charles: "*Plus ça change, plus c'est la même chose*".'

We walk on in silence for another hundred yards or so.

'Can I ask you something else, Jean-Claude?' I ask.

He smiles. 'You want to know whether I spoke with my ambassador. Yes?'

'Yes. You mentioned it when we had dinner on Monday evening, and again at lunch yesterday, and I understand that she might find the Foggin Island case interesting, but…'

We both stop and turn to face each other.

'Yes, actually I had quite a long conversation with Valérie yesterday evening.'

'But…'

'Charles,' he says. 'We understand that to you, this is just another case. But in French eyes, it was a case in which an English court recognised an important French interest under international law.'

'But it was clear from the evidence that the island belongs to France,' I object. 'What else could we have done?'

'True: but still, it's a remarkable thing for a court such as Bermondsey to find in favour of a foreign state, and against its own government, in such a sensitive matter. That is something worthy of note in international law, and it's not something that happens every day.'

We walk another fifty yards or so.

'What did your ambassador think about that?' I ask.

'She thinks the same as I do,' Jean-Claude replies, 'namely: that we cannot stand idly by while your government closes down such a beacon of international law as the Bermondsey Crown Court. In our view, the court must be preserved for posterity and properly recognised. We are not sure how much we can do, but we are agreed that we will not let it go without a fight.'

Cathy Writtle calls Jack Verity to give evidence. He's smartly turned out in his best City banker suit, as one would expect, but he looks terrible. He is pale and haggard, as if he hasn't slept for weeks. My first thought, as in almost every case, is that I'm seeing the accumulated stress of waiting for an impending trial; but given what we've been hearing about Verity's life in the fast lane, it wouldn't be much of a surprise to learn that this is his normal state. God only knows how he copes with a demanding job at the bank; then again, perhaps he doesn't.

'Mr Verity,' Cathy begins once he has taken the oath, 'the jury has heard that you are a banker by profession, is that right?'

'That's correct.'

'We haven't been using the name of the bank, but is that the same bank at which Miss Simmons also worked until she was apparently dismissed?'

'Yes, it is.'

'You met Miss Simmons through work?'

'Yes.'

'And a relationship began between you. How did that happen?'

'It happened much as she said. We started going out for drinks or dinner, and one thing led to another, and one evening we ended up at her place and went to bed. It went from there.'

'Leaving aside the sexual aspect of your relationship for a moment, did you have any arrangements between you about money? You were earning far more than she was. Was there any understanding about money?'

'It was understood that I would pay for dinner and drinks when we went out. We both liked cocaine, and I would purchase cocaine for her, or give her money for cocaine if she asked for it. As she said herself, she was quite capable of buying her own supply. She had her own dealer.'

'Your relationship lasted for some six months, didn't it?'

'Yes.'

'Can you give the jury some idea of how much money you were giving her during that period?'

'It started off modestly enough, fifty here, a hundred there, but she was always asking me for more. She said it got up to two or three hundred a week, but by the end it was up to four hundred or more and still it wasn't enough.'

'How did you react to that?'

'It disappointed me. I came to feel that she was only in it for the money, that she saw me as her sugar daddy, and to be honest, I got tired of it. The sex was good, but it was just too much of a hassle. I earn good money, but I couldn't afford to pay on that scale, and I didn't want to pay on that scale.'

'And did there come a time when you told her that?'

'I told her several times. I made it clear that it had to stop, or I was gone. She ignored me, and kept asking for more and more, and one day I said, "Enough is enough", and I told her that it was over between us.'

'What did she say to that?'

'She said if I walked out on her – that's how she put it – she would tell Megan all about us.'

'Megan being your wife?'

'Yes.'

'Did Megan know anything about your affair at that point?'

'No. It wasn't unusual for me to be out half the night entertaining clients, so there was nothing strange about my being gone in the evenings. No, she never knew a thing.'

'How did it make you feel when she threatened to blow the lid off your affair?'

'I totally freaked out. I panicked. I was terrified.'

'Why was that?'

Verity hangs his head in silence for some time.

'I love my wife. I was desperate not to lose her. I'd never done anything like this before. Well, there had been the odd one-night stand with a female client, but never an affair, never like what I had with Angie. And now Angie was going to betray me just because I wouldn't keep on giving her these insane amounts of money. I felt totally desperate, and I felt I had to do anything I could to stop her.'

'What did you do, in fact?'

'I threatened to upload the pictures on Facebook, or even put them up on the internet.'

'Mr Verity, do you have Exhibit one with you in the witness box?'

'Yes.'

'Just look through Exhibit one for a moment, would you?'

Unbidden, the jury take this as permission to open their own copies once more.

'Are those the pictures you are referring to?'

'These are some of them, yes. There was a far bigger collection on my phone when I made the threat – hundreds of them – but I've deleted them all since then.'

'These, of course, came from Miss Simmons's phone, as we heard from her. But do I take it that she would have had many more than the seventy-odd we have here?'

'Yes. I sent any picture I took to her phone on my way home every night, and we might do fifty or more in a night. She had every picture I had.'

'Now, you heard Miss Simmons tell the jury that she was reluctant to appear in these pictures, that she didn't like you taking pictures while you were having sex. What do you say about that?'

'That is just ridiculous. You only have to look at the pictures to see that she's having the time of her life. She thought it was just as much fun as I did. We used to look at the pictures together. It turned us on.'

'Did she ever ask you not to take such pictures of her?'

'Not at all. Not at all. She encouraged me. She loved every minute of it.'

Cathy pauses to consult her notes.

'Miss Simmons also suggested to the jury that the pictures were only one aspect of what she called your "domineering" behaviour towards her, which was based on your superior position in the bank, your higher earnings, and in contrast to her tender age of thirty-one, your more mature age of…?'

'Forty-five now, forty-four at the time.'

'Forty-four. Mr Verity, did you ever abuse your position in the bank to try to control Miss Simmons in any way?'

'Again, that's ridiculous. Angie Simmons isn't the kind of woman who would let a man control her. As an executive of the bank she had to be able to stand up for herself, with clients and with senior management, and to my knowledge she always did. She certainly had that reputation, and she certainly came off to me that way. She would never have put up with that kind of nonsense from me, or anyone else for that matter.'

'Did you ever suggest that you had any influence on her continuing employment at the bank?'

'No. I wouldn't do anything like that. I've never had anything to do with hiring and firing at the bank. That happens above my level, and Angie knew that as well as I did. Even if I had been involved with hiring and firing, I wouldn't have participated in any decision involving Angie, for obvious reasons.'

'Well, playing devil's advocate for a moment,' Cathy asks, 'she might have thought that you could put in a bad word for her with someone above your level, mightn't she?'

'Perhaps. But I never did, and I never would have done anything like that. And she never said anything to me about being worried about her job, ever.'

'Did you have anything to do with Miss Simmons losing her job?'

'No. Nothing whatsoever. I only heard about it after the event.'

'Do you know why she lost her job?'

'I really don't. The talk around the office was that she'd had a bad end-of-year review, but no one said anything to me directly, and I didn't ask. Once she sued the bank for wrongful dismissal, everyone stopped talking about it.'

'I think this is agreed, but I would like the jury to hear it from you, Mr Verity. Did you ever show any of the pictures you had taken of Miss Simmons to anyone at the bank?'

'No, of course not. If I'd done that, I would have been in far more danger of losing my job than she would. Relationships with more junior staff are discouraged in the best of circumstances, and if the directors had got wind that I was taking pictures like that, I could have been for the high jump myself.'

'In fact, did you ever upload any of the pictures to social media or the internet?'

'No. I did not.'

'Did you even retain the pictures after the relationship?'

'Only for a short time, in case Angie did try to tell Megan about us. But once she had been sacked, and she hadn't approached Megan, I just deleted them – all of them.'

'Mr Verity, looking back now, how do you feel about the threat you made to Miss Simmons to publicise the pictures you had taken of her?'

Verity is silent for some time.

'It's not something I'm proud of, but I genuinely felt I had no alternative. She was out of control, demanding money, threatening to tell Megan about us. I couldn't allow that to happen. I thought I was justified in making my own threat to bring her back to her senses.'

'And we know now that instead of going to Megan, Miss Simmons went to the police and made a complaint against you.'

'Yes.'

'You were arrested?'

'Yes.'

'And you were interviewed by the police under caution. We heard the interview read yesterday afternoon. Is it right that you told the police, at much greater length, essentially what you've told the jury this morning, and do you stand by what you told the police?'

'Yes. I've told the truth from the moment I was arrested.'

'Finally, Mr Verity, you were in court yesterday when I showed Miss Simmons a document we've been calling "document two". Is that a document you know anything about?'

'No. Megan found it, and I believe you will be calling her to give evidence later. But I knew nothing about it until she showed it to me.'

'In that case, I won't ask you to look at it,' Cathy says. 'But I will ask you this. As you say, your wife will be giving evidence on your behalf later. What attitude has she taken towards you since she found out about the affair?'

'She has been deeply hurt, obviously, especially in view of the very public way it has all come to light. But we've talked it over endlessly. I've promised her that nothing like this will ever happen again. She has said that she will stand by me and put it behind us, and I'm very grateful to her. It's more than I deserve.'

Out of the corner of my eye I see Jean-Claude smiling at me. I do my best to pretend I haven't noticed, without success. 'Or perhaps it's the only thing she can do,' he whispers, very quietly, in my ear, leaning in towards me. 'Who knows?'

'Wait there, please, Mr Verity,' Cathy says, signing off. 'There may be some further questions.'

There will be some further questions; there's no doubt about that. Roderick is already on his feet.

'Mr Verity, you say that you would have been for the high jump, as you put it, if the bank had found out about the pictures. But they did find out, didn't they?'

'Not from me.'

'No, but they did find out, didn't they? Tell the jury, please: what is your current employment situation?'

'I'm still employed, pending the outcome of these proceedings.'

'Whereas Miss Simmons was sacked without waiting for the outcome of these proceedings, wasn't she?'

'As I said before, I don't know why she was sacked. It may have had nothing to do with this case at all.'

'Is that a serious answer, Mr Verity?'

'Yes, it is.'

'Very well. I'll move on. Do you have a copy of the indictment with you in the witness box?'

Verity looks around but can't find one. Roderick summons Dawn, who speeds one over to the box.

'I'd like to take you through the indictment, Mr Verity. I'm sure you've been through it with your legal advisers, but I'd like to explore with you what parts of the definition of blackmail you don't understand.'

'There's no need for sarcasm,' Cathy complains, standing quickly. 'He can ask whatever questions he wishes to ask without being sarcastic to the witness.'

I can't help smiling. This is a definite case of the pot calling the kettle black. Cathy is the undisputed queen of courtroom sarcasm. I usually have to tell her off about it at least once per cross-examination in any given case. But it takes one to know one, and in this instance she's got him bang to rights; Roderick acknowledges this with a wave of the hand before I have time to tell him off.

'Do you have the indictment now?' he asks.

'Yes.'

'Good. Look where it says "particulars of offence". Do you see that?'

'Yes.'

'Good. The particulars allege, first, that you made an unwarranted demand with menaces against Miss Simmons. You did make a demand of her, didn't you? You demanded that she not tell your wife about your affair?'

'That's correct.'

'And you made that demand with menaces, didn't you? You threatened to upload those pictures in Exhibit one, and no doubt many others, if she didn't comply with your demand?'

'Yes, I did.'

'Yes. The particulars go on to say that you did this with a view to gain for yourself or to cause loss to another. It would be a gain if you could persuade her not to say anything to your wife, wouldn't it? You made that pretty clear to the jury this morning, didn't you?'

'Yes, that's perfectly true.'

'And by the same token, if you had carried out your threat, it would certainly have caused loss to Miss Simmons, wouldn't it?'

'I can't say that. As I said before, I don't know why she was sacked.'

'Well, the prosecution doesn't accept that, Mr Verity. But let's leave that aside for a moment, shall we? Forget about her job. Let's imagine that you uploaded those pictures, so that Miss

Simmons's family and friends could go online and see them for themselves. Could we fairly describe that as a loss to Miss Simmons?'

Roderick's legal research isn't as thorough as it once was. He referred to her family and friends during his opening speech, and I was half expecting Cathy to jump up then. But she was craftily biding her time. Now, she springs on him like a tiger from a thicket.

'Your Honour, my learned friend is misrepresenting the law to Mr Verity. He knows perfectly well that under the definition of blackmail, "loss" refers only to losses in terms of money or other property. It does not refer to an injury to one's reputation unless it would cause monetary loss, and there can be no suggestion that Miss Simmons would have lost money because her family or friends thought less of her.'

It's a bad mistake, and Roderick knows it immediately. A movement of his right hand suggests a momentary flirtation with looking it up in *Archbold*, but Roderick has been around too long to prolong a moment like this in a hopeless cause. He can see for himself that Cathy has *Archbold* open in front of her; she's not making this up. There's nothing to do but to beat a dignified and courteous retreat – something Roderick has become very adept at over the years.

'My learned friend is quite right, of course,' he concedes. 'I do apologise, Mr Verity. Let's forget about family and friends.'

'All right.'

'The fact remains, doesn't it, that she was sacked immediately after the board found out about the pictures?'

Cathy is in full tiger mode now; she has her claws in him, and she isn't about to withdraw them just yet.

'Your Honour, we've been over and over this. Mr Verity has insisted that he doesn't know why Miss Simmons was sacked. He wasn't involved with any aspect of that, and it would be wrong to invite the jury to speculate about whatever may have gone on in the boardroom. It may have had nothing to do with the issues in this case at all. It's unfair to Mr Verity to allow this line of questioning.'

There are in fact one or two not unreasonable responses to that, but being mauled by a tiger is a traumatic experience, and Roderick hasn't composed himself in time to think of them. In the circumstances, I don't feel like helping him out, and when he suggests that he will move on, I say nothing. Roderick makes a pretence of consulting his notes while frantically trying to work out where he can go from here.

'The particulars of the offence also allege, Mr Verity,' he says eventually, 'that the demand you made of Miss Simmons was unwarranted. Under the law – and I hope my learned friend won't have any problem with this, but no doubt she will let us all know if she does...'

He half turns towards her, but she half turns away from him and towards the jury, and it's fairly obvious that some smiles are being exchanged between them.

'As I was saying, under the law, a demand is unwarranted unless the maker of the demand believes one of two things. The first is that he had reasonable grounds for making the demand. Are you seriously telling this jury that you believed your demand was reasonable?'

'Yes, I am.'

'There was no other way to deal with the situation?'

'Such as what?'

'Such as sitting down with Miss Simmons, perhaps, to talk the matter over calmly?'

'We were beyond talking calmly at that stage. The only thing she wanted to talk about was my giving her more money. If I didn't agree to what she wanted, she was going to Megan. There was no reasoning with her.'

'In that case, what about sitting down with your wife, perhaps, taking pre-emptive action, facing up to what you'd done?'

'That didn't seem like an attractive option to me.'

'I'm sure it didn't, Mr Verity. But what the law requires is that you act reasonably. Was it reasonable to contemplate splashing these highly explicit pictures all over social media and the internet?'

'In my opinion, yes.'

'The second thing the law requires is that you believed that it was proper for you to reinforce your demand with that threat. No doubt you will say that is what you believed?'

'I believed it then, and I believe it today.'

'You're not telling the jury the truth, are you, Mr Verity?'

'I am telling the truth.'

'This was just another example of the bullying, hectoring behaviour you showed to her, wasn't it? You were making her submit to having those pictures taken, with the implied threat that you could influence her future career at the bank, and when she fought back, you threatened to ruin her.'

'That's complete nonsense.'

'Is it?'

'Yes, it is. She's trying to present herself as the innocent victim, but she's not what she claims to be: as you will find out when you see – what is it we're calling it – document two?'

Roderick sits down. His last question was pointless and it got the answer it deserved. It's not been his finest hour. There's the mysterious document two again, casting its long shadow over the case before the jury have even seen it. Objectively, the prosecution's evidence seems pretty strong, but I think I'm beginning to see the case slipping away – albeit not for the same reasons as Jean-Claude. Wisely, Cathy decides to quit while she is ahead. There is to be no re-examination, and Jack Verity makes the return trek from the witness box to the dock, bloodied a little perhaps, but as far as I can see, essentially unbowed. To the general relief of everyone in court, Cathy asks for a short break before calling her next witness. Coffee beckons.

In chambers, Jean-Claude and I concur about the direction in which the case is heading, though he still maintains that Angie Simmons is not the helpless victim she claims to be, and he still maintains that Megan has a dark side to her as well. I prefer the view that Cathy Writtle is doing a lot of damage to the evidence, and it's going to take its toll. Both of us find our conclusions disturbing, because the evidence suggests that Jack Verity has probably committed the offence of blackmail, even if you believe every word he's said.

We have longer to discuss this than we expected. Roderick sends word that he is asking for an adjournment until after lunch to consider the implications of document two and to take instructions from the CPS, which adds to the sense of disquiet. I can't really refuse him. It was a bit naughty of Cathy to drop it on him after the trial had started. Either way, I have to allow Roderick some time to consider his position.

And so to lunch, an oasis of calm in a desert of chaos.

I must admit that Jean-Claude's depiction of Bermondsey Crown Court as one of the holy sites of international law has sent my head into something of a spin, so much so that it's been quite an effort to focus on what's been going on in court during the morning. And try as I may to imagine it, it's hard to believe that Jean-Claude or his ambassador could persuade the Grey Smoothies to spare Bermondsey the axe on the ground that it's become a place of pilgrimage for devotees of the rule of international law. I'm still having some difficulty with the idea that we should even take credit for making the now infamous finding in favour of France. For one thing, we didn't have much choice; the evidence was clear. And for another, the result, whether against our government's interests or not, was a huge boon to yours truly. The Foggin Island case was a nightmare. If Chummy hadn't panicked at the thought of being deported to France and pleaded out, I would have been forced to give a very long and very public judgment about the status of Foggin Island in customary international law. I would almost certainly have made a complete pig's ear of it, after which any chance I might have had of making it to the High Court or the Old Bailey, remote to begin with, would have vanished for ever into the ether.

But Jean-Claude, and apparently his ambassador, seem to be in deadly earnest about it all. We talk at some length before going in to lunch. I ask Jean-Claude if we can let the others into the secret. He agrees, as long as we can agree to keep it confidential while he and the ambassador consider what to do. When I explain all this, he has the undivided attention of the judicial mess.

'Yesterday evening, I spoke with our ambassador, before joining Hubert for dinner,' he begins. 'She's an old friend from our university days.'

I'm struck by the renewed mention of friendship, and I find myself wondering whether there might have been a bit more than friendship involved during their university days.

'Valérie agrees with me about the importance of the case of L'Ile des Fougains to France. She also agrees with me that, because of the potential historical significance of Bermondsey Crown Court, it is important that the French Government should have the opportunity to be heard before any decision is taken to close the court. She and I each have our own contacts. I had already planned to return to Paris for the weekend, so I will see mine then. Valérie has suggested one or two names I should try to reach in addition.' He turns to me. 'Charles, I had planned originally to take a late afternoon Eurostar on Friday, but now, as I will need some time, I think I may absent myself from court, and leave for Paris early Friday morning'

'Of course, Jean-Claude,' I reply. 'Whatever you think best.'

'Valérie has promised to make some calls today, and her contacts,' he adds with the merest hint of regret, 'reach to a higher level than mine. If she can persuade them that action is needed, it will go to the very highest level.'

'Meaning?' Legless asks.

'Valérie is on the most intimate terms with the President of the Republic,' Jean-Claude replies. He smiles. 'I use the word "intimate" in the political sense, naturally.'

'Naturally,' I reply at once.

'But what would be the intended goal?' Marjorie asks.

'The goal will be for your minister to come under some pressure, so that he in turn will apply some pressure to – how are they called – the Grey Smoothies? We must hope that this will be sufficient.'

'And you want me to organise a meeting between the ambassador and the Grey Smoothies for next Monday?'

'If you would be so kind, Charles.'

'I'll get Stella on it straight after lunch,' I reply.

'But why would the ambassador meet with the Grey Smoothies, if the minister is involved?' Legless wants to know. 'Surely it would be better for her to deal directly with the minister?'

Jean-Claude shakes his head. 'The pressure on your minister must come from above, within your government,' he explains. 'It is Valérie's task to ensure that this is done. If she is successful, the minister will have no choice: Bermondsey will stay open. But then, for political reasons, the minister must turn to the Grey Smoothies to propose a plan to reform the courts while leaving Bermondsey open. It's very important to have this plan in place without delay, and Valérie is just the person to sit down with them and make sure that they cooperate.'

We are all smiling at the prospect.

'The important thing,' Jean-Claude adds, 'is to keep everything confidential for now. What is it you say in English? The loose lips sink the ships?'

'We really are grateful, Jean-Claude,' Marjorie says. We all chime in.

'It's my pleasure, entirely,' he replies.

'It's all very exciting, I must say,' Hubert pipes up, pushing aside the last vestiges of his steak and cheddar pie and chips, the unusually British dish of the day. 'All this cloak-and-dagger stuff. Reminds me of the Garrick, when they're trying to make us take women as members and we have to fight the buggers off: the Secretary running around like a chicken with his head cut off; all hands to the pumps, and don't say a word to anyone.'

Marjorie snorts and rolls her eyes.

'I enjoyed my dinner with Hubert at the Garrick yesterday evening,' Jean-Claude confides as we return to chambers, 'but I did find it odd that only men may become members. It's another thing I find strange about the British when it comes to sex.'

'So do I,' I confess.

* * *

Wednesday afternoon

'I swear by Almighty God that the evidence I shall give shall be the truth, the whole truth, and nothing but the truth.'

'Please give the court your full name,' Cathy begins.

'Megan Verity.'

'And are you the wife of the defendant, Jack Verity?'

'Yes, I am.'

'Do you also have a career of your own?'

'Yes. I'm a financial correspondent for a national newspaper.'

'How long have you and Jack been married?'

'Almost nineteen years.'

'And how would you describe your marriage during that time?'

She smiles and reflects for a few moments.

'I think the best way to put it is that, like all couples, we've had our ups and downs, but on the whole it's been a good marriage.'

'I take it that Angie Simmons has been one of the downs?'

She smiles again, more than a little bitterly this time, I think.

'Yes, that would be a fair way of putting it. There have been one or two others in the past: but nothing as long-lasting as this – mainly flings with some female client for a night or two, nothing serious. This bothered me a lot more. But –'

'And… I'm sorry, I interrupted you…'

'That's all right. I was just going to add, in the interests of transparency, that there have been one or two occasions when I've been led astray myself, so I can't find it in me to blame Jack too much. It was just the intensity of this one that threw me.'

I see the smile of triumph on Jean-Claude's face, and I can't stop myself smiling back. He passes me a note: 'These people really should come and live in France. They would be much happier.'

I scribble below his message: 'Can Valérie arrange political asylum for them?'

'I'm sure she can,' he scribbles back.

'We heard from Jack this morning,' Cathy is saying, 'that you are standing by him, and that you're working together to put it behind you.'

'Yes, that's correct.'

'Was that decision helped by something you found last week?' she asks rather mysteriously.

'Yes, it was.'

'Your Honour, with the usher's assistance, may the witness

please be shown what we've been calling "document two"?'

Finally. It's the moment everyone has waited for, and in the excitement Dawn almost runs from Cathy to the witness box to hand document two to Megan Verity.

'Do you recognise this document, Mrs Verity?'

'Yes, I do.'

'Please tell the jury what it is.'

'It is a duplicate of the pictures in what I believe is the court's Exhibit one.'

'And how does it come to be in your possession?'

'I went online and found it.'

'Explain, please.'

She sighs. 'When Jack was arrested, we were both in shock, needless to say. But even through the shock, Jack was insisting that he was innocent, and he was painting Angie Simmons as a demanding woman, who was trying to screw money out of him. There was something about her that didn't ring true to me. She just didn't sound like the sort of woman who would be too upset at having someone take a few candid pictures of herself. She sounded more like the kind who would try to make a bit of money out of them.'

'Your Honour, I would ask my learned friend to control her witness,' Roderick complains. 'It's for the jury to decide where the truth lies, not for this witness to speculate about Miss Simmons's character.'

'My learned friend is quite right,' Cathy acknowledges without waiting for me to agree with Roderick. 'Mrs Verity, just tell the jury, please, what inquiries you made.'

'I fed her name into various online requests, and this one came up – eventually. It wasn't easy to find, but eventually I found it.'

'You said it was a duplicate of the court's Exhibit one?'

'Yes.'

'Your Honour, may this now be Exhibit two?'

'Yes,' I agree.

'I'm obliged. There are copies for your Honour and the jury.' Dawn breaks into a virtual run once again.

'This is a printout of what you found during your search on the internet?'

'Yes.'

'Is there any indication of its origin?'

'Yes. At the top of the first page, there's the name of a firm called Jim Bishop Enterprises, with an address and other contact details in Sydney, Australia.'

'Is there any indication of what kind of business Jim Bishop Enterprises might be?'

'If you look at the photographs and advertising material on the first and subsequent pages,' Megan replies, 'it seems fairly clear that it's a combined escort agency and sexual accessories business.'

I glance over at the jury, who seem entranced and are studying every small detail. Jean-Claude seems mildly amused.

'Yes. Now, if you will kindly turn to page three,' Cathy says, 'did you find something of particular interest there?'

'Yes. The article on that page deals with a competition organised by Jim Bishop Enterprises to find the "best sexy home photos". Members of the public are encouraged to send in their entries, and there is a first prize of five hundred Australian dollars.' She looks up at me. 'That's just over three hundred and eight pounds, your Honour,' she adds helpfully.

'I see. Thank you,' I reply.

'Does the article go on to name the winner of the competition?' Cathy asks.

'Yes, it does. It names a Miss Angie Simmons, of London.'

There is a veritable gasp from the jury box as they find this information for themselves.

'And is there then a link to Miss Simmons's pictures? Did

you follow that link, and did you find the material you have produced for us today as Exhibit two, which, the jury will see, is identical to the prosecution's Exhibit one?'

'Yes, that's correct.'

'Have you found any evidence to show by what means this material came into the possession of Jim Bishop Enterprises?'

'No. I don't have the technical know-how for that. I'm hoping that the police might follow up on it.'

'I see DC Featherstone in court,' Cathy observes, and I see the officer in the case nod in her direction.

'If I may assist,' Roderick says, standing rather wearily, 'DC Featherstone and I have spoken to our expert to see what can be done. But I must say that it would have helped if my learned friend had shown me this at a rather earlier stage, rather than waiting until the trial has almost finished.'

Cathy raises a hand. 'Mea culpa, your Honour. We had hoped to get our own expert, but Legal Aid won't pay for it without the court's indication that it may be important to the outcome of the trial. If your Honour would give that indication now, it would assist.'

I shake my head. 'Even if I give that indication now, Miss Writtle, it could be a week or two before they get around to approving it. This really should have been done earlier.'

'Yes, your Honour.'

'I think our expert may be able to help,' Roderick says dispiritedly. Obviously, his heart is not in it, but Roderick is old school. The prosecution's job is not to get a conviction at any cost, but to be a minister of justice, and that sometimes means holding out a helping hand to the defence. 'It would help if your Honour would give us some time to allow the expert to work. His preliminary opinion is that he may be able to come up with something, but it's complicated and it may not be possible to do it overnight. We may need until Friday, and perhaps rather than keeping the jury hanging around unnecessarily tomorrow...'

I consider. Ironically, even if the expert finds evidence that Angie Simmons has sold her soul for five hundred Australian dollars, it doesn't mean that Jack Verity isn't guilty of blackmail. And why shouldn't she try to make a few quid from the pictures as compensation for losing her job? But on the other hand, it would show that she's told the jury something less than the truth, and that might well make a difference to the jury's verdict. My hands are tied.

'I'll adjourn the case until Friday morning,' I say.

* * *

Friday morning

Yesterday I suffered the fate all judges suffer when their trials have to take a day off: the list officer loaded me up with all the applications and sentences on the list, most of which would have held up work in the other courts as well as mine. That's fair enough, of course; it's how we always do it, and I can't complain: but neither can I put Jean-Claude through a day of that. He would be asleep after the first ten minutes, so I send him to sit in with Marjorie and watch her drugs trial, which is reaching an interesting point, with the two defendants beginning to turn on one another – as always, to the advantage of the prosecution. This morning, he's on the early Eurostar to Paris, and I find myself missing his companionship on the bench. But I'm hugely grateful to him for appointing himself as Honorary Ambassador of the Bermondsey Crown Court to the Elysée Palace, and I'm further consoled by the fact that he will be enjoying a decent lunch for the first time in several days.

The day begins with the Crown's expert proving conclusively that the transmission of the pictures to Jim Bishop Enterprises in Sydney came from a phone registered to Angie Simmons –

not the phone the police seized from her and interrogated, but another phone which the expert eventually tracked down by dint of trawling patiently through a series of servers and service provider records which, after many hours, yielded up the vital link. That's why it took so long and we couldn't go any further yesterday. Roderick takes him through it all as quickly as possible, and Cathy has nothing to ask him, so he's not detained in the witness box for long.

The question now, of course, is whether Angie should be detained in the witness box for rather longer, while she explains why she sent the pictures to Jim Bishop Enterprises, and why she told the jury she was desperate to suppress them. Roderick isn't keen on the idea, needless to say, but he can't resist it, and I will order her to return without hesitation if Cathy asks. But Cathy, rather uncharacteristically, declines the opportunity to beat Angie Simmons up again; she seems anxious to close her case. Fair enough, I reflect. Her train of reasoning would be: there's nothing much to add to what the expert has said, and the forensic pleasure of giving Angie a renewed mauling must be balanced against the possibility that the jury might have some sympathy with her, especially if they think she's been shabbily treated by Jack Verity. Good call on Cathy's part, I conclude. So we're suddenly ready for closing speeches.

Roderick's is mainly a rehash of his opening speech. But he has recovered his composure sufficiently overnight to make a strong argument that Exhibit two shouldn't affect the outcome of the case. Even if Angie Simmons did try to benefit from the pictures financially, in the scheme of things, the sum of five hundred Australian dollars is scant compensation for the loss of a good job with a City bank; and if Jack Verity was in any way responsible for depriving her of that career, it only goes to show that he is a ruthless man who made whatever threats he had to make to control her. A demand made in those circumstances can only have been unwarranted, and an unwarranted demand made with menaces amounts to the offence of blackmail. QED. Altogether, this is by some distance Roderick's best contribution to the case so far, and the pendulum seems to me to swing back somewhat towards the prosecution, despite the damage inflicted on Angie Simmons earlier in the morning.

Cathy launches the inevitable all-out assault on Angie Simmons, now proved by the Crown's own witness to be a liar and a perjurer. It would be wrong to base the conviction of a man of hitherto exemplary character on the evidence of such a witness, and may result in a miscarriage of justice with which the jury would have to live for the rest of their lives. Angie Simmons's story doesn't stand up to scrutiny, and she isn't the shrinking violet she claims to be – we can see that from Exhibit two alone. Far from being an emotionally vulnerable young thing, helpless to resist a man's domineering behaviour, she is a mature, worldly-wise young woman on the make, who knew exactly how to manipulate a man eager for her sexual services. Yes, Jack Verity made a demand of her with menaces, but it wasn't unwarranted. It was the only hope he had of stemming the tide of the endless demands for money, and the horror of being trapped in an affair that would sooner or later destroy his marriage and perhaps his career. It wasn't unwarranted, and if it wasn't unwarranted, it can't amount to blackmail.

We adjourn for lunch after Cathy's speech, which has been just as powerful as Roderick's. I'm not sure where the pendulum is now, and I don't envy the jury their task.

* * *

Friday afternoon

When I sum up, my main task is to keep the jury's eyes on the ball. What matters is the definition of blackmail, and whether

Jack Verity's conduct fits the definition. Was the demand with menaces he admits to making of Angie Simmons unwarranted? Are they sure of that? At the end of the day, that's what the case is about. I must do my best to prevent them from getting carried away by the prurient contents of Exhibit one, and by the sleazy aspects of Exhibit two and Angie's flirtations with Jim Bishop Enterprises. I keep it as short as I can, but by the time I'm ready for my concluding remarks it's after three o'clock, and far too late to send the jury out this afternoon. You can't risk a rushed verdict late in the afternoon, particularly a Friday afternoon with the weekend looming. So I ask them to keep an open mind until Monday, when I will make my concluding remarks and send them out to start work.

I'm apprehensive about Monday, needless to say, and before leaving court I ask Stella about the arrangements. Everything's in hand, she assures me. The ambassador has graciously agreed to come to Bermondsey for lunch so that she doesn't disrupt the court's proceedings – and because she's curious to see what this building of historic interest to the people of France looks like. Stella has found another room for the judges, so that the ambassador, Jean-Claude and I can take lunch with the Grey Smoothies in the judicial mess. Lunch will be catered in from Basta Pasta, a decent nearby deli – the last thing we need is to have the French Ambassador taken down at this crucial moment by exposure to the dish of the day. I'm having to finance this from my own resources – the Grey Smoothies will want to ensure that the public are not paying for lunch before sitting down to enjoy it – but in the circumstances I consider the investment to be well worth the expenditure. The Grey Smoothies will be represented by Sir Jeremy and Meredith, and by them only. To my surprise, and relief, they have taken my hint that a meeting like this might be a bit much for Jack at this formative stage of his career, so at least we won't have to put up with him as we debate matters of international comity. That's as much as we can do for now. We shall see what Monday brings.

* * *

Monday morning

To my amazement, Elsie and Jeanie, and George, tell me that Jean-Claude has been there before me this morning, and indeed when I arrive in chambers, I find him sitting at the side of my desk with a latte and copies of *Le Monde* and *Le Figaro*. He seems in an excellent mood, and if the demanding weekend trip to Paris and back has tired him, he isn't showing it.

'How did it go?' I ask anxiously.

He smiles. 'My contacts were very sympathetic, and they've reported to their superiors that something must be done urgently. So my part of it went well. But it's Valérie's contacts that matter, Charles. They are the ones we must rely on most, and she could only speak to them by phone. I spoke to Valérie late last night, and she seemed to think that it had gone well, but we won't know until later. She's told them that she needs some kind of answer before lunchtime, and some answer has been promised, but…' he shrugs, as if to add that it's all in the lap of the gods.

Well, of course it is. I'm amazed that anything could happen in such a short time frame, especially with something as big as deciding whether to close down a court or leave it open. It's the exact antithesis of our experience of dealing with the Grey Smoothies, in which it always seems to take aeons to get anything done, however simple. But that's the lesson, I suppose. If you want anything to happen while there's still a hope of achieving something useful, you have to go straight to the top, and we can only hope that's what's happened in our case. As I'm about to reply, there is a knock on the door, and Carol enters.

'Sorry to disturb, Judge, but I have counsel in the Verity case here. They want to see you urgently. Can I bring them in once I've found my hand-held?'

'Yes, of course,' I reply.

'Do you want me to...?' Jean-Claude asks.

'No, no need,' I assure him. 'Please stay.'

I'm fairly sure it's nothing so sensitive that it can't be fit for our honorary ambassador's ears. Roderick and Cathy enter quietly and we all sit. Carol switches on her recorder, inserts a tape, recites the date and time and the names of those present, and places it on my desk.

'The defendant isn't here, Judge,' Roderick says.

I glance at my watch. 'Well, it's not quite ten yet. He may be running late, traffic problems or what have you. Let's give him some time.'

But it wasn't so much what Roderick said – it was the way he said it. The sense I'm getting is that it's not going to be as simple as the Monday morning traffic.

'He's always been early for court, Judge,' Cathy says. 'Most days he's arrived before me, and he's very good about keeping in touch with his solicitors. But they haven't been able to reach him since Friday night. There's no answer on his home phone, and his mobile is going straight to message. Same with the wife.'

'Cathy, you're not telling me he's done a runner, are you?' I ask.

She nods. 'It looks very much like it, Judge,' she replies forlornly.

'Very properly, Cathy's solicitors notified the CPS on Saturday,' Roderick adds. 'We've had the police watching the house, and we've put out an alert to all ports and airports, but nothing yet. If he's gone, there's no way of telling where, or how long we will need to find him. It will probably mean bringing him back from Europe somewhere. Actually, that would be the good news. He's got enough money to go wherever he wants to go. If he's gone far enough, we may never find him.'

I shake my head. 'It seems a bit extreme to flee the country in this case,' I suggest. 'I don't know what you think, but it seems to me he has a decent chance of getting off.'

'We agree, Judge,' Cathy replies, 'but he's been a bit concerned with the question of whether his demand was unwarranted. Obviously, I had to advise him that a jury might very well buy the prosecution's case on that, and of course if he's convicted, you'd have to send him inside, and his career goes up in flames.'

I nod. 'So, you're telling me there's no point in adjourning. I may as well get on with it and send the jury out?'

'That's our considered view, Judge,' Roderick confirms. 'We might perhaps wait until eleven, just in case, but after that we might as well move on.'

'You and Valérie haven't offered the pair of them political asylum in France, have you, Jean-Claude?' I smile, once Roderick and Cathy have left.

'With the weekend we've had?' he smiles back. 'We've had enough to do trying to save Bermondsey. We would need at least another weekend to save Mr and Mrs Verity.'

At eleven, there is still no sign of defendant or wife, and I ask Carol to convene court. In this kind of situation, I have to tell the jury that there is no evidence of where Jack Verity is, and they're not allowed to speculate about why he isn't at court. They mustn't hold his absence against him. It's their duty to give him a fair trial whether he's at court or not, and they must put the fact that he isn't out of their minds. As a judge, there are a number of directions I have to give to juries that make me feel, and I suspect, sound, like an idiot, and this one is right up there at the top of the list. In fact, it's a perfectly logical direction and one necessary to a fair trial: but it's bound to occur to the jury that the defendant's unexplained absence means he's scarpered in what he believes to be the face of imminent disaster; and you have to fear the worst for Jack Verity at this point. I conclude my summing-up and send the jury out to start work.

And so to lunch… and whatever it may bring today.

When I'm introduced to Valérie Bernard I lose any sense of surprise at Jean-Claude's admiration for his friend from university days. She is extraordinarily elegant, tall and thin, her clothes restrained and formal but unmistakeably feminine, and in colours that perfectly complement her slightly dark features and stylishly short dark brown hair. Sir Jeremy Bagnall is clearly similarly impressed, and I'm secretly gratified to see that Meredith, in a pedestrian grey suit, seems rather overawed – the first time I've noticed any such reaction in her to anybody or anything. Lunch has been set out for us, and given the company, I've splashed out for a couple of bottles of a decent white Burgundy recommended to me by Jean-Claude. Ordinarily, this would horrify the Grey Smoothies, which today is fine because I would be happy to have them a bit off balance; but in fact, once they remember that the taxpayer is not funding the indulgence, they relax and join in with good grace.

'Madame Ambassador,' Jeremy begins, once we've all helped ourselves and taken our seats, using his best Grey Smoothie diplomat's tone of voice, 'it's very good of you to come out all the way to Bermondsey to see us.'

She holds up a hand. 'Valérie, please,' she insists.

Jeremy inclines his head. 'Jeremy and Meredith. Valérie, we're very conscious of the importance to France of the case of Foggin Island – or should I say, L'Ile des Fougains?'

'Yes, that's what you should say,' Valérie replies.

'Yes, of course,' Jeremy agrees. 'L'Ile des Fougains. And I need hardly say that we're all very impressed by Charles's handling of the case and the decision he made.'

'As you should be,' Valérie says.

With the aid of a sip of wine, I make a conscious effort not to agree out loud.

'Yes, of course. So we do understand why France finds the Bermondsey Crown Court to be of such great interest.'

'Thank you. I'm gratified to hear that.'

'But if I may, Valérie, I must explain that keeping the court open is quite another matter. That, you see, depends on making a business case for the court, and on providing value for money for the taxpayer. My minister has been quite clear about that.'

This time Valérie doesn't respond.

'And we don't feel that we can make the case for Bermondsey, you see, given that the prevailing economic model is for larger court centres. It's something we regret, naturally, but our hands are tied.'

Again, no response. Jeremy glances in Meredith's direction.

'What we thought,' Meredith adds tentatively, 'is that we might create some kind of memorial elsewhere, perhaps at the High Court in the Strand, where it would be seen by many more people, or perhaps even at the Supreme Court at Westminster, if you prefer: as long as the cost is manageable, obviously.'

Still Valérie does not reply.

'So, those are the matters we should discuss,' Jeremy adds in due course. 'Is there any comment you'd like to make on what we've said, Valérie?'

With no show of haste, Valérie takes a drink of her sparkling water.

'Not really,' she replies. 'Actually, if you've said everything you want to say, perhaps you won't mind if we now come to the point of today's meeting.'

'I rather thought that what we said *was* the point,' Jeremy replies after an awkward silence.

'Did you?' she replies, affecting surprise. 'In that case, I can only assume that you have not kept in very close touch with your minister.'

'The minister? I spoke with him late yesterday evening.'

Valérie nods. 'Ah. Well, that explains it, then.'

'Explains what, Valérie, if I may ask?' I sense Jeremy becoming slightly nervous now. His Grey Smoothie instincts are telling him that he's losing whatever grip he thought he had on the meeting, but he's not quite sure how it's happening.

'Well, you see, Jeremy, over the last day or two, Jean-Claude and I have spoken to certain contacts of ours in France, and our understanding is that it was intended for the President of the Republic to be informed of the affair yesterday, and for him to speak to your Prime Minister this morning.'

'The Prime Minister? This morning?' He hesitates. He's flustered now. 'What do you expect your President to ask of the Prime Minister, if I may be so bold?'

She smiles. 'Jean-Claude and I asked that the President approach the Prime Minister to guarantee that this court building, which is of such significance to France, be allowed to remain open. In that case, we would expect the Prime Minister to ask your minister to take the necessary steps for that to occur.'

'I understand,' he replies. 'But, if I may say so, Valérie, as I said before, my minister and I have concerns about the value to the taxpayer –'

'Perhaps I wasn't entirely clear, Jeremy,' she interrupts. 'These matters of policy are no longer for you to decide. Indeed, they are no longer for your minister to decide. The President and the Prime Minister will settle the matter.' She glances at her watch. 'Indeed, I would expect that they have done so by now. Perhaps you would care to check for any messages you may have received?'

Jeremy and Meredith exchange glances and both consult

their phones, which, as Valérie has suggested, do seem to have accumulated one or two messages.

'Our task this afternoon,' Valérie continues without any undue haste, 'is simply to propose a plan to keep Bermondsey Crown Court – the Ile des Fougains Monument, as we shall call it – open as a permanent reminder of everything it stands for: the rule of international law.'

Jeremy and Meredith are silent, their gaze fixed on their phones.

She pauses. 'I've heard wonderful things about you, Jeremy, and you, Meredith, from Charles. He says that you are very creative, always ready with a plan, responsive to change, and very innovative, and that the project will be in the best possible hands.'

'That's very generous of you, Charles,' Jeremy mutters darkly.

'Not at all, entirely deserved,' I lie as convincingly as I can.

One last look at the messages, and it's time to concede.

'We will do whatever is needed, of course,' Jeremy agrees quietly. Meredith nods, trying her best to smile through clenched teeth.

'Splendid,' Valérie says. 'In that case, I'm confident that we shall soon reach an agreement.'

'*L'Entente Cordiale*,' Jean-Claude beams.

'*L'Entente Cordiale*, indeed,' Valérie agrees. '*C'est ça*. I think this calls for another glass, Charles, don't you? Would you do the honours, as I believe the expression is? And after that, let's get down to work.'

* * *

Monday afternoon

The jury return to court just after three. Jack Verity still isn't with us, but they don't even seem to notice. Carol invites the foreman, a lady of Bangladeshi origins wearing a long, bright red dress and an impressive range of trinkets on her arms, to stand.

'Madam foreman, please answer my first question either yes or no. Has the jury reached a verdict on which you are all agreed?'

'Yes,' she replies.

'On the sole count of this indictment, charging the defendant Jack Verity with blackmail, do you find the defendant guilty or not guilty?'

'Not guilty,' the foreman responds at once.

'You find the defendant not guilty,' Carol continues after a momentary pause, her tone suggesting that she thinks she may have misheard, 'and is that the verdict of you all?'

'Yes, it is,' the foreman responds immediately.

'Perhaps it's time I retired,' Roderick says with a rueful smile, over tea in chambers a few minutes later. 'I must be getting old. Apparently, I can't get a conviction even when the defendant absconds.'

'Oh, these things happen, Roderick,' I reply reassuringly. 'We've both been around long enough to know that. And there is a certain irony about it, isn't there?'

'Well, it's some consolation to think of him sitting somewhere in darkest Europe, reflecting that he would be home free if he'd only stayed where he was,' Roderick concedes. 'I confess to taking a certain pleasure in that.'

'Not to mention,' Cathy joins in, 'the twenty thousand pounds his wife deposited with the court to guarantee his appearance, which is now subject to being forfeited. I'm sure the authorities will be able to find a use for that.'

'I'm sure they will,' I agree.

***

A Friday morning, about three months later

The decision to leave Bermondsey Crown Court open was announced within a few days of our lunch. The message that filtered down to Jeremy's minister from the Prime Minister was clear, and relieved both Jeremy and his minister of any pressure, and indeed of any choice in the matter. Good relations with France must come before fiddling about with economic models of the courts, and the minister would adapt his policy accordingly. Jeremy and Meredith duly prepared the quintessential Grey Smoothie plan: namely that the whole debate about the correct economic model for the London Crown Courts should be: 'Parked pending extensive consultation with all relevant stakeholders, other government departments, and the public'; which in Grey-Smoothie-speak, suggests that it will be left to lie in the long grass for the next couple of millennia. This, obviously, was good news for all of us at Bermondsey. But it wasn't until about a month ago that the true extent of the genius of the French diplomacy became fully clear.

About a month ago, I received an invitation to attend the unveiling of the 'Ile des Fougains Monument', followed by lunch, as a guest of the Government of France. The minister decreed that the court would close for the day, so that we could set up lunch in the main entrance hall to accommodate the large number of guests expected. The guests included: all our judges and senior staff, as well as the minister, Jeremy, Meredith, Jack, and other assorted Grey Smoothies; a sizeable contingent from the embassy led by Valérie Bernard; and, to our great pleasure, Jean-Claude, who flew in from Paris for the day. Until I received the invitation, I'd assumed that the 'Ile des Fougains Monument' was just a figure of speech used by Valérie and Jean-Claude, and had no physical expression. But the monument arrived with the invitation: a fine grey marble plaque, to be affixed to the wall in the entrance hall, opposite the Bermondsey Cannon exhibit, ready for the Ambassador to unveil during lunch. The plaque records, in French on the left and in English on the right, the role of the Bermondsey Crown Court in doing justice to France in the matter of L'Ile des Fougains, a shining example of the power of international law to put justice above narrow partisan interests.

It also records that, on the recommendation of the President of the Republic, Jeremy, his minister, and my good self have been named as '*Confrères de la Société Française de la Jurisprudence Extraordinaire*'. Quite what this *Société* does, other than being available for the President to create *confrères* and hold what I'm told is an excellent annual dinner in Paris, I have so far been unable to discover. But it doesn't bother me very much, and I'm quite sure that it doesn't bother Jeremy or his minister at all. Indeed, their reaction upon having the appropriate medal on its red ribbon placed around their shoulders by Valérie, with an accompanying kiss on both cheeks, seemed to seal *L'Entente Cordiale*. In view of the honour bestowed upon me, I'd made sure that the Reverend Mrs Walden was invited to lunch, and as the guests were dispersing afterwards, we stood together admiring the now unveiled plaque.

'I told you not to underestimate Jean-Claude,' she smiles.

'I don't,' I assure her. 'I only hope I'm not underestimating the Grey Smoothies.'

'There's only one person you always underestimate, Charlie, *mon confrère*,' she replies, 'and I hope this will be a lesson not to underestimate him in future.'

About Us

In addition to No Exit Press, Oldcastle Books has a number of other imprints, including Kamera Books, Creative Essentials, Pulp! The Classics, Pocket Essentials and High Stakes Publishing > oldcastlebooks.co.uk

For more information about Crime Books to go > crimetime.co.uk

Check out the kamera film salon for independent, arthouse and world cinema > kamera.co.uk

For more information, media enquiries and review copies please contact marketing > marketing@oldcastlebooks.co.uk